Sunday Dinners

Kellie Kelley

ISBN: 1546971009
ISBN 13: 9781546971009

Acknowledgement

A special thank you to life-long friends, Tommie and Tony, who encouraged me to fulfill my goal one day at a time. My appreciation goes to Donald and Matt, my technological support, for understanding I am computer and typing challenged. Thank you, dear friends and family, for enduring endless chatter from me trying to complete "Sunday Dinners" and for your support.

Sunday Get Together

Civility is not going to happen, because there is too much water over the bridge, and I am drowning in malice and contempt. Yes, I am going to be there, but I am not going with a pleasant smile, and pretending it has all been smoothed over.

"It" involves all the sisters, and their continuous feud over the leftovers of their parent's lives. I remember all the Sunday Dinners we had from years of happier times when all the family came together. There was laughter then, sharing at the table about our families and the occasional recipe scrutiny. We were always full of partaking, after all, our lives *could* and sometimes *would* center around food. We were true Southerners and all that the South represents.

Denise is the middle sister, lean with a streak of mean. Control comes easy to her because she is always hands on in any situation. She reacts quickly in all things, too quickly in some situations, and despite her awful vice of smoking, she remains strong as an ox and healthy for all I know. Of course, the smoking has taken its toll on her, her voice husky. When she speaks, it is usually gruff and sounds like a brother. She resents any comparison to a man. We have argued the point on several occasions. I support my theory by the fact that she wears men's shorty pajamas every night. She must have thirty pairs, from grey to blue stripes and plaids of all colors. I rest my case.

Denise and husband Tom have a three-hour drive to Mom and Dad's house. It is over the river and through the woods to grandmother's house we go. Sure, Tom knows the way, but he drives as slow as he works. If only he would talk about something that really matters, like Bingham's girl-friend. Bingham is Denise's son and Carly is Bingham's latest squeeze who spends too much money on tans and tattoos, hardly the southern magnolia Denise has in mind for her Bingham. She didn't think it was a good idea to bring Carly to the Sunday Dinner. Her appearance alone would send Dad into a major tailspin. Oh well, there are more" fish to fry" for the day. Carly will be on her own, and hopefully on her way out, just as soon as Denise could find the time to tend to it.

Of course, Denise would be late. God, her entrance makes me pithy. She greets mom with a cigarette kiss, and waves her hand to Dad. He never says anything to her, only glances, impatient for having to wait on her and her brood to eat. It is a quick glance to her, then back to FOX news, turning the television volume up even higher. It is always about him.

I put her pot of green beans she has brought in on the stove to fin-ish cooking them. Lifting the pot lid I gasp at the beans, floating in a sea of water and a life raft made of salt pork. She has a lot to learn about cooking I murmur. I turned to eye Tom carrying in a big pan of maca-roni and cheese, something only the kids favor. Dad always likens it to "hog corn" (big and yellow) True discerning Southerners only eat white young corn, he'd always say.

Denise has two big strapping' boys. They have been on the six-year college plan fully supported by Denise and Tom. Tom says that he had never had time for fraternity activities when he went to school, so let kids be kids. "Tom Jr. and Bingham have their whole lives to work!" he'll tell you. There is always an entourage with Denise and Tom. Lucky for us, they did not bring extra friends today. That's why Denise brings these banquet size dishes to our Sunday Dinners. She does not want any of the family saying she is not doing her fair share.

Carly walks in ahead of Bingham with a big smile and personality to match. "Hello, everyone, I'm Carly and I'm looking forward to getting to know all of you. Dinner smells delicious, my mom never cooks, and it's always been a passion of mine to learn. My Grandma Ora Mae is the cook in the family."

"Carly, where are your folks from?" Mom is starting the interrogation now, the piercing for information in order for the family to accept you. Yes, everyone is welcome after a fact. After all, that is only good southern hospitality but true acceptance in the family comes only whenever Momma thinks it is a fit. Momma says the Bible always states, "you need to be equally yoked."

Okay, the kitchen is getting crowded now, and hot. I glance at the clock and think it is time for the roast to come out. The cannibals always attack me about over cooking the meat. I am used to their rhetoric and abuse about me eating meat that is well done.

Carly has escaped Mom's questions, and wants to know if I am going to make gravy.

Bing has told her rice and gravy would be a regular on their table. Could I please show her how? My ego won't allow me to ignore her. I place the roast on a serving platter and place the roasting pan on a burner and turn the heat to medium. I pour a big glass of water into the pan with all the drippings, stirring with a big fork to loosen all the charred bits. I reach in the cupboard for some cornstarch and grab a bowl, and put several tablespoons in the bowl. I pour some more water in the bowl, and mix it with the same fork. The pan is crackling now, hot steam erupts, and I slowly add the cornstarch mixture to the pan. Stirring constantly, the gravy begins to thicken, now just a pinch of salt and pepper. Carly asks if I always use cornstarch. I'm thinking this girl is really interested, and I quickly explain the difference between flour and cornstarch. Carly seems completely different to me now because she has genuine interest. There *is* potential for her.

Carly thinks back to how her family spent their Sundays. She lives in her grandma's house and is alone most of the day. The windows are always drawn to keep the sunlight out because power bills are always less that way. Her mom leaves early everyday while she is sleeping. Her one meal is placed on the table, and that should last all day. The cupboards are locked so there is no extra snacking during the day. Often enough, her mom is always telling her that fat girls are not pretty, and most certainly men are not attracted to overweight chicks. Grandma does the majority of cooking for the three of them. There is grandma's chicken and rice, grandma's beef stew and grandma's soups, all one pot delicious wonders. Carly's favorite is slumgullion. Grandma makes it from all the leftovers in the fridge, places them in a pot and adds hamburger meat. The flavor is amazing. Seems like her mom is always too tired to eat when she gets home because she waitresses at a popular diner downtown. The Sunday dinner with Bingham's family is a different world to her, but Carly likes it.

The doorbell rings and Tom gets up at glacial speed to answer it. An elderly woman is inquiring where the Roberts' live. Dad yells out "tell them to go on down the road and look for the junkiest house with all the crap in their front yard." Yep, Dad has a way with words, not exactly the chamber of commerce president.

Rita and Roan are late. My oldest sister is a busy woman and she sure tells us often enough. She is babbling on that they have been up since five am, got in their walk, prepared their smoothies and attended the early church service. Mom asks if they had prayed for all us sinners. Rita said they did and inquires why Mom wasn't there. Mom is having some bathroom issues and thought it best to stay home. Rita expresses concern and lectures her on preventative care, and thinks a doctor visit is in order. Mom is a cancer survivor and considers herself impervious to another disease. Mom addresses Rita and asks if her kids are going to be late. "It's almost one o'clock now, and your Daddy is getting impatient to eat."

I just realize Denise is missing and probably having a cigarette outside.

The door opens again and Rene and Robert walk in. Rene is Rita's daughter, always luminous and she lights up any room. She is a beautiful blonde with big green eyes, and has a wardrobe that is stellar. She and Robert have been married twenty years. He is a dutiful husband but constantly nagging her about her excessive spending. Rita should take some lessons from her daughter on successful dressing, Professional Development personified!

"Rene, I ask, "Did you bring a dish or just your sparkling personality?"

"Yes, I did Auntie Dolly, I brought sweet potato casserole." Dolly is a nickname I endure, short for Amelia Dollene. Bingham catches Rene's eye and quickly grabs Carly's hand, and hurries to Rene's side, "Cuz, this is Carly Bedford, my girlfriend," Rene extends her hand but Carly leans in and gives her a big hug,"very happy to meet you Rene, I've heard a lot about you!" René is caught off guard. I think to myself, those *tattoos aren't going to rub off*, but Carly's personality is starting to rub in.

Dad is getting up and takes his regular seat at the end of the table. He fixes himself a salad and begins to eat. His wait is over and quickly we all pitch in and get all the dishes on the table for everyone to start eating.

It is traditional that we all stand in a circle holding hands and have prayer. Mom asks Roan to lead us. "Lord, bless this food that is prepared and help us to remember those that go hungry. Bless our family to remain family, and thank you for good health, and long life if it is your will Lord. In these things, we pray, Amen."

We three girls usually sit beside one another and husbands find their own place. Kids all eat together.

The food plates are being passed, and when the meat gets to the men, there is a pause and the meat platter is seriously reduced. *Roan, seriously? Tom, you're kidding me! At least save some for the rest of us!*

The rest of us indeed, I'm moving every piece of meat around to find some well done, my eyes darting on everyone else's plates. The cannibals have become Vikings! I help myself to plenty of salad, green beans and some squash that Rhett and Scarlett brought. Summer squash is still available in the grocery store, and this casserole is a family favorite. The rolls are soft pillows of goodness slightly browned on all their tops. Roan still thinks I make the best homemade rolls. Yes, I do! I buy frozen rolls in the grocery store, place them on a greased cookie sheet and allow them to rise for three hours.

Rhett is Rita's second child. The name fits. He is dashing, but there is a little scoundrel in him that makes you take a second look. He is a mover and a shaker. Literally, he moves in all circles, some dubious, and shakes down merchants to get the best price on everything he buys. And there is plenty of buying, more like accumulations, collections, surplus. He has high aspirations and is climbing up. He thinks to be a mountain one must be able to climb and stand alone. You take whatever comes against you and frankly, he has weathered his fair share of storms. He is widowed twice and currently married to a minister's daughter. Scarlett and Rhett are a team. Scarlett's father is a grief counselor in a therapy group where Rhett participates. Rhett always felt guilty that if he had been there with his wife when she when she was involved in a horrific accident, he might have saved her. The trooper said Kathy probably died instantly. Counseling helps him cope immensely.

Rene asks Bing how he and Carly met. Denise gives Rene the stink eye. Bing obviously wants to dodge the question too, but Carly quickly answers in an eagerness to fit in. "I am a waitress at Hooters." It's a .... Denise breaks in before she finishes her statement "we all know what it is." The table gets quiet. Dad shouts out "Who?" It is a laughable moment enjoyed by all.

Sanctuary Sunday

Sunday has passed now, and so has the laughter and togetherness. Now it is raw, a brawl that can't stop, between sisters. Dad has a massive seizure that night and never regains sight of day. At the funeral home, we three girls bicker about the details of the service. Rita wants a simple graveside service in our family plot. Denise wants the service at the Masonic Hall. I want to have it at Glenn Lake, surrounded by all the flora that represents his life. Mom makes the final decision to have it at the church in the sanctuary. Even though Dad didn't go every Sunday, all our family attended the First Baptist, even buying six of the stained-glass windows in the church. Whenever Mom threatened to change churches, Dad would remind her to get the windows when she leaves. Mom believed in tithing and told Dad often that "seeds sown with thanks to God produces big crops."

Making decisions is taking a toll on Mom. She begs for family unity and togetherness. The service will be on the following Sunday, and all the family will gather again. The church family is bringing over a roasted turkey and calls to remind us to have a family member at home to receive the food. Rita thanks them for their thoughtfulness on behalf of the family.

That week Mom is lost because she's always doted on dad. There is too much time in the day to try and fill. She looks worse than ever, and spends a lot of time in the bathroom. Lots of friends bring various food dishes over for our family. It is a casserole brigade of sorts. Some of the dishes are homemade but most are products of the local deli. Our family doesn't understand the concept of deli food, box cakes and coleslaw that is pureed in a blender with way too much sugar. We try to remember that it is the thoughtfulness that counts.

Rita tells Denise and me that Mom is suffering from chronic diarrhea and as soon as Tuesday, she will be taking her to the doctor. Suddenly, I realize how frail Mom appears to me and her weight loss is obvious. The black dress she is wearing today for the service accentuates how thin she looks. I think she has lost her spirit too. Sixty-seven years is a long time to be married to one man. It is all she knows.

The phone rings and it is Carly. She will be happy to stay at the house and get everything ready. We sisters are taken aback and surprised. How thoughtful she is. Denise remarks she must mention to Bing that he needs to tell Carly to wear something long sleeved, to cover up those tattoos. Small towns have big prejudices. Denise would insist on it. Denise is one third of the control squad and her directives are coming through loud and clear. Control is in our gene pool. I prefer to think of it as leadership rather than control like others may think.

Uncle Hayward is giving the eulogy, and tells all of us old army stories, fishing excursions and embellished stories about their weekly card games. Momma's brother is an Old Salt, man of the sea, a weathered angler who has lots of funny stories to share. This is supposed to be how one's life ends, in celebration with folks engaged in humor, and great memories of your loved one. Not at all like some preachers when at the pulpit, remind us that the deceased is almost a Christian. The service seems short I think, hardly enough time for people to take in my dad's eighty-seven years of life and not nearly enough time to notice all the beautiful flowers I have made for his service.

I am a florist, and it is my passion. It has become my life for forty years. I recall Dad always bought roses, so it is fitting that his casket spray be covered with eighty-seven roses. Two white roses are at the very top from his beloved 'Poopsie', because that is the name my Dad called my mom. He would buy her two rose blooms at a time. He would say that's all he ever needed for his Poopsie. The bottom half of the casket spray is cascading layers of leather leaf and plumosa ferns and it is breathtaking. I am teary eyed now. I just need to focus on the flowers before I totally break down.

We arrive home after the service and see that Carly has organized everything right by herself. She has gone out in the yard, picked some greenery and roses and found some vases in the laundry room to fill placing the vases on the tables. Remarkably, she has located tablecloths from somewhere. I laugh to myself because I know where the linens are stored, and I am sure a mountain of old gift-wrapping paper from the fossil years has fallen on top of her out of that closet. Clearly, Bing has relayed Denise's message to Carly about her attire because she is wearing a long sleeved white blouse and a super black and white paisley scarf. The white blouse makes her look tanner. I don't see any tattoos showing. Mission accomplished. I must tell her how nice she looks and how we appreciate that she volunteered.

Everyone separates into groups and families. Rita and Roan, Rene and Robert, Denise and Tom and their boys. Their plates are piled up with food and I see six rolls on Tom's plate. I glance at everyone's plate. Gosh, I hope there is enough for everyone else. .... a typical Sunday Dinner. I notice Carly in the kitchen, still dutiful, and so I join her. Now is the time to express appreciation.

"Carly, you look very nice today, and I'm glad you volunteered to help and it is really appreciated." Carly hugs me hard and said she is happy to help.

We fix our plates. Carly has small spoonfuls of food. It is like watching a bird eat; tiny, small bites, chewing slowly, carefully. I remark on her table manners, and she looks embarrassed. I look around and notice that we are all on our best behavior, even civilized. Mom seems content we are weathering the day without fuss and incident.

Carly and I begin to pick up the plates, and put the extra food away. Carly can't believe all the food that has been consumed. Something seems odd to me, perhaps her bewilderment. Clearly, she eats to live, not lives to eat. Finally, the kitchen seems in order again, and everyone is saying their goodbyes. Truthfully, we are all too tired to discuss anything more.

I am spending the night with Mom, so after most everyone departs, I retire to the bedroom to change, draw a bath, and hopefully get some much-needed shut eye. A hot bath relaxes me. I don't realize how much time has passed. I look in on Mom, she is just lying there, in her clothes from the funeral and she looks so peaceful. I lean over to give her a kiss goodnight. I whisper, "Momma you looked so pretty today. I think everyone enjoyed the service. Do you need help getting on your nightie?" There is no response, no sweet smile, nothing, just stillness. "Mom, Mommmm... I shake the bed, Mom, are you okay?" The only movement is mine, mine is the only breathing I can hear... She is gone.

I grab the phone on the nightstand and call 911. A voice answers this is Volusia County Sheriff's Department. Please state your name and emergency. I am trembling. My name is Dollene Diamond. I need an ambulance to 104 Glenn Lake Drive. My mother is unresponsive.

"Ma'am, please stay on the line while I dispatch an ambulance. I will need more information."

I think to myself, I have no more information.

"Ma'am, is there anyone else there with you?"

"No, I answer," I can hear a siren now, and see flashing lights reflecting in the window. "Ma'am, Ms. Dollene, the ambulance is arriving, please answer your door."

I hurry to the door, unlock it, and open the door as quickly as I can.

"In here," I wave my hand for the medics to follow me. A city policeman follows behind them.

Momma is the same. The medic feels for a pulse and shakes his head slowly, "I'm sorry, I cannot feel a pulse, "Ma'am, is your mom under a doctor's care?"

"Just regular visits," I answer, "my sister was going to take her to the doctor next week. My sisters and I have noticed a lot of weight loss recently." The policeman breaks in the conversation and explains the medical examiner must be called.

"They are in Deland, and it will be at least a couple of hours wait. We will stay here, and step into another room so your family can say goodbye."

"Say goodbye?" I ask, "our family just buried my daddy today and the people haven't been gone but three hours." I reach for the phone again, and call Rita. Roan answers. I am getting emotional and cannot stop crying. The medic takes the phone away from my ear and explains what the situation is. The policeman is talking to me directly. "They say they will be here shortly."

I sit down in the corner and just stare at my mom. *Dear God, what has happened?*

Quietly, Rita and Roan enter the bedroom. The medic hands them some paperwork and explains the medical examiner will have to be called. The medical examiner's office will be conducting an autopsy. Afterwards, they will release the body to the funeral home of our choice. Rita sits on the edge of the bed with Mom and takes Mom's hand in her own. How can it be that Mother is dead? There is no explanation, no reason, nothing makes sense.

Roan asks me when is the last time I spoke to her. "Had I called Denise?" I cannot recall even seeing Mom before everyone had left. I was in the bathroom a couple of hours. Rita is crying now, and garbles something like "how could this be?"

Roan said "Let's go over the timeline. First, let's call Denise and Tom. They are probably home now." Roan reaches in his shorts pocket and pulls out his phone. Denise answers.

"Denise, something terrible has happened and your mother has passed away. The police and medics are...... the phone hangs up. Roan says "let's give her a few minutes. I'm sure Tom will call back."

In a few minutes, another squad car drives up. The officer in the house opens the door and both officers seem to be in a quiet discussion. One officer comes back into the room.

"I am terribly sorry, but I have been instructed to ask you folks to leave now, leave the house and property, as this is believed to be a crime scene." He pauses.... "Apparently, a Denise and Tom Henry have power of attorney and have exercised that power. The medical examiner is an hour away now, and after they remove Mrs. Diamond's body, we will seal the front door. Everyone must vacate immediately. I am sorry, but my instructions are clear. Does everyone understand?"

Boiling Point

This is Denise, maneuvering in all her freaking glory. We are all stunned. I feel nauseous. Rita remains ashen. Roan looks shaken, "we heard you officer." "Rita, c'mon, let's go, let's go with Dolly, and go have a cup of coffee. Let's just leave now, so we can regroup and figure this all out. Let's Go!" He grabs Rita's arm and pulls her up off the bed. She's stumbling, and Roan moves to prop her up. He leads us both to the door. We make our way down the hall, and the officer waves us out the door. "I'm sorry folks, about the circumstances and appreciate your cooperation."

We're outside now and some of the neighbors are gathering and start walking toward us. Roan jumps out ahead of us and tells them that our Mother has passed away. "We don't know why. There will be an investigation as to the cause. We are leaving to go to our houses."

Rita and I are falling into her car. There are no spoken words between us. I think I am going to explode any second. Rita looks at me in the back seat and in a barely audible whisper she says, "We're going to need an attorney."

Bing texts Carly. She is already in the tanning bed with her protective eyewear on.

"Call me as soon as u can, B"

Well, he would just have to wait, geez. He is as demanding as his mom. It is ten o'clock and the last appointment the salon has for the night and I need to unwind from the day's activities. Bing's family is more than interesting and what a spread of food they enjoy. It is unbelievable! I have never seen so many side dishes. I wrote down the name of the person who made the squash so I can call them for the recipe. Maybe Aunt Dolly could get it for me. I turn over to tan on my stomach. I think back to my high school days. I am the palest kid alive and all my classmates call me "Powder." It is no wonder since I am never outdoors to absorb any sun, and with the blinds always closed, I guess I am ghostly. I need to tan because my job requires pantyhose legs and I look so much better in them *with* a tan. She phones Bing. "What's up?"

He seems really upset because I can hear that his breathing is so rapid. "My grandmother has passed away. Nobody knows what has happened. Mom and Dad have already left to go back there. Mom said she has to protect the family from the vultures picking the house apart."

"Who is your mom calling vultures?"

Bing doesn't acknowledge her question and tells her "that he will probably go back and forth until this is all sorted out. He's just letting me know. "Night, baby, talk to you tomorrow."

Carly freezes and thinks back. I just left from the family gathering. What could have possibly happened to Ms. Ellie? I remember seeing her coming from the bathroom with a pill bottle in her hand. She was slipping into her bedroom, away from all the offers of condolences and noisy people. I thought she was noticeably composed today and soft spoken. It was nothing like the first time when she and I were playing twenty questions.

It is midnight now and Rita, Roan and I are still in shock. We ride in silence a quarter mile away to my house. On the driveway, Roan shuts off the engine and we all sit in the car for a couple of minutes. Eventually, we open the doors, get out, and hobble together down the sidewalk to the front door and into my house.

We make our way to the dining room table. We need coffee. I go into the kitchen and begin making coffee for Rita and Roan. Rita is visibly shaken about the turn of events. Roan is calling Rene and Rhett to share the sad news before anything gets out on Facebook. People have no privacy these days, and with the police being at Rita's parents, speculation will be rampant. I hear Roan say "no, we're not there, we are at Dolly's. We do not know why but there is going to be an investigation and an autopsy. I imagine your dear Aunt Denise figures into this equation. Yes, your momma is stunned beyond explanation. We're dumfounded. We'll know more tomorrow."

The coffee is hot and I put some turbinado sugar in the three mugs, pour in the coffee and add half and half. Rita sips and asks what is different about the coffee.

"It is my newest elixir, and I tell her it is turbinado sugar. It has a hint of molasses in it. Ordinarily Rita doesn't drink coffee, and I notice she has both hands around the mug. It seems to be having a calming effect on her. Roan drinks his without conversation and we are all quiet, thinking, but I know the angst is in all of us. Imagine being asked to leave our parents' home, our home where we all grew up. We had played hopscotch together, and there are memories of making mud pies. We would pretend we had race cars out of match boxes and we would race around a homemade track.

The turf is divided now, and family is beginning to be foe. My beloved parents are deceased and there is a great divide opening. The sisters have opposing opinions on everything. We will be searching for answers. Attorneys will be hired and attacks will be personal.

Trust

Rita and I know that Denise oversees the family trust. Blu Diamond Farms extends twelve miles around Lake Glenn. Ten miles have rows and rows of *leather leaf* fern beds all the way up to the hard road. Surrounded by giant water oaks all around the fernery, the property is truly picturesque. The oaks drip a constant leaf mold that provides a superb growing environment for the fern. There is always dappled light overhead enabling the dark green fronds to look particularly lush. The farm also grows plumosa and springeri ferns commercially. My parents worked side by side in the early years, building and growing an empire, a legacy that shows a hard work ethic, and respect for the land. Blu Diamond Farms is a family business but depends on many laborers who traverse the vast beds and cut the leatherleaf fronds by hand. Harvesting requires bending over to cut the mature fronds at their base, careful NOT to cut the frond with spores. Fronds with spores will be a new crop and represents the future. Much had been discussed about bringing in something mechanical to harvest the crop therefore cutting down on expensive labor, but anything mechanical cannot distinguish mature fronds from the immature ones. Volusia County grows ninety six percent of the nation's leatherleaf and Blu Diamond is an industry leader.

Roan suggests I come to their house to spend the night, rather than be alone. I said I will probably take a sleeping pill, rather than cry myself to sleep. There is no telling what daybreak will bring. To be sure, there will be arrangements that need to be made. I am still waiting for the medical examiner's report.

I'm slow to rise the next morning. I need more coffee. I glance at my phone and have missed ten calls. I need to call my shop and let them know I will be late for work. Monday can be a little challenging with wholesalers coming in with the week's purchases needing to be made. I pick up the phone and Julie answers. "Bouquets Today, may I help you?"

"Hey this is me. ..Julie, yesterday's service was hard enough but last... night... I am crying, and having difficulty getting all my words out.

"My mom died last night," and I am having trouble communicating. "Look, I'll have to call you back Julie." I sit down and weep. Everything is too much to handle. I am overwhelmed and angry. My phone beeps and it's Rita texting.

D, r u up?

Texting is slow for me, so I call her. She answers the phone immediately.

"Yes, but having emotional incontinence."

"Have you heard from Denise?"

"You mean the devil incarnate? No."

"Roan went by the fernery and said her Jeep is there and a squad car."

"Should we go over there and ask her what the hell is going on?"

"Dolly, I'm not ready for her yet. I think we need some legal advice."

"Hang on, the store is calling me. I'll call you back."

It is Julie. "Hey, Dolly, an attorney is calling for you, I got his number 863 455 4500. I told him I'd give you the message, is there anything, anything at all I can do for you?"

"Thank you, no, I just need some time, thank you." I hang up.

I call Rita, I can tell she is having a moment too. "Rita, an attorney named Robert Fox is calling me."

"Yeah, he just called here too and wants to make an appointment to review the last will on record with the family, tentatively set for Tuesday at three."

I feel anxious, "Do we know anything about Mr. Fox? Where he's from, what kind of law does he practice? Seems like I saw some papers in the office with his name on it. Let's hope there isn't any surprises."

"I've got another call coming in that I need to answer and then I'm going to the store."

It is a number I don't recognize but I say, "Hello, this is Dollene."

"Ms. Diamond, this is the Volusia County Medical Examiner's office. We are ready to release your mother's body to the funeral home. We have finished our exam and we we'll be typing the report soon. We furnish one report to the family and that report can be faxed or mailed at a cost of fifty dollars each."

"Okay. Please send it to me. Are you ready to take my e mail address? It is dollenediamondintheruff@bouquetstoday.net. Thank you."

The store is where I work and is my sanctuary. Like any sanctuary, it is a refuge of my creative self, my home. I spend most of my time here serving the public and although they aren't aware of it, it is my lifeblood. Projects keep me focused and ideas become inspiration to create beautiful décor. I am an artist, and art can be a light source or a period of darkness. I have seen both and it is a see saw teetering back and forth and a struggle to keep myself in balance. I have known for years that simply surrounding yourself with beauty does not make beautiful. My therapist has repeated that mantra for years and it is her insight that I need to know what triggers my darkness, and learn not to react to it. Today I feel dark.

I check my e mail and there is e mail from the medical examiner's office. I click on it and I quickly scan on down. It is a standard form with momma's name, age, weight. I'm scanning down to the estimated time of death and cause. OH MY GOD, opiate overdose! I gasp, approximately 160 mg of oxycontin present, perhaps relative to stage four pancreatic cancer, metastasizing in liver, kidney. Two tumors approximately evidenced in right femur. Diagnosis is probable 4-6 weeks until morbidity.

Under notes: no evidence of valid RX for oxycontin. Per the police report, there is no medication found at scene, and no prescription. Over the counter 250 mg. Tylenol on night stand observed on a night table.

Mom had cancer and nobody knew! To my knowledge, she had told no one. She must have been in pain, yet no one was aware of that either. I am wondering how long she had known about her illness. I cried out, "Mom, we could have been there for you!"

I am weeping and do not realize that Julie is entering my office. I tell her about the report and we cry together. There is no understanding of anything. I cry until I cannot cry any more.

I am leaving my office and I give a list of flowers to Julie to order for the funeral. I am going home to sit with the captain. Captain Morgan is an old friend of mine. On occasion, he spends the night and I tell him stories. This is a big story. I need my old friend tonight and do not want for any other visitors.

I do not hear the doorbell ring or even notice someone has come in. It is Rita and she looks at the bottle, "Dolly, that's not going to be any good for you today or tomorrow. We need to go over to Mom and Dads and see Denise and make some funeral arrangements. Denise texted me and says people are stopping in with food and she needs help."

"Here Rita, read this," I reach over to the counter and hand her the autopsy report.

She is reading and stops. "Oh, my god, there was something wrong with Momma."

"Yep..."

"It's unbelievable,"

"Yep..."

"Do you think she overdosed on purpose?"

"I have no idea but look here. The police report says only a Tylenol bottle was on the night stand."

"Yeah, I see that."

"Yep..."

"Dolly, you need to go in your bathroom, and put a cold washcloth on your face and get yourself out of this funk. I'll give you a few minutes, then we're leaving and going to mom and dads."

I return from the bathroom to see Rita still going over the paper, shaking her head.

"I guess we need to take this to Denise, and let her see it."

"Yeah, it's going to be big surprise to her too."

Many times, I have been down the road to the fernery. It is always breathtaking to take in all the ferns and oaks. Closer to the house the lake offers a subtle breeze and the ferns want to dance. Maybe they are just saying hello. The fruit of our parent's labor is evident. Rita and I both stop and breathe in deep. God is good. Rita and I walk hand in hand to the house together, stronger, I think.

Denise is on the phone when we walk in and pass by the counter. There is a bowl of cigarette butts on the counter. "If it weren't for that bowl, she'd never have a hot breakfast!" The captain is talking now. Denise has started a list with friends' names on it who have stopped by the house with food, flowers and plants. It seems organized enough.

"Where have ya'll been?" Denise asks. Her mouth is tight now, but I don't give a rip. I have my captain with me.

"You mean since we were thrown out of our parents' house, you know, when the police came and said the doors needed to be sealed, since then, dear sister?"

"Well, I know how fingers can get sticky and then things start disappearing quick. I was looking out for all of us."

"Oh really," I bark back. "Maybe we should check your hands, your fingers, even your Jeep, and see what may have stuck to your fingers and have been removed from the house."

"Hey, now, let's stop the sniping and come to terms with what has happened." Rita is chiming in.

"The great facilitator has spoken," and my sarcasm is an open faucet. The captain is still talking.

"Denise, this is the medical examiner's report." Rita barely gets the information out when Denise spews, "Why do YOU have the report, where did this come from, why wasn't it sent to me?"

"It was probably when you were having your breakfast of cigarettes," I am sure.

"It is sent to me because I am the one that called the police, specifically my name is the one on record in the police report. I know I don't have POA attached to my name but I'm still a daughter in case you need reminding."

"I certainly don't need reminding of what a viper tongue you have." Denise responds in kind.

Rita reiterates that decisions need to be made, and details need to be sorted out. "could we just pretend we are sisters again? Mom is looking down on us now."

There are several knocks on the door, and a neighbor is bringing in a pound cake. "Juan is outside the door wanting to see Miss Dolly," she says as she places the cake on the table.

"Anything that needs to be said, can be said to me," Denise shouts as she accompanies me to the screen door.

"Oh for Christ sakes Denise," I am shouting. "STOP BEING A BULLY!" I open the door and Juan grabs me by the hand. He has heard my comment and whispers, "No, I do not want to speak to the bull!"

"C'mon Juan, let's stroll down to the fernery. What is it Juan? You do not have to be apprehensive... um... nervous."

"Miss Dolly, Señora Diamond say she need to go to town one day with me. The day before I find her on floor in office, she not hurt, jus tipsy, she ask me not tell anyone, she has medicine, everything ok. I take her three weeks ago, and we go to office round hospital and I wait for maybe two or three hours, maybe more. We not cut fern that day, we fertilize. I bring her home, she say no. Next you stop at drug store. I wait again. She come out with big bag of ty Len ole, she said Mr. Blu need for aches and pains, we go home. I think she not feel good after that, she looked thin, my Maria say she look tire, wormy, I very sorry Señora die now, maybe she was mucho sick." Juan shakes his head and starts talking again.

"Our family wants to honor your family and my Maria want to cook for you. We have all the food Señora and Mr. Blu like to eat, and all the family like we always see here. My Maria and me want big family to eat together like Diamond family. We bring to Mr. Blu house for everybody, an especial dinner."

"Thank you, Juan. Our family thanks you and Miss Maria from the bottom of our hearts. My daddy and momma loved you very much. Our hearts are sad they are gone now, but they are in heaven."

"Si, Miss Dolly, si,"

Mr. Blu is the name Juan always used for my dad. Juan had worked for my daddy while he was in high school, earned enough money to send for his childhood sweetheart from Mexico. He wanted to marry his Maria legally and have her live at the Diamond farm. Dad always said that Juan did two and a half times the work of men half his age and never complained and appreciated everything. Heck, he'd even hold the water hose out for my dad to take a drink of water from it when he saw dad coming toward him. Daddy always said, "all his boys were girls," and Juan was the closest to a son Dad would ever have.

The walk had sobered me up some. I returned to the door, and go inside to the kitchen. I reach in the cupboard to get a glass and fill it with water. Filling it again, I spy Denise and Rita eating sandwiches. I make me a sandwich too. Rita says they are discussing the service, particularly the music.

"Lord, didn't we just do all this?

"Oh, what did Juan want?"

I pause between bites and start to tell them. Denise lights up a cigarette, and I stare at her.

Property Management

"**S**urely, you have got the good manners to wait until we finish eating before you light up. Just because mom and dad are gone doesn't change anything. This is still their house and you didn't smoke in it when they were alive, so you shouldn't smoke in it now." I am pissed.

"Well, actually it's not their house anymore, I own it." Denise says it without emotion. "Which is probably what the attorney has called the meeting about, so ya'll might as well find out about it now."

I choke on my sandwich. Rita's eyes are like saucers, "what are you talking about?"

Denise begins explaining. "Two years ago, when dad had his first stroke, we sold a lot of equipment and the motorhome because we all thought, including Mom, that Dad wouldn't be able to drive them anymore. Long story short, they got hit with a bunch of taxes, which I paid, rather Tom and I paid, without interest, and they signed a promissory note that if anything happened to them, the note would be paid off first, before anything could be divided. That year, they suffered a major loss in fern production due to cold weather. The fern production is back now, and Blu Diamond should be okay, but this will be a job for the CPA firm to sort out and let us girls see what the financial report states.

"Is there no end that you will go to, to build your ungrateful kids an empire?"

"My kids don't even know about this Dolly. Is there no end to your heinous personal attacks? What is your problem? Don't poke the bear Dolly, you won't like what comes out of the cave!"

"Are there any other surprises that we don't know about? I'm referring to the attorney's meeting tomorrow."

Denise said, "she didn't know, that she had received a call just like everyone else. She knew he was the family attorney but thought the meeting was a formality of sorts."

Rita turns to Denise, "you still haven't read the medical report, I think you should read it."

Denise starts looking over the report, "can this be true?"

I start in, "we need to get the Tylenol bottle from mom's night stand, and then I'll explain."

"I threw it out this morning when l straightened up her room. It was empty anyway."

This is the shyest behavior I have ever witnessed from Denise.

"Well, it might have been empty."

"If you'll look at the report, it mentions residue of Tylenol. I'm not an investigator but I think it would be a good idea to locate the bottle and then notify the police."

"You're making no sense Dolly."

"I'm telling you both that I just had a talk with Juan who said he found mom in the office one day and she had fallen. On another day, he drove her to the doctor, then to a drug store, where she bought Tylenol. We need to get to the bottom of all this BEFORE our little community goes crazy with gossip and rumors."

"Let's look in the compactor for that Tylenol bottle. It might prove to be important. It might make sense of all that's has been going on."

Carly's phone rings and its Bingham. "Hey baby, mom wants all of us to go over to grandmas. Juan and Maria, you know the farm foreman, is cooking for our family. Tommy is driving in about four and I want you to go over with me and Tommy. The way the grown-ups are acting, it'll be better if we can leave when we want."

"I'll make a call to the manager, and see if it's okay. He will probably let me have off since I rarely ask off. Often, I've filled in for other girls when he needed someone to show up quickly. It can be slow on a Tuesday night. I think it will be okay."

Fox News

The offices of Robert Fox, Esquire, is in the neighboring city of Deland. I have been there many times to shop at the malls in Deland and know my way around. His office is an old house nestled in a cluster of crepe myrtle trees on the right side off Orange Blossom Trail. The crepe myrtles are in full bloom and some of the trees have dropped their blooms now and have settled on the cobblestone parking area. It looks like old Florida as I make my way around the winding cobblestone sidewalk. I pull the heavy front door open. Wow! It is an old house completely restored. The heavy wood molding is stellar and the walls have rich gilded magnolia wallpaper on them. There are two big comfy side chairs beside a table that each holds crystal oil lamps. Several nice coffee tables with big books are available for me to peruse as I wait.

The receptionist has a name plaque in front of her. Dorothy Williams stands up, and extends her hand to me, "I am Dorothy, how can I assist you today?"

"Thank you, I reply, I have an appointment with Mr. Fox. My name is Dollene Diamond from Pierson, Fl."

"Yes, Ms. Diamond, I will show you to the conference room."

The conference room fills the entire back porch, overlooking the cobblestone parking lot I have just left. The room has a terrarium feel to it because one entire wall is glass. The glass wall is sparkly clean and the room smells crisp with a hint of pine. Botanical print wallpaper covers opposing walls and is so realistic it looks like the outside fauna has come indoors to read some of the beautifully bound books everywhere. A beautiful marble topped table, no doubt an antique, has a colorful bowl of fresh fruit on it and some muffins are nearby under a glass cloche. It is not your typical 'boxed cookie and stale coffee in a Styrofoam cup' refreshment center. Crystal glasses sit on a glass tray on the conference table alongside two pitchers of water with sliced limes. With a good book, I know I can probably stay here all day. This is the idea I am sure, to make someone feel at ease and less nervous about the underlying event that will be occurring. I see Rita and Roan pulling in the parking lot and I find a seat and make myself comfortable.

Denise and Tom walk in. I have been engaged in looking at the room and did not notice Denise's Jeep outside in the parking lot. They seem to be having a disagreement, because she does not look especially happy.

In walks Rita and Roan, followed by a secretary carrying in file folders seemingly for everyone. A short white haired stump of a man enters the room too and walks over to each one of us individually and shakes our hand. "Just call me Bob, because I am an old friend of your parents. Please everyone, have a seat. Mrs. Harris will be glad to offer you some refreshment."

Robert Fox looks like an old country lawyer. Everything about him is conservative except his pizzazzy bow tie. He says, yes ma'am to his secretary when she offers him tea, followed by "always Mrs. Harris, always." Mrs. Harris leaves and returns to the room with four glasses of iced tea, placing one at the head of the table where he is seated.

"Mrs. Harris, I thank you." She smiles, and he continues, "if you would be so kind to share a folder with each party."

"Miss Rita, Miss Denise and Miss Dolly, if you'll permit me, ...the untimely deaths of your parents are particularly painful to me as they have been lifelong friends of mine since high school. If you'll permit an old man's laments... your mother was my sweetheart before she was Blu's. We had been dating just a couple of weeks when she met my friend Blu. Blu and Miss Ellie were a match from the start. Blue and I were in an agriculture project together growing ferns. Miss Ellie took it upon herself to nurture that baby fern like it was her child. Soon, Blu had won Ellie's heart, and the ag award. In fact, they honeymooned at the Florida State Nursery Growers annual convention. I went on to law school, but we have remained forever friends. I saw her on several occasions as she worked through her last will. Sadly, I found out several weeks ago, that she was ill and it was her wish that she add a codicil to her final documents, hence the reason you all have been called here today."

"Family unity was very important to Ellie. She loved to cook for her family and make Sunday's special. The reason your parents worked so hard is so they could leave a legacy but one that kept the family together, not one than divides it."

Denise interrupts, "Mr. Fox, what about the codicil?"

"Ah yes, Ms. Denise, the spirited one, ... he begins...

The trustee executer will remain the same, however there are some revisions.

1. The general foreman Juan will remain as the acting foreman and will receive an immediate bonus of ten thousand dollars. Thereafter, a yearly bonus of ten thousand annually.
2. Juan cannot be fired from his job except for gross negligence, and then it must be a unanimous decision from the three daughters.
3. Yearly division of profit will be after taxes, if there is minimum working capital and fifty thousand dollars on deposit.
4. Once a month, the family must come together for a Sunday dinner on the second Sunday of every month. Surely twelve times a year is not too much keep the family together. Absolutely no distribution of monies will occur without the Sunday Dinners.

Rita slightly waves her hand.... "Mr. Fox, what if it is impossible to clear your calendar, uh, make it, because of scheduling...

He lowers his eyes to look through the bottom part of his glasses, ... Dear Miss Rita, you must be the planner ... and the facilitator. Your mother felt there is nothing more important than your family, no friend, no job, no social engagement...she was unswervingly clear about this.

I spoke before I realized, and "who is supposed to cook these Sunday dinners..."

Mr. Fox is clearly agitated.... Miss Dolly.... The capable cook... You three can work out these details. Your mom led me to the conclusion that you three girls were smart enough and reasonable adults that could do this if you knew it was expected. Am I right? Are there any further discussions?" Mr. Fox is all business.

Denise, clearly frustrated, "and if I want to contest this ...this .... this new addition?"

"Ms. Denise, I understand that every hurt dog barks. But these are your mothers wishes, her strong desire for something she had come to realize wasn't easily attainable. Miss Ellie had stated that you three girls were hard headed like old Blu. She said your daddy had always told you that the helping hand you were looking for was at the end of your arm, that you were all different personalities, strong willed, so I'll give you some free council. In fact, your mother paid me two years in advance, anticipating some resistance. Please know that you may call on me for assistance, to air grievances, but ladies I know you can work this out, that you can reflect on your good times, on those fond memories when you were a 'family'. I plan on overseeing the implementation of this codicil to see that in comes to fruition. Now... Everyone has a copy of this codicil within their folder." He pauses.... "Again, I want to express my deepest condolences to all of you. I will miss your parent's friendship immensely and I look forward to coming to dinner once every now and then."

I could see why Mom and Dad and Mr. Fox were old friends. I bet he has some other old stories to share about my folks. I am sure they'd be another day to ask him.

I really don't know how I feel about what has transpired. Bottom line, I guess Mom thought FAMILY was more important than money. The family dynamic is changing, and it will take an attitude change from everyone. I will wait and see if there are any more worms crawling out of the can, so to speak. Denise will have to quit lording her power over us. There is a household of treasures to divide, we'd just have to see about all this.

Spanish Comida

The drive back to the farm, I keep thinking, there has been a mother lode of events the last ten days. Tonight, would be another family dinner. Juan and Maria were preparing Spanish food. Perhaps, the captain could let Jose Cuervo step in for him tonight. I arrive right behind Rita and Roan. All the family will be here, and good food always calms everyone down.

Juan and Maria had been preparing all day. There were tamales, chile rellenos, and big cast iron pots of pinto beans and Spanish rice. Every table had a big bowl of fresh salsa, and warm chips. Juan walks up to me and brings me a caipirinha. Juan makes this drink with Mexican tequila and pure sugar cane juice and lime. It is such a smooth drink, and does not take long for the drink to take effect. I didn't think I needed to keep a clear head tonight, so I think, "Bring it on!"

Maria walks up to me smiling, "everything good, Miss Dolly?"

"Of course, delicioso," I answer.

Maria adds ...."and we have soapapillia for dessert." Soapapillias are light and pillowy flour biscuits with honey inside. Maria always cut ice cream into small bricks and then heaps on some wine sauce while they are hot. It will be a sweet ending to a trying day.

Bingham and Carly are sitting together on a bench and Bingham has his arm around her, until he sees the soapapillias being served. He breaks away and slides in next to Maria. I'm next Ms. Maria."

"Ah, Mr. Bing. You and your brother are growing up big and strong."

"Yes, we like to eat Maria. You can tell my brother when he comes to get one that you don't have anymore."

"You tease me, si? Mr. Bing, you see we have plenty. Por favor, take one to your pretty senorita."

"I'll share some of mine with her. She likes the tamales best Maria."

Roan stands up and taps on his glass with his spoon. "Juan and Maria, the Diamond family says mucho gracias for the comida. You fill our tummies and fill our hearts with your friendship, much appreciated." We echo with claps, and smiles, and whispers of thank you all around.

It appears a small family discussion is taking place with Denise and Tom and their kids. Bingham and Carly have their arms around each other are nodding their heads in unison at Denise. In a few seconds, Bing and Carly and Tom Jr. ease over to Maria and Juan and say their goodbyes and goodnight. They are heading back over to the coast and we will see them when they return for the funeral.

I am ready to leave. It has been a long day. My head is starting to hurt and I just want to crash at my house. Thank God, it is a short distance to get there. I do not want to get into another heavy discussion with anyone. I look for Juan and Maria and make my way to them to say good-night. I thank them and hug them. The physical contact makes me weak in the knees, and I can feel my eyes flooding with tears. I break away and say "gracias, dear friends."

Walking to my car, the sound of people laughing, and soft guitar music echoes off the lake. The aroma of good food is replaced with the smell of good earth. This land my parents have worked with their hands surrounds me and I stop at the car door and just breathe it all in.

Reality Check

I do not know what time it is because my eyes are still closed. I'm dreaming about the country fair. Mom convinces me to enter a graham cracker cake in the baking contest. It is a family favorite.

I have taken first place and receive the people's choice award. I can hear people clapping and it sounds like they have gloves on. Damn, these thumps are text messages coming in on my cell. The phone is muted but the thumps are clear enough. Geez. I open my eyes and it is Rita calling. It is ten o clock and I have overslept. I turn on my phone and immediately it rings. It's Rita.

"Where are you? We're waiting here."

"Here where?"

"Where you're supposed to be."

"Okay, I give up."

"Are you coming? Did you just get up?"

"I'm not up and I'm half asleep, but I'll get ready, and meet you at the funeral home."

One look in the mirror, and I can see that it was a big night with big bed head. Into the shower I go. I'm thinking about the decisions that need to be made. This will be our first test between sisters.

The funeral directors are my people. I work with these folks weekly, but now this is more personal. I walk into the private family room and sit down. Good, Rhett and Rene are here.

"If I had known children could have input I would have insisted Bingham and Tom were present also," Denise tersely remarks.

"You know I have always admired the way you speak up, even if it is before you have fully thought it through ....all family should be welcome," Rita rebuffs.

Mr. Grady begins expressing his condolences. He is very sorry we are all here again so soon, burying our other parent. He hopes we were satisfied with the previous service he had provided. "I fully understand if there are different ideas with your mother. Please feel comfortable to change anything because we are here to help you in your time of sorrow."

He continues and asks if we have selected a date and time. We look at each other and in unison say SUNDAY... Rita asks two o'clock? Amazingly we can agree. There is HOPE for our family.

Mr. Grady asks if we have brought momma's clothing. "Did we want to use her regular hairdresser and did we have a recent picture? Is there special jewelry?"

Rita takes charge and thanks him. "May we have some privacy for a few minutes?"

"Of course, I will step in my office. Please press the intercom button whenever you want me to return."

Rita continues, "I think mom should wear one of her blue outfits. She recently had her hair cut so I think they are capable of handling her hair. After all, Mr. Grady knows what she looks like. We were all here just over a week ago. I think mom should wear her blue diamond necklace daddy gave her for their sixtieth anniversary, although I can't remember seeing it lately."

"It's probably in her jewelry box. Perhaps we need to take all the jewelry to the bank, until I decide how to split it." Denise interrupted.

"How YOU decide?" There is no chance of this statement getting by me, "Denise, there is plenty of jewelry to go around, and we will decide the democratic way who gets what. Maybe mom left a note with Mr. Fox about that. I can phone him."

"I will do the phoning Dolly. I have some other questions for him." Denise reacts quickly.

"Let's wrap this up." With that being said, Denise presses the call button and Mr. Grady answers.

"I'll be right in."

"If there are no changes to the obituary, we will submit it to the local newspaper and the greater Orlando area paper. Our secretary has mentioned that she has received several calls from nurseries including the Florida State Nursery Growers Association in Orlando." The funeral director reaches across the table and lays down an envelope.

"I have enclosed itemized expenses here in this envelope. If there are any questions, please do not hesitate to phone me."

Denise reaches down for her purse and pulls out her checkbook and hurriedly signs a check, tears it off and slides it on the table.

Mr. Grady clears his throat. "Oh, I didn't mean that it needs to be taken care of now. Whenever you are ready and satisfied with our services."

Denise retorts "it's good for whatever the amount," and she gets up and grabs her purse and exits.

Oh Em Gee! Who does this, who acts this way? I look at Rita and she shakes her head no, suggesting that I not say anything out loud.

Rita thanks Mr. Grady and picks up the envelope. Rhett shakes Mr. Grady's hand. I'd forgotten he and Rene were still here. I'm thinking this is typical Diamond children; should be seen and not heard. We all leave together and walk outside. Denise is smoking. Tom looks embarrassed. Of course, he is, we are all embarrassed.

"Can you be more of an ass Denise?" I shout. "You are completely psycho! Have you no manners or refrain? anything? These are my associates Denise. How would you like it if I went over to your town and acted this way in front of Tom's colleagues?" I barely get the statement out when she comes back with her usual viciousness.

"You wouldn't have a blank check to fill in Dolly because you spend every dollar you make. Her voice is loud now, "and if I get to mom and dads and I can't find that necklace then I'm going to call the police." Denise throws her cigarette down on the ground and takes her foot to stomp it out. She starts walking to her jeep.

I look down on the ground and see three cigarettes all snubbed out. "I don't know what possesses me but I lean down and pick them all up and hurry to catch up to her as she gets in her Jeep. She is buckling her seat belt. I throw the cigarettes at her and I am delighted they land in her face. "Here, smoke these. I may not have money but at least I have manners."

Everything is getting back to normal. I want to stab and wound as quickly as I can. This is war and I have years of pent up anger and aggression. I turn and see Rita and Roan leaving with Rhett and Rene in the back seat.

Rita never loses her cool and rarely participates in many barb exchanges. She refrains from personal attacks but just wait till she hears that Denise is accusing her of lifting the diamond necklace also. Denise believing, we are capable of stealing is wrong on so many levels.

Rita is in fact, Dr. DeRita Roberts, executive director of the Volusia County Consortium, twenty-four hours and seven days a week. She is all that and a bag of chips. It will be interesting to witness how diplomatic she is when called a thief.

My mother's necklace is stunning. Dad was extravagant for their sixtieth anniversary. The necklace has a center blue diamond that is a four-carat cushion cut stone surrounded by sixty channel set diamonds. The bale of the pendant is set with a top row of three diamonds and the bottom row has five diamonds, symbolizing their anniversary the fifth day of the third month. Momma was seldom seen without the necklace and she loved it dearly. Surely it isn't missing, perhaps stored somewhere else.

I don't know where everyone else is headed but I am going to the store to check on my business. All this emotional sparring is draining me of energy. I just want to sit down at my desk and unwind. I wonder if the back cooler has any wine in it. A small glass could take the edginess off and I could concentrate on mom's flowers, specifically her casket spray. I am thinking about a base of the best leather leaf fern our family grows. Maybe Juan can cut some of the new variety called Lacey to weave through it all the flowers. Mom always said the new fern was named for one of dad's old girlfriends. Everyone always laughs about it and mom will laugh about it too when she looks down from heaven.

Entering the store, I ask Julie how everything is going.

She tells me "I can take care of all this so why don't you go and be with your family?"

I look up at her and say, "I know you can handle anything, but right now, I'd rather drink a glass of acid rain than be with my family. Do we have many orders for my momma yet?"

"Yes, right now I have taken sixteen orders. There are a couple of large sprays ordered. The governor's office called. I first thought it was a joke, but he gets on the phone and says Rita is a personal friend of his and wants a floral tribute with presence."

"And does he have the money for a tribute of presence?" We both grin because we both know people want a world of flowers until there is a price tag attached to it.

"Oh well, you know my mom loved flowers, and I want her to look around in the church and see she that she was loved." I am getting emotional now. Over the years, I had hardened myself regarding funerals in general. Rarely did I lose it when families were ordering flowers for their loved ones. Some requests end up being a bit bizarre. I said I was going to write a book about funerals and flowers one day. One of my best stories is when an entire family comes in. Their favorite Aunt Molly was a gardener, and they wanted every flower we could possibly get and design a garden with an open gate, hang her garden hat on the gate all made out of flowers. Aunt Molly was this, Aunt Molly was that, and so beloved.

My reply was that it could be done. A base price of two hundred dollars was quoted and could run much higher. Before I could utter anything else about the pricing structure, one by one, the individuals started whispering and their necks stretched upward. There was a lot of clearing their throats...oh my, that much? they asked. "Well, it had been a while since they had seen her," Dear Aunt Molly wasn't so dear any more.

Through the years, I had made a lot of different floral designs that included a semi-tractor trailer, a dragline, an airboat, a Budweiser can, a grand piano, and even a ring of fire for a famous circus performer all out of flowers. I knew I could make my momma a tribute that truly honored her. It would be a labor of love.

Julie hands me a stack of message. The Smiths called, the church, mom's bridge group the Pierson Police Department. I stop looking at the messages and focus on the one from the police department. Investigator Price would like for me to come in for an interview at my earliest convenience.

The Interview

I'll call now. On two rings, I hear, "Detective Price speaking."
"Officer Price, this is Dollene Diamond." I am returning your
call."

"Yes, Ms. Diamond, I appreciate you getting back to me so quickly. I
know you must have a lot of details to attend to regarding your mother's
untimely death, however I would like to ask you to come in for a brief
taped interview...in my office."

"A taped interview? Do I need legal representation?"

"That will be your choice Ms. Diamond. I have also reached your
sisters and I plan to interview them separately from you. You are my
primary concern because you are the one that found your mother not
breathing. Based upon the medical examiner's report which I assume you
have read by now, it is our goal to try and piece together this puzzle and
come to a reasonable conclusion. Can I expect your full cooperation?"

"Of course, I want answers as well. I can come in this afternoon,
actually in a few minutes."

"That will be fine. I'll expect you shortly."

I get up from my desk and look at Julie and tell her I am walking
down to the police station. "I guess they're trying to put all the pieces of

the puzzle together. Maybe they have more information for me, for the family."

It is just two blocks south from our store. I walk in and a tall uniformed officer approaches me. I notice Detective B. Price on a gold name tag.

"Come right in, Ms. Diamond, and have a seat. May I offer you some bottled water?"

"Thank you, No."

Officer Price begins. "With your permission, I will turn on my recorder for the record."

"Oh, Okay."

"Ms. Diamond,"

"Please call me Dolly," I interrupt.

"The police report states you called them about 9:40 pm. Is that correct? "

"I really don't know what time it was, I suppose that is right."

"Why is that? that you weren't aware of the time, wasn't that the day of a family funeral?"

"Yes, everyone had just left and Mom was retired into her bedroom. I took a long bath and went in to say goodnight to her. I noticed she was laying down in her funeral clothes and I asked if she needed help getting into her nightie. She never answered me. I think I shook her and she was lifeless. It was then that I realized she wasn't breathing and I called the police. You have the ...the ...rest of the story."

"Are you aware she had a terminal illness?"

"To my knowledge no one in the family knew, only she knew, and possibly her doctor."

"I have spoken with her doctor and he has confirmed that she was under his care for pancreatic cancer. Dr. Wiley said the cancer was advanced and in his estimation, your mother had less than three months to live."

"Did your mother ever seem overwhelmed? Was she despondent or mention suicide?"

"Absolutely never. Lately she was concerned that my sisters and I remain civil to each other and get along. I admit that is a lofty goal."

"Why is that Ms. Diam...uh. I mean Dolly?"

"Why? Because I guess we're all different, competitive, and pig headed. The kids will include the word controlling, yes, all of that."

"And are you? Controlling?"

"I would like to think assertive with leadership." and we laugh together.

"Dolly, did you see any prescription bottle sitting around with OxyContin on the label?"

"No, never, I only recall seeing Tylenol."

"Do you have any further information that might be helpful?"

"Only that our farm foreman told me yesterday that he had taken my mother to a doctor's office several weeks ago. None of us sisters were aware that she had any appointments whatsoever. Juan, our foreman, found her on the office floor one day which was a complete surprise and I was shocked when he told me. I wish he had told me sooner, but Juan is fiercely loyal to my parents."

"That information is interesting and then Officer Price stands up. I thank you for your time and if you think of anything that might be helpful please call me. Here is my card." He hands the card over and extends his hand to shake mine. It is weird but I think of my Daddy's hands, a working man's hands.

I'm out the door, and up one block already when my cell goes off. The ring tone is Darth Vader's storm troopers anthem. I always laugh when I hear it. Rhett is calling from his mom's phone.

"Aunt Dolly, mom is looking for you and she's at your store, Are you on your way?"

"Yep, I'll be there in about thirty steps."

I step in the shop and am counting thirty-eight, thirty-nine, forty, forty-one. I lie. "forty-one steps, I'm here, what's up?"

Rita asks, "how'd it go?"

"Alright."

"Just alright?"

"Well, I haven't been arrested. I think they're just putting two and two together to try and get four. I did not feel interrogated and only slightly uncomfortable. He is nice guy and very good looking."

"Julie tells me the governor called for flowers. That is so thoughtful."

"Yeah, he wanted to spend the minimum, only twenty dollars. She said she told him if that's all he wanted to spend he might want to consider a packet of seeds."

"Don't tell her that! I didn't say that Rita." Julie shouts. "I didn't tell him that. He is very nice and ordered a big piece, said you were special friends or something like that."

"I know Julie, Dolly's just jealous because she doesn't have any famous friends. Are you getting many orders?"

"I haven't really been here to see." I yell across to the back of the room. "Julie, how many orders for mom?"

"About twenty or so. Most everybody says whatever the family would like is what most customers are saying," she answers.

"Well, Mom loved flowers, and I want her to have as many as she can. We do not want donations going to hospice."

"What are you planning on for the casket spray?"

"I want it to be a garden of everything; a seasonal kaleidoscope of color and includes roses, larkspur, snapdragons and verbena. I might even use some cut caladiums in it."

"That sounds pretty. Denise is going home to get some fresh clothes after her visit to the police department. For your information, she has been tearing the house apart looking for the necklace."

"It isn't there? Denise can't find it? Where do you think Mom put it? I can't remember when I last saw Mom wearing it. Was she wearing it on the day of Dad's service? My mind is blank but I'm sure it will turn up when we start looking for it."

The day is almost gone and it's almost five thirty now. Julie is starting to shut down the shop. I look at Rita. "I'm just not up for another family dinner. We probably all need some time alone don't you think?"

"Probably," Rita answers. We need to decide who's going to speak at the funeral. I need to call the church back and let them know how many will be at the service. I would think about the same number as dad's dinner after his service. The church secretary mentioned maybe a ham this time instead of turkey. Of course, she reminded me someone from the family will need to be there to accept the food.

"Carly did a great job last Sunday but I do think it would be imposing for her to do it a second time. It's just so hard to believe it's all been a week, yet so much has happened."

"Rita, I'm just so exhausted. I need to go home and rest so I can work on funeral work tomorrow. You and Denise must work out any more decisions that need to be made."

Rita frowns. "Working with Denise can be like working with rats on a sinking ship. She creates chaos and then she leaves the room or vacates when something isn't going her way."

"Take Rhett for support. He always seems to garner her favor."

"Yeah, that's a thought."

Rhett was taking some calls when Scarlett opens the door. She waits patiently for him to get off the phone. Rhett asks, "Do you mind if we go over to Granny's tonight? I think Mom needs some moral support with Aunt Denise tonight. She just wants to be sure Aunt Denise uses good judgement and that everyone is on the same page. She said we might need to set a few mouse traps," Rhett laughs to himself.

"What?" Scarlett asked.

"It's nothing, I was just 'foolin."

"Sorry, I'm late Mom, I stopped by the hardware store to pick up rat poisoning." Rita shakes her head but is clearly amused.

Rhett tells Scarlett to meet him there. On Wednesdays Scarlett plays the piano for choir practice. Her dad's church is a Pentecostal church with three hundred members and they have a lively church choir that can sing the old gospels till the cows come home. Scarlet had been playing piano since she was ten and is self-taught. Later in her teens she learned to read music. She likes to put in original little piano runs that are very entertaining. Sometimes in the spirit, when she is banging on those keys, her hair bounces up and down and it is a sight to behold. It is truly a God given talent. The audience is fed with the Christian spirit from her music. Scarlett has a calming effect on Rhett.

The Split

Denise is discussing to how to split up the contents of the house. She wants to do a family draw. The oldest daughter gets the first pick, then on down the line.

"What line, the kids, then grandkids?" Rhett asks. What happens if you pick the most expensive thing first?" No, I think a better way would be to access a value on the contents and divide it into three. Each daughter has so much spending dollars. This way, they can buy want they want from a fork to the farm."

"There are so many things you can't put a value on Rhett." Rita corrects him.

"Everything has a value on it Mom. Give me an example of something you can't put a price on!"

"Well, like pictures, frame, old letters, the family bible, mom's cookbook."

"Recipes can be copied, and if *your* picture isn't in a frame, why would you want it?"

"We're talking about pictures of Mom and Dad."

"Mom you get so emotional. Pictures can be copied too. I'm just saying Walmart Photo Shop copies pictures every day. I'm sure they can do this quick. As far as the cookbook goes, it's more important to fix the food, rather than fixate on a recipe. When is supper?"

"There is plenty to eat here. Fix yourself a plate. There's chicken and dumplings the Whitehouse's brought over this afternoon."

Rhett lifted the lid, trying to get a rise out of his momma and said, "Aunt Dolly would be making us some fried cornbread if she were here."

"Yes, she probably would, but you'll survive without it."

Everyone seemed to be enjoying the chicken and dumplings when Denise asked what else needed to be decided on about the funeral.

"Actually, lots. We need to ask someone to speak about Mom at the service, and what music will be playing while the video is being shown. They'll be a bigger group to feed afterwards because Mom's bridge group will be in attendance. I don't know how Dolly feels about what I'm going to say, but I want to forego the big dinner after the funeral and opt for a family dinner at home. We've all been through enough for two weeks, and given the circumstance of Mom's death, the less people means less questions asked about the investigation and less inquiries and gossip all around."

"Hmmm... Rhett responds. I'm on board for my family. We can announce it after all of the speakers and come back to Mom and Dads and try to have a quiet family dinner."

Detective Price has interviewed everyone. Mrs. Diamond's doctor had provided a bleak outlook on her physical condition and displayed no surprise that Ellie Diamond might have overdosed on pain medication given her despair and sadness. She had expressed to the doctor that she and her husband never wanted to be a burden to their children for any reason. She had told him on several occasions that she and her husband had experienced a complete life together and unlike many couples, they were ready spiritually to leave this earth whenever it was God's will. It was the doctor's opinion that Ellie had not had time to tell her husband she was ill, and perhaps in her mind she was ready to join her husband. The prescribed medicine oxycontin was to be self-administered as needed for severe pain. Mrs. Diamond had confided in her doctor, that she was tiring and had fallen a couple of times, probably from fatigue. He did not have a theory as to whether he felt the overdose was intentional, but did feel his patient had not shared the prognosis with any of her family as of her last appointment.

A secondary phone interview with a county psychologist confirmed many couples with a long-married life would choose to end their lives together given a choice. One thing was clear to him, that Blu and Ellie diamond had a family that intended no harm to either one of them. He wasn't sure the sisters felt the same about each other but would leave his personal feelings off the report.

A formal letter of the completed investigation would simply state that there was no evidence of criminal behavior, and death was caused by accidental means. Hopefully, the family would receive the letter soon and could begin the process of needed healing.

The captain and I are sitting on my screen porch and I am thinking about the events of the day. What was that old saying? When God closes a door, he always opens a window…. Yes, it seems my windows always come with jagged edges and eminent injuries. Both of my parents are gone now and although they provided me with a solid foundation to stand on, they also were the cause of my some of my insecurity and self-loathing. Outwardly I am self-assured and motivated. Inward, I am a mess of rum and ridicule. I need to be focused. Focus means survival. Survival can be success, and the big bus I'm on keeps on moving.

My mind drifts, and I can smell cinnamon rolls. I am only ten and its Saturday. Mom and I are going to make rock cookies. They take so long to make. I chop pecans for hours, candied cherries in red and green, and do the same with pineapple slices. There's a big stainless steel bowl I mix all of them into and add orange juice. I wake rested and for some reason could use a glass of orange juice. I intend to fill my day with beautiful flowers. I am inspired to create and make my momma proud.

On the way to work I stop by the fernery to pick up a couple of cases of greens. I see Juan talking to some workers on the loading dock so I pull my van into a side parking spot and then walk into the office. Understandably, the office is quiet, and there are small smiles on everyone as they acknowledge my entrance. Juan comes right in and says, "Good Morning Miss Dollene. I help you get fern boxes from cooler." We pass through the hallway and I can't help to see mom and dad's office door with green tape and a new lock on the outside of the door.

"What's this?" I shake the lock.

Juan answers, "Miss Denise, she come yesterday. NO one go in. No entrada! It's okay."

I nod my head. *yep, I'm on the bus, but I'm way in the back.*

Juan gets a box of leather leaf out of the cooler. I use my fingers to say two, and say "I need some of that new kind; *lacey, also,* just a couple of bunches."

"Si, I get for you."

I'm loaded, and ready to get cracking on the orders.

I drive to the store and I am so aggravated, talking to myself, and I realize I just need to calm down.

Julie is already working, and says for me to call my sister.

"Which one?"

"Both."

I call Rita and she answers, and I immediately say. "Look, I need to get something done today, I don't need a parade of problems."

"Have you talked to Denise?"

"No I but I went by the fernery. I thought she had gone home, but Juan said she was there yesterday, I guess long enough to put a new lock on the door and some tape. I guess it's official, she's in charge."

"Are there any marching orders yet?"

"We were talking last night. I suggested foregoing the big crowd, and dinner after the funeral to be for family only. That way we can warm up dishes ourselves, we don't have to ask anybody to help, just family, Denise agreed to it, you okay with it?"

"I suppose, it's going to be a long day anyway if we go to church beforehand. Okay, turn me loose, Ya'll decide."

Julie had already made several gorgeous standing sprays. It seems she has everything under control.

The casket spray will take me a couple of hours. I am reminiscing while I am cutting flowers about my mom and how she used to deliver some of the arrangements for me. One time she had left the recipients flowers with a neighbor. The recipients call up and say their door had been tagged for a delivery. The tag says the flowers were left with a neighbor. They didn't even know their neighbor. I called mom to ask where she had left them, her response was that they needed to get to know their neighbor. My mom was a dandy for sure, always smiling, and tried her best to be helpful in times of crisis. I was finishing now and Julie remarks that it is beautiful, one of my best sprays ever. I say my goodbyes, that I am going home. Tomorrow will be here soon enough.

I am walking in the door, when Rene calls. She has been away for a few days, covered in meetings and conferences. Could she bring anything for the dinner tomorrow?

"I guess everything is taken care of, and what isn't taken care of will just have to do. I think they have decided for the crowd to be just family."

"You sound tired Aunt Dolly, go to bed and get some rest."

"Okay." I hang up and search for my robe.

Denise and Tom phone their kids, and remind them of the appropriate attire for Granny's service. "Ok, Bing, if you really must, then bring Carly, "thank goodness Tom Jr. does not feel the need to bring any of his friends. Carly has been noticeably inquisitive about everything, and while I thought it is a good thing, she will need to be reminded I expect her loyalty. Changes are going to be made, and I need full family support. The gravy train from my parent's business that Dolly has been enjoying has a caboose. Dolly will soon realize she needs to grow up from "being the baby" in the family. I am going to ferret out what monies have been given to her and ascertain if they have been paid back."

Sunday has arrived and the family would meet at the church and go in as a group. The funeral home assures us parking space. I was glad Rita and

Roan offer to pick me up so that Julie could use the van to deliver the flowers by 1:00. We were all seated together, but somehow, I didn't feel close or embraced.

The video starts and it is the whole 'fan-damily' seated at one of our Sunday Dinners. Gosh, what a spread! I recall teachings from both my grandmas about cooking.

Dad's mother entertained a bit fancier. My other granny rarely measured. She would make biscuits and measure Crisco with her palm, quickly adding buttermilk with her left hand and mix everything together with her right hand. Yep, "with a quickness so one doesn't over-mix. Good bread, she'd remind me is the opposite and requires lots of mixing and kneading."

The video keeps playing. It is happy times. I wonder what the secret was back then...direction from our parents? There is kindness and respect, sorely lacking now. I wonder if Denise and Rita are seeing what I am seeing. I have lots of answers and no solutions.

I had forgotten we always followed dinners with games. We are playing volleyball with more family. It is our extended family with lots of cousins, playing in the lake, and eating watermelons. We should have done a video like this for Dad's service too.

Reverend Jackson steps to the pulpit now, and is stating that Mom "was a godly woman and represented helping hands for the church family. Service to one's church and community is a labor of love that does not cost money. All who serve the Lord will find their reward in heaven." He closes his remarks and introduces Robert Fox, a friend of the family.

Mr. Fox walks to the front, then side steps to acknowledge us girls one at the time seated on the front row, passing by each one of us, out stretching his hand, showing his respect, and whispering his condolences. It is brief, but I know it is heartfelt. I keep repeating to myself that he is a friend to our family. His voice is louder now than I remembered from a few days ago. I think it odd that he does not pull any sort of paper out from his vest and he begins speaking.

"I met Mr. Blu in my old college days. I was not able to come to his funeral last week, because of previous obligations, but I can tell you that I would have had something to say about the man that stole my girlfriend from me." There was a quick pause and then he laughs. "Yes, Mr. Blu and I were roommates in Gainesville. We both had ag scholarships from our FFA clubs. We were two rough neck boys who escaped the draft and whose parents thought we could use some more 'learnin'. We were full of vim and vinegar, equally competitive. We had the bright idea one night to take the club pig out for a joy ride. Yes, we stole Patsy the pig, put her in Blu's truck, and carry her over to High Springs, and let her run amuck in a corn field. Patsy was a lot heavier to pick up after she had eaten corn for few hours. We drank beer and just let Patsy graze a path in the corn field. It took both of us to pick her up, and put her back in the truck. The next day all the ag boys remarked that Patsy seemed fatter, you know all of a sudden like, they'd say. Some of the guys wanted to bar b que her right then and there. That night Blu told me that he'd have to tell me, that he was interested in Miss Ellie also, a girl I had been dating only two weeks. Later, we took on a fern project, and Miss Ellie took to liking Blu. Miss Ellie was a looker as we men would say, but she had goals, and she and Blu formed a strong bond that served them well for over sixty years.

In our small communities, unless published, we rarely see what our folks do outside of our community. I have been privy to know a couple that continued to grow in their knowledge of their industry, to foster programs, and support studies to enhance production of their products and preserve the land they were harvesting from. These actions were truly selfless, with anonymity, until now."

Miss Ellie served dutifully on the Florida State Nursery Growers Association board for thirteen years and it is her wish that family continue the good work this board does."

Thank you for allowing me to tell you about Ellie Diamond. She was a special lady for sure.

I guess we had been swept up in our own lives that we girls did not realize what our parent's legacy was all about. Time would tell if we girls would fully appreciate the fruition of their hard work.

Mr. Fox is thanking everyone for their attendance and for the many acts of kindness and then he announces the family would retire and continue to the cemetery for a private burial.

We stand up and file out of the church. Outside it is a typical Florida day, hot and humid.

The Family Plot

The flowers from Dad's funeral have been removed. Gosh, it was only last week. It didn't seem possible that we all are here again. There isn't the crowd of people now, just family. The grave diggers are off at a distance, and Mr. Grady stands reverently, patient as ever and quietly walks over to us and asks if we are ready to lower the casket. Finally, we agree on something.

It is an old cemetery where sand spots seem prevalent. Fire ant mounds are everywhere. The city needs to put out ant killer. Luckily, Mr. Grady has Astro turf under all our chairs because when fire ants get on your legs, I believe one ant says "Charge!" and then they all attack. There is little one can do except watch their footing and where they are going.

Looking around, I notice a police car and Detective Price is standing outside the door of his squad car with his hat over his heart. It is endearing to me and says a lot about his respect for bereaved families.

The drive back to the folk's house is silent. Of course, we arrive before Denise's family. It is typical for them to hang back and be full of tom foolery, and expect everything to be ready when they finally get here. It would be too much luck for Denise to have encountered any fire ants while she smoked at the cemetery.

Roan is slicing ham, and Rita is taking out the rolls out of the oven when everyone else walks in. Carly comes up and immediately hugs me like we are long lost sisters. She said she was so sad to learn Miss Ellie had passed away, "you must have been devastated to find her deceased like that."

"I was," I answer, "it still seems surreal."

I finish fixing my plate and find a seat in the dining room. I don't even feel like eating. I am in a tornado of thoughts. *I feel like I am riding in this bus, and I am in the back of the bus, there isn't a driver.* It was a good service, but where do we go from here? I look about and stare at all the "things" sitting on the tables and shelves; the mementoes, the *"glass kitties"* that define us. What would I want from my parents lives? All the leftovers need to be divided now, but how? My only wish is that I be given the family cookbook. I pray that it will not be another battle in obtaining it.

I hadn't noticed that Carly sits down beside me. Evidently, someone is keeping her informed to the latest information because she blurts out that she saw Momma leaving the bathroom last week with a Tylenol bottle in her hand on her way to the bedroom. Miss Ellie slipped into her bedroom away from the people and noise.

"I don't know why I think it is odd to be leaving the bathroom with a bottle still in your hand," she offers.

"I suppose," I respond. I am thinking... perhaps the medicine chest can provide some answers. I'll have to look.

I excuse myself when Bingham comes in to locate Carly and take my plate to the kitchen and place it in the sink.

I walk back to the middle bathroom where there is a big medicine cabinet and mirror and open it. Mom was never one to throw out anything, so it is no surprise that the cabinet is a smorgasbord of bottles containing capsules and pills for whatever ails you. There is a Caladryl bottle nearly empty from the year 1962 purchased in Idaho Springs, Colorado. God love her, Mom hung onto everything. So why couldn't she hang onto life? There it is, on the end what I am looking for. Ellie Diamond, oxycontin, dated three months ago. It is empty.

I grab the bottle and take it out on the porch where everyone can see it. "Look, what I've found."

"Well, it doesn't really provide any answers. We'll probably never know what was in Mom's mind," Denise utters. "We'd all be better served if you were to locate the necklace. I think that should be more worrisome to you."

"Perhaps you could devote some time to looking for it versus changing the locks on the cooler doors at the fernery."

"Perhaps, you can bring a business check the next time you come to the fernery."

With every exchange, I can feel everyone's sets of eyes volleying between us.

Carly stands up and asks if anyone needs more tea. There are snippets of laughter.

The telephone rings and I go answer it. "This is the Diamonds."

"Hello," a voice I do not recognize. "This is James Whitmore, reporter for the Deland Daily News. We are writing a story about Mrs. Diamond's passing, and we are investigating the drug overdose aspect. We are looking for a statement from the family."

"Mr. Whitmore, my mother was terminally ill, and had a valid prescription for the pain killer she was taking and was under a doctor's care. You might want to consider writing about the philanthropic work my parents did for this community instead of stooping to unsubstantiated rumors. I will have the police chief call you as soon as possible. Are you understanding our families position?

"Um, yes, I believe I do. Please accept my apology."

I quickly walk outside and call the number to Detective Price I have stored in my cell.

He answers on the second ring.

"Good evening, this is Dollene Diamond."

"Hello, everything okay?"

"I have three things I need to discuss. First, I just received a call from a Mr. James Whitmore from the paper who wants to do a story about my Mom's uh, accident, uh..demise. Listen, we can't, my family can't have that printed, where did they get that information?"

"And the second?"

"What?"

"You said there were three things."

"Yes, will you call him and try to put out that fire? Perhaps threaten him?"

"Well, I'm not in the habit of threatening citizens Ms. Diamond. I hear some anxiety in your voice, just take a deep breath."

"It's Dolly remember? And third, I want to thank you for being at the cemetery today. Your police presence was helpful, and the respect you demonstrated is appreciated."

"My mother pretty much insisted that I help you guys out, with budget cuts all over the place, squad cars aren't usually used anymore for private funerals, but I have to be a bit more flexible when my mom asks me. She's my cook and housekeeper. My mother and your mother were bridge friends. She says your mom had more southern spunk than anybody she knew.

"Begging your pardon, SKUNK?"

"No ma'am, I said **Spunk**!, you know spirit, spark, southern determination,"

"Oh, I laugh. I guess I better turn my belle tone up, I guess it's in our gene pool."

"Loss of hearing?"

"No, spunk. Well, maybe hearing too."

"Yes Ma'am, you are welcome."

"Goodnight," I pause.

"Yes ma'am."

I return to the inside and I must have a grin on my face. I feel like the grin needs explanation.

Rita asks, "What was all that about?"

Officer Price and I were having a breezy conversation about a reporter, and him being at the cemetery today."

"Did you say breezy?" Rita asks.

"Did I?"

"You did."

I sit back down at my plate and grin again.

Denise announces that she and Tom are going home in the morning, and that she will be locking the door to the house. "If it's okay with everyone, Tom and I will be back for the Sunday Dinner three weeks from now. Ya'll think about it and let me know what food you want us to bring."

Rita asked when will be getting together to access value on some of the household items. I do not believe that personal items of sentimental value should be your charge, comparatively speaking with that of the trust and those decisions, do you?" She gets up and says "I'll think about it. It will be my discretion." She grabs her purse from the hallway and makes her usual cig escape.

Rita looks over to Tom, "you can help the family by talking to her about letting up on some of that control she's lording over us."

Tom put his hands up in the air, "I think she'll calm down some with time. This has been a lot for everyone to absorb...I hope so anyway. I think her buttons are being pushed and she is just reacting. This is a big undertaking with little notice. We're all a bit defensive and edgy."

We all nod our heads yes, because we know he is right.

Rene says she and the rest of the cousins can clean up and divide the leftovers.

Rhett answers "we will?"

"Yes, brother, you, me, Scarlett, Robert, Bingham, Tom and Carly too."

"I'd love to help out." Carly immediately stands up and hurries into the kitchen and digs in for work detail.

Mondays aren't my favorite work days. There are buckets to be cleaned. Flowers need to be recut in every bucket and all buckets need to be sanitized for fresh product coming in. I get to work on time and go to my desk to make an early deposit.

The shop phone is ringing when I walk in and Julie hands the phone to me. "It's the Police Department." Somehow, I think that police calls are like Internal Revenue calls; they make her nervous.

"Hello, this is Dollene."

"Good morning Ms. Spark Plug. Much fire today?"

I am not amused.

"Three things... he starts. I talked to the reporter and he is revising his story. Two... I have a report I need you to sign. And three, would you like to go have coffee and a donut? If you agree to number three, we will have all three items taken care of."

"The thought of riding in your squad car in our small town unnerves me and may cause rumors."

"Okay, we'll walk then to the Corner Café."

"Walking is so crowded," I laugh.

"I see you walk all the time around town. I'll be there in the shake of a tail. Make that three tail shakes."

"Okay, bring money. I might want the big chocolate iced ones with sprinkles."

"Yes ma'am."

I hang up. "Julie," I yell over the running water sound, "I'm going to have coffee with the police." I amuse myself.

With that, Detective Price enters the front door, but NOT in uniform.

He looks completely different, in fact, he looks great. He's wearing a navy polo with khaki chinos and navy top-siders. He places a file folder on the counter.

"Okay, I am curious, "no uniform today?"

"Taking my mother to lunch and afternoon appointment with her banker."

"Alrighty then."

"Here's the report I need signed."

It is a report that states he will ask the reporter to revise his story in my behalf...

"Is this really necessary?" it seems odd to me.

"I don't want to appear assuming. The report states that the request was officially made in behalf of the Diamond family. It keeps everything above board, you know, the sunshine law approach."

"Gotcha."

There are some heads turning when we reach the café and sit down. He immediately looks over at me, "with your permission, and because I am paying," he turns to the waitress.

"We'll both have coffee. I'll have a sour cream donut and Ms. Diamond will be having.. the waitress says it in unison with me, "a large chocolate iced donut with sprinkles.

"What can I say? I'm so transparent and predictable."

She brings us over the treats and pours hot coffee in our cups. "I brought your special additive."

I clap my hands up to my face and wiggle all my fingers. "Yum!"

Detective Officer Price looks on as I help myself to a large table-spoon of turbinado.

"You know you really need to expand your horizon and try something new in your coffee, you know, a **spark** of the unknown," I am teasing him.

"Yes ma'am, it wouldn't be polite to not try it."

"You're right, it's just good ole southern manners."

"Yes ma'am."

"Can we lose the yes ma'am?"

"Yes ma'am." I mean yes.

"You don't eat a donut with a fork or I don't. One must bite in, full impact, simultaneously," we both pick them up with our fingers and take a big bite. We are both grinning, and he motions to me I have excess sugar on my lip.

"Oh," a bit embarrassed, I start to fidget.

He is grinning and says, "gotcha!" For once, I didn't have a comeback.

We finish our coffee and donut and the waitress brings the tab. He gets out fifteen dollars and the waitress says she'll bring back the change.

He answers, "No change needed, thank you."

I repeat thank you and "thanks for remembering the turbo." We get up and walk out and start toward the flower shop.

"Where are you taking your mom for lunch?"

"McDonalds, of course."

I look in horror. He said "No, actually we're not going there, we're going to the Olive Garden. My mom gets a strawberry margarita, and then we have soup and salad."

"Alrighty, we're here. "Enjoy the rest of your day and thank you for the breakfast treat."

"You're most welcome." "If you need anything, reporters threatened, citizen shake downs, you know, normal stuff. You know how to reach me."

"Regards to your Mom. Margarita huh? My kind of person!"

Monday afternoon comes quickly. Julie tells me we should be getting rain about two o'clock. I plan on going to the cemetery to check out the flowers and clean up, and remove any plants. But if rain is coming, maybe I'll go home, get with the captain and start writing thank you notes.

I drive by the fernery and from the drive by everything appears to be business as usual. I notice there is a semi loading at the dock as I pass.

I pull in my garage and go into the house and retrieve the captain from the cabinet. The air is cooler now that the rain has started. A weather alert appears on my phone. I glance down to look at the radar. It is a mosaic of color and I can expect a thunderstorm soon. There is nothing like a Florida thunderstorm. It is like a short story, strong elements, lots of action, and usually a lightning show in the sky.

I start a fire in the fireplace and say hello to the captain and sit in my comfy chair. I am thinking about the next family dinner and what will unfold.

I wake up to a porch chair bumping my patio door in time to see some of my potted plants skipping across the brick pavers. Wow, the rain is pelting all the patio furniture and my newly planted marigolds. The storm will be over before the captain and I can find a raincoat and my wellies.

My phone is ringing but it is barely audible because of the rain. The voice mail and I answer together. It is Rita.

"What are you doing? Julie said you left work early."

Yeah, it was going to storm and I thought I could get a head start on thank you notes."

"How many did you get done?"

"Uh, none, yet."

"Oh, why don't you and I sit down one afternoon and do it together? I'm going to be leaving for Tallahassee tomorrow so let's plan on next week. They don't have to go out this week. There is no rush."

"You have no idea how many phone calls we florist get from customers asking if their flowers were delivered because they haven't heard from the intended recipient. They'll say, I know they would have called me or dropped me a note. It's crazy that people don't acknowledge the senders. Many times I have sent flowers to funerals from Mom and Dad and there has been no thank you. I tell Julie all the time I'm going to make an app for that, a checkbox that sends a printed note for you....I could get rich don't you think?"

"Umm, how personal it sounds, I wouldn't go out and spend those millions yet." She is laughing. Oh, Roan mentioned he wants to go to Parker Island this Saturday or Sunday for a cook up. He and Rhett are going to cook some ribs and swamp cabbage. Rene said she'd bring a salad and we can put some potatoes on the grill. We were thinking you can make a dessert, not that anybody needs it, but it will be like old times.

"Well, Saturday would be better for me, because on Sunday I need to go to an apparel show."

"Okay, Saturday it is."

"Alright, turn me loose, and let me get to my bath."

"Yep."

Waking up this morning there is a blanket of fog all around as I look out my glass door. The air is cooler now and undoubtedly the ground has been cooled down by the thunderstorm. The winds have blown some of the Spanish Moss out of the trees and I will have to pick it up before I go to work because my lawn guy will charge me extra for picking up the moss. I lump all lawn guys in the same group. They just mow, blow and go.

I quickly make coffee, standing over it while it perks as if that will hurry it along. I glance at my reflection in the mirror in the hallway. Oh Em Gee, there is no beauty before coffee. Saturday can't come quick enough.

Parker Island

Old times involve all the family kicking back and relaxing with some good southern grub.

Parker Island is forty-eight acres of pure paradise set back off old state road 629. It is about seven miles out of town and the family can spend the whole day here. It isn't an island at all, but aptly named because it does represent a bit of isolation remote from the entanglements of town.

Someone will start the bacon in a big cast iron skillet and cook it over an open fire with a homemade welded grid over it. There is a combination of salt pork bacon and hand sliced fresh bacon, cooking slowly to a crisp, then it drains on some newspaper and paper towels. Everyone waits their turn to grab the finished bacon and put a couple of pieces of it in a slice of light bread and a long green onion. Latecomers must wait for the next batch to cook. Undoubtedly one of the Grannies say, "ya'll are going to fill up on that and be too full to eat." The bacon keeps cooking and the last batch is poured over the swamp cabbage pot boiling away.

There is an art to cutting the cabbage and readying it for the big pot. Some of the men folk will take the Polaris to spot three or four cabbage palms. An ax is used to cut down the cabbage palm and then the boot of the palm is shucked down like corn, to reveal the heart of the cabbage palm. Select pieces are recut with a pocket knife into little circle medallions, then shucked for a second time to keep the tender morsels coming from within the boot of cabbage. The pot boils for a couple of hours with the leftover bacon and drippings. Salt and pepper and a stick of butter are added in the last thirty minutes. Our family does not add milk like some southern families do and there is never any left over to take home. It is a special dish that requires a lot of labor but so worth the effort to enjoy in the woods.

Ribs require some preparation as well. We'll order a case of ribs and lay the sides on some brown paper and cut the thick side off and take a sharp paring knife to scrape and remove the extra fat off the meat. We salt and pepper the ribs throw them on a big grill with oak limbs that have been burning down. Dad used to put the ribs high up off the heat, and sprinkles them with white vinegar. He'll cut small holes into the lid of a white vinegar bottle and use it as a sprinkler for an hour and a half, all the time turning and sprinkling. The ribs are divine, never burned. The vinegar helps the fat burn off the ribs. Everyone brings their own lawn chair and we'll hang out by the fire feeling blessed.

My specialty is making coconut cream pies. I have perfected my recipe over the years and am secure in thinking they can win any blue ribbon. A good coconut pie has a thick filling in a flaky crust and has to be made and eaten the same day. Refrigerating the pie just ruins the crust and meringue or so I think. I usually return home with empty pie plates so refrigeration is rarely an option.

We had a cold front come through during the night and I need a flannel jacket as I head out to Parker Island. I pull into the gate and am greeted at the cattle guard by a white-faced cow. She is bellowing as I pull in and drive past her. Apparently, I am the last to arrive because everything is underway.

"Any bacon ready yet?" I ask.

"Look in the aluminum pan," Rhett calls to me. Rhett and Roan are busy grilling the meat. It smells fantastic. The last time I had ribs was Easter Sunday and I am looking forward to getting as full as a tick.

Rita asks me what I brought for dessert, "any chance of coconut cream pies?"

"Yep, just got them out of the oven, guaranteed to exceed your calorie count for the day. We can worry about that tomorrow."

We are centered around the fire in our lawn chairs and Rene asks, "if I have heard from Aunt Denise lately."

"You know the second Sunday of the month is next week," Rene continues.

"I haven't thought about it. Gosh, it came so quick."

"What does everyone want to bring?" I am suddenly concerned. "Taking count, there will be at least twelve.

"Ordinarily I'd say we could check Mom and Dad's freezer to see if they have a roast or something, but Denise locked the house. I must admit I have no ideas as to a menu."

"Is there going to be a family meeting after dinner?" Rene asks. Maybe ya'll should call a preacher so no one will act out."

"I'm ashamed to say that having a preacher there at the table wouldn't stop me. Denise annoys me so much I can't control myself."

"There's enough hostility from all of us. The relationship between all of us is corrosive beyond understanding." Rita interjects.

Rene chimes in and again and says, "I'm seriously considering giving Doctor Phil a jingle and see if he can straighten us all out."

"Go for it! I say. Now that is a man I'd miss a meal for!"

"You are so crazy Aunt Dolly."

"Yep. Certifiable."

Rhett announces it is time to eat and for us to gather round. "Aunt Dolly, did you say you were going to miss a meal? Did you mean today?"

"No, not today, tomorrow's not looking good either."

Rhett leads us in prayer and I can feel Rene gently squeezing my hand as the prayer ends. She is so sweet.

I reach for a potato, some ribs, and a big scoop of salad. I'll get a separate bowl for my swamp cabbage because I need to add some pepper sauce. Suddenly it gets quiet because everyone is eating. Life doesn't get any better than this.

Looking around, I realize the land hasn't changed much over the years. There are a few more stumps from trees that have enjoyed a full life and are now decayed. Yet the stumps offer a new life to fire flies for the future. It is nature at its best; every phase of life to explore. My grandparents had vision when they bought this property, and I hope it will remain in the family for generations.

The day has passed quickly and we begin gathering up our belongings. We pitch in to *put everything back like we found it.* That is the Diamond Family way that is steeped in us in everything we do.

I say my goodbyes and get in my car and drive out to the hard road. The white-face cow had moved on to a greener pasture. In a few minutes, I will be home with the captain. No doubt he has been patiently waiting for me.

Tomorrow is the apparel show and I really need to attend. I'll see how I feel when I wake up the next morning.

I can hear music most of the night and struggle to fall asleep. The neighbors must be having guests and entertaining outside. I get up to visit the *sandbox* and decide to stay up and watch Law and Order, one of their million or so episodes. I think of Detective B. Price and realize I don't know what the B stands for. I will ask Julie if she knows on Monday.

The rain wakes me up. I peak through the blinds and decide it will be a good day to sleep in.

Sunday morning and noon have come and gone before I open my eyes. Apparently, my body and mind need rest. Finally, I wake and walk outside to my porch chair. It has rained for hours. My phone is ringing but I catch it before the party has hung up. I glance to see who is calling. Darn, I have missed many calls. I phone Rita.

"Where have you been?" Rita asks the question and answers the phone in the same breath.

"Right here, I was sleeping in."

"Oh, we looked for you in church."

"I think I am caught up on church for a while."

"We are never caught up Dolly. As Christians, we need to be fed by the Holy Spirit every day so that we can witness and walk with God because he will reveal his purpose for all of us."

"Well, his purpose was clear to me last night. Get in bed and rest. I am drained. I need to regroup."

"Well, while you were sleeping, Denise called, and said Bing and Carly are engaged. She is obviously sour on the relationship and has been from the start."

"I found Carly a little different, but certainly likable and it appears she really has a connection to Bing. We all need to give her a chance. Remember Mom always saying, "if you can live with them, then I can certainly live with them."

"Yes, Mom had a lot of little sayings. We should have written them down in a journal."

"Dolly, nobody expects you to do all the work next Sunday. We need to come up with a plan, and give some directives. The kids can bring a covered dish."

"We still have fish in the freezer. We could do a fish fry since the weather is cooler now."

"Yeah, that sounds good, with some grits and coleslaw and hush puppies. Sounds like a good plan."

"Let's work on the thank you notes this afternoon. Okay?"

"1 will see you about four o'clock." *Great, hone in on my time with the captain.* "Alright, I'll see you then."

I don't feel like company or a shower. I need coffee immediately if not sooner.

When the coffee is done, I pour myself a big cup. I take it to the porch because it is so inviting. I sit in my rocker and look out and take in the birds singing. They have enjoyed the rain too.

Good Grief, the doorbell rings, and it's Rita. My me time has expired. I open the door and tell her I need to gather up the thank you cards and a couple of writing pens. "We can use the dining room table."

"You sure you're not going back to bed?"

"No, I think I'm ready to get started," I hand her a list and I keep a list for myself and sit down. "What else did Denise have to say when you talked to her?"

"She mentioned she and Tom were coming on Saturday, spending the night at Mom and Dads and perhaps do some cleaning out."

"Oh, she can clean out but the doors are locked to any of us that might want to clean out. She's completely blind to the injustice of it all. Did you say any of that to her, or are you so politically correct in every facet of your life, so full of let's all get along attitude that you can't address any of that. You can't make waves because you are saturated from the association of your cadre of educators and have lost your courage. You just accept what she says **all the time?** Damn, it makes me sick that you just standby and say nothing to check her. If you're not part of the solution, then you are part of the problem."

"Well, that is some diatribe you spewed! Are you finished? Did you get it all out of your system? I hope none of that is written on one of those thank you notes. Take a breath! Heck, I want to breathe for you. Where does all this anger come from?"

"I'm so just tired of all of this mess; the big mess of the estate, the accusations, the inference that we are thieves and the fact that there is no trust and no sisterly love."

"Listen, perhaps we all need to see a counselor. I think part of your anger is grief. I think some of it is frustration. But whatever the reasons, a professional can help us all. And frankly, sisterly love can only come from the hearts of all of us."

"Perhaps you have a point....I will ponder it."

We begin writing our notes and for about an hour we share silence at the table.

"I've finished, do you need any help with your list?" Rita asked softly.

"I've got three more, I'll just finish them at work tomorrow."

"Okay, Roan was expecting me some time ago so I'll be on my way."

I am feeling low now, "leave them all and I'll mail them from the store."

Rita hugs me, and says quietly, "feel better Dolly and leave the captain alone tonight."

I start to react but something pulls be back. I decide to make myself a sandwich. The day is practically gone, and I will feel better after I eat. I glance at the clock and it is fifteen after seven.

Dinner is quick and I want to get into it with the captain, but wander into the bathroom and draw a bath. I pour half of a bag of Dr. Teals Epsom soak into the water and step in. It is an immediate fix to my mental state. I will soak and then sleep, a winning combination.

I am pulling the sheets back and my cell rings.

I reach for my phone on the nightstand, "Hello...

"Aunt Dolly," this is Carly. "I hope I have called at a good time. Did you hear that Bing and I are engaged? I was completely surprised when he proposed but I am so excited."

"Yes, I heard, and yes, you sound excited. I'm excited for you."

"Well, Bing says you are full of ideas, and I'd love to meet with you, and see if you can help me plan, and establish a budget. Can you help me?"

"I'll certainly try Carly. Have you set a date?"

"Not yet. Bing will graduate in six weeks. That will give me some time to save some money."

"Well, I'll do whatever I can to help you sweetie. Start gathering up some magazine pictures of things you like, and make yourself a notebook. Please don't buy anything yet, just look first and formulate some ideas. Okay?"

"Sounds like good advice. Thank you. Momma and Grandma seem overwhelmed when I tell them you're helping me it will calm their nerves."

"Okay, goodnight, congratulations to you both."

We both hang up the phone simultaneously. She is excited and eager to plan her big day. I keep thinking what a breath of fresh air Carly is. I placed the phone back and drift off dreaming of white flowers all around me.

The first days of the week fly by. On Thursday Denise calls and is inquiring what she could bring to our Sunday dinner adding they would be getting here on Saturday.

"We're having a fish fry with the usual side dishes that go with fish," I replied. "It's all been taken care of for this Sunday, perhaps, for the next Sunday dinner you can be in charge of the menu."

"On another front, I understand Carly has phoned you about her engagement. I wouldn't be too hasty in making plans just yet. Just sayin…"

"Just saying what?"

"Well, Bing has to graduate first and I expressed my reservation about moving too fast with marriage. After all, she doesn't bring much to the table… her job is .. uh.. mediocre. She doesn't even have a vehicle that is particularly roadworthy."

"Well, I remember Granny always saying that a cheap ride sure beats a proud walk. You shouldn't downgrade Carly because she isn't a sorority girl. She has demonstrated a big heart, and many selfless acts of kindness. She is Bingham's choice and she deserves a chance Denise."

"Obviously spoken from a person with no children. I think I am quite capable of steering my own children Dolly. I would prefer you don't give her so many ideas so quickly, could you do that for me?" *Do that for her? I would give it a lot of thought, more than she could ever realize.*

Julie sticks her head in my office, and asks if I can come do a few arrangements so the delivery person won't have to wait.

"Sure, I quickly find my knife and begin to poke posies. I make a bubble bowl filled with white and yellow daisies. It so simple, yet the bouquet says so much. I hope the person who is receiving it finds their day sunny. I make a couple of mixed vases, then go back to my desk to do some bookkeeping.

Birthday Boy

I answer the second phone line to hear a definitive voice on the other end. "Hello, may I speak with Ms. Dolly Diamond?"

"This is she." I do not recognize the voice.

"This is Janet Price. I am Boyd's mother. "

"Forgive me, Mrs. Price. I do not recall knowing a Boyd. Are you sure you have dialed the right number?"

"My dear, Boyd is Detective Price with the Pierson Police Department."

"Oh, oh, oh, Mrs. Price, I apologize. I am not aware of his first name. Boyd, that's an interesting first name."

"Yes, it is a family name. People want to shorten it and call him Boy, so he doesn't use it very often. It was his father and grandfathers name."

"Oh, oh."

"Yes, I believe you said that. Anyway, I am planning a small dinner gathering for Boyd's birthday on Saturday. I wanted to invite you, mind you, I am not match making, just including interesting people his age for a casual surprise dinner. Are you available Ms. Diamond? About six o'clock?"

"Yes ma'am. Please call me Dolly. I have not made plans yet. May I ask your address?"

"Of course, it is 3000 Banyan Tree Drive. It is a casual affair and I look forward to meeting you Ms. Diamond."

"Absolutely, thank you for inviting me."

"Goodbye."

My mouth is still open with surprise as I hang up. I look over to Julie. "You'll never guess what, that was Detective Price's mother on the phone asking me to birthday dinner for him Saturday night."

"Really? Do you know her?"

"No, I do not know her and she certainly comes to the point quickly, a bit short I'd say."

"Julie, I didn't even know his first name. It's Boyd. I was going to ask you if you knew what his name was. Apparently, it is his birthday."

"Well, are you going? Do you even want to go?"

"I admit I am intrigued by him. We have had a few discussions. Maybe his mom is trying to get him to be more social."

"You mean like you? You are the one that never goes anywhere! You just retreat to your house after work."

"There is nothing wrong with going to one's home after work. I happen to like my own company and my house. It's where I relax away from phones and stress."

"Well, are you going?"

"I said I would. Gosh, it's his birthday. I need a gift for someone I barely know...something creative, something original..."

"Here we go, sounds like you might like him just a little."

"A little... I'll let you know if this is the man I'd miss a meal for..."

We both laugh. Julie has heard me say this often enough. I return to my bookkeeping and open some bills and post some checks.

I am having difficulty focusing because I am thinking of the birthday dinner. It is casual, she stated...hmmm. I'm so sure Mrs. Price did not envision my casual moo moos that come to mind. I am having a private moment of self-mocking that makes me laugh again.

I review the orders for tomorrow and order more flowers and call it a day. There is still a few hours of daylight left when I get home. It is a good opportunity to weed along my sidewalk and trim up some plants. I walk around to the back of the yard and into my greenhouse to see if I have any orchid plants in bloom. There is a gorgeous yellow oncidium

I pick up to put out front on my glass table near the door. Finally, work has ended for the day.

I put a leftover eggplant casserole in the microwave and head for a bath with a glass of wine in hand. I'm thinking it is going to be a full weekend. I'd have to see what unfolds because I did not have any preconceived notions of any one person or thing.

Guess Who's Coming To Dinner

Saturday afternoon is here too quick. The store closes early on Saturdays at two o'clock. I need to make the coleslaw for tomorrow's fish fry. I listen to the radio as I cut the cabbages, both green and purple. Hand cut slaw is so much more appealing than slaw made in a food processor. After all, you eat with your eyes first. Refrigerating the slaw a day ahead melds all the flavors into a delightful dish. I will make a dessert tomorrow morning early for the awaited family dinner.

I have decided to make a dinner coupon for my house out of card stock and wrap it in a little box for Boyd's birthday gift. It is Julie's idea and I like it. It shows creativity and will show a side of me that Boyd does not know. I will cross my fingers it will be a hit. It isn't that personal, and I am not assuming anything. I do not know why I am so concerned or why I am over analyzing.

I put some rollers on the top of my hair and proceeded to take a bath and add some of my favorite bath crystals to moisturize. I want to look sharp this evening at the Prices. I call it my plucked in, sucked in, and tucked in effect. I know my crazy is showing.

Navy capris and a navy gingham collared shirt is my choice of clothes to wear. I put on a scarf to dress it up a bit yet it is still casual. I had a pedicure yesterday so my navy sandals will look good and complete my outfit.

I arrive on time and ring the bell. Several cars are already in the driveway. It is six on the dot. The door opens and a young blonde and a little girl open the door.

"Hello and welcome," the woman speaks instantly. With that, the little girl comes around and takes my hand and says, "We're having a birthday party for Uncle Bo."

"Come right in," the blonde waves me in. She offers no name but says "we're all on the back lanai having cocktails." I have my small box with me expertly and colorfully wrapped. I also have a cello wrapped bouquet of loose flowers for the hostess.

"Is that for Uncle Bo? I can take it to him." the girl asks.

"Okay, can you tell him it's from me?"

"What's your name?"

"My name is Dolly," *this little girl is precious.*

"I have a dolly; her name is Mandy."

She runs off with my box in her hand. I follow the blonde who isn't overly friendly. Mrs. Price's home is beautifully decorated in black and gold and bold. Immediately, an elegant looking lady comes up to me and extends her hand.

"I'm Janet Price and I'm very happy to meet you. I was sorry to learn of Ellie's passing. We were occasional bridge partners as I was a substitute for her regular club. I found her delightful, a real gem, and I shall miss seeing her and hearing her laugh."

"Thank you so much for your kind words. I brought these flowers for you and I appreciate you inviting me."

I look around the room and feel completely out of my element. If the captain was here, he would be providing me some liquid courage. *What was I doing here?*

Someone tugs at my arm, I look around and there is Bo, uh, Boyd, holding the little girl in his arms.

"Hi there, he smiled. "Good to see you again, you look pretty and somewhat more rested. I worry about you, that you are under too much stress."

"You do? Worry? Please don't, I am fine. Hope you are having a great birthday, I'm happy to be invited. I brought you a little gift that this precious one confiscated at the door."

"Yes, she came running to me with it, wanting to open it. She could not resist the bright wrapping and all that ribbon. Thank you. I look forward to opening it with you. He reaches over to hug me. I am caught off guard.

"Lordy, he smells great, or is that dinner I smell?

"Did someone offer you a beverage? What would you like?"

"Whatever you are having," OMG, I am having a sudden identity crisis. "Um, wine will be fine."

Boyd said he'd be right back, took the gift and set it on the table. He was getting a beer for himself and a glass of wine for me.

"Did you meet my mother Dolly?"

"Yes, she is very gracious, and said some lovely things about my mom. I am touched."

"Did you meet my sister?"

"Well, yes and no, she met me at the door, but I didn't catch her name."

"It's Rachel. She is visiting from Atlanta. She and Mother tolerate short visits with each other, and she is leaving sometime tomorrow."

"Oh," I nodded in complete understanding.

Janet announces dinner is ready and asks that we be seated. Boyd tugs at my hand and gestures where my seat is. Oh my, I am sitting next to him and his sister is beside him. His mother and his niece, and another middle-aged couple complete the table seating.

Boyd turns to me and introduces another couple as the neighbors next door, David and Nancy Waggener.

"I'm happy to know you," I respond.

Mrs. Waggener responds, "I understand you own the Bouquets Flower Shop downtown."

"Yes, ma'am," I started when I was eighteen."

"Oh, my word," she seems startled. "Did you attend a special school to learn design?"

"Yes ma'am, I completed floral school but the real education is experience you gain by doing and trying to improve your craft every day."

"I imagine that's true."

Janet raises her glass up toward the center of the table and said she would like to propose a birthday toast to Boyd on his 55 th birthday. She states she is very proud of him, in awe of his kindness and respect to people and wishes him a happy and healthy life. We all raise our glasses and I turn to Bo, "Double nickels huh? "He grins and I think he looks so young and carefree.

Boyd picks up a platter of meat and places a piece of chicken on my plate.

"Thank you, looks yummy." I reach for the potatoes in front of me and I help myself and in turn, place a portion on his plate, then pass the potatoes to Mrs. Waggener. The asparagus bundles reach us next and we help ourselves. Everything looks delicious.

I cut into my chicken and it reveals a layer of fresh spinach inside with bits of bacon and herbs and butter. Each bite is moist and tender. Mrs. Price is an experienced cook I can tell.

"Mrs. Price I am really enjoying the chicken and would like to have the recipe."

"Of course, I will be happy to share it."

"Dolly, Boyd shared with me that you have two sisters. How are they doing with all that happened in such a short time?"

I swallow hard, "we're experiencing some struggles as we make our way down the path our parents envisioned us to take. We need prayer and reasoning," I swallow again. Boyd reaches for my hand under the table and squeezes it. I look at him and swallow a third time. Somehow, he knows what I am feeling.

There are questions I want to ask about his family but this isn't the time or place. Rachel glances my way and I have never felt more vulnerable. She asks her mother "is there birthday cake?"

"Of course, Boyd requested a Hummingbird Cake. I hope everyone likes it." Excuse me while I get some fresh plates."

"May I help clear some of the dishes?" I stand up and gather some plates and follow her to the kitchen.

"Thank you Dolly, but you are a guest."

"It won't take me but a few seconds, I'd love to help. Let me say again I really enjoyed your meal. It is superb." With that I turn back to procure the other dishes from the dining table.

Boyd is engaged talking to the neighbors, but looks up at me and whispers, "thank you."

"Of course, glad to be of help."

I have entertained enough to know how appreciative you can be to have someone clear the dishes for you while you are preparing dessert plates.

Out of the corner of my eye, Rachel is completely oblivious to her little girl opening Boyd's gift. I guess it is just too much temptation for her.

"Oh, I forgot to put candles on the cake, maybe just one on Boyd's piece."

"Sure, that will be fun and we can all sing Happy Birthday!"

"Good idea."

"It's a beautiful cake Mrs. Price. It's one of my family's favorite also."

She puts a single candle on a piece of cake, and strikes a match to it. "Thank you, now let's go eat some."

I pick up two dessert plates and follow her out. Janet starts the chorus "Happy Birthday" as she is walking out to the table. We all join in finishing the rhyme quickly.

I get back just in time to witness the box and its contents being pulled out. "Look, Uncle Bo, all you got was some paper!"

This is not going the way I thought it would. I look over to Boyd and he grins, "well, let me see."

He reaches over and is reading, and looks my way. "Dinner? Home cooked meal?"

I stutter and say, "I think there is an expiration date on that."

"I don't think so."

Everyone seems amused as we all start to eat cake. Mrs. Waggener was first to comment that the cake is outstanding, she loves pineapple.

"Coffee? Anyone?" Janet asks.

Everyone agrees that we are all fine. The evening is winding down and the Waggener's are saying their goodbyes and commenting they have known Boyd since he was a skinny little kid. Boyd seems to take it in stride.

"It is a big family day for me tomorrow" and I am talking to Mrs. Price. I enjoyed the dinner immensely. "Thank You again for including me."

Boyd stands up and says he will see me out to my car.

"Thank you."

We reach the front door and he steps outside and takes my hand and we head to my car. He squeezes my hand. "Thank you for coming and for being my dinner partner tonight, and for my dinner coupon that I'm really looking forward to. You are a trooper Dolly. There are so many surprises to you." He leans over and plants a kiss on my forehead. "Until the next time."

I climb in my car, and he shuts my door for me. "Drive safely."

I start the car and begin to drive away. This guy... this guy is starting to get to me but I know there is a lot to know about him before I let my guard down... and before I miss a meal. LOL. It is almost eight thirty when I pull into my garage. I'm going to go to bed early because I want to get an early start tomorrow. I am restless and keep waking. Finally, I give in to my inability to stay asleep. It is five o'clock in the morning and I might as well start making my strawberry cake for the Sunday dinner. It is grandmother's recipe but I embellish it with fresh strawberries between the layers. It is worth the extra effort for taste but I'm not sure the extended family is worth the extra effort.

Guess Who Eelse Is Coming To Dinner

Rita and Roan are in charge of any fish fry. After all, it is their fish. Our family has vacationed in the Florida Keys since we were small kids. Rita and Roan keep up the tradition bringing home fish and lobster and conch. Today, mahi-mahi will be on the menu with coleslaw and grits and hushpuppies. We make our hushpuppies with a great deal of minced onion and buttermilk. Of course, there is a ritual; a batch of fish followed by hushpuppies, then frying additional fish. The hushpuppies cook at a lower temperature so between fish batches the oil has time to reheat and accept another load of fish. Simple.

Denise and Tom are already here but they've been ferreting out the bedroom probably in search of the necklace. I guess it doesn't concern Denise that Rita and I would like to sort through Mom and Dad's personal items as well. Here we are fixing Sunday Dinner for her family. Nothing is ever going to change.

The fish are frying and I busy myself setting the table and making tea. The doorbell rings. I can barely hear it for the massive irrigation system at the farm running. I answer the door and open it to find Mr. Fox standing there. He is casually dressed: no bow tie or suit. I must look surprised. He asks, "am I at the right place? something sure smells good."

"Mr. Fox, it's nice to see you again. I had no idea...

"No idea that I would be coming to the first Sunday dinner? Oh, I have them on my schedule and I must say it is a lovely drive down here. I am impressed with what Blu and Ellie have done with the place. They have come along way and the work shows."

"Won't you come in, we're just about to eat."

He walks right in like he has been here a hundred times. I follow him, I cannot wait to see the faces on everyone when they see him. He gets to the edge of the porch, waves his hat, and shouts out, Hello...ooo., I hope I'm not late."

Everyone stops what they are doing. I see bewilderment, shock, amusement, and daze. Yes ma'am, it is going to be a Sunday Dinner to remember.

I see Roan turn off the gas under the fish. There is a big pan of fish and hushpuppies that Rita is bringing to the table. She places it on the long buffet along with the slaw I'd made the night before. There is a big pot of grits, and some sweet bread and butter pickles. I have added some pickled beets, and cut wedges of fresh key limes and place them on the table.

We all gather hands, because some habits never go out of style. Mr. Fox asks if he can say grace. No one utters anything. We all just bow our heads.

"Lord, we give you thanks for your blessings today. Today is an important day as this family continues to heal and make their way on your path that you have laid before us. We are grateful for the loving hands that have prepared us this bounty. May we all be mindful of your continuous grace and grant us patience and love toward one another. Amen."

The silence is golden. Bing and Carly are first in the line, and as if there is a hand on Carly's shoulder, she steps back and says to Mr. Fox, "after you, you are the guest today."

Silently, I say to myself, Carly you are a gem."

Mr. Fox has a comin' appetite, as we say in the south. He has a heaping plate of everything. It is a compliment that he must think everything looks good. I hope he enjoys it.

Everyone is seated now, eating away. I think it is good time to fire away.

"Mr. Fox," I am anxious.

"Please call me Bob."

"Okay, Bob, how far does the power of the trust executor extend? By that, I mean, specifically does Denise have an obligation to consult, discuss, with Rita and myself the personal items, the furnishings, and the division of such items?"

"The fish is outstanding, and cooked to perfection. I am so enjoying this family. I want to know the details of this catch. "Who can share the details of that with an old salt with no boat?" He pauses, "and after our meal, we can have a round table discussion with any questions you all might have."

Denise is relishing in delight I am so sure, that Mr. Fox has deterred my question. None the less, the time will come for her to be reined in.

Rita and Roan smile, and Roan begins to answer, "we wait for a quiet day, with little or no wind, take lunch and runout as far as we can and look for a weed line in the water and birds above it. This means there are usually dolphin running underneath the weed and debris. One dolphin will strike and others will soon follow. On a good day, we can fill the boat with more fish than you want to clean. We usually cut the blood line of the fish before we package it. That way the fish isn't strong, especially when you're freezing it."

"Mmmmm..mmm. It is good. Could you pass the pan around?" Mr. Fox is enjoying himself, and it is heartwarming to witness.

Carly turns to Bing and asks if he will be taking her out fishing like that after they are married. Mr. Fox looks over and asks, "is there going to be a wedding soon?"

Looking a little embarrassed, they both grin, and Bingham turns to Mr. Fox, "this is my fiancé, Carly Bedford."

"I am delighted for you both. You have some fine examples of marriage all around you."

Carly looks my way, and smiles real big.

Denise looks too, and if looks can kill.....

"We have strawberry cake for dessert. So, save some room for that." I announce.

"A big piece for me Dolly, please," Tom pleads. "It's been a long time since I had some of your strawberry cake."

"Denise can fix some coffee for us, I know you want to help sister dear."

"Yes, I do, I'll make a full pot, more caffeine will be good for the afternoon."

Bob Fox announces "he generally steers clear of desserts, but he could not resist the temptation, and it looks like it is well worth the extra calories. I want to thank you for one of the best meals I've ever had. I'd like to help too, so I can clear some dishes and then we can have a talk."

He stands up and stacks some dishes, and makes his way to the kitchen. Everyone follows suit and soon the table is clear.

Bob excuses himself, and goes to the front door. When he comes back, he is carrying a zip up file folder of sorts. He swings by the coffee pot and pours himself a cup of coffee.

It seems we are all on the edge of our seats, waiting, like dogs waiting on bones.

He clears his throat. "A person in charge of a family business often sacrifices a lot for the betterment of the group. That person must have support and sometimes unlimited encouragement because they know that people are counting on them. Their decisions affect many. It is a burden, a weighty endeavor to please everyone. A trust is as simple as it sounds. Trust should be blind to control and power. From all angles, trust is given freely, yet it is earned, it should not be provoked, or undermined. It must be a solid force where small insignificant things or even colossal events can not affect it. Trust isn't a short trip but rather a long journey that you take and the destination is worth all the inconveniences it endures. The personal treasures of a family can be an emotional roller coaster. There are memories that surface with the association of a special keepsake. Denying a person the right to hold on to a token or memento is not reinforcing the trust that a person places in you and that confidence they place in you begins to erode."

"So...ladies and gentlemen of the jury...it is imperative that your family stay the way your loving parents intended, and you do that with trust and kindness and respect."

One question gets us all a sermon on the mount. Reverend Fox speaks and the congregation listens.

I want to take my big mouth and go home.

Mr. Fox gets up and states he is available to any of us any time. He reiterates he has enjoyed the Sunday Dinner more than we can ever realize. He is leaving, and I watch him drive away in an older Jeep Grand Cherokee. For all I know, it could have been a green national guard armory truck. I feel fear and guilt.

I walk back to my parents' bedroom. It is the first-time I have been in there since my momma has died. The room looks like a robbery and a bomb has taken place. I cannot get out of the house quick enough. I am gone.

I speed down the drive, onto the hard road and push the pedal for home. Into my house, I sit in the dark and bust out crying. Like the crab I am, I retreat to my shell and tuck myself into my little hideaway of a home. The captain and I spend the next two days alone because I can. I text Julie I am feeling poorly and I am going to be home.

Please refrain from telling anyone where I am
I am okay just taking a couple of days to unwind
GWL
Julie will know that means great white leader.

Drinking with the captain always leads to bouts of despair and eventual accountability. It is another reason I am not married. That accountability thing, where have you been? Why did you buy that? Do you really think you need that? How much was it?

In two days, I have managed to get myself in a real mess. I look around my house and count six empty bags of microwaveable popcorn. I call Julie, and say I am ready to come back to work. Has anything earth shattering occurred?"

Julie says I have messages, two from Boyd Price. She is dying to know how the birthday dinner went.

"Did he like my present? He sure seems to be interested in where you were on Monday and Tuesday. How did the family dinner go on Sunday?"

"I'll tell you all about it when I see you on Thursday. Go ahead and take your Wednesday day off."

I decide I will fix me an omelet for supper. Yes, that will be tasty. I collect my phone and realize it has been off since I last texted Julie. I turn it on and messages pop from Rita, Rene, Carly, and Boyd.

Of course, I open Boyd's text first.

> *Good morning*
> *The sun is shining, it's 70 outside, a beautiful day!*
> *You know the police have tracking devices we place on ve-hicles to know a subjects' whereabouts, I hope that won't be neces-sary to use department equipment.*
>
> *My car hasn't been moved from my house so your device cannot be beneficial*
> *In obtaining any nonsense surveillance*
>
> *Are you ill? We have ways to make people talk, ie waterboarding.*
>
> *I'm a water sign, I love water, Bring it on.*
>
> *You're not trying to get out of my dinner, are you?*

Not at all, McDonald's or Wendy's is so handy these days
Okay, you win

You give up too easy!

Duty calls. Talk to you later.

This is the brightest spot on my last two days. I decide to call Carly, gosh, she probably thinks I was ignoring her on Sunday. I bolted, because I was upset and didn't say goodbye to anyone.

I dial her number, and she immediately answers." Aunt Dolly, thanks for returning my call. Have you been sick?"

"No honey, just need to do some things at home, what's up?"

"Well, I want to make an appointment to talk about the wedding, I'm working on my budget and thought establishing a base plan would help me make decisions."

"Okay, sure. Next week on a Tuesday or Thursday will work for me. What time did you have in mind?"

"I can be there at ten o'clock on Tuesday."

"Carly, do you have your colors all selected? Because it would be futile to discuss flowers without knowing colors and number of attendants, etc."

"I have it all done, you'll be pleasantly surprised how organized I am."

"That will be refreshing Carly. Will you be bringing your mother?"

"It will be just me, but I have their blessings and I already have their input."

"Okay, I look forward to Tuesday. Goodbye honey."

Rita could wait. The omelet was calling me, then a long bath.

I clear my counters from all the popcorn bags, and put the captain underneath in the cabinet. I grab a couple of eggs out of the fridge, and lay them on a towel to keep them from rolling. I find some spinach in my veggie tray, and some cheddar cheese to add once I have beaten the eggs. Supper is ready in less than five minutes. After so much alcohol for the last two days, I need to eat something that will make my stomach settle.

I watch the news while I am eating. This is another bad habit I have, but when you live alone it is normal.

I clean up the kitchen, wash all my bar glasses, and head to my bath. My soul needs soothing, and it is going to be a long and warm one. I hear my cellular ringing. I figure it is Rita and I don't feel like talking much. Tomorrow will be soon enough to rehash Sunday.

The morning starts off good. I am up ready to go by 7 o'clock, and make it to the store, ready for business. I look at the orders for the day and quickly make six arrangements. Four will be going on deliveries and two of the bouquets will be for the front cooler showcase. I like being busy and creating beautiful arrangements. So far, I have not been distracted by wholesalers calling. Julie has done a good job ordering in stock the day before. We are a good team and I value her immensely.

Back At It

When I slow down, I am tempted to call Boyd, for no particular reason, only to say hello, and have a good day. I resist because for once in my life, I want to be pursued and not the one making all the initiative. That is a good thing about being older, I'm not as apt to make stupid advances, and I can tell Boyd is reserved and a thinker.

Lunch comes early. I order an antipasto and the delivery girl wants a sub. Selfishly, I want to eat outside on our picnic table and get some vitamin D. Today, there is a slight breeze. It's such a good idea. Lunch interrupted. My sister is calling.

"Hello,"

"I asked you politely not to go ahead with Carly and any wedding plans. Now I hear you have an appointment with her next week." *Dam, this is the wrong sister.*

"Here's the thing. It is business Denise. Carly seems very organized, and ready to establish a budget, and make herself a plan for their wedding. You cannot control what is inevitable. I'll say again, give the girl a chance. Nothing she has demonstrated warrants your animosity. I repeat, she has done nothing I can see to embarrass you, or make assumptions. She's thoughtful, and respectful." My voice is getting louder.

"She doesn't have a clue Dolly," she is shouting back.

"I think you are the one that is clueless. You can't expect to gain anything by alienating her. You are smarter than this Denise. You need to think long and hard about what you are doing to undermine Bingham's choice."

"You should know about undermining. Every turn and decision I make for the family is attacked and ridiculed."

"Here again, you demand instead of accepting there may be alternatives to what you are doing. Did it ever occur to you to share the duties of cleaning out Mom and Dad's bedroom? It looks like a bomb went off in that room."

"I was looking for the necklace Dolly. What occurs to me is that you are not concerned at all, because you either have it or know its whereabouts."

"We could have looked together Denise, but you just insist upon being a solo act!" So go ahead, at warp speed, and see how many riders you can pick up on your starship. And here's another flash, DON'T ASK ME FOR ANYTHING! I hang up the phone.

I look over at my employee, obviously needing to explain whatever, and say, "I'm auditioning for a play...how'd I do?"

She said she wasn't paying attention. "Good answer."

Someone has come in the store. I walk out front to the counter to see a man who looks so very sad and has tears in his eyes. He asks, "How much is a rose?"

This is always such a loaded question because a rose can be loose in cello, in a bud vase, or in a simple water tube. He keeps talking in a whisper, "I just want one. I have two dollars, it's for my wife. She needs to get well, we have been married sixty years," and I want her to have a rose."

"I will go get you a pretty one."

I leave and go back to the cooler, select a beautiful one and add a piece of baby's breath and some greenery, place it in a water tube, and wrap in cellophane with a bow. I hand it to him, and he beams.

I whisper, "I hope she gets well very soon."

He hands me four quarters, and turns to leave. It occurs to me that's all he can do to help her, and he wanted to show her love. I feel so sorry for him, I would have given it to him but I recognized he had pride.

I am still watching him through the window making his way along the sidewalk, thinking of my parents.

To my surprise, Boyd walks in, "I hope you didn't overcharge that man."

"He was so pitiful I told him they were on sale for a dollar. He only had two dollars. It's probably been forever since he has bought any flowers. I would send him into a heart attack if I charged him five dollars."

"Are they really five?"

"Yes, on an average, in a water tube, with all the fluff,"

"Gosh, I have been enlightened, that I definitely can't afford a dozen," he smirks.

"Well, I always tell men customers, because men think that roses are the only flowers women want. I tell them, one rose will do what six will do, and six will do what 12 will do, and let them think about it."

"More and more, I am convinced how aloof you are."

"Aloof? Never has anyone said that to me," I am laughing.

"Yes, I think you keep your distance, reluctant to care, maybe care is not the right word, but slow to commit, don't want folks knowing you can be tender hearted."

"Now I have been enlightened, you're not only a detective but a multiple personality therapist."

"Well, I am a detective."

"And does the detective need a dozen roses today?" *I could spar all day.* I can make twelve water tubes with twelve roses, Or I can make twelve budvases with one rose in them each, I can make a dozen roses in one vase with lots of baby's breath, or I can make, wait for it…. A dozen roses wrapped in cellophane, with all the fluff, like a presentation bouquet that you could present to your Miss America! *I did not realize how loud I was getting.*

"I really came in to see if you are feeling better. "Hey are you okay?" He comes closer and he can see that I am not okay. He grabs and holds me, "hey now, hey, don't cry, I know something is wrong." He just holds me tight, and I am still. He shifts a bit and pulls out a handkerchief. I am sniffling, *and I hate myself for it.*

I look up, because he is picking my face up, "whatever it is, you're going to be okay, I got this, it's alright."

"I'm a mess… Boyd, I'm a mess."

"No, you are not a mess, you've been through a lot in just a few weeks. You need time to heal, to catch a breath, and slow down. I know I'm right, maybe a grief counselor could help. Hey, I'm not going anywhere, I am here for you. We can talk it out. Are you hearing me? Lean on me. I want you to lean on me. Lord, I'm talking too much." He kisses my forehead and kisses my nose. *I feel like a kitty cat.*

"Thank you, I apologize for my melt down. It's been a rough couple of days. I do feel like you are my friend, and one day, we will talk more. I do need you. I am still looking into his eyes, and he leans in and kisses my lips, and as quickly as he does, his lips leave me, and he gives me a big tight hug.

His radio goes off, and it startles us.

I speak up and say "I'm okay. Thanks Boyd."

"Okay, I have to go, feel better. May I call you later?"

"Sure, go, catch some criminals!"

I turn away, and he leaves quickly. Well, that didn't go well, I cannot believe I lose it in front of him. Thank the lord, there are no customers that walk in or someone calling on the phone; *Hello, China Direct, please hold, one of our real live basket cases will be with you shortly.*

The pity party is over. I still have his handkerchief in my hand, a corner of it is monogrammed with BFT. I lift it to my lips. It smells like him. I dab my eyes with it.

The phone is ringing, and on the third ring I reach it, "Bouquets Today"

"Dolly, it's me, are you okay? I didn't want to leave you like that."

"I'm fine, I have your handkerchief and I have it close to my face, it's comforting."

"Oh, good. Keep it. My mom keeps me supplied. Hate to cut this short, but I wanted to be sure you are better. Smiling again? I hope so."

"All smiles, you made it happen. Talk to you soon."

I am a lost soul. Everything IS getting to me. I am completely cognizant that I if I keep these mood swings Boyd will lose interest. I have never cared about someone losing interest because usually I had already lost interest myself in that person. This is becoming different. I will have to figure it all out.

I close a little bit early, because I want to stop by the fernery to get some ferns for the shop, and say hello to Juan and Maria. It is quitting time for Juan too and he meets me in the driveway with a big grin.

"Miss Dolly" is good to see you again, you very busy?"

"Not really, how about you guys?

"Busy, moving furniture into the new office for Miss Denise. She say we have meeting soon for everybody." Today we ship out full semi-truck going to Carolinas.

"Are you happy working here Juan? I want you to be happy, even though my parents are gone, it is still our family business. You can call on me any time. You have my phone number Juan."

"Si senora Dolly."

"I mean it, Juan, ANYTIME! you can call me.

"I'll get some fern boxes while I am here."

"Si, you have to sign ticket," for Miss Denise she say.

I am fuming inside, "Okay Juan, I sign ticket." Before I realize, two boxes are being carried out to my vehicle.

"Please sign here," Juan says softly.

I give him a hug. Gracias.

I'm driving off, thinking about the new rule. I phone Rita.

Rita knows it's me on the phone from caller ID.

"Well, it's about time you check in with me. You haven't been at work, you left in a flash from the Sunday dinner. What in heavens name is going on with you?"

"I'm alright, I fell apart when I saw how Denise and Tom went through mom's room like a wrecking ball. I've just had enough. And get ya some of this, tonight I stop by the fernery and Juan says they are moving stuff into a new office, I actually had to sign a ticket for taking two boxes of fern. Apparently new policy."

"Well, that's news to me." I can tell Rita is taken aback too.

"Do you think we should call Mr. Fox and ask him if some sort of communication is expected or demanded from the executor of the trust."

"Well, he did tell us he was available to ask questions, and it doesn't cost anything."

"Did I mention Denise called me and wanted, actually demanded I not help Carly on her wedding plans?"

"You're kidding!" Rita is surprised.

"I wish I was. I told her to give Carly a chance, and then of course she makes her usual accusation that I must know where mom's necklace is. Did u get a look at that room she destroyed under the guise of looking for it?"

"No, when I realized you had left, Roan and I cleaned up and left right behind you."

"Julie is off today and I've had a restless day, and I got in a bad mood. I've a lot on my mind these days."

"Yeah, all of us do, I want to tell you Roan and I are going to the condo this weekend. Would you like to come and wind down?"

"Sounds like a good idea, but I need to know what's on the board for orders for the weekend, so I'll just have to let you know. I'll call you tomorrow night, okay?

"Sure, bye now."

A weekend at the beach sounds fantastic, and I hope Julie is okay with me taking off. I think it is Julie's turn for a Saturday off. Generally speaking, we trade often, I just hoped she has not made plans already, we'd see tomorrow.

Thursday starts off with a bang, the phone keeps ringing with orders for the day but so far, the weekend looks slack. Of course, Julie is encouraging me to take off. "It will be good for you to get away. Go have fun, and don't come back with a sunburn."

There is something about the beach that is all encompassing. After all, I am a crab. It is just natural.

I ring up Rita and say, "I am ready."

"Ready already?" She laughs.

"Yep, all ready, bag is packed."

"We'll swing by in a few."

Rita's condo is in Daytona. They had bought the time share about ten years ago, and it is right on the beach on the top floor. It has a great view of the pier. One only has to open the sliding glass doors to enjoy the beach night life. There is always great island music to listen to and there were some great restaurants in the area that had feature a fresh catch daily.

We get underway about four o clock and arrive about six. The conversation is light in the car, and I am glad. Rita and I are making plans to make a sandwich first thing after breakfast and take it to the beach, lay out like lizards and soak up some Vitamin D.

Rita planned on a hamburger for supper. We busied ourselves preparing all the fixings, and soon we were eating burgers and drinking beer. Roan cleans up the grill, and then sits down to enjoy the breeze and the waves coming in. He lights up a cigar and said, Viva La Voya!"

We all laugh at the same time, because we know he is talking about his retirement account that made the whole condo acquisition possible. He is referring to the orange money retirement squirrels you see on the television. Orange color was the inspiration to decorate the condo in corals and oranges. Rita actually bought Roan an orange squirrel for his birthday one year, as a joke, because he obsessed about how the plan had paid off for him. The condo was bright and welcoming, and Rita had quite the collection of seashells she had collected over the years while walking on the beach. She had purchased a colossal glass fish to house all her unique shells, and sharks' teeth. Years ago, they had found a unique driftwood coffee table with an extraordinarily thick piece of glass on top of the twisted wood. It was always a topic of conversation to all who visited.

I could tell Roan and Rita were having a few romantic moments, so I said goodnight, and retire to my guest room. No counting sheep for me, I was in heaven.

There is nothing like a Florida sunrise at the beach. Mr. Sun was up early, the tide was rushing in and all the sea birds were wanting breakfast. I smelled coffee, Hallelujah, there was a spring in my step as I made my way to the kitchen, "Top of the morning to ya," I said, avoiding all other conversation to pour me a cup. Yes, please, cream and sugar, big sip...ahhh... "and the balance of the day to you too, my Irish friends."

"Her crazy is showing again, Roan, she'll break out in that old Florida song soon."

"Yum, my compliments to Juan Valdez, coffee maker extraordinaire! I remark.

I walked over to the sliding glass doors, and look out, "I'm coming," I yell.

"Hopefully, you won't feel the need to make any more announcements to the other tenants," Rita adds as she is laughing.

"Thank you for including me guys, it's just what the doctor ordered."

"Of course," it is our pleasure Sis," Do you want breakfast? We have eggs, cereal, bagels, she's asking with her eyes.

"More coffee," I answer.

I take my second cup down the hallway, to my boudoir, brush my teeth, run a wet comb over my hair, put a hair clip in, and turn to my suitcase; Bathing suit, beach bag, sunglasses, sunscreen, phone, and grab my coffee and a towel and whistle back to the kitchen.

Rita and Roan are dicky birding around.

"Would you like me to make you a sandwich dear sister?" I am pulling ingredients out of the refrigerator.

"Lordy, you are in a mood today, like a child at Christmas, Rita is smiling.

"The early bird gets the worm, I retort. With that, I stuff my sandwich in my bag, and add 3 bottles of water. See 'ya on the sand."

The elevator raced down. Good for me. Tenants are still sleeping. It stops. I have arrived.

This is not rocket science. I do not need to walk a country mile to find the right spot. I drag a beach chair to me, assumed the lizard position and close my eyes. I just listen, and my breathing and the waves coming in are one. I guess about twenty minutes has passed, and I open my eyes and sit up. I decided to take a dip in the ocean to cool off before I apply some sunscreen.

I find the water refreshing, and plunge under to wet my head. I head back to the beach and apply a generous amount of sunscreen. I wonder what is keeping Rita, maybe I should give her a quick call. Dang, I missed a call from Boyd. Immediately I return his call and he answers on the first ring.

"Good Morning, thanks for calling me back."

"Top of the 'mornin to you my friend, "I couldn't resist, because it is a glorious morning indeed.

"I hope you haven't made plans yet for the weekend because I would like to ask you to go fishing. The chief let me know last night I could have two days off. I thought it too late to call you. You said you were a crab, I thought the ocean might be fun. Would you like to go? but I warn you I am not a catch and release guy. You'll have to clean what you catch."

He was trying to be cute. Little did he know I could clean a fish probably as good as he could but I'd keep that my little secret. "Well, that sounds fantastic but I am already at the beach. I came over with my sister, Rita and her husband Roan to their condo in Daytona. Why don't you come over here, and we'll all go out to dinner? It will be fun, and we can all trade fish stories."

"What is the address? I'll just pack a change of clothes, see you about five o'clock. Since I'm not fishing, I think I will mow mothers yard before I come.

"Okay, I'll text you the address when I speak to Rita.

"Looking forward to a nice evening D. Bye for now."

He just called me D. I guess that is a new nickname for me. I think I like it.

Rita appears before I can call her. Even though she is my older sister she looks great in a bathing suit. She sits down her bag on the sand and walks over to fetch another lounge chair.

"Were you talking on the phone when I walked up?" Rita asked.

"Yes, I was talking to Boyd," I answer.

"Whose Boyd? Someone at the shop?" Rita sounds serious.

"Boyd is the Pierson Police Department detective. You are probably not aware of his first name. I just asked him over to the beach and out for dinner. He'll be here around 5:30 p.m." I giggle.

"You asked him? Are you kidding me? Why?"

"Well, he just called and asked me to go fishing, and I said I am already at the beach so I asked him to join us when we go out to dinner this evening."

"This is big news Dolly. Do you even know him?" Rita is still probing.

"Sort of, I mean I am getting to know him and I admit I like what I see so far. I went to a dinner party at his Mother's for his birthday. Time will tell Rita."

She wasn't going to stop with the questions I could tell. "Is he spending the night? Or will time tell that also?"

"Yeah, that's it. Time will tell," I said.

Rita shook her head sideways, "you never cease to surprise me sister."

"Relax, I said, we're not on a roller coaster, it's more like bumper cars."

"Well, let's hope there are no accidents anytime soon. We have a reservation at six at the Green Turtle, the Thunderbirds are supposed to be playing there at nine."

"I need to text him the condo address now." I continue to look at her and she responds, "6510 Ocean Drive."

I take my phone in hand and started texting the address, I ended the text with see you by 5:30 p.m. D."

"Do I need to think about what to wear?" Rita is worrying now, I can hear it in her voice.

"I guess we will wear what we brought. It wouldn't be my first choice but there isn't another option."

"I'd rather stay sun bathing than go shopping." I answer her.

"Have you already eaten your sandwich Dolly?"

"I haven't, and I'm not very hungry now. Imagine that."

"I'm trying to." Rita is teasing me now.

The sun is at twelve o clock now, and I applied more sunscreen. I definitely did not want to look like a lobster. Tanning was easy for all of us girls because we were used to the harsh sun and kept a nice tan. Sea gulls were all around us now because there were little kids tearing up bread pieces to entice the birds. They do not know better and today was not my day to patrol the beachcombers. I glance over to Rita and she has her eyes closed underneath her big hat. She was nodding off and I wanted to remind her about sunscreen but she is a big girl. I'll give her a few minutes before I say anything else.

It is low tide now and shell seekers are combing the sand for unique treasures. Some have those box scoops that can sift through a pile of shells and sand simultaneously. People on the beach fascinate me. I suspect they come from all walks of life, always unencumbered about their attire, ignoring all what other people might think and going about their business with ease. That's what the ocean does for you, cleanses, and washes away ones' strife.

"Rita, are you awake?" I gently shake her towel.

"Just a little," she whispers.

"You need some sunscreen, maybe we should go in now, you look a little pink. You don't want to be miserable tonight," I say.

"Okay, I feel like a shower and an early cocktail."

"That sounds like a plan." I grab my bag, and retrieve a water bottle to drink on the way back to the condo.

"You need some?"

Rita shook her head no, "I'm good."

It was a short walk back, and we stopped at the back and used the water hose to get the sand off our feet. We stepped into the elevator and punch the tenth floor. Roan is watching television when we walk in but manages to tear away from the program to ask "how was the beach?"

Rita said "hot."

I said "beautiful."

Rita tells Roan we are expecting a guest for dinner, could he please change the reservation to four?

"Of course, who is coming?"

I figured I should jump in here, "I have a guest, Boyd Price, from the police department."

"Is this official business or ..."

"It's a date Roan, so try not to ask him too many questions, can you give us a break?" I am pleading.

"Of course, I'll try and refrain from embarrassing you."

"Is this your first date with him?" he asks.

"Kinda, we have seen each other a couple of times, he asked me to go fishing and I told him I was already at the beach, so he said he'd come over. You don't mind, do you?"

"Well, since you told me he was a fisherman, and not some clarinet player in a band, I'm up for it."

I had dated some doozies in my time, and the family always felt the need to share their opposition to each one without being asked. I was the baby in the family and had experienced some real disasters in the dating game.

My one and only trip to the altar was three years of pure hell that nobody would forget. Since then, the family had learned not to wag their fingers at my moral shortcomings because they wanted me to have a life, and live life again.

Rita is showering and I walk to the kitchen to make a drink. Looking in the bar, I eyed the captain, and he winked back. With drink in hand I walked back to my room to think about what I would wear. I brought a sundress with me but it seems too casual. The Green Turtle isn't fancy but the Thunderbirds are playing and it should be 'rockin' tonight. There is a denim skirt hanging in the closet I spied and I wondered if it still fit from last time I was here. In fact, the skirt was a little loose, and thankfully not too short. I went through my suitcase for a blouse that looked sharp. I'd wear a turquoise tee, and turquoise sandals. I'd better check with Rita.

Rita yells from the kitchen and asked me if I want a glass of wine. Apparently she has not noticed the captain on the counter, but she will, and will not resist telling me to leave the captain alone for the evening.

I take my outfit in to the kitchen and ask Rita what she thinks.

"Hmm... let me look at what you brought. She returns with me to my bedroom and looks in my suitcase. "What's wrong with the sundress?"

"I think it is too casual, I'll try it on and you can see."

"Well, it shows off your tan really great and looks 'kinda sexy. Try on the skirt and tee. That looks nice too. Which one are you more comfortable in?"

"I'm just concerned that with great music and possible dancing, I don't want my ass to shake in the sundress."

We both laugh and fall on the bed.

"Maybe I have a scarf for you to wear as a belt." She carries her glass of wine with her, waves me in to her room and we go through her closet. "Here we go, this is perfect."

It is perfect. We tie it through the belt loops and give it a square knot.

"I'm going to the shower now, so I can concentrate on my hair. Thanks Sis."

The shower feels good. Looking in the mirror, I did get some color today at the beach. My signature fragrance is Ysatis by Givenchy and I am going to layer it on my body, first lotion, then powder and finally perfume. It is my *fate de complete*. I am annoyed at myself in making this dinner date such a big deal. Bo has seen me at my worse, and he is still interested. Confidence is what I need, not perfume. Too late.

Normal women use mousse for their hair. In truth, I need to use elk. I want my hair to stay set yet movable. I have the blow dryer on low and my hair is falling into place, I think. Or am I falling apart? I need to speak to the captain.

Roan stands in the doorway and whistles. "Smells fetching in here," I look over to him and he is smiling.

"Seriously, you look great and I hope he is worth all of this effort."

Thanks, Roan, you're the best! I give him a quick hug. He pulls quickly away, "don't mess my hair up."

I bust out laughing, "am I being that vain?"

"I'll take the fifth," as he brushes by me.

I call out to Rita in the living room and join her. She is already dressed. She stares and me and announces it is 4:45. "Have you heard from him?"

"No, but I have no reason to be worried. You didn't comment on how I look. Please don't tell me I should change."

"Absolutely not, you look cute and sassy, for an old girl. I'm excited for you and I have never seen so much fuss from you to go out."

"I just want to look attractive for him, that's all."

"I have some crackers and cheese over there on the counter. You should eat something if you and the captain are keeping company tonight. You know how I feel about him."

"I know, I have had my last drink." I take a cracker and cheese and screw the top back on the bottle and put the captain away. I open the refrigerator and grab a bottle of water and begin drinking it. I can hear a vehicle beeping downstairs and it is making me nervous.

Roan is ready and comes out to join us. "Okay, we need to be leaving for the restaurant soon," and we hear the doorbell ring. Roan goes to the door and opens it.

"Hello, and extends his arm out to Roan for a handshake. "Good to meet you, I'm Boyd Price.

"Welcome, come in, I'm Roan, the brother n law...we've got an anxious lady in here panting for your arrival."

No, he did not just say that. I am going to kill my brother n law.

"I've been beeping my horn downstairs." He pauses and says "just kidding, that was another car in the lot." He walks over to me, gives me a small hug and a kiss. "Hello," you got some sun today, and you look rested." He turns to Rita, "nice to see you again."

"Yes, thank you, let's all go before we're late for our reservation." Rita waves us to the door and out to the elevator. Bo grabs my hand and rubs his thumb over it back and forth all the way down to the ground floor.

"Perhaps, you guys need to follow us down to the Green Turtle, so we can all leave when we want."

"Sure thing," Bo replies, takes my hand and leads me to a black Tahoe and opens the door for me. I turn to him to be sure I am climbing up lady like. He shuts the door and walks around to the driver's seat. "Seat belt please, as he smiles at me, you look wow in that skirt."

"Oh good, I was afraid I just looked r e s t e d."

"That too," he answered and we're down the road following Roan and Rita.

"Tell me about this restaurant. Do they have a specialty?"

"Yes, seafood, any way you like it, although I'm warning you, you might not get a chance to look at it the menu much before the questions are fired at you like a cannon."

"Okay, duly noted D."

"I like that you call me D but wonder why."

"I don't know, I just want to get to you, I mean start to talking to you as quickly as I can." He tugs at me and says "move closer to me please."

I push my skirt down as I move down the seat closer to him. He is saying everything I want to hear. I look up at the back corner of the headliner and there is a leather sling holding a gun. "Um, I see your gun, do you always carry it?"

"Yes, always." He sounds serious now, not light hearted.

"Oh, just curious."

"It will always be with me, you will get used to it and it then it won't bother you so much." He squeezes my hand again. We are pulling in the parking lot and pull in beside Roan and Rita.

They are getting out and Bo opens his door, reaches for my hand and I slide out ever so carefully. I'm standing upright at the door and he leans in and kisses me on the lips sweetly and says he is looking forward to tonight.

I look up at Rita and it did not go unnoticed. Roan puts his arm around Rita, and kisses her lightly, "I can do that too."

Not very funny Roan.

My Bo looks awesome. He has got black jeans on, and a salmon colored polo shirt on, with black boots. He certainly doesn't look like a fifty-five-year-old. There's some greying around his temple around his ears that look distinguished. I am proud to be with this guy and so anxious to know him better.

The restaurant looks crowded but we walk right in to our table. Roan pulls out the seat for Rita and Bo follows suit. The waitress appears with menus. We all open them up as she asks if we are having drinks. Roan says he'll have bottled Budweiser, Rita will have wine, and he looks over at us. Bo asks me what I'd like, wine for me too please, red Cab if you have it, and then Bo says he'll have a Bud also.

We begin to look at the menu, and Roan asks Bo how long he has lived in Pierson. I tap his leg under the table.

"I've been here two years, retired from the FDLE and moved to this sleepy hollow away from the city. I like it, and I'm getting to like it more and more," and glances over to me with a wide smile. "My dad bought acreage in Pierson a long time ago with big banyan trees on it. It's where my mother built her house." He is interrupted by the waitress ready to take our orders for dinner.

Boyd turns to me, "what are we having babe?"

"I am thinking about the Halibut with asparagus and salad. Balsamic dressing please."

"That sounds great, two of those please ma'am."

Roan looks at Boyd, "hey, want to share some oysters on the half shell with me?"

"Sure thing."

'Good, they're always fresh here. An order of oysters please, and we'll have the seafood pasta for two."

The waitress smiles and hurries away.

Boyd and Roan seem to be getting along well talking about fishing, and itching to go fishing. Rita and I are sipping wine when the salads arrived. I finish my wine and drink almost a glass of water.

Bo offers me an oyster, I sweetly decline, and say for him to enjoy them. *I hate oysters, they aren't worthy of my persnickety pallet. Lordy, how can anybody even taste them before they slide down your throat. Must be a man thing. Oh, yum, dinner is here.* I wait till everyone has been served and look over to Rita. *Blessing?*

Roan says a short prayer, and in unison we all say, "Amen."

"Good choice D. The fish is cooked to perfection. It's been a long time since I have eaten halibut." He seems to have a hearty appetite. I think he's going to fit right in. Our waitress returns to ask about more drinks.

"D, another wine?"

"More water please."

I look over at Rita. She gives me a thumb up.

The band is starting to set up. I lean in to Boyd to ask him if he likes oldies music. *This could be a deal breaker.* He puts his arm around me and says "there is no better music." Luckily, our table is close to the dance floor. We have finished eating, and our table is cleared.

"After dinner drinks guys? Before the show starts? I get pretty busy when the band starts up," the waitress announces.

"I'll have a Kahlua and cream, thank you." Rita nods, "that sounds good."

Roan orders a beer, and Boyd asks for water.

Dang, the band opens loud, a classic, *Ebb tide by the Everly Brothers.* Bo leans over and kisses me on the neck.

I whisper I need to visit the sandbox. Uh, bathroom."

"Do you want me to go with you?"

"I'm pretty sure I'll be okay."

He pulls out my chair, Rita says she'll join me.

In the bathroom, Rita and I barely get there when she says "looks like ya'll are pretty smitten with each other."

"Why does he call you D?"

"It's cute, don't you think?"

"Is he planning on spending the night?"

"Rita! Uh, I don't know, I want him to. Heck, I want him, but I can't go there yet. I'm sure of that."

"You'll know when the time is right Dolly."

"That hasn't always been the case Rita."

We walk back to the table, I bump Rita to the dance floor because the band is nailing *"Let's Dance"* Rita and I are moving like we're in a dance contest. We move back to the table and I lean in to Boyd "did we win the dance contest?"

He laughs, "in my eyes, yes."

The band starts "when a man loves a woman" and Boyd grabs my hand and stands up and leads me to the floor. He holds me so tight and starts singing in my ear, *he'll trade the world for the good thing he's found...*

"You are winning my heart, Detective Price," I whisper back to him.

"I need more time with you D."

"Let's get this right Bo. No rush. I'm not going anywhere."

The song ends and we sit for the next hour enjoying one hit after another. The band breaks and the conversation turns to calling it a night. Roan waves down the waitress, and asks for the check. She smiles at Boyd and says he'll have to work it out with him. "Thank ya'll," and she was off.

"This was going to be my treat Bo," Roan is matter of fact.

"Next time is yours, I just appreciate being invited."

"You're slick, I'll say that." Are ya'll coming back to the condo?"

"Yes, we'll follow you, but D promised me a talk on the beach when we get there."

We walk outside and get in our vehicles. Bo lets them drive away and pulls me to him. " I have waited long enough to really kiss you. He holds me tight, one hand on each side of my face, and plants his full mouth on mine. He touches every part of my lips and when he stops, my eyes are flooded with emotion. "You are my second chance at love D. I want that second chance only with you."

"Okay, let's go." He starts up the Tahoe, pulls my hand up to his mouth and kisses my hand. "Would you buckle up?"

"That kiss tasted like more, and you want me to buckle up? I'm in need of oxygen I think."

He grins and I see a dimple, "let's get to the beach and we can talk."

We drop our shoes off at the bottom floor, and I grab a towel to put on the sand so we can sit. Boyd has been the perfect date, and I know my guard is coming down.

It is a short walk to the beach and the moonlight beams across the ocean. The mighty sound of the water rushing in silences our conversation. I put down the towel and sit. He joins me and seconds go by before we speak.

"You mentioned leaving a big city Bo, what city was that?"

"Atlanta," he sighs.

"Miss it?"

"Not at all, I lived in Georgia all my life. Went to police academy there, worked two years for the sheriff's department, then transferred to FDLE. I was married once, but.... I did something my wife could not forgive me for." He swallows so hard that I hear him.

"Were you unfaithful?" *I was scared to know the answer.*

"No, although she might have forgiven me for that. I met Dina in college, and we both were taking criminal justice classes. Dina had a twin brother that she was very close to. He was fun loving and they shared the usual bond that twins share. Danny was always in trouble, wanted to make easy money, smoked a lot of pot. Dina dismissed his bad behavior as harmless. She had a psychology degree and tried her best to talk to him, enabling him, making endless excuses about why he didn't keep a real job. His pot habits turned into drug use." Bo seems lost now, like he is being sucked out with the tide.

"Bo?"

He just keeps staring out and then starts talking again. Our department had worked several months working undercover, paying informants, to catch some high-profile drug buyers. My unit sets up a sting operation to break up that ring of buyers, sellers, users. That night Danny was a part of that ring, and he opened fire on us. I shot and killed him that night. I didn't even know it was Danny until he laid dead. Dina never returned to our home again. She said she never wanted to see me ever again, to lay her eyes on me. She was filled with hate, anger, blame, reserved all for me. She had her parents move everything that was personally hers, out of our house, and sent me a message she didn't want any part of me or our life again. There was almost two years of investigations and internal affair probes that followed the shooting. The investigators wanted to know if I knew Danny was dealing, if I had covered anything up, suggestions I might have shot him to cover up my own involvement. Every part of my life, our marriage, our financial records were put under a magnifying glass. During those difficult days, my mother revealed to me that Dina was pregnant and received an abortion. I lost my life as I knew it, my wife, and my child all due to work. I had to re-evaluate every aspect of my life and so I check into a center to receive intense therapy. After all that happened, I decided to retire and get a fresh start in life somewhere else. I don't even know where Dina lives. My one letter I gave to her parents a couple of years ago was returned to me unopened. I have not dated or looked at another woman until you. I feel like a new life has begun. He turns to me and says, "now is your time to run if you want to."

"I don't want to run anywhere." I swallow hard too. "I know that story was painful to share. No matter what happens between us, I will always covet that you trusted me to tell me." I put my arm around his waist and nuzzle my head on his chest. I feel so very close to his soul. He kisses my hair, my head.

"Bo, I don't want you driving home tonight. I can tell you have a heavy heart with all that's been said. Please stay here. I want to be close to you tonight."

He stares at me, I feel him searching deep in my eyes and he pulls my chin up and kisses me deeply and softly says, "me too."

He gets up and pulls me up. "Its past midnight, I think."

"Want to go skinny dipping? He is shocked at the thought I can tell. "I'm just kidding you, but maybe one day we will." He swats me on my backside and I feel like Bo has returned.

"Did you bring any clothes with you, a bag?"

"I always carry one because I never know where I will be overnight. I'll get it from the car."

I wait for him and we walk to the elevator and get in. Rita and Roan are asleep it appears and their bedroom door is closed.

"My room is in here, and there is another guest room with another bathroom. If you stay here with me, I'm afraid there will be a few conditions. I didn't bring any footed pajamas but right now I feel like I might need them." I giggled and he laughed.

"Give me a couple of minutes in the bathroom, and I'll come out to talk."

He takes his bag and goes into the guest room. I hurry to the bathroom, check my hair, makeup and brush my teeth and put on a sleep set. *This is no time to be without my glamour.* My pajamas have pictures of doughnuts all on the bottom capris and the top shirt is captioned *Donut Disturb.*

I walk out to the living room. "Would you like some water?"

"I think I'll have a doughnut and some water, Dolly, you make me laugh all the time." And he is taking a hard look at my attire.

"Doughnuts aren't on the menu tonight," I grab a glass of water for us both and sit on the couch. He sits next to me, and leans over and sprinkles my neck with small kisses, and lays his hand on my inner thigh. Dolly, I know tonight is not the night I have been wanting and thinking about with you."

"You have? You do?"

I had to say something, "Bo, I know the difference between sleeping with someone and sleeping with someone you love but this not the time or place. Oh, I want you, and it would be so easy to start out kissing like this," and then I demonstrate what I have in mind, his ears, his lips, his neck, his chest. My hands are underneath his shirt and they are moving up and down his back. I pause for a second, and he says, "I'm listening."

We both laugh again. "I want you too, all of you. I don't know how long we should wait, because I don't want to wait, we're not teenagers, but I sure as heck feel like one when I am with you."

"Okay then, I'm going to tuck you in and say goodnight, before anything else happens."

He pulls me up and we walk to my room. I pull down my cover and slip in the bed and lay down. He pulls the sheet up on me, kneels down and puts my head in his hands, and kisses me so softly and tenderly. "sleep tight D." He shuts my door. *I am in heaven eating doughnuts.*

Rita is knocking on my door, "Dolly are you up? We're having coffee."

"Okay, I'll be right out."

I go in the bathroom, OMG, there is a raccoon in the mirror with me. Quick action is needed; Makeup remover, toothbrush, comb, brush, clip, light compact powder, dabbing some lotion on neck. I walk out and do not see Bo. I look around and they look around. Everyone is looking around. Rita and Roan start laughing. "He went to get a paper."

"You guys, honestly."

"Well, the roof didn't fall in, we didn't hear the bed fall, guess ya'll made it through the night."

"There is a time for joking, and this is not the time."

"I have the say, "this isn't the normal way we see you come out in the mornings." They are still laughing. I begin laughing too. There's a knock on the door. I hope it is Bo. I open it.

"Good morning sleepy head, you must have had a good tuck in last night."

"The best, Good morning to you too, I'll have my coffee now if everyone is through making sport of me."

Roan says, "You're such an easy target."

"Dolly, were ready for pancakes, and we need you to make them. We've been patient. Pleeeeese Sis!"

The skillet is on the stove. I wash and dry my hands and grab a bowl from the cupboard. I reach for the self-rising flour, and guesstimate about three cups. I put about three tablespoons of oil, a pinch of soda, add an egg, and start stirring in some buttermilk slowly. I reach for a fork to stir because it gets my lumps out quicker. The skillet is hot now.

"Rita, perhaps we could use two skillets, you know to cook the short-cakes quicker."

Rita places another skillet on the stove top burner on medium. I spray some vegetable oil in the skillet and ladle some batter in. I can get two pancakes in there, so I pour another in. The pancakes are bubbling all around the edges, and they are ready to flip. I work both skillets till all the batter is done. Rita sets the table with plates, and silverware, napkins. She grabs orange juice from the fridge and puts it on the table with some juice glasses. The pancakes are ready now. There is a platter of them. There is already a variety of some syrups, and honey and butter. Rita had already cooked bacon in the oven, super crisp. Chow is ready. I am need of more coffee, so I bring the pot to the table.

Bo is sitting at the bar pretending to read the paper while I am cooking. He looks so fresh and crisp. I wondered what time he got up. I should have left a note to Rita that he was here so she would be prepared that we had company, but I didn't. I'd find out later the morning scenario.

I smile at Bo, and he smiles back. "Are you doing okay?

"Yes, I lifted a weight off my back last night, found a life line, and I'm going to keep hanging on till you let me go."

"I'm not going to let you go at all or give you much slack, either. I'm going to keep bringing the rope in closer."

"That's my girl,"

I beam.

We're at the table, and to my delight the pancakes are light and fluffy. I am excited to spend some of the day with Bo. Bo and Roan compliment the cooks and retire to the living room and start talking fish. I ask Rita if I can beg off dishes, to go get a quick shower. "Sure, thanks for breakfast."

I am in a hurry and wash and condition my hair in a flash and lathered up in my favorite body wash.

There is no wasting time. I do not want to seem like a prima-donna, spending too much time on me. The truth is us older gals need to spend a bit more time on ourselves because we didn't do it when we were younger. Moisturize, Moisturize. This is the key to better looking skin.

I finish my hair and put on that sundress until I find out what the days' activities are going to be. Everyone is in the living room hanging out. I sit beside Bo and he pats me on my knee.

Reel Him In

Roan asks, "what's on the agenda today? Are you two going beachside or do you want to do a little fishing?" I know that when fishing is an option all other votes are canceled. Fishing it is.

Rita volunteers us to pack a lunch and the men head out to get the boat ready and fill some ice chests with some bait and drinks.

Last night's romantic evening has faded to memory because the guys are focused on a big catch for the day. Rita keeps a lot of supplies on hand for fishing trips because she and Roan go fishing all the time so we are ready in about thirty minutes.

Of course, I change clothes into a swim suit and a cover up, and my lucky fishing hat. There is always a competition on the vessel as to who will catch the biggest fish. It's about a twenty-minute drive to the marina where the boat is. We're on board in a matter of minutes and motoring out in the ocean. I have already lost my boyfriend to Roan who seems to have all his attention. We're heading toward a glory hole according to Roan's loran. Rita and I are making small talk and I confide in her that Bo has shared something very personal to me and I am having the best weekend ever. Rita and I take turns applying sunscreen to each other. I hold up the bottle gesturing to Bo if he needs some. He shakes his head no.

Roan says we are getting close and suggest we get some bait and reels ready. He wants us to drag some jigs over the area and hope for a hit. Shazam! looks like the girls are going to take in the first fish. I am excited and look over at Bo. He smiles, gives me a thumb up, and hustles over and ask if I need help reeling my fish in.

"You're kidding me, game on!

Bo says, "You Diamond women are fierce."

Roan chimes in he has trouble keeping his manhood and confidence up. We are all laughing. Rita and I both catch a grouper and both are of legal length. Bo's line starts singing and the reel bends over. Of course, I rush over to help the poor guy, but he declines my offer. Roan makes another pass back over the area and there is more action. The captain is having a lucky day or is it my lucky hat? We catch six fish within one and half hours. I think we have emptied the hole and Roan kills the engine. It's time to grab some lunch. We have some turkey and pimento cheese sandwiches already made. Rita passes around some pickles and oranges. We all have a cold beer and thank the captain for putting us on the right spot. There's another place he wants to try and we start up and Roan gives the boat a full throttle and we're off to new territory. Bo comes up front and sits on the center console beside me. "I am pleasantly surprised you knew how to handle a four ought reel, but then you are always surprising me.

"I can also make a mean peanut butter and jelly sandwich in the dark."

"And I'm looking forward to it D." with a full-face grin. He adds, "I'll hold ya to it."

"Want something else to snack on?"

"Thanks, no."

The captain of our boat yells out "one of you try here with a line out," and Rita gets her line out immediately in the water. She feels a tug before she can even place her rod in the holder. She moves to one of the chairs and begins the back and forth reeling in line. All eyes are on the reel when the rod bends and breaks. Crap, I guess the big one gets away. For two more hours we troll without results. We have fish in the fish box and it has been a good day we all agree. Roan asks us to put up our rods because he plans on running in fast. "Hold on to your hats. Since the girls are catching the most fish, I think they can clean 'em while we drink beer, how 'bout it Bo?"

Rita answers "that'll be fine, as long as you and Bo unload the coolers and package up the fish."

"I never win Bo," and Roan is trying to act defeated.

It is about five o clock when we tie the boat up. This is the worst part about fishing; the cleanup that follows. Rita and I unload and load most everything in the vehicle and go up to the condo. I take some zip lock bags and a pan down to the fish bench where Bo and Roan are filleting out the fish. A couple of bystanders are asking the guys where they found them, and Roan points and says, "way out there in the ocean."

"Need anything?" I am looking at Bo.

"Probably some sunscreen,"

"Too late now, and as Rita would say, "I don't want to hear you complaining."

Bo looks at Roan "these women are harsh."

"Stick with me long enough, and you'll be eligible for sainthood like me,"

Rita and I both are showering now. The cold water feels good on my back that is sunburned. I quickly finish, get dressed and put a head band on my wet hair. The guys are upstairs talking boats and have rinse off in the garage shower. Bo is already dressed.

"Do you want to ride back with me tonight D?"

"Sure thing," I look to Roan "are you and Rita going back tonight?

"yeah, we're going to shove off right behind you guys."

"I'll go get my bag Bo and then we can leave."

Rita meets me in the hallway and I ask her if she needs help with emptying out the refrigerator.

"Nope, it is all under control."

I get my duds and come out to the living room and Bo is trying to give Roan cash for some boat gas. Roan replies "it's on the house, in fact

he welcomes another man on board so Rita and I will stop bossing him."
Geez.

Rita is coming from the room and says, "I heard that."

We say our goodbyes and take the elevator down to Bo's SUV. "Are you tired?" he asks.

"A little, the sun saps my energy right out. I'm fine," I smile.

Road Trip

We zip out of the parking lot and on our way home. Bo immediately tells me that he really enjoyed the fishing trip and spending time with my family. You guys seem to kid around a lot with each other. I tell him one must have a sense of humor to fit in with all the antics that go on, "I think you're holding your own detective."

"Oh, I see we are back to detective, are we?" He smiles.

"Just trying to give you your due."

I feel so lucky I spent the weekend with him. I have new energy and my heart feels big. I hope it just keeps getting better.

"I need to turn my police radio on. I hope you don't mind. How often do Roan and Rita go over to Daytona?"

"I really don't know, sometimes I think their kids go there without them." Rita is traveling all the time for the consortium. She is always in Tallahassee hanging out with the governor, and learning about new grants being offered."

"Dolly, I had the best time this weekend and I hope we can have many more weekends together."

"How many weekends do you get off in a month?"

"Not many, because the Pierson Police Department has a small staff. I'm also on call from the county sheriff's department for special assignments. Can you take off every weekend if you want?"

"It all depends on the workload. Funerals are our priority and all the holidays fall on the weekends. I really don't take many, but maybe that will change."

"Hey, are you hungry? Do you want to stop and have dinner? Or do you want to try making that mean peanut butter and jelly sandwich? It will be dark soon."

"Touché, detective, paybacks are hell. Yes, let's stop and experience some fine dining, perhaps, beef Wellington, surf and turf, or chateaubriand? It will be a stiff penalty tonight detective for sparring with me, one that will cost you some of your hard-earned bucks."

"Money well spent. Do you know of a place on our way home?

"I think there is just the usual franchise restaurants. I am not hard to please."

"Why do I find that hard to believe?

"Because this yellow hair squaw woman speaks with forked tongue."

"Yes, I think so. Whatever the price, I think I can manage it. How much for sleeping in teepee with me for night Yellow Hair?"

"Oh, em gee, you did not just try to proposition me, did you? For your information, I am saving myself for Chief Thunder."

"This Thunder, he big chief?"

"Okay stop, I can't take it anymore."

Bo has gotten the best of me. He pulls into an Outback. "Let's eat here." He parks and just stares at me. "You have the craziest sense of humor." He gets out and before I know it he is at my side opening my door. There are so few princes left in the world. I am exiting right into his arms and he exclaims "you are hot, I mean sunburned."

"I like the other word better, you know HOT,"

"I'm having trouble keeping up."

We're in the restaurant now and seated at the table.

"I know what I want to eat. I'll have a strip cooked well, with a salad, and fresh vegetable. I have to visit the sandbox."

"Cooked well, you say?" Looking at me like I had two heads.

"Yes, we'll have to discuss why when I get back. Can you handle that?"

"I'm like Roan, I'm beginning to doubt I can handle any of you, losing my manhood, isn't that what he said?"

"Then try harder." I am amused but I really have to go to the bathroom now but I'm loving every minute of his fun-loving way. I return to the table and there is salad.

"You shouldn't have waited."

"I didn't, I had a piece of bread."

The restaurant doesn't appear to be that busy and the steaks arrive quickly. Bo takes my hand and bows his head, "thank you lord, for this meal and for this crazy girl you have introduced me to." He squeezes my hand, and says "I mean that."

"That is so sweet of you, I will behave for the rest of the night."

Bo opens the door for me once again. My head is spinning from all of the attention I am getting. We are still an hour from home. We pull out onto the road.

"Tell me about your parents Bo."

"Mother and Dad were married fifty years and then Dad passed away. He had a heart attack playing golf. My father was a judge in his later life. He suffered too because he was on the bench when I shot and killed my brother n law. I almost gave up law enforcement, but realized I couldn't be happy in any other profession.

"Have you always been a florist?"

"Yes, since I was eighteen. It's a rough business to command, but I get to work with some of Gods best creations of beautiful flowers. It has its merits."

"Are you happy D?"

"Most of the time although it has been a sad time for myself and my family recently."

"Time will heal most anything."

"There are some things that time can't erase Bo. I am willing to forget the past but I am not willing to forgive everything. My family is fragmented and right now I'd say we are ripe for destruction."

He is silenced by my words. And maybe I am caustic but he doesn't know what I have been through. There is no band aid for the hole I have in my heart caused by someone that betrayed me at the highest level.

He remains quiet for a while, and I guess I have run out of fuel. I lean my head back against the headrest and nod off. It is my wedding day.

There are so many beautiful flowers and it is spring. My bridesmaids have floral chiffon print dresses in shades of blues and yellow. My fiancé, Kerry has just given me a new thunderbird car for a wedding present. He has worked for the Ford dealership for six years. Kerry is a smooth operator, and too good looking for his own good. He flirts and can be over friendly with all my girlfriends. "It's just part of the job Doll. That's what I do, sell, and I'm good at it." In hind-sight, I never truly know if he makes any real money at it, but he looks the part of confidence and financial success.

"Dolly, we have arrived at your place." In a louder voice, Bo is call-ing, "hey Dolly"

I am startled, "oh, we're here. I must have taken a power nap."

"Yes, I think you did." With that he grabs my bag from the weekend, opens my car door and walks me to the door.

"Do you want to come inside?"

"No, thank you, tomorrow will come early. I will see where my queen resides another time. He tilts my head to the side, and caresses my throat with his fingers, and kisses me deeply for a long time. I wrap my hands around his back and he continues. My lips are moist when he finishes. "Sleep tight. I'll call you."

He opens my front door for me and he turns and leaves.

I meander in my house, and look around. Yep, it is just the way I left it. I get a glass of water and draw a bath. I'll be ready for the bed soon.

Today is Monday and I take my coffee to work. As soon as I walk in, Julie tells me Denise has called.

"How was the beach? You look like you got some sun. You look like a brown berry."

"Wearing sunscreen is the key. You never guess who came to the condo. Best weekend ever."

"It has to be Boyd to make you this happy."

"We had dinner, he spent the night, and the next day we went fishing."

"Wait, wait, back up. He spent the night?"

"Yes, and we decided that we could wait till we were both ready. He shared a very personal part of his life with me."

"And did you share your secret with him?"

"No. That is something I could not even tell my parents so they could understand what turned me upside down. It is buried in that hole I have in the core of my body that is too painful to relive. I need to make an appointment to see the my therapist. The demon is resurfacing again."

"If Denise wants to call again, I'll talk to her, but I won't make an effort to return the call."

"Give me some orders to do, and catch me up on our sales over the weekend."

The phone is ringing. Unknown Caller. "Hello, Bouquets Today,"

"Aunt Dolly, this is Carly. I hope you remembered our appointment tomorrow. I took your advice and I am ready with pictures, and thoughts I have about my wedding."

"That's great, I love an organized bride. Can you be here at ten o'clock or shortly after?

"Yes ma'am. I am so excited."

"I can hear it in your voice. See you tomorrow sweetie."

Julie hears my side of the conversation and tells me she hopes it doesn't start another battle with Denise.

"I have nothing to base this feeling on, but I suspect Carly will surprise us. Once in a great while, a bride deserves everything extra we can do for them."

Noon time comes and goes, and I agree to sit down with a sales lady cold-calling. She steps outside to get her samples and catalogs. I make a space on the conference table and go get some bottled water for us.

I think back to some time ago that a salesman missed his appointment by twenty minutes. He came in with this exasperated story why he was late. I gave him such a hard time, but he offered to buy me a drink after work to apologize. I felt bad I could not see his product until the next day so I agreed to a drink after work. He had a traveling showroom uniquely arranged that he parked at the hotel. One drink led to several and dinner. We had lots of fun sharing crazy stories about this business we are in. I was very comfortable and we had chemistry between us that led to a rendezvous in the bed at his hotel. He was a real teddy bear that loved being physical and afterwards we were just lying there cuddling. I glanced down at his lower right pelvic area and there was a patch on his skin. I shyly asked him if what I was seeing was a nicotine patch to quit smoking. He looked puzzled and raised up a little bit and looked down at it too. As soon as I heard him say no, what are you talking about? A feeling came over me like I was on stage singing in my birthday suit. I was looking at my own hormone replacement patch that had stuck on his skin during my Mrs. Toad's wild ride. Immediately, I laughed so loud at my own ridiculousness and told him what it was and that it belonged to me. You could have knocked me over with one of the feathers which incidentally he sold. Meekly, he asked what was going to happen to him. I kept my humor and said his voice might be elevated some for a few months. That story is one I tuck away in my black book referenced single life.

"Is this where you want me to unload the catalogs?" my saleslady is back.

"Yes, come right in and grab a chair."

I place a three-hundred-dollar order to ship in September and I assure her I will look at holiday product after Labor Day.

It was past five and Julie had started closing procedures while I was wrapping up my order. We both wanted to get to the grocery store.

"See you tomorrow" as we both get in our cars and leave.

I arrive home quickly and started preparing supper. Rita is blowing up my cell. I have groceries I am putting them away but answer her anyway. She is so impatient as is the whole of society. Everyone expects instant gratification. Geez.

"Denise called again, and is ranting that you have not returned her call."

"I wasn't aware that I owed her any money."

"What does that mean?

"It's a joke Rita, because I don't owe her any money. Yet she snaps her fingers and I am supposed to answer her every beckon. Won't happen."

"Roan said he really enjoyed Boyd this weekend. Frankly, I think it boosted our love life."

"That's funny ha ha and funny peculiar."

"Have you heard from him today?"

"No I haven't."

"Are you concerned?"

"Well I wasn't until you just mentioned it"

"Sorry"

"Turn me loose so I can finish up supper and put these groceries away. Oh, by the way Carly is coming for her appointment tomorrow at ten. Call me if you're available for lunch."

Here Comes The Bride

Carly is punctual and greets me with a big hug. She sets her notebook down and exclaims "I love your store."

"I hear that a lot and I have to say it is a team effort to make beautiful displays and keep product moving."

"Your dedication shows."

"Let's get to planning."

We cover all the preliminary questions about date and time and venue.

"Tell me about your dress."

"Here's the thing. I find this outrageous vintage dress in a store called Second Hand Rose. The owner shared with me that this elderly lady brought it in and it was her dress she wore in 1950. She brought in a picture of her wedding day wearing the dress which I brought for you to see. The lace is old but real thick and has a quality feel to it. Grandma says the trim on the hem and sleeves and neckline is called eyelash lace. You see the detail Aunt Dolly?"

"Yes, I bet the lady had a very swanky wedding."

"Did you notice her flowers? She looks a movie star or a queen for a day."

"I'm sure you will be too."

"I bought the dress because I was enamored with this woman's story how long they had been married. The owner of the shop says the lady is a kind and sweet person. It was good Karma walking out with that wedding dress. My grandma is going to make a new lining for the whole dress including long sleeves in a color that matches the aged lace. That way my tattoos on my arms will not be a problem. I know Mrs. Henry, uh, Denise is not pleased with the tattoos I have.....I'm trying. During high school, I struggled with an identity crisis and when I graduated I fell into a group where everyone got them. In hindsight, I realize you don't need to keep adding them to be noticed. Bing makes me feel beautiful and I want his family to support our marriage.

"Okay, let's hear about how you envision your special day."

"A perfect day would be Bingham's mother not coming. Of course, I am kidding. It's just that I try so hard to please her and I just get this sense she has this big distaste."

"Carly, the best advice I can give you is to be yourself and respectful. I think she might come around if she is not provoked but like all of us sometimes the words we say can become weapons that ricochet back to us."

"My grandma has a big collection of old tatted and crocheted table scarfs and large circular doilies. In keeping with my vintage dress, I would like to use these somehow on the table linens. It would make her so happy to see them used on the tables at the reception. I don't want big flower arrangements that would take over the vintage feel. I definitely want to carry the same flowers in the picture. Momma keeps calling them canna lilies but now I know they are calla lilies. My grandma still tats and I am asking her to add tatting on the edge of some linen handkerchiefs I'm having monogrammed for my bridesmaids."

"I will put my thinking cap on to come up with a centerpiece for the tables. How many tables do you think there will be?"

"I have three bridesmaids and a few customers from my work and I am thinking maybe thirty guests on my side. Bing thinks he will have one hundred plus some. Let's plan on fifteen tables.

"Another thing, uh problem, is that I need to convey to Denise without offending that my Grandma and Momma are not pretentious people. They both worked hard all of their lives and saved money for my wedding. I don't want to spend all of that money on the party and not have money left for my marriage. I have been to Mrs. Henry's dinners and parties and even though I am in awe, I think some items are needless and wasteful. Please don't tell her I said that. I really do wish she could give me a real chance because I know I can be a good daughter n law."

"Awe, keep being yourself and I think she will come around when she realizes how much you and Bing love each other."

"Aunt Dolly, why aren't you married? You are fun and pretty and a good cook. Don't you want to be married?" I asked Bing and he said that you canceled your wedding."

"Yes, I did because I got caught up in the hype of a wedding and lacked the respect and trust that I was supposed to have in a marriage."

"Momma said I should give you a deposit today. Is five hundred dollars enough?"

"That will be fine Carly." I enjoyed hearing your ideas and together we will make your special day memorable. Are you driving back now? I thought we could have lunch with Rita."

Lunch Dates

"Okay, it you know somewhere quick."

"I'll phone Rita now."

I phone Rita and she picks up. "The time frame has passed for me. I thought you would call earlier so I can't make it. Gotta run. Bye."

I grab my purse and tell Julie that Carly and I are going to lunch. "Let's take my car. It's parked in the back."

Carly takes a second and walks over to Julie and gives her a hug and then joins me.

The restaurant that I drive to is a local favorite that features daily specials. We walk in and we're seated immediately and given menus.

"I definitely don't want chicken wings," and Carly laughs.

"Oh, I guess not. They make really good salads here. I usually get the Greek with chicken."

"I think I'll have that veggie burger."

"How are you today Ms. Diamond?" Our waitress is Sandy and I know her from church.

"I'm good Sandy. This is Carly who is marrying my nephew."

"Okay, what can get for ya'll today?"

"I am going to have the Greek salad, and Carly would like the veggie burger. I'll have water."

Carly chimes in "me too."

I hand back my menu and look around and there is Bo with a woman who is laughing and patting him on the back. The police chief is with them and looks like they are all having lunch. I guess "I'll call ya" didn't mean yesterday or today. My neck cannot be more strained to see what is going on at Bo's table. Bo is smiling back at her now and curiosity is about to do me in.

"Do you eat here often?"

Carly said something to me. *Not now, Carly.*

"What is it? I asked. No, I usually eat lunch at the shop," *although this restaurant seems to be an eye opener. I might have to change my water to Captain Morgan.*

"Do you know them?"

My flamingo neck is still stretching. "Who?"

Carly is giggling. "The handsome policemen,"

I turn back to her. "I'm sorry, I guess I am surprised, that's all."

The food has arrived but I have lost my appetite. I scoot everything around on the plate with my fork and finally eat a piece of feta. Carly is eating and looking at me and then turns to look at Bo and whoever SHE is. *Oh hell no, they are leaving now and he is likely to see me.* I don't know how he could notice me because he is seeming to be enjoying her company.

I know he is standing over me. I look at Carly. She has her mouth on her burger and is frozen in time and her eyes are giant balls that have appeared from nowhere. Bo puts his hand on my shoulder. "Hey, I called you last night and left a message."

"You did?" All is well. "I guess I didn't look at my phone. Did you have a nice lunch with your friend ..s...?"

"Yes, the chief treated today."

"Good for you. I'd like to introduce Carly. She is marrying my nephew in September. This is Detective Boyd Price."

Bo acknowledges her "very nice meeting another member of the family,"

Carly nods her head and swallows. "Thank you."

Bo squeezes my shoulder. "Talk to you soon."

He departs out the door. I look at my plate and I have managed to spill my salad all over the edge of the plate on to the table with my fork still in motion.

Carly wipes her mouth with her napkin. "He is pretty dreamy."

"Dreamy? I hadn't noticed."

I get a text on my phone and it is Bo. "Excuse me a second."

Jealousy is a side of you I might enjoy
She...is a safety instructor from Sanford
And can't hold a candle to you
Dinner tonight with Chief Thunder?

Me jealous? I think you are tripping.
Very animated discussion for safety instructor.
Yellow Hair will be ready at six for pickup

The check comes and I hand twenty-six dollars to Sandy. Outside on the sidewalk, Carly asks me if everything is all right

I answer, "it is fantastic." We return to the store and say our good-byes. "I'll be in touch." Carly gives me a hug goodbye and a big smile "and good luck on your police guy that you are trying to convince me is not on your mind."

I walk in the shop. Julie asks if I had a good lunch.

"Yes, but I didn't eat much. I'll probably be hungry this afternoon."

"I'm ready to make the deliveries, Okay?"

"Go ahead."

The afternoon is uneventful and I look at my notes about the wedding. I hope I can come up with something that will make Carly overjoyed. I'm out front straightening a table up and barely catch the phone, "Bouquets Today."

"Bingham tells me Carly came in for a wedding consult. I can just imagine that she probably wants to use cheap silk flowers or worse yet burlap." *Oh joy, it is Denise.*

"I don't ordinarily discuss another customers' requests but since it is Bingham's wedding I'll make an exception. Carly has some lovely ideas that I think are original and unique. Actually, her bridal bouquet will be stunning out of white calla lilies and we will probably carry that theme throughout in the centerpieces."

"If she thinks I am going to fork over thousands for calla lilies, then she is mistaken. Aren't they expensive?"

"Well, it's relative to how many we use on each table."

"Bing also told me she has already found and bought a used dress at some store. That's laughable. She is going to ruin Bingham 's wedding because she has no taste."

"Did you say ruin a wedding? That is rich coming from you. Don't repeat that ever again to anyone or I am warning you I will tell Bing how you ruined mine. You are black with sin and you disgust me with your high and mighty attitude. And for your information, I am quite sure she and her family are paying for everything despite the fact your guest list will far outnumber Carly's guests."

A long silence follows and I think she is paralyzed by fear. I am confident I have made my point. Now that my parents are gone she better believe that my threat is not an idle one.

"I repeat Denise, she is a hardworking and thoughtful girl. If you would just step back and take a second look, you'd know this. On the other hand, maybe you deserve a daughter n law that is a first-class bitch. Goodbye."

I am unaware that Julie is back and up front with a customer. She finishes her sale, and steps back to my desk, "I thought for a minute there, I was going to have to ask you to calm down. Your voice was getting louder and louder especially when you said the B word. You must have been talking to Denise."

"The one and only. I know she pushes my buttons and I lose control. Do I need to call the customer and apologize for my potty mouth?"

"I don't think so. Just go home and relax. I will finish out the day."

"The Lord looked down on me and blessed me the day I hired you. Thank you, friend. I haven't had the chance to tell you I have a dinner date this evening with Boyd. So, I will go home and start getting ready."

There are so many events unfolding lately that are unsettling me. It is time to call and make that appointment with my therapist. I'll call tomorrow for sure.

It is half past four and cocktail hour. I'll just have one with the captain to unwind my screwball head and head to the bath. A great soak is a quick fix for everything. I am thinking about what I will wear tonight and I don't have a clue where we are dining. There was much anxiety in my day today. I wouldn't mind skipping dinner in exchange for being held by Bo for hours.

Reservations Required

I'm dressed in jeans and a long sleeve blue and white stripe shirt monogrammed with my initials. I'll take a baby blue sweater in case is it is cold where we are going.

He is punctual. I like that in a person. A date once told me he looks at three things in a lady; her fingernails, her lipstick, and whether she can be on time. I have always remembered that. I believe every date I have ever encountered has taught me something. The doorbell sounds.

"No horn honking tonight Detective? Your manners are overwhelming." I cannot believe he is holding a bunch of daisies in his hand and says, "for you, a little road-side-ea."

"You are over the top, but somehow I don't believe you picked these alongside the road. Daisies? Is this she loves me, she loves me not?"

"Something like that." Are you going to invite me in?"

"Entrada, mi casa, su casa."

"You speak Spanish?"

"Si, that was it."

He grabs a hold of me, "Hello" and we kiss like he has just returned from a furlough.

"Let me get a vase, gosh, imagine me receiving flowers. You make me happy." I get out a blue delft vase and recut the stems and add some preservative.

"Your home is exactly like I thought it would be. Fresh and tidy, homey and welcoming. Beautiful, like the person you are." He is looking, walking around and studying pictures. Are you going to give me a tour?"

"Of course," I take his hand and show him around from one end to the other. When I get to my bedroom, "Wampum needed in here."

"How much?"

"It's negotiable," I answer.

He pulls me again close to him and gives me a short smooch. "Let's get going."

We're out the door and at his Tahoe. He leads me to the passenger side and opens my door. I'm in my seat and he reaches over and buckles my seatbelt. "I'm checking for safety. Today I had an attractive female instructor teaching me today."

"I guess I deserved that."

"You were looking pretty green in the restaurant today. I could see you through a mirror and never had to turn my head. I enjoyed it."

"Smug is not attractive on you."

He shrugs and he has that kid grin on his face. He gets in and buckles his seatbelt. "I'm taking you to one of my favorite restaurants. He starts driving south and I am thinking there are no restaurants this way. He makes a turn on the highway. "My mothers." He takes my hand and squeezes it.

"I'll try not to smack my food." I hear him snicker.

"That will be appreciated."

We arrive in a couple of minutes. The landscaping looks freshly manicured. He knocks on the door but goes in anyway. "Mother, we're here."

Janet Price appears from the lanai. "So good to see you again Dolly."

"And you as well, Mrs. Price."

"Please call me Janet."

"Thank you."

"A glass of wine Dolly?"

Bo takes his hand off my shoulder and looks in my eyes. "I'm coming right back."

I sense Janet is looking me over. "Dolly, you look rested. I assume the beach agrees with you. Bo told me he enjoyed his weekend immensely. I have you to thank for his happiness these last few weeks. I am sure... Bo is back with glasses of wine for both of us.

She holds her glass to mine. "Cheers"

Bo is drinking a beer. "How are my favorite girls? Mother, something smells good."

"Thanks son. We can go in and begin with our salads."

We are dining in a different room off from the kitchen. She has fresh daisies in a vase also. The tablecloth is black and white buffalo check with white glazed dishes everywhere. Janet has a gift for decorating. Bo has been brought up with some extravagance I can tell.

She sets our salad in front of us and sits down. "Dolly, this is a recipe that my grandmother used to make." The salad is fresh snow peas, small green peas, and water chestnuts tossed with bacon and purple onion. I suspect both mayo and sour cream are mixed in and it is delicious.

"This is so delightful. Cold and crisp is a great combination, my compliments."

"Would you like some more? How 'bout you Bo?" We both decline seconds.

"I'm only declining because I surmise something special is coming next."

Janet prepares our plates at the stove. Bo refills our glasses of wine and surprisingly pours himself one. He responds, "Real men drink wine too." He winks at me.

I move my salad plate over as Janet places my dinner plate in front of me. It's a thick pork loin slice with a peppery sugared crust. There are sweet potato medallions with a pat of butter and Brussels sprouts. I have never been able to make Brussels sprouts that are tasty and I have tried several times. Everyone has their plate and Boyd takes his mother's hand and mine. Janet reaches and takes my hand. It feels like family. He closes his eyes and says a blessing.

I share my dismay of never being able to cook Brussels sprouts with Janet. She remarks it took her a little while to get it right herself. The pork is divine and moist and the outer edge of the meat is at least a quarter of an inch.

"Is there a food you don't particularly like Dolly?"

"Not many, I don't care for liver and malted items are not my favorite. I love quality food, experimenting with new recipes and I love cook books."

"Sounds like you have a command of the kitchen too."

I am sipping my wine between bites. The truth is I could eat from the stove it is so good.

"I understand why Bo told me we were going to one of his favorite restaurants."

"You had not idea you were coming here?"

"I did not. This is a pleasant surprise. That's two for the evening." I glance his way.

"I've got to keep you guessing."

Janet, whenever I have dinner guest, I love it when people eat everything on their plate and I'm letting you know I intend on being a clean plate club member."

"Well, I'm delighted you are enjoying everything."

"I am."

Janet asked Bo how his day went.

"I went to lunch with the chief and an instructor form Sanford. It proved interesting."

I'll add gloat to the smug list...and handsome, and thoughtful.

It's about eight now. Janet rises to clear the table. Bo stands and I join in. "May I load the dishwasher while you put away the food?"

"Thank you, that will be helpful."

I rinse them off and place them all in. Three in the kitchen make fast work of cleaning up. I sit back down and drink the last of my wine.

Janet opens the refrigerator and removes three parfaits. "It's just a light dessert with Greek yogurt and homemade granola."

It is beautiful and creamy with a crunchy nutty topping. I have met my match in the kitchen. That homemade meal I promised Bo will require some homework.

"This is super Janet."

"Thank you, Mother." Bo gets up and gives her a kiss on her head. He picks up his dish and ours and places them in the sink.

"You guys go now, I appreciate the company tonight. Come back soon Dolly."

Bo pulls out my chair for me. I say goodnight and we make our way out the door.

"The gardener does a good job here on the grounds."

"That would be me. Mother helps too. She keeps active."

His good manners never get old. I think to myself about all the stories I have heard from singles dating who declare they are always stunned when manners are short lived and romance wains and there is burping and all the other unacceptable social habits that appear in the relationship. No wander people can't stay married.

We're leaving, and I tell him, "Your mom is certainly a grand hostess. You must be very proud to be her son."

"That is nice for you to notice. She is and was very supportive of me especially when Dina abandoned me. She handed me some brutal honesty that was hard to accept."

We're at my house. "Would you like a night cap, maybe a Kahlua?"

"Okay, sounds nice."

He sits on the couch as I fix us a tumbler of Kahlua and cream. I sit down beside him and we both take a sip. He puts his arm around me and draws me close and sweeps my hair from my face. "Dolly, I know we have chemistry. I feel it when we are together. I know we have a lot to learn about each other but I don't want this to be a game for you because we have fun together. You make me laugh every time I am with you. I believe we share a lot of the same values. I need you to know I am invested and I want us to move forward. He picks my chin up and looks in my eyes. I love your eyes. They sparkle and I'll never get tired of looking in them and seeing the beautiful woman you are."

He has so much passion and I am responding to his deep kiss. My eyes flood and I utter "I'm afraid."

"Of me? Tell me why." He is holding me tight. "I'm scared to death that when I let my guard down that I will be vulnerable and unprotected. Trust is not easy for me. Hold me and never let me go. I want you more than ever. I want to surrender everything and let you love me, but I have some issues to work on." He is kissing me more. "Bo I'm afraid I will disappoint you, that you're expecting an angel which I am not, a partner, when I have been doing and making my own decisions for so long. He's still kissing me.

"You're making it difficult for me to talk."

"I want you so much. I want your commitment to us from this day forward. Can you tell me that?"

"Yes, I am committed to this relationship. I love everything about you. I know I am falling in love but I want more than lust and physical satisfaction. Bo, have you heard what I've been trying to tell you?"

"What was that part about you surrendering to me and letting me love you?" He is kissing down my neck and I'm feeling weak.

"Bo, when I make love with you, I want the night and the morning and the next day. I don't think this is the night. Is it?"

"I thought it was." He stops and gives me a short kiss in my mouth. He pulls me in closer and whispers "I love, love, love, being with you." He's breathing hard and sighs. "I hope you know you are turning me out in the street and missing the opportunity of a lifetime."

"This is my only chance?"

He pulls me in close again. "We have the rest of our lives. You are the one for me. Believe it." He pulls me up from the couch. "I'll say good-night." He walks out the door and I am still in the doorway.

"Bo," and I walk toward him and kiss him once more.

"Soon," he whispers in my ear.

I go back and lean against the door. *I love this guy so much.*

At eleven thirty I receive a text from Bo.

I want you to know that you are my greatest adventure in life and

I want all of adventure whenever you are ready. B

I am in the bed, and can only imagine how special our first night will be. I know it will be soon. Early in the morning, I get another text from Bo.

Good morning my love. Happy Day. B

You are the sweetest. D

My day starts off on a high. Sometime during the day, I will send an invitation to Bo for him to redeem his coupon for a meal at my house on Friday.

Rita phones me and tells me Rhett is grilling chicken tonight. Do you want to come over?"

"May I invite a guest?

"Sure, bring a salad. See you at six."

"Okay."

I call Bo on the phone. "Hey, sweet guy."

"I try."

"Rita's son Rhett is grilling tonight. Want to go with me and eat some dead chicken?"

"Love to, but I can't. I'm taking mother overnight to Atlanta for some business."

"Oh, okay. I'll miss you. When are you coming back?"

"I'll be back on Saturday and I'll see you then."

"Would you like to redeem your birthday coupon for Saturday night? You realize that coupon has an expiration date on it."

"There is no expiration date with us. I'll text you what hotel I'm in tonight. Miss me."

"I will. Tell your mother hello. Bye."

This is disappointing news I admit, but I will be excited for Saturday.

I call Rita and say, "just one for dinner. He is going out of town tonight with his mother."

"Alright, see you at six."

Finally, I get to the store. "Good Morning Julie."

"You sound happy and you deserve it."

"The restaurant Bo took me to was his mother's house. She is an excellent cook and I can't help being a bit jealous. Bo reveres her cooking. I can tell they are close. I also notice that he has great respect for her and I applaud that."

"Do you think she approves of you?"

"I don't know. I hope so. I think him taking me over there gives her more insight about our relationship. I am willing to bet she has influence on him." Anyway, he's out of town for two days and on Saturday I am having him over for a romantic evening."

"I'm looking forward to you doing nothing for two days around here, and talk, talk, talk, about Saturday." Julie is teasing me but she is so right.

"Your orders I need you to do as soon as possible are on your bench."

"Gotcha," I quickly do them and we stay busy. She is out front and I cover the back by answering the phone and making more arrangements. It is after five and I still need to make a salad. I'll just go by the store and buy the ingredients and make it at Rita's.

The chicken is phenomenal. All I want to eat is the meat and salad.

Rita asks me how the wedding appointment went with Carly.

"Actually, very good. She was prepared and had some unique ideas. Her dress has been purchased and it is vintage heavy cut lace. She told me her grandmother has lots of old lace tablecloths and doilies that she has tatted and she would like to incorporate them in the wedding flowers somehow. Carly did not tell me her budget but said there were funds allocated for her wedding. I got the impression she could have an extravagant event but chooses to save some to start her married life. "Of course, Denise thinks she is a gold digger and won't give her any benefit of any doubt. We went to lunch and I said I'd get back to her with some ideas."

"If anyone has good ideas it will be you."

"Thanks Sis." Speaking of ideas, I need some for a romantic dinner Saturday night with Bo. I was thinking about seafood, maybe some crab cakes with a creamy dill sauce.

"Roan and I are available too if you need a foursome." Roan is shaking his head yes.

"If you come you must leave early because I am planning something special for us."

"Hope we don't have to leave before dessert, do we?" Roan is moaning as he speaks.

"I guess I wouldn't be very hospitable if I threw you out before dessert."

"Sounds like there is hanky panky planned." I suppose you deserve intimacy after all these years."

"What do you mean all these years? I have had the red bulb in my outside light out for a long time. And you should not be talking about this. My life isn't an open book you know."

"We can set our phone alarms and say Rita is ovulating and we need to leave immediately."

They are both enjoying themselves at my expense.

Rita is laughing. "You wish that was the reason Roan."

"Okay, that is quite enough or they'll be no dessert for you two."

Rhett was out of the room and wanted to know what all the laughing was about.

"Nothing son, just your Aunt Dolly and the tangled web she weaves."

"Rhett, the chicken is tasty beyond description. I'm going to take a piece for my lunch tomorrow.

"Of course."

"Dolly, the Sunday dinner is coming up the next Sunday. Have you any thoughts about the meal? I expect that Denise will want to discuss dividing the personal affects. Hopefully she will also have a report about the changes she has made with the office."

Our family calls all the little statues and momentous that sit around on bookcases and shelves glass kitties. It is agonizing to go through treasured items from happier days sorting which to keep and which ones to trash. There is usually some sentimental value to the things you want to keep. I am usually a sucker for old linens and old dishes because I remember all those Sunday dinners when our family was whole.

"Again, I enjoyed the chicken Rhett."

"I need to motor on home and get some things done at my house. I guess I'll see you and Roan about six on Saturday." The reason I need to rush is that I am hoping Bo will call and I don't want to be at Rita's when I answer the phone.

It is almost ten and I am already in my bed when my phone rings. My heart beats because I am excited to talk to my man. "Hello,"

"Hey there, I hope I didn't call too late. You don't need any beauty sleep."

"You must be joking, I could use all the help I can get. I am just thumbing through recipes wondering how I can top your favorite restaurant's dinners. Your mom is tough competition. Are you in a hotel?"

"I am in the Marriott on Peachtree in the heart of downtown Atlanta. We booked a suite and Mother is next door. We have an appointment downtown in the morning, and then we're going to do a little shopping. Anything I can bring you to make you smile?"

"Just yourself."

"Did you go to Rita's?"

"Yes, I've been back about an hour. You missed some great chicken Rhett cooked."

"I hope they'll be other opportunities. I enjoy your family."

"Absolutely, you're in this for the long haul remember?"

"Yes I am. We are checking out in the morning and going to my sisters for dinner and we're going to spend the night there. She's in the outskirts of Atlanta. We want to avoid the morning commute traffic due to our appointment."

"Dinner with your sister will be nice."

"Yes, but she eats late, almost nine most nights, so I probably won't call you tomorrow night.

Oh, okay, I'll try to keep occupied with girl stuff. I miss you."

"Miss you more, goodnight baby."

"Night Bo."

It is a great way to begin sleeping with Bo on my mind.

I wake up early. Apparent the house across the street is getting a new roof and the roofers are loud. It is a sure bet I'll be to work early.

"Good morning Julie, and top of the morning to you."

"You're in a good mood."

"Yep, life is good."

"Have you heard the news about Derek Shaffer?"

"What news?'

"The rumor is that he committed suicide. I already contacted the funeral home. They said the family would be in at nine."

"Oh god. How tragic. He called me two or three days ago. I saw it on my cell but he didn't leave a message. It has been two years since I have dated him. We did not have a lot in common and so I can hardly call it a romance. He was cute though and really fit. I guess that was part of the problem for me. I thought he was too much into exercise and strict dietary guidelines. He took steroids which I was concerned about and told him so. His lifestyle was an oxymoron. You eat healthy but you take steroids. That isn't healthy. He was fit but very myopic about the path he was taking to achieve those results. It ended on a good note. I feel horrible for the family. I saw his mother a couple of times in the grocery store. Confidentially I think his mom wanted us to get back dating."

"Wow, do you wish you had answered his call?"

"Of course, especially if he was reaching out to me, but how could I know that? I don't think for a minute he was despondent over me. We didn't have that kind of relationship."

I walk to my desk and sit down. The news about Derek makes me sad. I hope he is at peace now in his soul. I reach in my drawer and pull out a special card and address it to his parents. I write a personal note to them expressing my sorrow and sign my name.

"Julie, can you make a nice bouquet so that we can deliver it today to Derek's parents?"

"Of course. I feel sad too."

"His parents have a strong faith and that will give them strength."

Julie and I have an early lunch. During lunch, we check with the funeral home to find out information. The body went to the medical examiner's office and the service won't be until Monday. We are interrupted during our lunch. The Shaffer family wants to select a casket spray. I walk out to the front and hug Derek's mom and tell her how very sorry I am and I will be thinking of them every day. Derek's parents are bolstering each other up. I retrieve the floral tribute binder that shows a multitude of sprays in all colors and flower combinations. She explains his casket is silver and they like the red and white one with red roses and white carnations. I tell them I will take care of it for them.

Mrs. Schafer says, "I know you will honey."

I return around the counter and assure her she need not worry and they leave the shop. His death is so needless. I feel horrible they are having to deal with all the unanswered questions.

I make a list of the flowers we will need and order them. I wonder if Julie and I are thinking the same thing.

"Julie, have you sent those flowers out to be delivered yet?"

"Yes, they left shortly after you finished talking with the family."

This day had been difficult to get through.

I'm on my way home and Rita calls. Rhett told me the news about Derek. "Do you know any of the details?"

"None about his death, only that the service is Monday. The family was in and visibly distraught. I feel terrible for them trying to cope."

"You didn't date him long, did you?"

"Only twice I think. It's still sad."

"Have you heard from Bo?"

"Last night. He said he probably won't call tonight. That's good, because I'm going home to get my house in order for my dinner soirée on Saturday. I'm going to say goodbye Sis."

Detect This

I didn't want to talk about Derek. I wanted to avoid the captain tonight as well and keep busy.

I start in my bedroom and clean the bathrooms till they sparkle. I put everything away under the cabinet so my counter top in the bathroom looks pristine. I'm making a list as I go through the house cleaning. I write flowers for bathroom on my list. I spend an hour on my bedroom and move to the living room. This room doesn't require much since I tore into that over a week ago. I add 'new orchid plant or hydrangeas and get a candle' from the store to my list. It's about ten thirty now and I have made great headway. The kitchen is spotless, and I have polished my grandmothers silver, pressed the tablecloth and set the table. I have all my serving plates to one side. I review my menu in my head. I will shop tomorrow for the groceries and make my guava cheesecake for dessert tomorrow night. I'm coming out of my kitchen and barely hear my phone. It's Bo.

"Hey there. I didn't think I would hear from you. How's your mother and Rachel?"

"I have left them in the living room. Dolly are you Okay?"

"Of course, better now that I can hear your voice. What's wrong? Are you worried for some reason? Gosh, I have lived by myself for a long time. I assure you I'm okay."

"Dolly, please listen."

"Alright, what's up?"

"Tonight, I am reading a report from the police department where they have pulled telephone call analysis regarding a suicide. It has your number on the report and you are flagged for an interview. Has anyone called you asking you to come in?"

"From the police department? No."

"Did you know the guy who committed suicide?"

"Yes, and the family. I dated him some. He did call me a couple of days ago, but he left no message, therefore I did not return his call. I saw the family today. They were in the shop ordering flowers. It is so sad."

"You dated him? For how long?"

"Bo, you are sounding like a detective and I don't know where you are going with this."

"Dolly, with every suicide there is a police investigation. Questions are posed to all that had contact with the person in the days before their death. When I get back, I will have to recuse myself as the lead detective of the department because of our relationship. In all probability, another investigator will probably contact you in the morning and set an appointment up with you for next week. Are you up for this?"

"I suppose, will you be there?"

"I just told you I must recuse myself."

"So you did." *I am not liking his tone.* There is silence between us.

"Dolly, they will ask you some pointed questions, personal questions. I am trying to prepare you, shield you."

"It doesn't come across that way. I haven't spoken to him in probably a year to two years. I didn't break his heart Bo if that's the information you are seeking. We didn't sleep together. I probably only had two dates, maybe three with him. I can make you a list of all the winners and losers I have dated if you want."

"D, Baby, please stop."

"No, you stop."

"I can hear in your voice I have hurt your feelings. I have the utmost respect for you baby. I wish I was there to tell you and show you how much

I care for you. I am sorry if you are offended. Forgive me. I was trying in some small way to help you fend off intrusive questions that may be asked. Tell me all is well. I need you to tell me D."

"Well, you might try cutting out your tongue and painting your Tahoe red and going down Main Street letting everyone know you have wronged your Yellow Hair."

"Lord, you are a fierce negotiator."

"Too much, huh?"

"Yes, but I hear you smiling again and it makes me happy. I'm either going to whip you or love you to death when I see you."

"I can sign up for either one. I really miss you. It has been a sad day since I learned about Derek taking his own life. I don't know why he called me. I believe he was messed up on steroids and other pills. I'll talk to you about him on Saturday. Thank you for caring so much about me."

"I hope so. Goodnight Love. In my sleep, I will hold you all night."

"Night."

I had a lot to think about what Bo told me. The hair raised up on my back for a minute. I don't know if I'll ever be able to share with him my darkest hour if I can't trust him completely. I have loved others and was betrayed. Fear will be my blanket tonight. I sit down and stare at the television. *I do not want to be needy or dependent.*

At three o'clock I wake up and go get a glass of water. I come back to my bed and pull my blanket on top of me.

I drag into the store a little after nine. "I'm sorry I'm late."

"You're late all the time, why the apology today?

"Thanks for reminding me."

"I thought you would come in all excited, telling me what you are cooking for your big night."

"There might not be a big night."

"What happened?"

"Bo called me and asked about Derek's suicide. I felt demeaned. He said the police were going to call me because my number showed up on Derek's phone calls. He said he was trying to shield me but I felt he was probing. For a minute, I felt cornered. It wasn't a good feeling. And I over reacted. You know how I am, hard shell on the outside, but subject to injury when I stick my neck out. I'm very conflicted, not about the way I feel about him but about trust or my inability to completely trust." My visit with Dr. Mallory is overdue. I will call her immediately."

The Doctor Is In

D r. Mallory's door is unlocked. She is expecting me. She hears the door open. "Come in Dollene." She stands up and walks over and gives me a hug. A fair amount of time has passed since my last visit. She seems older and weathered.

"Sit down please and get comfortable. It's good to see you. I pulled your file from your last visit. It has been two years since I have seen you. You look great Dollene. I hope you are sleeping well."

"It's been sporadic due to the loss of my parents."

"I am so sorry Dollene, I read both of their obituaries and wondered if you would call me. Tell me what is troubling you."

Dr. Margaret Mallory was not one to waste a patient's time or money. She practices candor and seeks to uproot problems at their base and up through their branches. I came to see her after my wedding day. I was here for four hours and went through every emotion a person can. She is a lecturer and author and someone I deeply respect. She found the unfindable deep in my core and for years the exercises she proposed to aid me made a profound difference in my life. During my visits, we have laughed and cried together. Although we have never publicly acknowledged one another, I call her my friend and she is as close to me as the captain.

"How is the captain?"

I knew she would ask. "He's still around. There is no need to be vague. He visits a lot lately."

"Do you ever see Kerry?"

"No, I did hear he married someone very young."

"How are your sisters?" I imagine Denise overseeing the estate is making you anxious. There is a long pause. "I can wait."

And she could; Wait until I was ready.

"Denise and I have been battling. The old hostilities are resurfacing. One of her boys is getting married. My helping the bride is a blister that is growing. Of course, she is lording her trustee title over Derita and me. The family trust is being tested daily as all three of us differ in the direction the farm should take. Doctor Mallory, I have a boyfriend that I am crazy about."

"I am so happy for you, I hope he is worthy of you Dollene. Tell me about him."

He is a detective with the police department and retired from the FDLE. He is so caring and passionate, and I believe honest. I haven't slept with him yet but I want to more than anything. I know I am no spring chicken Doctor. He has shared his previous marriage story but I haven't told him why I am a spinster.

"Is that the way you feel Dollene, like a spinster?"

"I know you abhor when I portray myself like a loser. Through your counseling, I am confident once again I am not a loser, but those trust issues still exist for me."

"And they probably always will Dollene. If you want to be a part of the world, then you must get out there and get in it."

"The detective and I are in a whirlwind. Saturday night he is coming for dinner and I'm afraid I will not be able to say no one more time."

"Dollene, you have slept before with people you don't even care about, so why worry about this man?"

"He touches my soul. I believe making love will not be exercise for him. He is a good man with a moral compass. He is worthy Doctor."

"Have you shared your heart ache?"

"No, and I don't think he has witnessed my vitriol that springs from nowhere. Of course, if he ever witnesses how much I hate he might not be so interested. He is kind and respectful and treats me like a queen. Maybe I don't ever need to tell him or speak of that day again."

"I know the bar has been set high Dolleen. It's time for you to give yourself another chance."

"He told me that I am his greatest adventure in life Doctor."

"Then take that opportunity to trust your instinct. TRUST Dollene. .....And that life adventure will unfold. I think we're almost out of time Dollene."

"It has been a fast romance, and I realize I'm not a teenager and neither is he. I need to show him I am in love. Thank you, Doctor, for seeing me on such short notice. Today I learned someone I dated a couple of years ago, took his own life. It made me so sad, yet all I keep thinking this afternoon is that life is so short. I have wasted a lot of time on guys I had no intention of marrying because I didn't give them a fair shake. I don't want to lose this opportunity. I believe my heart is whole again."

"Call me anytime Dollene."

I stand erect like I did my wedding day but it is different now. I am not lost. I have found my way. I am glad to have the afternoon with Dr. Mallory. I am resolute that I must give love a chance with Bo.

I am walking to my car and glance at my phone. There are three voice mails from Bo. I ring him back.

He answers. "Dolly, I have been trying to reach you."

"Oh, I have been in a meeting." *not exactly.* Are you on your way home?"

"Yes, mother and I are on our way home. Have you heard from the police department?"

"No, not that I'm aware of. I have been out of pocket visiting a friend. I am headed for the store."

"We'll be getting home so late that I doubt I'll see you tonight but I'll call you in the morning. Are we still having dinner tomorrow?"

"Of course. Roan and Rita are coming also."

"Sounds like fun. I've missed you."

"Me too."

"I feel better now that I've spoken to you. Goodbye."

I check in with Julie. "Anyone call important?"

"The sheriff's department called and left a number for you to return. We have some orders for Derek's service."

"Let's go ahead and do the orders because I only want to work a half day tomorrow. Company coming."

"Yes, I remember. Hot springs tomorrow!"

"Julie!"

"You will share the intimate details want you?"

"We'll see."

I phone the number Julie leaves on the message pad. "Hello, Dollene Diamond calling Detective Mullins."

"Detective Mullins speaking."

"This is Dollene Diamond returning your call."

"Ms. Diamond, can you drop by the Pierson Police Department and speak with me on Saturday."

"I'm afraid I cannot. I have made plans for that day already."

"Oh, I see. Is Monday more convenient for you?"

"Monday afternoon is available but in the morning I am attending a funeral."

"I see. I will pencil you in for Monday at two o' clock. I hope that time is acceptable to you."

"Goodbye."

I write police appointment on my calendar on Monday.

After a couple hours of designing Julie and I are finished for the day. I'm heading to Publix where shopping is a pleasure. I have my list hoping to zip through the aisles. I'm out the door and on my way home. I pull into my garage and notice the lawn guy has mowed today. Good. I put all my bags on the counter and turn on my oven.

Guava marbled cheesecake is my own recipe I invented several years ago. I purée guava paste with canned guavas that I drain reserving the guava juice to make a drizzle for the top of the cheesecake. I know it is not a competition cooking for Bo but I want him to think my cooking is comparable to his mom's. While the cheesecake is baking, I cut the blue hydrangeas I brought home from the store and place them in a vase. I decide on some blue salvia and greenery for my bathroom in a small cobalt vase next to a candle on the window sill above the tub. I make another small vase for the sink countertop. My bedroom is clean and orderly. My side chair and nightstand have all the catalogs and magazines removed. I put a small orchid plant on the stand next to my reading light. Everything is perfect except me.

The oven timer is beeping and I take my cheesecake out. It looks great. I will make my glaze so that when I am ready, I can criss-cross ribbons of guava glaze on the top and add some toasted walnuts. Tomorrow afternoon I will concentrate on the dinner. It is time for beauty rest and it is no surprise, I fall to sleep quickly.

My bridal bouquet is gorgeous beyond words. The fragrance of the yellow garden roses is heavenly. White peonies and blue tweedia surround the roses in my hand-held bouquet. The Baptist church is almost full of friends and family. Dad has planted maiden hair fern pots to put at the ends of every pew. They are so beautiful. We added garden roses in water tubes in the pots and blue ribbons. A canopy of lush draping ferns is at the altar. The kneeling bench is set back a couple of feet under the canopy in the middle. I wanted candles everywhere but mom reminds me candles should be used after three o clock. We would save candlelight for the reception. She had seen to every detail because I am the baby and last to marry. Kerry and I are going to Disneyworld for our honeymoon and stay in the Polynesian hotel already reserved for Mr. and Mrs. Kerry Williams. I wake and my pillow is wet because I am crying. I get up and sit in my side chair. It has been a long time since my mind was here. I sit there long enough to doze off and wake again to my phone ringing.

"Good morning sunshine."

"Oh, hey good morning, "I was fast asleep."

"I'm sorry I thought you were an early riser."

"Not always. I'm getting up and heading down the hall with phone in hand to the coffee pot. What time did you get in?"

"About one a.m. Do you want me to bring you breakfast?"

"Thank you, no. I going to get cracking and go on into the store since I am getting off early to cook for tonight."

"We can go out if you would rather."

"Oh no you don't try to wiggle out of redeeming your coupon."

"I wouldn't dream of it. If you don't need me I will stay and mow the yard for Mother."

"Okay, I'll see you tonight around five thirty or six."

I look around my house and see my table set. I'm glad I have tended to things early. I never know when I can actually leave on Saturdays from the store.

I am ten minutes from the store and now Rita is calling.

"Are we still on for tonight?"

"Yes."

"You sound cranky."

"No, just hurrying to work. I woke up late."

"Were you and the captain together last night?"

"We weren't. I was busy making my dessert and getting chores done. I've got big shoes to fill."

"Why do you think that?"

"Because his mother is a great hostess, cook and housekeeper. You can tell Boyd has been raised in an elegant home. His father was a judge. I bet they entertained all the time."

"I wouldn't worry. Roan and I will try not to embarrass you with our manners. Want us to wear overalls and blacken in some of our teeth?"

"I don't think that will be necessary. Just be your normal podunk selves."

"Want me to bring some wine?"

"Wine, heck, I forgot wine. Yes, please"

"See you at six."

Julie greeted me with a huge grin.

"You look like you swallowed a Cheshire Cat. What's going on?"

I see a rose in a bud vase sitting on my desk. I glance at the rose then back at her.

"There's a card on it." I walk over and open the card.

I'm hoping one will do what six will do. Looking forward to tonight and every night with you. Bo.

I swallow. "Every night?"

"I didn't read the card. He came in person as I was opening the front door. I think he thought you were here and when he found out you weren't, he said he wanted a rose for your desk. He gave me a twenty-dollar bill."

"Well, this is another surprise, and I like it."

We are both smiling. "Okay, ready to work?"

"I beg your pardon, I've been at work."

"Touché."

"Did you want to make Derek's casket piece or do you want me to make it? I assumed you'd go the funeral and everything should be ready by Monday morning."

"Yes. Go ahead and start it."

It's already ten and my mind is elsewhere. Julie is in the cooler getting flowers and I need to answer the phone.

"No one has one called me about the Sunday dinner. Am I supposed to be cooking?"

It's Denise. She does not know the meaning of a pleasant greeting. "You can do it if you like. Perhaps make the entrée and we can fill in with the rest. The weather is getting warmer now. We could go down to the lake and if all the kids are here we could swim and ski."

"Cook what? We live 2 hours away."

"I don't know. You're the one that suggested it. Have Bing and Tom cook chicken. You can figure it out."

"I'll talk it over with my family and get back to you tonight. Later."

"Geez."

Julie is at the design bench working away and glances my way. "I take it that was Denise."

"You take it right, always a delight to talk to her about nothing. It's always a ferris wheel of arguments."

"How does this look?"

"Beautiful. The family should be pleased. What a shame Derek did not realize how much he was loved."

"Hey why don't, you go on home and start getting ready. I'll finish up here."

"You are too good to me Julie. I owe you."

"You do."

It doesn't take me too long to get my purse and leave. I'm in my car and remember my rose on my desk. I go back and rush in to pick up my rose. I'll give it a special place. He'll have to explain the card he wrote.

The kitchen is so clean I hate messing it up. I'll get the French onion soup underway so it can simmer a couple of hours. That will be my small appetizer so no one fills up. Next, I wash the spinach and my strawberries so I can pat them dry. I'll make the crab cake mixture next and the dill sauce and refrigerate it. The rice can cook while we're having soup. There are two packages of green beans that I need to snap the ends off. I'm going to sauté them in my wok with garlic and olive oil while the crab cakes are cooking. I pull out my check list. I don't have bread. No, I'm okay without bread because I'll have a slice of baguette in the soup. I don't want too much food. It's almost four, and I am going to the bathtub and relax.

I'm redoing my hair and makeup. I am satisfied I am at the top of my game. I pray Bo thinks so too. Making such a fuss about dinner tonight has made me forget about all the family drama. That's a good thing.

I decide to have a cocktail and calm my last nerve. The captain is close at hand and gives me the familiar wink.

The candles are lit in my bedroom, and I light the small one in the guest bathroom. The only thing I am missing is one of those big coffee table books. I need the one entitled "How to Commit Suicide."

Finally, someone is here. I answer the door. It is neither of my guest. It's the Jehovah Witness folks. Their timing sucks.

"Hello," *I see Bo driving up.* They begin their spill, I have no choice but to cut them off. "I'm sorry, I have dinner guest coming and one of them is here now. Please come back another time." I knew this was not going to be easy. Immediately, the lead spokesman begins, "Do you know God's Kingdom World awaits you?"

"Absolutely, thank you, I must say goodbye."

Bo is by my side now and I take his hand, and pull him inside the door and shut it. Our eyes meet and it is instant. I am leaning against the door and he kisses me full and hard. When he finishes, I can barely get out the words, "Welcome. I hope you're hungry for dinner too."

He laughs. He smells so good, and I can't stop smiling at him. The door is trying to open, and I hear Rita say, "Is the door stuck?" *Oh, crap.*

I open the door. "Hey."

"Is your door stuck?"

"No, it's okay. Come in."

Rita and Roan are inside. Rita brings in two bottles of wine and puts them on the counter and asks me if I just ran off the Jehovah Witness and I say "yes."

"Are we having a séance? There's a lot of candles lit in here." *Oh hell no, Roan did not just say that.*

"Yes, instead of eating, I thought we could try and contact your mother, you know the one responsible for teaching you manners."

Roan walks to Bo and shakes his hand. "Good to see you again."

"Likewise."

"Drinks? Bo? Would you like beer or wine or scotch or …."

"Bo gets up and says, "I'll help you."

Rita chimes in says "I'll have wine."

Roan lets me know he started with vodka and grapefruit so he'll continue with vodka for one more round."

"That explains a lot."

I look at Bo and tell him on the porch is a bar with vodka, ice and a refrigerator with grapefruit juice in it. "Here's a glass. Do you need another glass for you or are you having beer?"

"I think I'll join Roan. We men have to stick together."

"Really? You may be eating under the table. Knock yourself out."

"I love it when you spirit up," and he winks at me.

I pour Rita and myself a glass of wine. I hand her a glass and clang mine against hers, "Down the hatch."

Rita is laughing.

"This isn't starting like I wanted. Breathe". ......

I cover the soups with cheese and put them in the oven and set the timer.

Roan has joined Bo on the porch. We girls walk out and join them. "Did you find everything you need? I go over to him and he puts his arm around me, and he pecks me on the cheek. "I had no idea you had this back yard. It's beautiful."

"It's getting to be too much for me to take care of."

"And, you have a greenhouse?"

"Only orchids. Regretfully, I have about thirty dead ones. I let them go while all this has been going on with my parents. Hopefully, I'll get back to them soon."

"I'll help you with it one day soon."

Roan blurts out, "That's the best news yet. I used to be her "rent a husband."

I look at Roan in complete disbelief. "Are you high or in a drunken stupor? I'm ready to break your plate."

Everyone is laughing except me. The timer goes off. I'm in the kitchen pulling out the soups. I put each one on a paper doily on a saucer and add a spoon. I stick my head out on the porch. "Let's eat."

We're all at the table and the soup is hot. Everyone is sipping their cocktails as we attempt to start on the soup.

"This is really good Dolly." Roan is getting a big scoop of cheese.

"Good Boy, finally." I pour Rita and I another glass of wine and smile at Bo. *He is so handsome.*

Rita asks if this is my own recipe.

"Yes, I use a little of turbinado sugar for caramelizing the onions."

Bo looks inquisitive.

"It's the same," I say. He knows what I'm referring to.

"What kind of cheese? Rita is needing to know the recipe right now, I guess.

"Tonight, I used Gruyere."

Bo squeezes my thigh with his hand... everyone is almost finished and I retrieve the salad dressing out of the fridge and toss my beautiful salad. It is spinach and water chestnuts, purple onions, sliced strawberries, crumbled bacon and toasted walnuts. I add the raspberry vinaigrette and toss. I put the bowl on the table, and pick up the soup bowls. Rita serves and says this looks "yummy."

I glance at Bo's glass and it is empty. "Another drink, or wine or beer?

"I think I'll join you in a glass of wine."

"Roan?" He immediately points to his wine glass. "I'm way ahead of you."

I step back in the kitchen and put the crab cakes in the oven on a lower degree, and take the dill sauce from refrigerator for it to come to room temperature. The rice is still on warm, and it's okay.

Roan asked Bo if he plays golf and he answers, "Occasionally."

"Are you any good?" Roan keeps going.

Bo responds, "pretty good." Roan laughs and says, "Well, we won't do that then."

I almost choke swallowing my wine.

Roan asks Bo about an accident on Old Albee Road today. Bo said he heard it on the police radio, but he had just returned home from Atlanta last night and didn't work today. He didn't know the details.

"I see a card on the rose, a thank you Dolly?" Rita is nosey beyond belief.

"From one of my ardent admirers." I look at Bo.

Roan says, "you're starting off way too strong Bo, you're 'gonna spoil her, and you're making me look bad."

Everybody laughs, "I think that started with the séance comment." I look over at Bo, "It never ends."

I pick up the salad plates and take them to the kitchen sink. I turn to the oven and remove the crab cakes. I place two on each plate, a scoop of buttery herbed rice and drizzle the dill sauce on the cakes. I add a lemon wedge on the side. Everyone is served now.

"Does anyone want any iced tea?" They are too busy starting to eat.

I'm happy with the way everything tastes. I am still drinking wine but I need to start drinking some of my water. Rita wants to know if I purchased the crab meat from Publix. She said the last time she bought crab it had a lot of shell in it. I tell her you should buy lump meat and you won't have that problem.

Bo tells me the crab cakes are incredible and he's glad his coupon is still in effect. I ask if he's saving room for dessert.

"Of course."

"What's for dessert?" Everyone knows Roan has a sweet tooth... uh.. fang.

"Peanut butter and Jelly," and I chuckle.

Rita sighs, "everything is scrumptious Dolly but then it always is at your house. Surely, you have told Bo that our family is full of mischief and endless joking."

"I'm sure he has come to that conclusion all by himself."

We are all finishing our dinner and it dawns on me that I have forgotten the green beans. I guess my face shows some expression. I look at Rita and I say, "Well, I guess I forgot to sauté the beans."

Rita adds, "We didn't really need them Dolly, no worries."

I clear the plates while my guests are chit chatting with each other. It doesn't take but a few minutes to load my dishwasher and pick up my kitchen.

I grab some dessert plates from my cupboard and get my cheesecake out of the fridge. I have the guava glaze in a plastic tipped applicator bottle and place it in the microwave for fifteen seconds. I decorate each piece of cheesecake by criss crossing the glaze on top. I'm proud of my guava marbled cheesecake recipe that required many attempts to perfect the recipe. I hope Bo thinks so too.

"Something sweet for someone sweeter," and I set a dessert and clean fork at Bo's place.

"Thank you."

I get two more ready for Rita and Roan, and cut myself a small slice. Oh, everyone is waiting on me. We all dig in. Rita is the first to give me kudos out loud and when I look at Bo, he smiles and gives me two thumbs up. I am a super star. *Maybe.*

I'm trying to look fresh but the truth is I'm pooped. It's nine thirty and I start clearing the table. To my surprise, Bo and Roan both bring dishes into the kitchen. Bo leans in to me at the sink, puts his hands on my shoulders and says the dinner was amazing.

"You don't have to flatter me, I wasn't going to ask for help with the dishes." Suddenly I am refreshed.

Roan and Bo retire to the living room and Rita and I finish the kitchen. I go sit by Bo on the couch. Rita tells Roan they better be heading home and that she is ready to go. Roan gets up "Great dinner tonight Dolly."

Both Bo and I accompany them to the door and say goodnight. The door closes.

"How's my cook holding up?"

I smile. "I survived."

"Are you tired Bo, from driving back and mowing the the yard today?"

"No, I was anxious to get back to you."

"You're here now and that makes both of us happy."

He pulls me in close and just holds me tight. "I am in love and I hope you are too."

"I am and it's the best feeling ever."

"You surprise me all the time. You are fearless and you've got grit. I think you're clever and funny, bold and beautiful and I want to spend my life with you."

"You've not seen me first thing in the morning yet."

"I don't think that will change my mind."

"I hope not, but some days, I don't know why, but two heads appear."

"Good, I can kiss both of them." He kisses the corners of my mouth and then kisses me deeply. I am ready to lose myself in this guy that I respect and admire. I take his hand and lead him to my bedroom and he sits on the edge of my bed.

"Give me a second, and I'll be right back." I close the bathroom door behind me, use the bathroom and slip on an aqua lace negligee. I am refreshed and walk out. I look at Bo. "Tonight, my answer is yes."

"Come here. I have so much love in my heart for you." It is everything I want to hear. He leads me in the dance and we spend the night giggling, talking, laughing and loving. We share stories of our lives and our desires for the life ahead that we want. He is closing that hole in my heart and I am happy, beyond what I thought was ever possible. We sleep, we wake and we plan. It's morning now and Bo gets up and goes in the bathroom. I comb my hair and get up to make coffee. He has his pants on and no shirt when he comes in the kitchen. He has a slight beard and rubs it against me up and down my neck. "I'm checking for two heads."

"Very funny."

"Are you making me breakfast like a good wench? Or shall I take my lady out for breakfast?"

"You're going to need your energy for round two."

He reaches in his pants and pulls out a small box. He holds up my face and looks into the depths of my eyes.

"Someone as special as you should not have to wait. I am committed to you today and all the rest of our tomorrows. I want to marry you." He opens the box.

It is the most extraordinarily unique ring and breathtakingly beautiful. I am shocked and speechless.

"This is you Dolly, unique and sparkling, bold with depth. I love you D. I don't want to waste what time we have on rules and other opinions why we should wait." He slips the ring on my finger. The stone is set horizontally and it is enormous.

"This is a deep blue step cut diamond considered rare like I know you to be. I went to Atlanta to my mother's jeweler to find you something very special. I hope you love it but if you don't, we'll go shopping together."

"I love, love, love it and I love you. Yes. My answer is Yes. After all those honeyed phrases, you have rendered me powerless. Lordy, how big is this stone?"

"It is 2.76 carats of deep blue diamond and almost three carats of baguette diamonds surrounding the blue diamond. It is you Dolly."

"You had that ring all last night and I didn't have a clue. Had you already decided before you went to Atlanta? Tell me what your Mother said."

"She is very happy for me, for us. I know there are those who think we should wait until we know each other better. The truth is you have been here all your life. I can't think of a surprise that would dissuade me from marrying you."

"You have made me the happiest girl ever. I adore you. This is crazy good. You are certifiable crazy."

"This ring must have cost a fortune."

"It did, but I have a fortune to spend on the woman that has captivated my heart. Tell me when we can get married Dolly. Tell me what kind of ceremony you want."

I don't know what to say. I look at my ring and cannot believe that this big blue diamond is mine. "You realize my Dad's name was Blu." My eyes are flooded with tears.

"I hope those are tears of joy. Yes, I realized. My mother reminded me about your father. She said I had exquisite taste. That comment coming from Mother sealed my purchase. When D, when will you be my wife? Next Sunday suits me."

"You are absolutely crazy. Do you want any friends there or just family? I can't think. Let's go get a shower so I know I am not dreaming."

We walk toward the shower kissing along the way but our passion gets the best of us in the bedroom and we fall into the bed. "I hope it will always be like this." Bo says. "Spontaneous."

I answer "Crazy."

He adds "Passionate."

I answer "Crazy."

He whispers "Scorching."

I utter "Crazy in love." He is soft and tender. He is strong and driving, and he is mine."

"D, let's go get that shower." And we head to the shower again.

My phone is ringing just as I am stepping in. Bo says he'll start without me. It's Rita.

"Hey." *I know my voice is elevated and giddy.*

"Is Bo still there? Roan wants to know if you had hot sheets last night?"

"Yes, and Yes."

"Oh my. We're cooking hamburgers about one. You guys want to come? I thought you could bring your cheesecake."

"I'll ask him and call you back."

I walk to the shower and he is finishing. He is grabbing a towel and leans over and grabs me just as I am getting wet. "No kiss for your fiancé?"

I respond, "Today they will be frequent and free."

I hurry and lather up, shampoo and condition my hair. I am out in a shower wrap and he appears with a cup of coffee for me.

"Before two heads appear," he smiles and hands me coffee.

"Do you need a toothbrush, paste?"

"Thanks, no, I got my bag out of the Tahoe. Were you able to catch the phone?"

"Yes, it was Rita." *I am blowing my hair dry.* "She invited us for hamburgers at one."

"Did you tell her?"

"No, I want us to tell them together. Shouldn't we stop by your Mothers, maybe take her a piece of the cheesecake? I want her to try it."

"This is why I love you, because you are thoughtful. Yes, that will make her happy that we include her. I'm going to dress now."

"Okay, I need to put my makeup on and get dressed too." I am done with my hair and putting my face on. Bo has already dressed in tan shorts and a green polo. I guess I will wear shorts too. I find a green short set and put some lotion on my legs.

"Your eyes look green in that outfit."

"Yes, sometimes when I wear green or purple or lavender, they will look green. And sometimes …I grow two heads."

"As long as both of them have the same blue eyes, I'm good."

I walk over to the bed and begin to make the bed up. He pushes me down on it, half kissing me half playing around. "Maybe we're not done here just yet."

"Sounds good, I will never turn you down Bo."

"Never?"

"Only when you forget my anniversary or my birthday."

He pulls me up and smacks a kiss on me. "Ready?"

"Yes. Let me pick up the coffee clutter."

"Where are we headed?"

"To Mothers, then Rita's if that what you want."

"Okay, give me a second to cut your mom a piece of cheesecake." I grab the rest covered in tin foil and head outdoors. I unlock my car and retrieve my purse and sunglasses. We're on our way.

"D, I need to travel to Deland tonight for an early meeting in the morning, but I'll be back and meet you back at the police department for your interview by two o'clock.

"I had almost forgotten. You already knew about my appointment? I don't recall telling you."

"Detective Mullins told me. He also told me that Derek Shaffer left a suicide note and your name is mentioned in it. There is probably nothing more to it."

"Probably?"

We are here and I am dumbfounded. Bo comes around to my side and opens the door. He catches me in his arms. "Don't worry, I'll be there with you. I won't be allowed to say anything, but I'll be there." He puts his mouth on mine, "are your kisses still free today?"

"Absolutely." His kiss is wet and taste like more. I turn and get the plate with Janet's cheesecake on it. We are holding hands up the walkway, and he unlocks the door and ushers me in. He calls out to his Mother.

Something smells good. She appears. "Hi son, have you and Dolly had lunch?" I walk up to her and hand her the plate. "from last night's dinner, guava marbled cheesecake, my own recipe."

"Gracious, thank you honey. Now let me see that engagement ring on your finger."

"You knew he'd give it to me last night?"

Bo smiles. "I was nervous."

"It's good to know I have that effect on you." I pick up my right hand and show her and say "I'm thrilled beyond belief. Thank you for taking him to your jeweler."

"You'll find he has ideas and creative thoughts on his own."

"I have been warned. Thanks."

"Dolly, I'm delighted to have you in our family. Bo is the happiest I have seen him in a very long time."

I look at him and he picks up my hand and he rubs his thumb over my ring. "I whisper "me too," and he kisses my hand.

"Mother, thanks for the invitation, but we're going to her sisters for lunch."

"Your welcome son, you kids go on now, don't be late."

I go up and hug her. "I hope you enjoy the cheesecake."

Bo hugs his mother goodbye also and we walk out to the Tahoe. He opens the door for me again and I get in.

"Buckle up please."

I am preoccupied and do not buckle up. "So, if I have this right, everyone knew but me you were going to pop the question last night. But you waited until you popped my cherry to ask me?"

"What did you say?"

"I didn't stutter, you heard me. I personally believe virginity is retroactive after so long. Here's the thing, you waited till you defrocked me before I got the ring?"

He pulls over on the side of the road. He is laughing, and pulls me hard over to him, pushes my hair away from my face. "Listen, that defrocking was awesome, and damn near wore me down. I have kept my eye on the big prize, YOU. If we never have sex again, I will love you every day of my life because you have captivated me body and soul." *He is way serious now.*

"I was just wondering if I should have kept my vaginal vault still sealed." We are both laughing hysterically on the side of the road.

"The vaginal vault, and he can't compose himself enough to quit laughing, as you refer to it, would have been worth an extra three carats of diamonds. I love you so much you crazy girl."

"Sufficient answer." And I kiss his neck up and down and land a short kiss on his ear."

"Now buckle up. I need directions," and he is still snickering.

Rita and Roan live in a gated community. It is 12:45 p.m. I guess Rene and Robert are here because I recognize their vehicle. I didn't know they were invited. I'm so happy, and I cannot wait until one of them notices my ring. I get the cheesecake out and turn to Bo. "Still captivated?"

"More than ever."

We go through the pool gate because I am sure everything is happening on the back porch. I hear Rita saying, "There they are, hey, you were supposed to call me back."

"Sorry, we were tied up."

Roan says, "I hope that was a figurative term."

"I heard that."

Rene looks over at us. "Mom has just shared with me that your Aunt Dolly has a beau. And here you are, the two of you."

Rene and I hug each other. "Rene, this is Boyd Price."

"Bo, this is my niece Rene, and Robert is her husband." Robert shakes Bo's hand. "They are both educators Bo, so be forewarned. Please don't mention title one, grants, school board, testing, or leave a child behind, any of that stuff, just saying...

Bo answers, "What?"

Rene jumps in, "She is joking with us. What do you do for a living Bo?"

I blurt out, "He just got the manager position at Pizza Hut, here in Pierson."

"Congratulations, now what do you really do, because I know Aunt Dolly would never date a Pizza Hut manager. She has dated some doozies, but she has some standards, so...?

"I'm a detective," and he gets out his wallet and shows his badge."

"Let me see that, I haven't even seen that."

"Well, I wouldn't have believed him but now I do," Rene is still curious.

Rita announces, "We're ready to eat."

I look at Bo. "I bet you are hungry."

"Admittedly, the vault was more important."

I hug his chest, and he kisses my forehead. *I am pretty darn sure I have met my match.*

We fix our plates and I point to where we will be sitting.

"Did you guys go to church?"

"Yes, we barely made it on time."

"Aunt Dolly, what are we having for the next Sunday Dinner?"

"I don't know. At one time, I was thinking about a brunch. But I'm game for anything."

I look at Bo.

"What are you guys talking about?"

"Our Sunday Dinners. It is our parent's plan to keep our family together. Once a month we must have a family dinner. Mandatory attendance is required to receive any drawing out of our inheritance."

Finally, my hamburger has all the fixings on it and I am ready to sit down. "Bo, I'll get you some iced tea. Sweet or Unsweet?"

"Sweet please."

I realize I know very little about Bo's food likes or dislikes. I will try to communicate more and find out. Bo and I sit down to eat. Roan leads us in a short prayer of thanks. I cut my hamburger in half so I don't wear it home. It is really tasty and tell Roan I appreciate him cooking me a well-done burger. Bo shakes his head in disbelief. He tells me we're going to have to talk about eating my meat well done. *I don't think so.*

Roan seizes the opportunity to tell him that the family has been working on that for years to no avail. "Good Luck on that one," and he is talking to Bo directly. I continue to enjoy my hamburger and then Rene screams out, "Aunt Dolly, oh my God, that ring!"

All the table is looking at me, and immediately they look at my hand. Everyone stops chewing their food. I look at Bo and swallow my last mouthful. He puts his arm around me. In a loud voice, Rene exclaims, "That looks real! It can't be, is it? NO. Yes... spill your guts Aunt Dolly."

"This handsome man next to me with impeccable taste cannot live without me. I realize ya'll don't understand this rationale but we are engaged officially."

Rita said, "you had better be telling the truth."

Roan stands up and shakes Bo's hand. "You're supposed to run these things by your brother n law first, especially a rock like that. Rita, don't look, it's just a promise ring, I think."

"Good Lord, how much do detectives make a year?" Rene's voice is still pitching. "I am just kidding...not.."

Bo is at a loss for words.

"It's a good thing Bo is not asking to marry any of you. I think the words you should be saying to us is "we are so happy for you and Congratulations."

Rene says "yeh, yeh, yeh, all that, may I see that ring closer?"

I put my hand up to her face and I am so proud. I glance at Bo and I think he is a bit overwhelmed, but still smiling.

Rita asks "When? We were just there last night. You already had the ring?" Rita is analyzing. "When is the wedding?"

I take my hand back and look to him for the answer.

"Very soon." Bo answers matter of factly.

Rene says she feels faint and she needs vapors.

Robert shyly speaks up, "Thank God he is not a Hispanic or Cuban or some other nationality that needs government clearance and papers showing ethnicity." Everyone laughs but the joke is lost on poor Bo. I whisper to Bo that Robert is Cuban. Bo nods.

"Still captivated my love?"

"I'm here for the duration."

Rita is breathless. "Okay, it is my turn to gaze. Is that a blue diamond or a blue topaz? I am not believing that cut of diamond. It is unusual. Roan, go get our jewelers loop."

"Okay ya'll, don't make my man sorry he asked me. Are ya'll through joking?"

Bo is laughing. "I'm okay with it," and puts his arm around me again.

"Seriously," and Rita is, "When is very soon?"

"Maybe Friday or Saturday or Sunday."

"In other words, you don't know."

Bo answers, "I am ready tomorrow, or whenever. Whatever kind of wedding or ceremony D wants, I will be ready." He leans over and kisses my cheek.

Rene is in complete disbelief, "Ya'll look so happy and so much in love. Robert, did we ever look that way?"

"I don't think so. Uh I mean, yes, dear."

Rene ask me, "Do you know what kind of ceremony you want or dress?"

"It won't take me long, you know I am in the business."

"Are you going to live in your house?"

I look at Bo. He steps up and addresses them all. "I have some options I want to talk to D about. Whatever she wants I will make it happen. I want her to be happy. That's all that matters to me."

Rene turns to Robert, "Are you listening? Dad, did you hear him?"

"No, I did not. Right now, I am feeling like milquetoast."

Everybody is laughing so much.

"Enough, I can't take it anymore," I reply.

"Bo, would like another burger or something to drink? I think Roan has some scotch in the bar if you need a stronger drink to get through this family's antics."

"Yes, I do. I think everybody could use a drink."

It seems all of the news has thwarted everyone's appetite. I ask if anybody cares for cheesecake. Everyone shakes their head yes. I get up to start serving.

"Best cheesecake ever Aunt Dolly." Rene chirps.

"Ditto," Robert adds.

"Well, I'll say one thing. Bo, you are getting one of the best cooks around."

"Awe shucks, Roan, I answer back, it's going to be peanut butter and jelly at least three times a week."

Bo knows what I am talking about, and I think back to my defrocking comment and remember he said I damn near wore him down. *I am so much in love. I hope my forehead does not look like a neon sign that goes on and off* **love, love, love.** *I'm amused.*

"D, we better be leaving. Remember I said I needed to leave for Deland tonight."

"Okay, sure. I'm sorry I forgot. I'm ready."

"We need to shove off. Thank you for lunch."

"Good grub! Love you guys."

We're all hugging each other. I think I see a few tears in Rene's eyes. She is such a softie.

We're headed to my house. Bo says he'll drop me by my house and then stop by his Mothers, and pick up a change of clothes and his uniform, etc. "I'll stop back by to say goodbye before I leave town. Okay with you D?"

"Yes. It's all good."

"Your family is really comical."

"That's a polite way to say dysfunctional I think."

"My sister and I never have these kinds of exchanges. I was entertained and I am still captivated. I move over to him over the bucket seat part and kiss his neck and nuzzle him. I love his scent and he kisses the top of my head. We drive up and he tells me, "I'm going to miss you the first night of our engagement."

"I know. I am thinking that too." I make a sad face.

I unlock the door, and he is at my door opening it for me. He tells me he'll see me within an hour. He gently kisses me and turns to leave. I watch him drive off and say to myself, I'll just do whatever I usually do on a Sunday before I became engaged. Clean. I vacuum my bedroom and clean my bathroom. It smells like pine sol. I light a candle in my living room and wipe off my kitchen counter. I check my hair and makeup. I want to look good when I say goodbye because I want to leave a good last impression. I dab some perfume on me. I hear him drive up and he knocks on my door. I'm almost at the door when he opens it.

"Are you ready to go? Do you want me to fix you a sandwich or something to eat before you go?"

"I'm only hungry for you. I don't think you know how pretty you are. I want to taste you again before I leave you for the night." His arms go around me and his hands are on my back and he pulls me in tight. He starts out slow and deliberate. I feel he wants more than a kiss.

"You alright?" I manage to get the words out.

"Very happy, just don't want to leave."

"You have two options. Miss me tonight and we'll make up for lost time when you return, or I will take whatever time you give me now." He smiles that great smile. "I don't want to short change you. I'll take door number one."

"Okay, and I kiss him deeply. "We'll make tomorrow night special."

He reaches in his wallet and pulls out his credit card and hands it to me. "I'd like you to start on the wedding. Buy your dress or whatever you want and buy whatever I need. I would like to have my Mother to be present. I know you'll make our wedding beautiful. I'll see you at two o'clock at the police department. He picks up my face between his hands. "I love you Dolly, you are my everything." Quick kisses, and he says bye. He looks back at the door, "Till tomorrow."

I'm on the verge of crying. I don't know how I feel about being someone's everything. I'm upset. I'll talk to the captain. I fix my drink and go out to my porch and review all that has happened. I call Rita.

"Hey, we still can't believe it." I am upset and she senses it.

"Rene and I will be right over."

Save The Date

$\mathcal{I}$'m on my second drink when they bust through the door.

"What's happened?"

Rene looks at me. "Well, the ring is still on your finger."

They sit down. "Dolly, it's time to talk."

"Bo is gone to Deland on business. He'll be back tomorrow and he said he would be back in time for my police interview."

"Okay, catch me up."

I get it all out, and include the everything part and the credit card.

"Dolly are you ready to commit to him?"

"Yes, I am sure of that."

"I ask you because ....and I never wanted to mention to you ever... but you were not ready many years ago when you walked out there in your wedding dress and said there would not be a wedding."

"There were different causes that factored into that."

"Have you told Bo about that?"

"No, it is doubtful that I ever will."

"Dolly, do you need to see Dr. Mallory?"

"I saw her three days ago."

"Are things going too fast for you?"

"No."

"Why are you drinking?"

"Because it is what I do, depend on my captain."

"You have a new captain Aunt Dolly. His name is Bo. Trust him because I think he has enough strength for both of you. He obviously loves you very much. Heck, take that credit card and we will make you a bride in a few days. Is that what you want?"

"Yes, I want to marry soon too. I want us to be together. "I want God and everyone to bless this union. I want something small with family, that is, if you guys want to come. What about on Sunday down at the lake since the entire family will be there anyway?"

Rita and Rene look at me and at each other. "Let's do it. Let's tell everyone that they must wear white or khaki because we're having a complete family picture being made."

"That sounds fantastic."

"We need a dress, decorations, food. That idea about a brunch is great." Champagne can be flowing. Mom, you make a list and I will make a list. We'll combine our lists tomorrow."

"Do you feel better?"

"Some. We have one week. I cannot meet tomorrow night. I promised Bo a special night since he had to leave on the first day of our engagement. He is very romantic and I don't ever want to diminish that trait of his. We have both been alone for so long."

"I understand."

"Do you?"

"Dolly, has Bo ever been married?

"Yes, a long time ago. It was a sad tale I do not intend on repeating."

Rita gets up and puts the captain up in the cabinet. "Dolly, every day I want you to do small things that depend on Bo and demonstrate trust. Talk to him about that. Renée and I are going to go ahead and leave."

"I think you're feeling a lot better now. Try and have a good night's rest and know we are all very happy for you and Bo." They leave shortly and I take myself and my phone into the bathroom and hope that Bo calls me soon and he does. I answer the phone and he suspects I am a little upset.

"What's wrong. What's happened?"

"I just fell apart when you left."

"Why? I can't believe that. You're the strongest woman I've ever met in my life."

"Bo, I'm strong in some regard. I have this hard shell on the outside but I crumble when it comes to trust. We'll talk tomorrow when you get home. I have some trust issues."

"Not with me I hope." Please tell me we have a wedding date Dolly."

"How does Sunday sound to you?"

"That's my girl, what do I need to do?"

"What do you think about having it down at Glenn Lake where my parents have the fernery? There's a lot of natural decoration down there and I can decorate at the bank or on the dock and I thought we would just keep it a surprise and just invite a few friends and family. Renée has this great idea to ask everybody to wear either white or khaki under the pretense that we are having a family picture made."

"Sounds perfect."

"I'll get together on Tuesday and get our lists synchronized and everyone that's involved with the planning can take care of a small part. It should come together."

"I can ask my mother to coordinate the food and beverages. She can do all of that if you want. She would not want to overstep her bounds. I will preempt mother but I know she would want you to call her yourself before she takes over coordinating food."

"Yes, please call her and I will follow up tomorrow afternoon with her."

"Dolly, please get some sleep tonight. I love you and I will see you at two."

"Love you more."

Not A Good Fit

This morning is sad as I ready myself for Derek's funeral. I am dressed in a black suit with a white lace tank. I am uncomfortable about seeing Derek's family because my name is mentioned in his suicide note. Perhaps my appointment with the police department will enlighten me as to why Derek called me.

It is a small hometown crowd at the church. I see several buff men no doubt friends of his and patrons of the Fitness Gym in attendance. I imagine they have been interviewed already by Detective Mullins. I will be next. The speaker is another fitness instructor with an ill-fitting suit that delivers the eulogy. He tells us Derek was committed to a daily regiment to obtain a fit body. His arms are so tight in his sleeves that I think he must be uncomfortable standing there at the pulpit.

I am sitting at the back of the church and leave quickly before the last hymn is finished.

Julie asks me how the funeral went.

"Like most funerals, Julie." His fitness friends attended and they looked possessed by exercise. The speaker whom I surmised was another fellow fitness trainer talked about Derek's dedication to the gym and programs they offered. I felt at times, he was auditioning for a commercial."

"It's almost time for your appointment."

"I'm leaving now. But I haven't had a second to tell you about this." I hold up my hand.

"Are you kidding me? Good God, that is beautiful!"

"When?"

"Sunday and Sunday."

"Are you crazy? One week?"

"Yes, I'm starting to believe I am."

I walk into the police department still dressed in my funeral attire and tell the receptionist my name. I'm looking around for Bo. Maybe he is already in the office.

"Please have a seat over there, and points to a cluster of chairs lined up. She said someone will be out to get me in a few minutes. Twenty minutes go by and I am beginning to fidget. A door opens to a conference room and Detective Mullins steps out to greet me. *No show Bo is not in here.*

He extends his hand, "I am Steve Mullins. I'm happy to meet you. Please be comfortable." *Right.*

"I'd like to turn on my recorder for the record. Is that Okay?"

"Yes, if that is protocol."

"He speaks into the recorder, Case File DS75669, interview with Amelia Dollene Diamond. *Bo could show give him a few pointers about making an interview more comfortable. Where is he?*

"Ms. Diamond, we are questioning you today as part of an investigation regarding the suicide death of Derek F. Shafer. In checking telephone records, your cell number was one of many telephone calls made in the last week prior to his death. When was the last time you spoke with Derek?"

The door opens and it is Bo in his uniform. He looks tired. He walks over to me and kisses my forehead, "Hello," and Steve stands up and shakes his hand. "Good to see you again." *Really, this is not old home week for me."*

Bo sits down next to the table.

"My question is...."

"It was some time ago, probably a year and half ago."

"What was the nature of your relationship?"

"We were friends from high school, and the last time I saw him is when we were dating."

"How did it come about that you were dating?"

"I recall I ran into him at a store, and we were talking about school days. He asked me for my number."

"When he called you the other day, did you recognize his number?"

"Not at first, but it did come to me later."

"Did you return his call?"

I pause a few seconds. I would think you would already know the answer to that question but I will tell you anyway, NO."

"Why is that?"

"He did not leave a voice message, therefore I didn't. I have lots of calls daily that I do not return from salesmen, wholesalers, family members. And I am not in the habit of phoning men."

"You said you had, I believe three dates."

"Two or three,"

"Did he pick you up for these dates?"

"Yes."

"At your apartment or home?"

"My home."

"Why did your relationship end?"

"I would not call it a relationship, we were friends. I was not interested in continuing to date him. I told him I thought we were not compatible in our lifestyles."

"Explain further please."

"Derek was a fitness fanatic. I did not approve of his constant dietary supplements he was taking, his food restrictions and general obsessiveness about exercise and training. I felt like he was taking abundant steroids, and testosterone injections. His mood swings made me uncomfortable."

"Was your relationship sexual or ever become violent?"

"Friendship Detective, not relationship. It was not friends with benefits." I look over at Bo. He is pensive.

"Did you feel threatened by his mood swings?"

"No, not particularly, I did comment to him I thought he was experiencing some. I cautioned him about all the steroid use and told him he was not making healthy choices despite the fact he considered himself to be very healthy. I even recommended a clinical psychologist to him that I know and encouraged him to seek help because I thought he might have some issues regarding women."

"Issues?"

"I thought maybe he had the wrong idea about what women want, uh, characteristics women seek in a relationship…that all women do not want a Mr. America or Mr. Olympic."

"Ms. Diamond, Derek Shafer mentioned you in his note, that he should have listened to your advice you gave him. We did not have a full understanding of what that advice was. I would think you could take comfort in the fact he regretted not heeding it."

"May I see the note?"

"No ma'am, that is personal information that was given to the family."

"I understand."

"This concludes my questions. Thank you for your time." He turns off his recorder and stands up. "I'd like to offer my congratulations on your engagement to Boyd."

"Thank You."

Bo is already up and takes my hand. "I'll walk you to your store. I'll be right back Steve."

Bo and I walk out of the department and on to the sidewalk leading to my store. "I've never seen you in heels before and a suit. You look pretty."

"There is a first time for everything."

"Are you upset?"

"Kind of. It's been a crap day. It will get better I'm sure."

"I have to be in my office till six o'clock and we can go out to dinner, okay?"

"Sure."

"I'll be at your house at six fifteen or so, and I'll change there."

"Sure."

He kisses me on the cheek. "Bye." He exits and I walk to the back of the store.

"It's me Julie."

"How did it go?"

"Unnecessary questions I thought. Personal, none of your business kind."

"Did Bo say anything during the questioning?"

"No, he didn't."

"Did you expect him to?"

"I didn't know what to expect."

"You're upset. Dolly, it can all be done. Give me a list. Don't worry anymore about the wedding."

"Me worry? the Runaway Bride?"

"Tell me what I need to do for Sunday."

"I need an arch. We can use pots of ferns everywhere. Call Juan and ask him how many large ferns they have planted that we can stagger up the bank next to the have lots of ferns as a backdrop. I think the ceremony should be on the bank under the shade with the lake in the background. I need a bridal bouquet and boutonnière. I need centerpieces. Plan something beautiful and elegant. I need to go to the computer and go online to find a dress."

I type in buy crème or coffee lace dress for wedding. The Gods are in my favor. I find one that I love.

My Favorite Place

*I*t is six o'clock and I need to hurry home. I dash out the door and tell Julie, "see you tomorrow. I am barely inside when Bo arrives. He knocks then comes in. I will give him a key tonight." I am down to my slip and hose and heels when he comes into the bedroom.

"Nice look."

He starts taking off his uniform shirt, and sits on the edge of the bed, and takes off his shoes. I walk over and lean in.

"Are you sure you want to go out?"

"I was pretty sure," and he's looking at my cleavage. "Not sure at all now."

"Want to join me in a bubble bath?

"Only if you let me wash your front."

"Want a glass of wine or cocktail?"

"I'll get the drinks and you get the bath ready."

The lights are off and I have lit three candles that smell like gardenias. The water is foaming and I put two towels, two face cloths and two shower wraps out on the stand. I put my hair up in a clip and get in. This is what I need. I press the remote to my Bose and my latest cd of Barbra Streisand's duets. Bo comes in with a bottle of wine, a wine glass and he has a cocktail.

"Watch yourself getting in, the water is a little silky. He hands me my glass and I put the bottle on the window sill. He is in. "Whoa." He reaches up and pours my glass full. "A toast to us."

"Thank You sweetie, doesn't this feel good?"

"I'm not usually a bath person but I like what I see." He is sliding to me and with him comes a mountain of bubbles into my face."

"Careful,"

He pulls me close and we are locked.

"You taste like wine."

"You taste like rum. And how was your day Detective? catch any criminals, run over any old ladies, shake down any hard-working florist?"

"Just one, you are a pro, articulate and beautiful. You blew the lead Detective off his game. You were composed, fearless, a lioness, and I am so proud of you."

"Bo, my friend has died."

He sighs, and kisses me so tender. "I know, I am sorry."

I pour myself some more wine. "Want some?"

"In a little while."

We just look at each other and stare. He picks up a facecloth and lathers it up, "turn around, I'll rub your back. Relax Dolly, I know you are troubled, like that day the man bought that rose for his sick wife." He slides me into him and nuzzles my neck. "You smell like a gardenia."

"It's the bubble bath, my favorite scent." I'd have them all over the place if they were not so expensive."

"I want you to have some in your bouquet when we marry. I'll buy them for you. I'll call Julie tomorrow and order them."

I turn around and gaze in his eyes." I don't think there is anything you wouldn't do for me. Have you had any blood work done lately? Did you hit your head on something, been thoroughly checked out?"

He pulls me again to him and holds me so that I can't move. "What has someone done to you that you can't believe it is possible that any man wouldn't treat you like a queen if you gave them half a chance. I count my lucky stars every day that you gave me that chance."

"It is the uniform, the front please. Keep your promise."

I don't know, I think you are going to be a twenty-four hour a day job, a lot to handle."

"Frustrated?"

"Captivated. In this candlelight, you are so beautiful Dolly." He takes the clip out of my hair and puts his hand up my neck and hair. "Do you know how much I love you?"

"No. Yes. I hear you and I know you have touched my scarred heart, but I'm not perfect. A backlash of bitterness rears its ugly head within me occasionally, and you won't like this lioness as much."

"I won't like it, but I will still love you. I promise you nothing will shake my loyalty and I hope nothing diminishes your spirit and zeal for our life together. Let's talk about trust. That five-letter word that is building a fence between us."

My head is down, looking at the faded bubbles. I turn the water back on to warm up the water.

"Talk to me. You have an issue and I want us to work on it."

"That's what Rene and Rita advised me to do. Give you a bit of trust every day and demonstrate I believe in us. They said you were strong, that I needed to lean on you." I am emotional now and look up with my eyes so glassy and on the verge. "I believed in love a long time ago. Believe is probably the wrong word to use. I trusted too much then and it was a disaster. I placed such faith in two people I loved that I was blinded by a big wedding, a big celebration, lofty ideas of happy days ahead. I reach for the wine, "here you need some of this and me too." I finish pouring out the remainder of the bottle.

Bo puts my head against his chest. "Hear my heart pounding D? I cannot stand to see you this way. I'm asking you to put some faith in us and what we have started, the greatest love story I have ever experienced. It's you and me and God driving the bus." *He said bus. I heard him say bus. God must be steering.*

"Sitting in this tub I think I have lost my manhood in here. D, are you going to sleep in here?"

"No, I'm actually hungry."

He stands up in all his glory and pulls me up beside him. "Since I am the new manager of Pizza Hut, I'll order us a pizza, and we can sit in bed and eat pizza and drink beer. Yes, in your bed. Sometimes you just must expand your horizon and try something new. A lady I met a month of Sunday's ago told me that one day. She is absolutely correct."

I had my 'donut disturb' sleep set on when the pizza arrived. Bo took care of everything and I was laying up when he brought the ice bucket in of beer to the bedroom, a pizza box, and a roll of paper towels. So much for the romantic first night of our engagement. He laughs when he sees them. "After we eat, those are coming off and you will be disturbed. It's a promise."

We chow down and drink beer and laugh and giggle. Finally, I click on a western movie with Indians in it. He turns to me and says, "Chief Thunder ready, you already ate the wampum."

The next morning there are crumbs in my hair. I'm in the shower. I don't know where Bo is, but I come out soon. He said he has already showered in the other bathroom, hands me a cup of coffee, and mutters, "before two heads appear." He is in street clothes with his badge on his belt. "I gotta go baby, I let you sleep as long as I could. "Kiss me Bye."

"That will be my pleasure." He put his arms down at my waist and I lift my head up and place my lips in the wet spot of his lips and linger there. It puts a stir in both of us. He whispers five more days till you are Mrs. Price."

"I know, and so much to do before them."

"Make a list for me today and I will step over to your store and get it."

"I will."

He leaves me with my wet hair and longing.

Sunday Countdown

On my desk, Julie has sketched out a design for me to look at with cost of everything we will need. She places an order for gardenias after Boyd calls her.

Bo listens to me and I know he wants our day to be special. I call Rene, and she and Rita have handled the cake, and secure a photographer because we are going to take that family picture. She says I will be pleasantly surprised on Sunday on the decisions they have made.

I call Carly prepared to leave a message and she answers the phone.

"Hey, Aunt Dolly,"

"I was going to call you today. I realize I am going to see you on Sunday but wanted to tell you I have a great idea for your wedding centerpieces, but Sunday has so many activities planned, there might not be ample time to sit down and discuss anything."

"Yeah, Rene sent out a group text about the family photo at the lake. It's a cool idea for everybody to dress that way. I love that most everyone considers me a family member before we are legally married. *Heck, legal, add license on Bo's list.* I've seen pictures done like that on the beach over here. Bing handed down an ultimatum to his mother about her undermining our wedding plans. He told me he told her she had to stop being the alpha and omega, the be all and the end all, or she would be driving a wedge that could not be repaired. His brother backed him up. I think she cried, and agreed to stop her reckless talk and shape up."

"That's a hallelujah for sure. So be gracious and keep including her Carly like nothing negative has transpired. Kill her with kindness and I believe there will be a stark difference in her attitude."

"I don't know what you said to her the last time but Bing said she was shaken after she talked to you. Thank you for being on my side."

"You are welcome."

"How is it going with the policeman you were turning green about in the restaurant? Have you been seeing him?"

"Carly, we are inseparable, and you were so right. He is dreamy." We both laugh and I tell her she will see him on Sunday. I hate to cut this phone call short but I am busy at the shop today, just wanted to let you know I have not forgotten about you and I'll see you Sunday."

My next call, Janet. I ring her up.

"Hello Dolly, Boyd said you might call today. I'm delighted to help if you want me to. Is today good for you to drop by?"

"Yes, I know you play bridge on Wednesday so this afternoon is fine. Please tell me what time you would like me there."

"If you haven't made lunch plans, we can share lunch and then get at the task of planning."

"Oh, okay. I can be there at twelve. Thank you."

"You're welcome honey."

Lunch Landslide Afternoon Avalanche

I look over at Julie, "Everything is going too smoothly. I hope my balloon doesn't burst anytime soon."

"Are you going to lunch?"

"Yes, to Boyd's mother. I hope she likes the brunch idea."

I check my computer and look at my e-mail to see if my dress has been shipped. Yes, it will arrive tomorrow. I pray it will fit. I make a list for Bo; Preacher, license, liquor, beer, champagne, count of friends invited.

I check my cell and there is a group text from Rene and Rita and Roan. They have handled the following: wedding cake, ice, parking, family all notified about attire for picture. (Denise not happy) Mr. Fox.

Mr. Fox? I did not even think of him. In fact, I have not thought of any of my friends. I'll talk to Bo about the guest list and find out his thoughts. I text back, "great work, love and thank you, everything is coming together, cake type?"

Reply; we're surprising you

I ask Julie if we need to go down to the fernery this afternoon to look at the lay of the land.

"I think we should. It's been a long time since I've been there."

"When I get back from Janet's, we'll go there."

Both shop phones are ringing.

Julie tells me it's Denise, she'll catch the other line.

I mutter thanks for nothing. "Hello,"

"Who decided about this family picture?"

"It's a good idea don't you think?"

"What is wrong with navy and khaki?"

"Well, I think we are taking the photographers suggestions."

"Did you decide on the menu?"

"Oh yeah, we're going to do big brunch."

"What?"

"A brunch."

"That doesn't sound like any Sunday dinner we've ever had."

Rene wants to host it, just let her take her turn and you worry about getting over here on time."

"You don't need to remind me about time Dolly. I guess Bing and Carly are driving themselves. Tom Jr. Is coming with them."

"Good. I 'gotta go. I have an appointment at twelve. Bye."

She hangs up. No goodbye, no pleasantries, *always a joy to talk to her.*

Julie steps over and tells me she has called Stephanie to deliver since I am frantic with all the things that need to be done.

"Crap, we need to tell her about my wedding and include her and John as guests."

"Julie, do you think Justin is available for music on Sunday? To dee jay?"

"I'll call now." She picks up the phone and calls JAM Inc., Lake Placid, FL. to schedule him if he is available.

"I'm going to leave and I'm leaving this list for Bo."

I'm getting in my car and Bo comes through the back door.

"Hey, you just caught me."

"I see I did."

"Leaving for Mothers?"

"Yes."

"Take a breath, I can tell you are getting nervous."

"Bo, I left your list with Julie, we need to talk about how many guests you're inviting."

"I'll make a list. He takes my hand. Breathe D."

"I need to go by the fernery at five with Julie, check the lay out and invite Juan and Maria."

This time he holds my hand. "D. Look at me. It's just us. Remain calm." He smiles and kisses my hand.

"Does anything rattle you?"

"One or two things."

"I guess I'm going to find out what these things are."

I start the car, "Get your list from Julie," and I'm driving off. He is shaking his head in disbelief. He's right. I am getting nervous and stressed. I glance at my ring. It is so beautiful. I should be more relaxed. I ring Janet's doorbell. She opens it and hugs me.

"Oh good, you brought a notebook."

I walk beside her and she has my plate already sitting there with iced tea. "I'm a little late, I apologize." Bo appeared just as I was driving off and was telling me to relax. It's great for him to say. *I'd rather have the captain here instead of iced tea.*

I sit down and take a sip. I am parched. I take my notepad and write in the margins: hair, manicure, pedicure.

I look up at Janet and she is waiting on me. "Are we ready to eat?" She takes my hand and says a blessing.

"Amen."

"Dolly, I just made a chicken salad sandwich and some fruit for us today."

"Looks beautiful. Thank you so much. Everything is so rushed. I can't blame this on Bo, I want to get married soon too. I am too old fashioned to live with someone without marriage. One week is not much time to get everything done. I want to look back and know we had a beautiful ceremony. I cut my sandwich again. Janet looks over at my plate. I look down and I have cut it again. My sandwich is now in seven pieces. Any more cuts and I will be eating them with a fork.

"Janet, would you like to invite any friends?" My last guest count is about twenty-five without you or Bo's count included."

"How can I help? Would you like me to coordinate the food for you? Bo said it was going to be brunch."

"A hearty brunch. Our family has a Sunday dinner scheduled this Sunday. It is part of the legacy our parents outlined for us. We have a family attorney who will be here from Deland who attends every Sunday Dinner assuring we are all present. It's funny, my parents added this codicil to their will, to ensure our family will keep family traditions. We cannot draw any inheritance unless we attend. So far, so good. No one has been injured yet.

"Did you say injured?"

"Yes, that is just a joke." *If she only knew.*

"That is a novel concept."

I eat a piece of fruit.

"Dolly, what are your thoughts about the food menu?"

"I need suggestions. My thoughts are everywhere. Ordinarily, I would love to make the food but with the decorations, I have my plate full. We have asked our family to wear white and khaki under the guise of a family picture."

"Sounds lovely. Creams and whites, how many tables?"

"Julie and I think five tables of ten, a cake table, a beverage table and buffet table. We will have a champagne fountain on the beverage table with liquor and other beverages. The liquor and champagne is on Bo's list. We have ordered ten round linen tablecloths, and a beautiful Battenberg lace topper with matching lace trimmed napkins. Julie and I are thinking glass bubble bowls with white hydrangea, roses and peonies. Candles are out because it is brunch I don't know how long this celebration will last...

"From what I've witnessed from you and Bo.... a lifetime."

I pause and let what she just said sink in... "Thank you," I am moved and full of emotional weight. I dab my eyes with my napkin to keep my mascara from running, "I apologize."

"Oh honey, every bride gets emotional."

"Yes, I have already experienced a nightmare of unparalleled proportion in the wedding category."

"I know Bo has shared his first marriage with you Dolly and I asked him if you had shared your first marriage with him. He told me no. I will confide in you that he let me know it did not matter to him how many times you had married; the bond and chemistry was life altering for him. I know my son to be a great judge of character. He has been in law enforcement all his life. He has witnessed all walks of life from poverty to tremendous wealth. He believes you are one of a kind Dolly."

My eyes are flooded. I apologize again. "I hope I am worthy of his devotion. He is miles from ordinary. I know you must be very proud. I haven't shared my heart ache with Bo even though I carry it almost daily. I have told him I have trust issues and it is an internal struggle that manifest itself a lot."

"I want to be as polite and delicate as I can be Dolly. I have heard the story about you calling off your wedding from a friend of mine I play bridge with."

"I'm sure you have. Yes, I changed my mind at the last minute and chose never to discuss the reasons with anyone except for my therapist and the woman that works with me, Julie. Julie worked tirelessly for my wedding designing the bulk of the flowers. My wedding was a floral showcase where a nursery of beautiful greenery collides with a florist. In most folk's terms, the decorations were over the top. No expense was spared for my big day. I owed Julie an explanation. I never told my parents or family the reasons. My parents knew me like you know Bo and accepted my judgement that I knew what I was doing. Despite the thousands of dollars they put into a five hundred guest wedding, they never probed or plotted to know the answer."

"I can see you are in pain and I want to help in whatever way I can."

"I imagine you are concerned I will become the runaway bride again."

"I pray that will not be the case. He loves you very much and I have come to love you too."

Tears are beginning to drop off my bottom eyelashes.

"In hindsight, perhaps I should have told my parents. I carry a lot of guilt around about it. The embarrassment I created for my family was overwhelming and I have spent a lifetime trying to make it up to them. I was the baby girl, the last to marry and they wanted me to have a mate to grow old with, someone to take care of me. Today, I am fiercely independent. A few days ago, when Bo left for Atlanta with you, he told me I was his everything. It affected me so much, I had a meltdown. I wasn't sure how I felt about being anyone's everything. Every man I have ever dated or had any kind of a relationship with has been like leaning on a broken reed. And now I have met someone who embraces my strong will and loves my spirit and fire, all facades to cover trust issues. You understand the stronger I am, the less I need to trust or depend on anyone."

"Here Dolly," and she hands me a tissue and a glass of water.

"I dated Kerry for about eight months. He worked for the Ford dealership, even gave me a new thunderbird for a wedding present. He had movie star looks and a titanic personality. He was teeming with friends and female admirers. He explained his flirtatious behavior as expected, part of his job training to sell and close a deal. I took it all in stride. After all, I was the one he asked and wanted to marry. The monstrous truth is that my fiancé was cheating on me right up until the wedding ceremony. Quite by accident, I learned of his sordid affair about fifteen minutes before I walked down the aisle. The music was playing and my father stood waiting with my five bridesmaids and three flower girls. It just took a few seconds to dash back in a little choir room to get my something borrowed, something old, something new. Kerry was talking to a woman behind a curtain. I listened in horror as he said he wanted to continue their affair. I left the room immediately, only to see the back of the woman as she was leaving. I told him I listened to him and there would be no wedding. His explanations were chameleon. He denied it, claimed I misunderstood, then stated she never meant anything to him. It was crystal clear I didn't mean anything either. It was another insult to my injured ego... He did not believe I would cancel the wedding, that I didn't have the courage."

"My father was waiting patiently and I asked him to go sit with my mother. I didn't want people to be standing for me when "Here Comes the Bride" music started. I walked down to the end and stood erect like a soldier in front of a firing squad. I thanked them all for coming but I told all of the guests I had changed my mind. I would be returning all their generous gifts and even though there would be no wedding, I felt an abundance of love from all of them that attended.

I pick up my glass of water and drink it all down.

"The woman......my sister. I never confronted her. An ugly filthy secret doesn't need a laundry line to hang it out there for more people to see. I spared her reputation because of our family. I believe Kerry might have told her I knew it was her. I believe she thinks if she never faces me about it, she doesn't have to acknowledge it ever happened."

"Is this information that needs to be shared? It is my problem, not Boyd's. I don't want him spending a lifetime proving himself trustworthy. Sacred trust will come to us because of the person he is."

"Janet, am I worthy of this man who tells me I am his everything?"

"Yes, I believe you are, and I realize now why Boyd is captivated by your everything; your warmth, your sincerity, your honesty, your strength, your perseverance. I will be so proud to call you my daughter n law."

"Thank you."

"Dolly, please let me do the coordination of the food for you. I will make some of it myself and order some things. It will be a wedding present for you and Boyd. If you will procure the cloths and flowers and set the tables up, I can get the buffet there. It is getting late. Boyd said you were going to the fernery at five. He'll be worried about you."

"Yes, I'll be going." I get up and I am weak and I have eaten none of my lunch. I hug my new mother n law and kiss her cheek.

I'm on my way down the road. Boyd has called twice, Julie once. I get to the fernery and they are waiting for me.

"I am sorry Julie for being tardy."

"Are you okay? You look like you have seen a ghost."

"I have, a ghost from the past. I told Bo's mother the whole ugly truth. She is worried I am going to break her son's heart. Let's move on and walk to the lake." Juan comes out from one of the fern canopies.

"Miss Dolly, how are you, you have lost weight."

"Have I?" Bo joins me and kisses my neck and whispers hello.

"Hey there," and he takes a second look at my eyes.

Juan is looking at Bo's badge.

"Juan, this is Bo Price, I am going to marry him Sunday here at the lake."

"You say marry? He is surprised, I can tell.

"Yes, you and Maria come to wedding and party at twelve o'clock here at the lakes' edge. We make beautiful with flowers and your ferns. The family is all coming. Can we use some pots of ferns that you have big and full?"

"Si, I bring down here and you put where you want."

"Thank you, Juan," and I hug him. Juan smiles again and looks proud.

"Okay your thoughts, Julie," I make another note in the margin; chairs.

Julie says she has an idea what she'll be doing. "I have it all in my head now."

"Boyd, shall we get married at the embankment or on the dock?"

"Wherever you want to baby. This is your day."

"No, it isn't, it's our day."

"You're right it is our day." I'm slightly irritated.

Bo quietly asks, "What's next on the agenda?"

"I hope nothing."

"We should probably talk and get on the same page.

"Like? Unbelievable, I don't know who you want to invite or how many people are coming, etc."

He takes my arm and is ushering me to my car, "I'll meet you at your house." He puts me in my car. "I'm going right there," and he walks off and gets in the Tahoe.

"Fine." I get there before him and go inside and bring out the captain. I'm on the porch when Bo arrives. He comes back and sits beside me. "What's going on?"

"Specifically?"

"For starters, you can cut the cryptic language. Something is amiss. I'm a pretty reasonable guy but I am baffled by your tone and abrupt answers. What is not going right? We are three to four days out Dolly, and you are freefalling to God knows where."

"God knows where?"

He gets up and gets a beer. And I get up and get another dose of the captain.

I return to the porch and he has moved to a chair. That's fine.

"What are you drinking?"

"Would you like some? It's good for what ails you."

"And what ails you Dolly? Don't tell me it is this trust issue that I have tried so many times to understand."

"Okay I won't."

"If you aren't going to communicate then I don't need to be here."

"Okay, then don't." I gulp so hard I almost choke.

"When you are ready to talk call me. He grabs his beer and walks outside and leaves.

This calls for another drink. I take my drink with me to the bath tub. I am weak, and emotional and drained. Maybe marriage doesn't agree with me. On Sunday Denise will be here. How can I concentrate on a new wedding when I haven't been able to forget the old one? Well, that wasn't really a wedding. This is a fact. I probably need to give the old girl a break. She and I have been carrying a cross on our backs for years. But she seems unscathed by it all. She did me a favor, yep, the old girl did me a service. It opened my eyes better than the drops you use to dilate. My eyes hurt. Needless crying. No wander I do not feel better because there is no water in my bath. I make my way back to the captain, one more for the rough seas I say. I'm back in my tub now with water and bubbly. My clock says 9:45 or is it quarter till 12. I take the facecloth and cold water and hold it on my face; one face, two heads. I look up from my cloth. Bo is back.

"Can I join you?"

"Yep, steady now, rough seas."

He takes the cloth and rinses it and holds it to my face. I do not know which head it is on. He pulls me to him and holds me against his chest. He strokes my back, and kisses my neck. He feels good and safe. I have found an anchor. Bo takes the cloth again and wipes my face again repeatedly.

"You are a mess yellow hair."

"Where did you go? A storm came up."

"D, what am I going to do with you?"

"Love me, love me tender, love me true, never let me go. He turns on the cold water and fills up my glass.

"Drink this. I went to my Mothers and told her I didn't understand women."

"This is sobering news. Did she tell you?"

"She told me enough. She told me to get my ass back here and tell you how much I love you. And I do Dolly, with all my heart, love you. Both heads. There's just one now, beautiful almost sober head." His fingers are stroking my back and he lathers up the face cloth and washes me all over.

"Are there little horns on my head because you are doing that to me?" He is smiling.

"Let me take you out of here. You need to eat something. He wraps a towel around me and helps me out of the tub and we are both in the towel and he is drying me off.

"Let's dress and go to eat."

"You want to go out? I look like Maleficent, you know evil doer. I can make us something here. I have a dead chicken in the fridge."

"That sounds real gourmet. Please get dressed. Mother said you did not eat anything. She thinks you have lost weight. She is worried about you. I'm worried about you."

"Don't worry, the captain and I go back twenty-five or thirty years."

"Maybe the captain needs to relocate to another port, set sail somewhere else."

"After he has been so supportive of me?"

He puts his hand around my neck and pulls me to him. "You have me for support now," and he kisses my lips, and side of my face.

I have managed to change and put a hair clip in my hair and look presentable. We walk out to his car and we both get in on our own side. I'm in and cannot resist saying "I guess the honeymoon is over, no door open for moi anymore?"

Bo jumps out rushing around to my door, opening it and buckling my seat belt. "The honeymoon will never be over for us." He is back in his seat now, "Where would you like to go for our honeymoon? It's one of the items I think we need to discuss. What place sounds interesting?"

"How many days can you get off?"

"I was thinking four to six days, unless you want to wait and take a couple of weeks and go somewhere for a longer time."

"Four days is good, surprise me. Bo, how many guests are you inviting for Sunday? I need to get a count for food and drinks. Anyone you need to send a personal note to or are you going to call them?"

"There's a special lady in Sanford, my safety instructor."

"Very funny, regretfully, I suspect she will be unable to attend."

"How would you know?"

"Broken leg, food poisoning, something will keep her away." We both giggle a little.

"Detective Steve might want to come and get his head bit off again."

"Is he married?"

"Yes, happily with three little boys. He thought you were very attractive."

"Well in that case, he can come."

"The police chief, maybe the Waggoner's."

"Were you successful in reaching the minister?"

"Yes, my list is completed. What can I do to help you be less stressed?"

We pull into the parking lot of "Roosters."

"Is this a good place to eat?"

"Yes, I ate here a lot when I first moved here."

He is over at my side opening my door and I slide out. We're greeted at the door by Mary who takes us to a corner back table for two. It is close quarters.

"Are you hungry?"

"Not really."

"I'll order for you so I can be sure you eat."

The server is a at our table ready to take our order. Bo orders two orders of pork roast, sweet potatoes, and green beans. Iced tea please. Do you want a salad D?"

"No thanks." The server is gone. Bo takes his hand to the side of my face and rubs it, holds up my chin while he talks to me. "I am sorry that I slighted you. I underestimated the importance of trust to you. I have not been wronged like you were and I haven't walked in your footsteps to know how bumpy that path you took was. But I do know how it feels when someone can't forgive you. We're starting a new life, a life full of love and respect for each other. And when you hold malice in your heart, it's hard to give someone else all your heart. Will you think about, just give it thought, for us, about forgiving you sister, and putting all your trust in me, because when our commitment to each other becomes strong it becomes powerful. We won't be able to recall the hurt. We'll be too happy to hang on to that old resentment."

His fingers are still at my chin and I move my hand to push his fingers in my mouth and I slowly kiss his fingers. I am silenced thinking about what he is saying. He smiles at me and rubs the side of my face again.

A different waitress sets our plates down with some silverware. The food looks good and Bo looks over at me. "EAT, please, this isn't negotiable."

The pork is moist and tasty and the green beans are bright green similar to beans I sauté at home. I treat my sweet potatoes like dessert and save that for last. I have finished my tea and my glass of water. I don't eat all my meal but enough of it and excuse myself to the bathroom. I return to the table and Bo has ordered us a crime brûlée to share. Sweet. Bo is still serious. "Talk to me about where you want to live. Would you like to build a house or buy one?" He takes my hand and puts his hand over my hand and his thumb is rubbing my ring.

"I don't know. It never occurred to me you wouldn't want to live in my house. Are the finances there for us to build a house?"

"I have more than enough to buy or build 'my everything' anything you want."

"Did you get a raise at Pizza Hut?"

"Something like that."

"It's a good thing I sobered up so I can remember all of this in the morning."

"And lastly my love, you don't need the captain anymore. I'm putting in my application for his position. You can drink libations with your husband and drunkenness is strictly prohibited."

"This is a lot of requests, uh demands before we are even married."

"Too much?"

"Not from my everything."

Bo leans over. "I love you."

It's a quiet ride home. I am tired and I think Bo senses that. I'm not sure my head can handle what I have crammed in it."

"Bo, did I screw up things with your mother today?"

"No, no baby, she has more respect for you than ever. She told me she was the one that asked you about your wedding day. She said she thinks your dam finally busted and it upset her to see you in that much pain. You scared me today, you were so distant. We have to keep that second head of yours buried. "We're home, I have arrived home safely, and hopefully in your arms soon."

I am leaning on Bo all the way along the sidewalk, still quiet, still thinking. We both head for the bedroom. The nightlight is my only source for seeing as I reach in my chest of drawers and pull out a sleep set and lay it on the bed. I look at Bo and he is staring at me. We both know I won't be needing them. He pulls the covers back and we get in the bed.

I wake up by myself again. I smell coffee and my coffee boy is not here. I go in the kitchen and find a note in my coffee cup sitting beside the coffee maker.

I had to be at the department early
You looked at peace sleeping. NO sign
of extra head. I'm a phone call away. B.

With coffee in hand, I head to my shower and ready myself for work. It does not take me long. Bo has straightened up my kitchen from last night's pity party. He cleans too, another surprise.

Back in the kitchen for a second cup of java, I reach in the cabinet to take the captain out and pour it down the drain. The captain has vanished. Gone.

Another Day Another Dollar

"Top of the morning Julie,"

"I'd say so, it's ten o'clock, Bo has already called and told me to run his credit card for the money you are spending."

"Are you kidding me? He seems to think of everything. He removed the captain from its quarters."

"That is probably a good thing."

"When we left yesterday from the fernery, I was upset and emotionally drained, aggravated, and scared. I started drinking and we had a little tiff. He left and I kept drinking, and I hadn't eaten, I became wasted. It wasn't a pretty sight. He came back and we worked it out and talked through it. He did all the talking. Bo asked me to try and forgive Denise, to put my trust in him and what we have so that we can start fresh without looking back. I have wasted so much time being angry and he has a special way of talking to me. I calmed and I realized it is time to quit tearing myself up inside.

"He is a special man Dolly."

"Whoops, Rhett calling...Hello,"

"Why am I the last to hear about this ceremony on Sunday? I was blown away when Rene called me. Listen, I just talked to one of my friends and they have an abundance of picked strawberries. Want me to get four or five flats for the wedding? Mom said she and Rene can decorate them with chocolate or dip them, whatever you do to make them fancy shmancy."

"We were trying to keep it a surprise. Yes, to the berries."

"Hold your thoughts Julie, I must make a quick call."

Janet answers immediately. "Hi Dolly, don't worry, everything is going great."

"Thanks Janet, you are my guardian angel. I just hung up the phone with my nephew, and one of his cronies is giving us four or five flats of strawberries. My sister and niece are going to decorate them with chocolate stripes. Is that okay with what you have planned?"

"So many? I was planning a fruit skewer with a strawberry in the middle. I will omit the strawberry then. Perhaps we could use some in large silver bowl near the champagne fountain. Do I need a tray for the chocolate dipped ones?"

"I have crystal or silver or white trays. I can tell them to do either and place them on paper doilies."

"Silver I think. Sounds lovely."

"Is there anything you need? How are you fixed for extra refrigeration.? I can have Juan at the fernery clean out a space for anything."

"I believe I have it all covered. Rachel and her husband will be here on Thursday. She is very excited for Bo and of course Amanda has a new dress with all the trimmings. She keeps trying it on every day and driving Rachel mad. "Dolly, you sound less stressed. I hope you are not upset because I shared some of your story with Boyd. Men brush over women's feelings sometimes because they aren't as emotional. Boyd's father was a straight arrow and I had to teach him a few times that issues can't be resolved with a snap of ones' fingers."

"I cannot thank you enough Janet for your support...and love."

"You are so welcome dear. Don't worry. It will be a beautiful day. You'll see."

Fed Ex is at the door. Julie signs for it. "This looks to be a special de -liv —er- ry!"

"It must be my dress."

Julie already has a knife in her hand to slice open the white and silver box. "Close your eyes, and I'll hold it up for you. Okay, ready?" I open my eyes, and it is totally me.

"Try it on so I can see."

"Okay, we might have a customer come in. I'll put the 'gone to make a delivery, be back in five sign' on the front door. Everyone can wait. This is a lot more important."

I am in the bathroom slipping it on. The details are better than I expected. It feels a little big.

"Here I come."

"Wow, it is stunning and way sexier than I thought you would wear."

"Really, sexy?"

"Yes, and beautiful on you, but I think you might want to take it in a bit. Let me pin it so you can see what I'm talking about. We step into our 'spotlight section' of our gift store where we sell ladies apparel, all black and white pieces. There is a full-length mirror in there and I take good look. The neckline is a deep vee with a four-inch lace ruffle trim on the vee neckline. The lace ruffle lays flat on the dress and has the tiniest of crystals and cream beads within the material. The bodice is the same lace pattern but a thicker heavier cut. Julie pins in at the midriff and waist. I gather up my hair with some hair pins.

"I wish I had my mom's necklace to wear."

"Dolly, you don't need anything but a pair of crystal danglers."

Julie picks up the phone, "Hello, Grandmother, could you take in a dress for me by Friday?" Julie pauses on the phone and is listening. "Yes ma'am, I will bring it to you tonight. Thanks Granny."

"Julie, you are my rock."

I call Bo. "I missed you this morning. My coffee boy I mean."

"Is that all I am to you, your water and coffee boy?"

"Don't forget my pizza delivery man, my doctor, my psychologist, my love."

"I like the last one best."

"I was just talking to your mother, and she mentioned Rachel would be here to help, and that Amanda has a new dress. What do you think about asking her to be a flower girl? That is, if it won't distract you from keeping your eyes on me throughout the ceremony."

"Well, there is my safety instructor from Sanford to eyeball too."

"Geez."

"That is very sweet of you to ask her. I think she will be thrilled and Rachel too that you included her."

"Okay, I'll handle it, I want to give her a little surprise when I do it, so mum is the word."

"Are you having a good day?"

"The best Bo, my dress came in. I love it but it's a tad too big."

"Mother said she thought you had lost weight."

"Bo, Julie told me you gave her money for expenses. That wasn't necessary."

"Necessary and I wanted to."

"I need to give your mother money for the groceries she is buying."

"It's been taken care of, besides she needs something to spend her money on."

"Seriously?"

"I must go, by the way, Steve and the chief are coming, but not the safety instructor. She ate something bad, and she's down for the count. I can see your eyes sparkling. Bye baby."

"Julie, we need to add a little flower girl basket with fancy ribbons to our list."

"I heard you. By the way, Justin is available but wants to know what kind of music you want played throughout the day. He has a worksheet he needs you to fill out like your favorite songs, time of events, etc. He's going to e mail to you."

"Julie, I need a suggestion for a wedding present for Bo."

"Why don't you ask Roan or Rhett for one?"

"Good idea."

"I call them both and leave a message."

"Oh Julie, we forgot the front door, we better unlock it."

"We didn't forget, I did that twenty minutes ago. And your beautician phoned and asked if you could come in earlier."

"How much earlier?"

"About two thirty."

"Mother, may I?"

"You haven't done much anyway these last few days," and we laugh.

"Are we going to start on the wedding flowers tomorrow?"

"Yes, the big urns and the top of that wrought iron arch and probably some centerpieces. Rene called me about the cake and since I ordered some gardenias. I thought we could use a couple on the cake for decoration."

"What kind of cake?"

"Can't say, it's a surprise."

I text Bo and let him know I am going to the beauty shop for cut and color and personal grooming and I will stop by and bring a steak home so we can eat steak and salad for dinner.

He answers; Personal grooming? Waxing?

I scream out. Julie rushes beside me. "What's wrong?"

Detective Price just asked me if I am going for waxing. Now what would he know about that? He'll have to explain that one."

I reply, "Why sir, only ill-bred and vulgar Yankees speak of such things in the presence of a lady. Seriously, you've got some explaining to do with that comment."

"LMAO" is all I get back on text.

"Julie, I'm off to my magician, I mean beautician. I'm getting the works, hands, feet, and hair. I'm taking my list to check things off while I am there. Oh my gosh, shoes, I need shoes. No, I think I have some already."

Amy has been doing my hair for years, and she always listens to me when I want something different.

"Your hair has grown. It's been awhile.

"Both of my parents passed away and the days have flown. I would like to show you something I got that is really special. I hold up my hand and she screams. "Get out of here! That is unbelievable."

"I still can't believe it. It's a special day for my family on Sunday and I am going to surprise the family with a wedding, or at least half of the family will be surprised.

"Stop it, you brave, amazing, lady."

"Yep, I am so happy I want to pinch myself."

She starts on my hair and I tell her I want to go a little lighter."

"How light?"

"Platinum to light wheat."

"Okay, I can do it."

I tell her about my dress and Bo, and our whirlwind romance. Under the dryer, another girl works on my feet. She asks if I want siren red on my toes.

"I beg your pardon."

Amy hears us and tells she's talking about the color of toe nail polish.

"No, just the palest pink, almost like a French without the white tips." *I think we have a different kind of wedding in mind.* I am back in the chair and Amy begins to cut.

"I am wearing a cream tea length lace. It has a plunging v and so I am thinking about clipping it up with a fresh gardenia in it."

"Sounds very elegant."

I look down on my nails. "The same color on the nails please," being sure the girl understands.

"You sure you don't want red? "I have big apple red."

"No thank you.'

Amy blows my hair out and it looks soft and pretty and healthy.

"Thanks Amy."

I go to pay and the receptionist tells me the bill has been paid including a tip for all the girls. "What? Who paid?"

"Boyd F. Price."

He really knows how to stay one step ahead of me.

"Best wishes Dolly."

I stop by Publix and get our steaks and some salad material. I'm in a hurry...

My New Yard Boy

Boyd is already home and in the greenhouse working away. I make tea and salad and a great horseradish sauce for the steaks. I step outside to turn on the grill and let it burn off.

"How long till we eat?" he is yelling through the screen in the greenhouse.

"Oh, I'm eating at seven, but I thought you wanted to continue working. I just ordered a load of paver bricks for you to add another layer to my wall. There is still a lot of daylight hours for you to be working. Paybacks are hell."

"What have I done now?"

"Beauty salon, flowers, food, what's next?"

"It will come to me."

"You're not going to have money for our honeymoon."

"Pizza Hut manager gave me an advance."

"Enough already."

"You've got thirty minutes before we eat."

"Yes ma'am."

In a few, Bo comes in all sweaty with his Georgia Bulldog shirt on. I'm afraid you have more dead orchids than thirty."

"I suspected."

"Do you want me to cook the steaks?"

"If you want to get a shower, then do that."

"I'll cook the steaks."

"Well done for me please."

"How do you do that? Do you look for a piece of charcoal on the grill? You know I'm not responsible for the appearance of well-done meat."

"You burn my steak, and I will demonstrate some waxing techniques on you tonight."

"Yowzah, I hurt already."

"And for your information, Georgia tee shirts aren't allowed. You live in Florida now Bub, so pick one."

He kisses my neck, "checking for an extra head." I like your hair, very nice, looks straighter."

"I'll go get the steaks."

I hand him the steaks, a pair of tongs and a cold beer.

"Well done, not burnt."

"See you in an hour."

"I just thought of what I could get you for a wedding present. A choke chain."

"Ouch."

I put a tablecloth on the porch table, light the lantern, put two wine glasses out, a wine cooler, and silverware and napkins. I step back inside and get the salad bowl and my horseradish sauce and make another trip in for two glasses of water. I'm sitting at the table and pour myself a glass of wine. I'm talking to him through the screen door, "would you like another beer?"

"No, I'm good."

He brings everything in and I ask him if he turns off the grill and the gas too.

"Yes ma'am."

"I might want to keep you around, I'm thinking seriously on it."

"Wine Bo?"

"Okay."

"I looked for my captain to have one for old times' sake."

"You know that old codger left first thing this morning, said he didn't feel welcome any more here."

"Really? I have one word for you."

"Is it thanks?"

"Wax..... tell me how is it that you would know about such intimate things my sweet and innocent husband to be?"

I just remember when Rachel got married, it seemed she spent all day in the beauty shop, from sun up to sundown, you know legs, brow, bikini line, it seemed like it cost a lot. Did you wax? Are you?"

"Not today, tomorrow isn't likely either."

"My steak is just right, I swear you're starting to be handy."

"I like the dressing on the salad. And this horseradish sauce is outstanding. I know Mother would like the recipe."

"Your mother said Rachel was due in with her husband. What's he like?

"Banker type, golfer, country clubber."

"Are you close?"

"Yes, most of the time. He's a bit competitive. I always let him win at golf."

"Let him?"

Yes, I'm a better golfer even though he plays five times a week. But if I don't, he gets so sore and he's in a bad mood until I leave."

"Sounds childish."

"Exactly."

"Are they happily married?"

"You be the judge on Sunday or whenever you meet them. Dinner was great. I saved room for dessert. Want to join me in the shower?"

"When I clear the dishes,"

"Okay don't wait too long."

"I'll be right there."

I have never loaded the dishwasher quicker. I had a delightful idea. I stepped into the garage and undressed, put my yellow raincoat on, my yellow rain hat and my yellow wellies. I'd show him dessert.

I go in the bathroom and turn out the light. He is shampooing his hair and the soap suds are everywhere. "Hey, I can't see." He opens his eyes. "What the hell? you look like a duck. You don't need this" as he is unsnapping the rain coat and surveys I have nothing on. "That's more like it, you can keep the hat and boots on because they look cute. Now come here and let me wash you, then you can wash my back. I have to wonder what you did for shits and giggles before I came along."

"You're not going to believe this, but I spent most of my time in the local library and knitting in my bedroom."

"You're right, I don't believe you."

"Are we done?"

"Almost," and he begins kissing me. The shower water is a steady drip off the rim of my yellow rainhat between his face and mine. He pulls the hat off in one quick move, "this is better" and plants a wet, lingering kiss in my mouth. He shuts off the water and hands me a towel, and takes one for himself. I stop by the sink to brush my teeth. I put on a shower wrap on, and gather up my play things to put them back where they belong. I take a minute to call Julie on the phone.

"Are you out shopping?" *the girl is a night owl.*

"How did you know?"

"Because I know you. I have a favor to ask, can you look for me a child headband with crystals on it for Bo's niece, the flower girl?"

"How much do you want to spend?"

"Whatever it takes, I'm going to wrap it up cute in a box before I ask her."

"That will be sweet."

"Thanks a lot."

"See you tomorrow."

Bo is sitting on the bed watching television. "Who are you talking to?"

I called Julie to see if she could pick up a cute sparkly headband for Amanda. I'm going to ask her and give her a present when I do."

206

Bo holds out his arms and I get up on the bed and nuzzle in his chest.
"Your hair smells so good. I whisper three more days. He nuzzles my
ear, "I know baby. Are you happy?"

"Very, more than I could have imagined. Are we leaving Sunday or
Monday?"

"Sunday late,"

"Are you going to tell me what sort of clothes to take?"

"You don't need any sleepwear." I'm kidding you, take what you want,
shorts, bathing suit, couple of sun dresses maybe that short skirt you
have."

"Bo, I want you to wake me up in the morning when you get up so I
can make you breakfast."

"I was going to tell you I need to leave at five. I'm traveling to Lake
City to take a deposition for the sheriff's department so I'll be getting up
at four. Sorry, I don't think you want to get up then."

"I do. Please wake me so I can say goodbye."

"I won't be back till Saturday morning. Will you be alright?"

"I'll be fine."

"Now let me show you how much I'll miss you. I love you D, and holds
my face and starts a deep slow kiss."

At four, I am awake because I cannot sleep knowing he is leaving. He is
sleeping peacefully and I place my hand on him, and move my head to
nuzzle on his chest. I give him small kisses all over his chest and he stirs.
I keep inching up, to his neck, and he says "Good Morning Beautiful.
I like waking up like this with your lips on me." He lifts me up to his
mouth. "I will miss you" and he holds me so tight. I whisper in his ear,
"I need you."

Bye Bye Love

Bo is showering and I start some sausage and grits and eggs. I am having coffee and he comes out shaved and is in his uniform. I never know where he keeps his clothes or what he has with him. With everything that is going on, we don't have a lot of time to work out simple things, but I know we will.

"Thanks baby, for breakfast and getting up to say goodbye." I will call you tonight from the hotel. I know it's not a good time to leave but it can't be helped. You have my credit card. Why aren't you using it to pay for things? I'm sorry I haven't done a better job of discussing finances before now. I don't want you to foot the bill for this wedding when I have the money. Use the credit card please. "Dolly, be safe while I'm gone and get some rest if you can." He kisses me quickly, "love you," and he takes a cup of coffee with him out the door.

It's five o'clock and too late to go back to bed. I'm going to drag out a suitcase and start to pack some clothes for my honeymoon. That will be another chore done before Sunday. I still need to get him a wedding present and time is running out.

Time for my shower and getting to work. Today will be a full day designing flowers and prep work. I want to check in with Janet and hopefully my little flower girl. I am going on in to the flower shop and take care of some book work since I will be gone and be sure Stephanie is aware I expect her to fill in during my absence.

To my surprise, Julie beats me to the shop. She shows me the headband she found for Amanda. It is precious. I think I'll add a couple of tiny cream satin roses and sew them on to coordinate with our theme. We keep several arches available at the store for rentals. The flower arrangements we add to them can be simple or simply elegant. I want to utilize all the ferns available to me and combine them with seeded eucalyptus for a lush effect. We'll plug in big flower blooms for an elegant look. The iron arch will stick in the ground so we can transport and install it easily. There are so many oak trees around the fernery, I plan on hanging lanterns from the trees and shepherd hooks along the path that hold vases of assorted flowers and greenery with coffee and crème colored satin ribbons hanging to the ground.

Final count is about forty guests which includes our families. I want the music to be romantic all afternoon and with the breeze coming off the lake, I will be a happy bride.

The flowers are here, and Julie and I open the boxes and my wholesalers have added some freebies because they know it's me that is getting married. The gardenias are waxed and packaged individually so we refrigerate them without breaking the seal on the box. I concentrate on the small vases for the hooks and centerpieces while Julie works on the big stuff for the archway. We work and laugh and talk about funny things that have happened to us about weddings we have designed. Planning is a big part of the wedding and one time I told her I was planning a wedding with a potential bride and ask her if she had an aisle runner. She replied, Oh God, do I have to buy them a corsage too?

It is a crazy business, not for the faint of heart. We snack while we work and the work day has ended before we know it. I take a few minutes to wrap up my headband in special paper and fancy ribbons to go over and see little Miss Amanda.

Julie asks me if I am getting nervous yet. I said maybe about my dress, and Julie tells me she is picking the dress up tonight."

"Let's have a beer. I have something special for you."

I go get the beer from the back cooler and she goes to her car and brings back a beautiful box with a card on it addressed to me. I open it and read it aloud. "You have been crowned with love and I can see it in every part of you. You deserve every happiness that life can offer you. Knock him dead and rock his world. Enjoy! Love to you both." Julie.

"That is the sweetest message ever, and I am so happy marrying this guy that God sent my way. Thank you from the bottom of my heart Julie." We are both sniffling and they are happy tears. I open the box and it is light weight. I fold back the tissue and say, ooh-la-la. I pull out this white lacy negligee and silky panties that is so sexy. I should be twenty years younger to even purchase it let alone try it on and think about wearing it. But I will wear this number and hope to God I don't knock him dead from shock. I could text him a picture of it, but the shock of seeing his face with me wearing it will be worth it on Sunday night. Shazam Julie, this is breathtaking. I love her to pieces and she is such a special friend.

The In And Out Laws

I load my presents in the car as Julie is leaving and I dial Janet's phone.

"Hi, this is Dolly."

"Hello, how is everything going? Have you heard from Bo today since he left?"

"Not yet. I wanted to come over if I can and see Miss Amanda. I have something to ask her from me and Uncle Bo."

"You don't have to phone Dolly, just come on over."

"I'll be right there."

I arrived in less than fifteen, ring the doorbell, and Amanda and Rachel come to the door.

"Hey Sister n law to be. Let me take a look at that engagement ring that cost my brother a fortune." I walk in with my box and hold out my right hand, and she whistles." I told him that it is a mighty short romance for such a big diamond." I am not exactly sure I know what the comment means. Maybe Bo brought my captain over here and she has sampled some, or a lot of it. She is unmistakably out there in the deep blue sea no doubt oaring around in circles. Janet comes from the kitchen and gives me a hug. Rachel stumbles back a bit and Amanda is trying to get everyone's attention.

"Is that box for me?" Amanda asks me twice. "But my favorite color is purple." *Dam, two strikes...*

"It's for you. Open it and then I want to ask you something."

"Okay." She tears open the box and gets out the headband and puts it immediately in her hair.

"What do you say?" Rachel is prompting her.

Very shyly, she says "Thank you."

"I wanted to ask you to be my flower girl at the wedding when Uncle Bo and I get married. Will you?"

"You mean next year? Momma said ya'll should wait a year."

There it is, strike three. I look up at Rachel and she shakes her head and says, "I think she misunderstood."

I smile. *So sure that is not true. If I could find the captain, I know he'd want to go home with me.*

"Was that a yes Amanda, will you?"

"I guess so."

Janet takes me by the hand, "that is so sweet of you to include her, come meet Rachel's husband Everett."

My eyes sweep the room when we walk in, "Everett, come meet Dolly" your soon to be sister n law. Everett gets up from the sports program he is engrossed in and walks over to me. I wasn't expecting such a tight hug, and he looks square into me. I feel undressed and uncomfortable. He is good looking and so full of himself I know this for a fact. He's tan from the outdoors, reasonably fit, but wearing way too much cologne. I am sure he has marinated in it. He has a gold heavy chain around his neck and bracelet to match. *Real men do not require embellishment. Ugh.*

"Won't you join us for cocktails and dinner Dolly?"

"Thank you, no. I have so many little items to take care of; *knitting, library books, besides there isn't enough liquor here in this house to keep me here without Bo, Bo may have gotten the better deal on families, just sayin.*

"Do you know our head count is about forty?"

"Yes honey, Bo called me this morning."

"Is there anything you need from me?"

"Oh no, I have everything under control, but I need to check on dinner cooking right now. Excuse me. Everett will see you to your car."

Before I could say anything, we are at the door walking out. *I am pretty sure I can find it by my lonesome.* Everett is standing way too close in my personal space.

"May I have your key?"

"My key?"

"To open your door,"

"Oh," he puts the key in and opens my door and hugs me again. Tell Bo golf on Saturday, okay?"

I tell him bye. He shuts my door. Too bad he is not close enough now for my car to run over him. He is a creep of the highest order. Bo doesn't know it yet but there will be no more sacrificial golf games. Just sayin.

I'm almost home, and I just need a hot bath and I could use my captain if I had it anymore. But I will respect Bo's wishes and have a big glass of water instead.

I take my phone with me and lay it on the sill. I am removing my makeup and my phone rings.

"Hi, we are cleaning strawberries. Actually, Roan and Rhett are eating them as quickly as we are cleaning them. Want to come over?" It is Rita.

"Rita, I just got home and jumped in the tub. Big day today with all the flowers and I just left Mrs. Price's house where I met my future brother n law Everett, reminded me of a taller Jack Nicholas and a sleazy car salesman."

"Ugh."

"That's what I said to myself of course. I think Bo is getting the better side of n laws."

"Awe, thanks sis. You're all loyalty."

"Are you getting excited and nervous?"

"Some, trying to keep busy, Bo has traveled to Lake City for the Sheriff's Department."

"Oh,"

"In fact, he is calling in now, bye."

"Hello My Love,"

"I've missed you today. What are you doing?"

Taking a bath without my captain. Per chance did you take that over to your mothers? I would swear Rachel was imbibed and ready to walk the plank when I saw her this evening."

"Are you serious?"

"Yes, definitely, I'll tell you about my short visit over there tonight when you get home. I went over to give Amanda a gift and ask her if she wanted to be flower girl."

"Did you meet Everett?"

"Yes, indeed, we met."

"Is there a story here, you are being all mysterious."

"Let's just say, a woman's intuition is usually spot on."

"Yeah, I think he thinks of himself a ladies' man."

"Thinks?"

"Okay, give it up."

"I felt like he was undressing me with his stare, and for the record, you are NOT to be letting him win any more golf games. Are you hearing me?"

"I think everyone in the motel heard you. Thank God, the police chief is in another room. Bo is laughing way too much……"

"Dolly?"

"Dolly? Are you still there?"

"Waiting till you get through laughing."

"You want me to show no mercy huh?"

"You got it. He's expecting a game on Saturday. I'd almost volunteer to be the cart bitch just to see him get whipped really good."

"Cart what?"

"Cart Bitch. When I played golf, we called the girl that drove around on a golf cart with cold beverages the cart bitch. They always wore low cut tank shirts, with lots of cleavage, always flirting with all those old men."

"Do you play golf?"

"Played. Past tense."

"Are you calling me an old man?"

I start laughing now. "Yes, you're my old man. I miss you too. One more night till you're home. Are you and the chief bonding?"

"Like super glue."

"I asked for that."

"Were you busy today?"

"Doing wedding work for a very lucky bride marrying a real prince. She seems to be head over heels in love."

"I know the feeling. Goodnight D. I will call you tomorrow. Sleep tight."

"I cannot because you are not here."

Remarkably, I did sleep well and ready myself for work quickly. I am going to stop by the fernery and pick up some leatherleaf and remind Juan that I am expecting him and Maria for the wedding on Sunday. I also need to touch base with Justin from Jam, Inc. about the music selections. The tent Julie ordered for the patio should be delivered and erected. Florida is hot year-round and it will provide protection from the sun beating down on food and family. I turn down the road and see that Party Rental is already here unloading. I pull beside the delivery driver and get out to speak to the man in charge to be sure he understands where the tent is to be placed. Oh good, I see Juan.

"Good morning Juan," and I feel like hugging him.

"Miss Dolly, good to see you."

"The men are putting up a tent and tables and chairs. They won't be parked on the road long."

"Si."

"If Miss Denise calls…"

"She call this morning."

"Oh crap. What did she say?"

"She say big family picture on Sunday, wanted some ferns on dock."

"Whew, Juan did you say anything about the wedding?"

"No, I never have time to say anything, she always talk, talk, talk so much always giving orders, she does not wait for answers." He shrugs his shoulders.

"You still coming on Sunday, aren't you?"

"Oh si, Miss Dolly. Maria put out my special pants for wedding and shirt. Maria wear pretty dress from Mexico she wears for quinceanera."

"Please keep wedding secret. Miss Denise find out when she gets here. Comprende?"

"Si, grande sorpresa,"

"Yes, surprise." I hug Juan again, "Gracias"

I walk toward the lake and Juan has already set huge pots of ferns along the path. There are ten in number on the embankment. I only made eight vases with handles to hang on the hooks so I will make some more, or something else so it does not look monotonous. I hadn't thought of the inside of the house. I will add a couple of vases of mixed flowers. The tables are already under the tent. These guys work fast. All the linens are in boxes, and sitting on a table. Looks like Julie has thought of everything. The man in charge walks up with ticket for me to sign. I scribble Dollene Diamond with his pen.

"Oh, wait sir, there is no total here. Are they faxing it or putting the charge to "Bouquets Today?"

He glances at the ticket, "No ma'am, this has already been paid by Boyd Price."

Of course, it has. I am starting to think I need to bring some money for the honeymoon, at least a roll of quarters, because he is clearly going broke. I'm afraid if I have to bail him out that I will have to tell him I started with nothing and I still have most of it left. The truck is departing and I am right behind them. Juan is waving to me to halt. "Your flower shop call, say she need more fern, please wait."

"Heck, I had forgotten all about it. I need to give those girls a raise. The boxes are loaded and I leave. Destination: "Bouquets Today."

I walk in the store and my dress is hanging up. Stephanie has arrived to lend a hand. "I love your dress. It is simply elegant. Looks expensive."

"No comment. I happen to think I am worth it. I have waited almost thirty years to get married. My biggest concern is the fit." Julie and Steph want me to try it on. Let me go get my shoes from the car. I step into the bathroom and slip it on with my shoes. I walk out and their eyes are big with astonishment.

"Well?"

Stephanie blurts out, "That dress is you" and Julie agrees.

"It's true. Stunning. Go look in the mirror. I can see a difference in the waist." They follow me there.

"What about a veil?"

"I haven't given it a second thought. I don't think I need one. I'm older, and I think the gardenia in my hair is more sophisticated."

"Yeah, you're right. Thanks girls, you are a better support system than my captain. Okay, enough, there is work to do."

Julie says Rita and Rene have called.

"Oh, let me undress, and I'll call them back."

I hang my dress up. Tonight, I will get everything together and take everything I need to Mom's bedroom so Boyd won't see my dress when he returns home.

I telephone Rita.

"How's the bride?" Everything coming together?"

"Yes, I was just at the fernery, and Juan has helped a lot with all the ferns. The tent is already there.

"How is your schedule for Saturday? Rene and I and Scarlett want to take you to lunch and have a mini shower with some mimosas."

"Okay, sounds fun, can't stay all afternoon, 'cause Bo is due home. I have really missed him."

"Ain't love grand?"

"It is. My cup runneth over with blessings."

"We will pick you up. We're going to the Magnolia Tea Room."

"Sounds like fun."

"We're just wearing pants suits. Do I need to call Rene back or is that what she was calling about?"

"Yeah, that was it."

"I'm going down my list. Justin. I ring him on his cell and he answers.

It's about time you got back to me."

"Is that any way to treat your oldest bride ever?"

"I got you covered. You want oldies but goodies, right? I got it all lined up; Tennessee Waltz, Don't Come Home a Drinking by Loretta Lynn, You Ain't Woman Enough by Tammy Wynette; How am I doing?"

"I think that it is the B list, in case you look around and see the guests looking like they need oxygen machines. I'd like to hear Ebb Tide, by the Everly Brothers, and Elvis' *The Wonder of You*", and I must have, I repeat, must have Percy Sledge's *When a man loves a Woman*" because Bo sang that to me on our first date."

"The details are making me blush with envy. Do you want to have any announcements?"

"Uh no, there's only forty guests, we pretty much know each other."

"What time are we 'going to wrap it up?"

"Not sure. But we'll see how it goes. In a couple of minutes, I'll mail you a bad check." I am laughing.

"Well, thank God your groom paid me already, so I don't have to worry about your lack of finances," and then he laughs.

"Really?"

"Really."

"Yep, that's why I am getting hitched, so I can wear his checkbook on my forehead and remind myself why I am married."

"On a serious note, he's getting a heck of a lady, you're disappointing a lot of old men out there on Sunday by going off the market and all."

"Enough, I'm glad I not paying you for all that extra comedy."

"See you Sunday."

"Thanks Justin."

"Dang, I am going to have to start a ledger named "Bo's Blow" subtitled 'how my fiancé broke me before I said I Do.' It should be a best seller."

Julie and Stephanie start laughing. "Did you mean to say that?"

"Yes, every turn I make, he pays for everything."

"That's a bad thing? Stephanie is puzzled.

"No, I guess I'm not used to all of this spoiling. I don't want him thinking I am extravagant and expectant."

"But you are extravagant and classy."

"I'll take that as a compliment."

Stephanie reminds me it is lunch time. "I think your running on adrenaline."

"Okay, please order me a salad with chicken."

"On it."

"Julie, have I forgotten anything?"

"I don't think so, we have a diagram of the table layout so it shouldn't take too long to set up."

I explain about the ten colossal pots of urns already in place, and ask her for ideas for something different along the path.

"How bout we call Robbins Nursery and get some white impatient hanging baskets and some of those jumbo white petunia plants. That will add some fragrance."

"Good idea. Let's order a dozen total."

"Lunch is here."

We're eating and Stephanie asks me if I know where we are going on the honeymoon.

"It's a surprise."

I need to get him a wedding present and I am coming up blank. He is not a jewelry person so cufflinks are out. A watch is an idea, and I thought of an engraved money clip.

"You have two days to get it engraved."

"That's what I'll do, I know a personal engraver. I going to call him now."

Julie tells me there is no need for me to stay." Go home and pack and get Sundays' clothes all together."

I let her know that I'll be gone for lunch with the girls tomorrow. "Oh, and I tried on the negligee last night. Lordy, it looks dangerous. He'll probably laugh at me."

"He better not laugh at you."

Julie and I finish all the decorations and the only thing that remains is the bridal bouquet and Bo's boutonnière. Julie asked me if I want to make my own bouquet. I look over to the vase of crème peonies that are opening beautifully. I'd like some variegated lily grass and some Italian ruscus greenery. It is a softer green and will lend itself to the soft edges of the peonies and the gardenias. If you would like to make it, that would be special, but I would like to make Bo's boutonnière. I can come by Saturday after my shower luncheon and make it. Rita and Rene and I will probably dash to the fernery and be sure everything is in place. The hanging baskets arrive and I send them with Stephanie to the fernery. Anything transported today will be less to deliver Sunday.

Julie brings me the phone. It is my engraver.

"Thank you so much, I apologize for waiting to the last minute. I would like "Invested Forever" D., relatively small block font, you'll know what will fit. Please call me and I will pick it up or you can drop it by my shop on Saturday afternoon. I can give you my credit card number now. I really appreciate it Jim. Thank you and goodbye."

I look at Julie, "I cut that close."

"You sure did."

It is almost five and I am calling it a day. "Thanks girls, for helping me not go crazy."

I grab my purse, grab a diet root beer and get in my car. Driving off, I call Rene.

"Hi, this is the love-sick bride calling. I'm available if you guys need help."

"Come on over, we are having wine and cheese Auntie Dolly."

"I'm on my way. I need some company."

I knock before entering and make my way to the kitchen and it looks like a disaster. Rita and Rene are striping strawberries and placing them on paper towels. "Are the strawberries tasty?"

Rene answers they are very good."

"Be sure to reserve some for the big silver bowl that we're going to use next to the champagne fountain. I need to write myself a note to take my silver tongs to use in picking up the strawberries. Immediately, Rene pins a note to my shirt. I look down at it and smile.

"Aunt Dolly, would you like a drink, the captain?"

I sigh, "sadly the captain and I have parted ways. He was too much of a male companion for Bo to look the other way. He said liquor and love, they just don't mix. He told me the captain needed another port of call. It's okay. I will adjust."

"Then wine it is... and she pours me a glass of Chardonnay. Are you all packed for your honeymoon?"

"Yes, except for makeup. I have all my wedding attire grouped together. It's hard to believe Sunday is a day away. "Rene, is the photographer taking the family picture after the ceremony?"

"I suppose."

"Do I need to call him and ask to take some wedding photos?"

"Aunt Dolly, that's what we paid him for."

"Oh, good."

"Just going over things in my head, right now I am a little scatterbrained. In fact, I think I will motor home, and call it an early night. I will see ya'll tomorrow."

He Thinks Of Every Thing

*I*t is a good idea to come home. I open my door and I smell cleaner, like I have just finished mopping. Looking around, the glass top on the dining table has been polished and everything has been moved and dusted. I walk in the kitchen and there is a card. "Merry Maids was here. Kindly phone us if you find anything out of place. A phone number is provided and the name of the maid, Corrine."

I am not understanding how they got in here. I am in my bedroom and there is a arrangement of a dozen white roses on my nightstand. I pluck the card out. "I'm under the influence of love and even though I am not there, you are in my every thought. B." Julie has kept this under wraps all day, I am guessing. I'm undressing and walk to the bathroom. Another dozen is on my window sill with an organza bag of gardenia scented bath crystals. There is a gardenia candle and I look down to see petals in my tub. This crazy guy. It's sheer lunacy. I am scared to look around the corner, afraid there will be a jack in the box at every turn. I am rendered powerless to his attention and romantic gestures. I get my phone and set it next to the roses on the sill, finish undressing and turn on the warm faucet water and add some bath crystals. I sink into the water and unwind. All my thoughts are on this man I am about to marry. I cannot believe my good fortune. And speaking of fortunes, he is spending one on me. In a short time, Bo is acutely aware of how I unwind and what makes me happy.

It's after nine, and Bo must be working late. No worries, I have no plans to leave this utopia any time soon. Finally, my cell rings and I know it is him. "Hey there,"

"Miss Diamond, this is Chief Merrill."

"I'm sorry, who?"

"Chief Merrill, ma'am."

"Is everything alright? Has anything happened?"

"Ma'am, if I can continue please. We are on assignment in Lake City taking a deposition from a victim of domestic violence. The perpetrator is sitting in our county jail. Detective Price in official capacity, was attacked today by the accused brother while interviewing the victim."

"Please tell me Boyd is alright."

"Yes ma'am. He sustained minor injuries. He was transported to a hospital by a squad car for an overall evaluation. He is in good spirits despite his ordeal. Thank God he had his police vest on underneath his shirt. Boyd always follows safety procedures and this time his precautions probably saved his life."

I catch my breath, "Chief Merrill, what are his injuries?"

"He has some abrasions on his upper arms, a small laceration on his scalp that requires a few sutures. There is concern about his left knee, MRI imaging will dictate exactly what the injury is...Ms. Diamond, are you there?

"I can barely speak, what is the name of the hospital Chief Merrill?"

"Lake City Medical Center."

"When do you anticipate talking to him, and traveling home? Has his mother been notified?"

"I personally have not called his mother. He gave me his cell phone to advise you. I am on my way to see him now. I can give you another call when I get there."

"You have Bo's phone, is that my understanding Chief?"

"Yes." I stayed on scene to be sure the brother was charged and was on his way to jail. Bo delivered some self-defense blows and was able to apprehend him, and handcuff the attacker.

"I'm going to call the hospital now. I may not be able to gain access regarding his condition. Please, please call me when you lay eyes on him. I will be waiting up to hear from you Chief."

"Yes ma'am, don't worry we'll get him back there for Sunday."

"I'm counting on you chief, should I telephone his mother?" I think I will. "Please call me in a few minutes when you have additional news. Bye for now."

I telephone Janet.

"Hello Dolly, is everything alright?"

"Janet, I just got off the phone... let me catch my breath... Chief Merrill and I just spoke and Bo was injured today and I do not know the full extent yet. It will be a few moments before I know specific details. I was told he was in good spirits, just being thoroughly checked at the hospital."

"What ever happened Dolly?"

"I am being told he was attacked by the brother of a person being held in our county jail. Bo was taking a deposition from a victim of domestic violence. I believe he is okay, He gave his phone to the chief to call me. I know it's late but felt you should be notified as well."

"Thank you, sweet daughter, is he badly hurt?"

"A small cut on his scalp, abrasions, possible knee injury. Chief said he was wearing his vest and saved him from a lot of further injury. I will talk to you in the morning, I think they will release him soon or maybe in the morning and then they will be enroute home. I'll know more in a few hours. Janet, try not to worry."

"Okay, Dolly, please keep me informed."

"Yes, yes I promise."

I cannot wait. "Siri, please call Lake City Medical Center, Lake City, Fl.

"Lake City Medical Center, how may I direct your call?"

"Emergency Department seeking information on an emergency patient please."

"Emergency Department, Anne speaking."

"Anne, my name is Mrs. Boyd Price, I am calling to find out information regarding Detective Price who came in a few minutes ago."

"Please hold while I check."

"Mrs. Price, transferring you to his room."

One ring, two rings, "Kathy White, emergency."

"Is this Detective Boyd Price's room?"

"Yes, who is calling please?"

"Mrs. Boyd Price."

"Dolly?" and I hear him laugh.

"Thank God it is Boyd, my heart is still racing. "Are you okay? Tell me you are okay."

"I'm fine, very lucky Baby. I hear your voice cracking. Please don't worry. Nothing is broken, I am better than okay. I will be home tomorrow as planned. Did the chief call you?"

"Yes honey, I just started breathing again. Bo, we can postpone the ceremony."

"Not on your life. I'll be home tomorrow. I'm going to keep ice on my knee on the way home. The worst part is that the chief is the driver on the way home and it will take us longer. He just walked in and he said he's going to drive forty miles per hour. Torture."

"Don't tease with me Bo. I'm not in a joking mood."

"Since when? Dolly, all parts are working, all of them. I might have a black and blue eye for our wedding picture."

"I can tell everyone you got out of line with me."

"The chief was praising you for wearing your vest."

"That's true or I might have some broken ribs."

"Do you have an idea when you'll be discharged?"

"I'll ask the chief when we are leaving. I'll be sleeping on the way home with some Tylenol three according to the nurse. She said regular Tylenol from then on. She did say I am going to need lots of nursing care, specialized care."

"Really?"

"Yes, hour long back rubs, chest massages, lotions, kisses, excessive acts of endearments."

"Boyd, you have no shame. Kissing might promote germs, I'm thinking complete alcohol and antibacterial disinfectants."

"You can't spare any consideration for an officer injured in the line of duty? My mother used to nurse me with the slightest scratch."

"Then call your mother."

"Ouch. Did you get any surprises today?"

"Yes, you are spoiling me, I was skinny dipping in the most glorious bath when the chief called me. The roses were phenomenal and I smell gardenias throughout the bedroom. I wish you were here."

"Tomorrow, and we will be together."

"I'm going to call mother and tell her I have spoken to you and you are full of it and must be okay."

"Do you realize you said Mother? I like it that you called her that instead of my mother."

Goodnight D, I Love You."

Immediately, I phone Janet and I know she must be restless waiting for information. "Janet, I just spoke with Bo and he is in good spirits and is fine. He needs to ice his knee on the way home and he'll be home tomorrow. He was joking and telling me he needs 24-hour care. That's when I realized he was truly okay."

"Very good news, Dolly thank you for calling back. I won't worry any more tonight. Goodnight."

Very good, indeed. I go to the bath tub and there are petals floating around. That was such a beautiful surprise Bo organized for me. Bath time has passed now and I want to put my nightie on and fall asleep and dream of our life together.

It's almost ten when I wake up. Bo will be home today and I am as impatient as ever. I get a shower and dress for the luncheon with Rita, Rene and Scarlett. If we sit outdoors on the patio, I can get a bit of sun on face and shoulders. I choose a yellow sundress, and in an hour, I am ready. I call Bo to find out his ETA. He picks up, "I was going to dial you in a minute or so. I thought you might be still sleeping."

"No, I was at the drug store buying Ben Gay and other medicated liniments. Some of the labels say, 'might cause burning, gosh, I hope they aren't too stringent."

"You're kidding,"

"No, you told me you needed extra specialized care, I remember."

"I believe I still have strength to put you over my sore knee and give you a proper spanking."

"Promises, promises, that's all I ever get, reminds me of a country song."

"I am going to lunch with Rita, Rene and Scarlett, sort of a mini shower and lunch with mimosa's." Call me when you hit town and I will come home immediately."

"Is someone else driving?"

"Now, who's worrying?" guess Everett is disappointed about the golf prospect going down the drain? I was so worried about him, I could not sleep."

"You really don't like him, do you? Did he offend you?"

"I don't want to make anything of it, I know the type. Like you, I have been single a long time."

"I'm glad you waited for the right one to come along, like me."

"Me too, I'm the luckiest girl in the world."

"Flattery like that will get you everywhere."

"Don't forget to call me when you and the Chief get here. Tomorrow I will be Mrs. Boyd Price."

"I thought you already were, you know hospitals have rules about giving false information."

"Do you mind? I knew I wouldn't get anywhere unless I said that."

"Always thinking on your feet D. Talk to You later."

Tea Room Surprises

The girls are here and I meet them at the door and hurry out. Happy times ahead. The Magnolia Tea Room is an old Pierson landmark. Magnolia trees surround the property and is owned by two elderly sisters, who are still living in the age of white gloves, old lace and old-fashioned ways. There is an order to everything. Ladies are to curtail themselves from outburst, eat and drink slowly, and maintain a certain decorum. The food is charming and scant because we are notably watching our wasp waists. Overdoing anything is discouraged. We'll see. For that reason alone, it will be best to be outdoors.

While we were waiting for another round of bubbly, I share the story of Bo's trip to Lake City and his injuries and how I was worried but that after I talked to him I knew he was fine.

Rita has ordered for all of us. Lemon, basil and walnut pasta, cantaloupe with a goat cheese medallion drizzled with white fig glaze and a poppy seed muffin. We begin with a mimosa, and Rene makes a toast to the happy bride. That's me. They all start talking about my old dates that never had a chance. A few alcoholics, and men that failed to tell me they had girlfriends or worse yet wives. There was the UPS driver who got lost every time he was on his way to my house, the radio disc jockey that sounded like Alvin on the radio, and the drugstore cowboy that didn't own a horse, and he had never heard of John Wayne. Bo has missed his opportunity to go over that loser list when it was offered. We were laughing a little too loudly and managed to clean our plates and have three flutes of mimosas apiece.

"Strawberries and crème for dessert ladies?" the waitress asked. She has been clearly amused trying to listen to our dating stories. Thank the Lord, those days have ended, just memories. Glad, we could provide entertainment for all the ladies on the patio.

They produce a gift bag and present it to me. I am elated to find another sexy nightgown. Bo will need resuscitation if I make it through to the second night following Julie's contribution to my honeymoon. There is a bottle of my favorite perfume too.

"Awe, thanks guys. This has been fun."

"Do you think Bo is home?"

"I insisted he call me immediately, I don't know."

"I think Bo is the one who will do the insisting in this marriage Sis. It appears you have been hypnotized with his influence and missing some of the meals you said you said you never would."

It is nearing four and I have yet to hear from the boy. Enough. I telephone him. Four rings no answer. Five, six, voice mail. "This is detective Boyd Price, Pierson Police. Please leave a clear message about the nature of your call and your phone number."

Clear as a bell. "This is Dollene Diamond, 1800 D E S P E R A T E, reporting a missing fiancé, last seen on Interstate Four, traveling south at a snails' pace. He could be under the influence of drugs, incapable of finding his way home. I'm afraid if I don't hear from him soon, I am calling my friend, Captain Morgan."

The girls drop me by my house, and I thank them for a great lunch and the present. I need to add it to my suitcase. I'm in the house and taking my new gifts to the bedroom. I'm startled, because I am not expecting a man in my bed. It's Bo, fast asleep. His phone has a slight beeping. It is letting him know he has a message. He has a package of frozen peas on his knee. I lean over to kiss him and notice the bandage on the back of his head. I hope the cut is not as large as that bandage. There's a couple of bruises on his neck, and small nicks on his ear. He hasn't shaved and who could blame him. He is home and safe. I pull back the covers on my side and climb in to lay beside him. I need to be close to him. I am nestled and he moves his arm and puts it around me. "Hey, D, miss me? He sounds groggy. I look up to his eyes, and reach up to kiss him. He responds so tenderly and kisses me with so much passion.

"How are you feeling?" I whisper. This man could ask for the moon and I would go find it.

"Better, I didn't realize I was that tired, it might be the meds. Did you have a nice lunch?"

"Yes, it was super. Are you hungry? Want some iced tea?"

"I just want you like this to hold and cherish." He rubs my face with his stubble cheek. I'm thinking about growing a beard for the wedding tomorrow."

"Alright, I like beards."

"What's come over you? Where's that spit fire I'm used to?"

"I'm saving it for tomorrow night."

"What about tonight? No fire for your injured policeman?"

"Just liniments tonight, doctor's orders."

"Come here and let me show you how much energy and strength I have."

My phone is ringing, saved by the bell. I mouth, "It's your mother. Hi Janet, yes, I just got home and he is asleep on the bed. He is waking up slowly."

"I was calling to invite you over for flank steak. Everett has volunteered to grill it. I didn't think you would want to cook tonight."

"We'll talk it over and one of us will call you back. Bye."

I relay the invitation, and tell him I need to go the store for about thirty minutes. "If you want to go over there, I can swing back by from the store and pick you up. Where's your Tahoe?"

"The Chief was going to have one of the guys drop it by, I don't want you to cook, because we're leaving and we will be gone for four days."

"Where?"

"Secret, remember?"

"I thought the drugs might have you forgetting to keep it a surprise."

"Can you call her and let her know? I'll be twenty minutes, tops."

"Yes," and he is already dialing.

In my eagerness to see him again, I have forgotten to make his boutonniere for the wedding and need to pick up my wedding present my engraver has finished. I am at the shop making his lapel flower and find his money clip on my desk. This was a great idea. I find a small box and wrap it up. I do not need a card. The engraving says it all.

I put the bout in the cooler with all the flowers that Julie will bring tomorrow. Tomorrow...is almost here. Tomorrow I will see Denise. Bo has not mentioned her since the night the Captain over served me.

I drive back to home, go in, and Bo is up, and walking slow but good.

"I want to get a quick shower. I sat in the sun today and feel like I need one to freshen up. I'll be a couple of minutes."

I rush but feel renewed when I step out. I dress quickly. Bo is on the phone talking to someone. He glances over and smiles at me. I walk over to him and he puts his arms around me.

"New perfume?"

"You notice everything."

"Yes, I do, where you are concerned," and he kisses my nose. "Are you ready?"

"I am."

Bo opens my door. I watch him go around my car and he is definitely walking slower. He gets in and comments, "This is a first, me driving your car."

"Bo, are you in pain?"

"A bit. I should take some regular Tylenol."

"I have some in my purse." I retrieve two from my little pill box and hand them over. I grab a bottle of water from my back seat and hand it to him.

"Thank you, sweetie," he reaches for my hand and rubs it back and forth.

We approach the driveway and turn in. I tell Bo "don't let yourself get too tired tonight. Okay?"

Bo and I go on in and he closes the door behind us. We walk to the back lanai.

Mother rushes to Bo, "Son, so thankful you are okay. Oh my Lord, your head. How many sutures?"

Bo answers "six."

Everett gives him a half hand shake and hug, "missed the golf game today, afraid of a little competition huh?"

"That's it."

Amanda runs from one of the bedrooms, and runs up to him. I see him flinch as she tries to get him to pick her up.

"Uncle Bo can't pick you up tonight sweetheart."

I am deeply concerned that Bo hasn't been totally honest about how he feels physically. Tomorrow will even be worse because of soreness. I am going to insist on a bath with a muscle soak for him tonight.

Everett gets Bo a beer, "What for you Miss Dolly Parton?"

"Wine please, thank you,"

I inch closer to Bo and take his hand. He knows exactly what I am doing and he squeezes my hand and gives me a short kiss on my neck.

Everett appears with my wine and hands it to me. "You smell divine Miss Dolly."

Rachel asked if he would get her a glass of rum and coke. *I knew it, it was rum.*

Everett begrudgingly goes to the bar to fix her a drink. *What a complete ass.*

He is still the ringmaster and he asks everyone how they would like their meat cooked. I remain quiet. I hope Bo will have my back and he does not fail me.

"Dolly likes her meat well done Bro. He mutters something to Bo. I see Bo shake his head no and it seems he is being a tad animated. I step into in the kitchen and offer my help.

"Thank you Dolly, could you put the salad on the table for me and salad tongs and plates?"

"Of course, anything else?"

"The butter dish and this hot plate with the rice that I'm bringing out of the oven now."

"Water glasses, Janet?"

"Thanks again, I have forgotten. Dolly, how do you find Bo, sore? He seems a little low key."

"I notice him favoring his knee. I believe everything is temporary. I am going to insist he have a soaking bath, or something for soreness."

"That will be good, but Dolly, do you want to see him before the wedding on your day?"

"I will be lost and unable to sleep without him. Confidentially, mother, he might need a night off to heal." I laugh and she laughs. I hug her, "I can't believe I just said that to you."

"Dolly, you are a special jewel."

We are seated when the flank steaks come in. Bo brings me a special small plate. "Here you go."

"Thank you," he presses my shoulder. I look up and ask if needs another Tylenol.

"In a few," he answers.

Janet asks that we bow our heads in prayer. "Lord, we come in thanks for Bo's safe return to his family and to his bride." Bo takes my hand and holds it tight. Bless this food to the nourishment of our bodies and us to thy service. Amen."

We begin eating and I ask Janet "if she needs any help tomorrow getting the reception food to the fernery. I can ask Juan or my girls to come aid."

"Who is Juan?" Everett inquires in his usual arrogance.

I am irritated. "He is a valued friend and employee of our family for over twenty years. He is an invited guest, but he would be honored to help me any way he can."

"An invited guest?" Everett continues to show out.

I have to respond, "I believe I said that clear enough for you to understand."

"Bo, you might have trouble handling her, she's beautiful and bold, a dangerous combination."

"Yes, Dolly is all that and more. She is her own person, and she has more grit than both of us combined. I respect her and I expect all my family to respect my wife because I chose her much like my sister has chosen you Everett. Perhaps it is liquor that makes your lips loose and offensive and if that is the case I will overlook it but at any rate, I think an apology is in order to Dolly, and I think we are all ready to hear it."

Everyone is still and looking at Everett. He is surprised and contrite. He clears his throat, "my apologies dear Dollene, I am exhibiting poor manners and I am sorry."

Amanda looks at Janet, "Grandma do we have dessert? I have finished my dinner, please."

"In that case, Grandma will go and get it. Aunt Dolly can help me."

"Excuse me," I take my plate and follow Janet into the kitchen.

Janet takes my plate immediately and takes me and hugs me." Dolly, please forgive, we are not ill mannered and I am so embarrassed."

"It is nothing Mother, please don't dwell, he spoke before he thought. His opinions are not important to me. Let me serve him dessert in an effort to make everyone feel comfortable, please, please hand me two, one for Amanda and one for Everett."

For Bo's sake, I will kill him with kindness. It is no no wonder Rachel drinks and is so miserable. She is downtrodden from living with that chauvinistic pig. I will endeavor to reach out to my new sister n law to pull herself out of her misery and get some renewed strength within herself.

Rachel goes to the bar and makes herself another drink. It does not go unnoticed by Bo and myself. Bo tells his sister he'd like to take a walk with her on the eve on his wedding around the grounds. She beams and sets her glass back down on the bar. I look at Janet and she smiles. Everett seems a little confused and excuses himself to the TV room.

"Thank you for the excellent grilled steak Everett" I say as he brushes by me. *kill him with kindness*

"Bo didn't touch his dessert, and you hardly ate any of yours D." Janet is surprised and seemingly worried.

"I know, I'm sorry, may we can take it home on a paper plate?"

"Of course, dear."

I am admiring some of the silver platters setting around the kitchen. I assume they are being used for the reception. "Janet, these are beautiful."

"I am happy to be using them again for a beautiful occasion. I hope that I have not prepared too much food."

"Doubtful, we have hearty eaters in our family. Again, someone can drop by to transport for you."

"I have three servers hired to assist with the buffet Dolly, and they are expected to come by here early."

"You have made so much effort Janet," I lean over and hug her, "thanks mother, let me finish clearing the table while you put the leftovers away."

I finish the kitchen and I notice Janet has put our desserts on the plate I sent over with my cheesecake on it.

"Dolly, that cheesecake was superb. I managed to enjoy it several meals and would like to serve it to my bridge group one day. Dolly, are you ever able to fill in one day as a substitute? Your mother told me you played."

"Give me some notice and I'll make a point of it." I can see Janet will be pleased if that comes to fruition.

Rachel and Bo return and she seems to look brighter.

"Are you ready to go D? Big day tomorrow, unless you've changed your mind."

Before I can say anything, Janet jumps in, I say this unequivocally, no one is changing their mind because Rachel and I have prepared too much food."

"Thank you, Rachel for helping so much." I give her a hug too. Bo and I take each other's hands and I hold the dessert plate in the other.

Bo yells out, "Bye Bro." and Everett mutters something back.

"Goodnight." and we are out the door.

Bo sits in the car a minute without starting the engine. "Everything okay my wife to be?"

"Never better."

"You never disappoint me D. I can't believe my good fortune. Slide over here so I can be close to you." He kisses the top of my head and whispers, "Tomorrow."

"We're home and Bo's Tahoe is sitting in the driveway as expected. "We need to talk about some closet space in that closet of yours for your husband."

"Really? I laugh. "I thought we could wait a few months to see if the marriage works out."

"Trust me, it will work."

"I'll get right on it Detective."

Nurse Diamond On Call

"*I*'m drawing you a bath with some Epsom to get rid of some of that soreness you are experiencing."

"Okay, I'm ready for that and some Tylenol too."

"Go ahead and get in while I go get you some pills."

I gasp when I get back into the bathroom. Bo's left side has black and blue bruises from the shoulder down. "God Bo, you, you, you look like you should be in agony. Do your legs look this bad?"

"I can't see them, and I've had a long sleeve shirt on today."

"Oh lord, you should be asleep in the bed." I take the face cloth, wet it with solution and let the Epsom water stream down his shoulder. I do this repeatedly and give him small kisses all over. He is relaxed."

"Are you getting in?"

"No baby, you need to outstretch that knee. Keep it under water. You look rough, with that beard coming on, I'm starting to think I've switched boyfriends."

"How long do I need to be in here?"

"Probably an hour. Do you have somewhere to go that's pressing you?"

"Very funny, I am shriveling up in here."

"You'll survive, stay in there a little longer." I go back to his shoulder. Bo, did you and Rachel have a special talk?"

"Yes, my sister is retreating. Everett is becoming over bearing. Mother has been worried about her. She's not strong like you D. She's insecure and needs support. She asked me when I get home from my honeymoon if I could talk to him about some counseling or I think she might leave him. She suspects he is having an affair with his secretary. I almost decked him when he called you Dolly Parton. He thinks that is humorous. It is offensive that he notices your chest and comments. I didn't want to make everyone uncomfortable at the table but I won't allow him to disrespect you or your opinions. You were so gracious D; such a class act you are my love. He pulls my arm around and pulls me closer to him and takes my face between both of his hands and kisses me so softly and tenderly. I have missed you terribly and he stands up, bringing me up to him again. He whispers, it's been three days D."

"I know, I know," and we are wrapped in each other's arms. He kisses me all along my neck and the tops of my breast.

I grab a towel. "Please go lay on the bed. I'm going to rub some muscle cream on your shoulder and on your left side. Tylenol helping?"

"Yes, I'm on the mend." He walks over to the bed without the towel and lays down. I bring the towel with me and am going to try and restrain myself. "Turn over on your side baby."

I start at the top of the shoulder, and rub the muscle cream in deep. "Does that hurt?"

"No. It feels good. I love your hands on me."

"Your knee has some broken skin on the back side, it looks swollen."

"I believe that guy hit me with a piece of PVC."

"Wow, there is a big long red area right behind your knee."

"Yeah," his voice is lower now and I think he is nodding off. I lay a thin blanket over him and tell him I'm getting a shower. His eyes are closed and he is barely audible, "okay."

I let the water out in the tub and scrub it with soft scrub. My white roses are fully open and I think back to my gardenia bath. I get a quick shower and put on a nightie. Bo is fast asleep still on his side. I straighten the kitchen, and get the coffee pot ready for the next morning. I turn off all the lights, and ease back into the bed. I want to wake him but he needs rest and he shall have it.

I feel a stir about four o'clock and Bo turns over flat on his chest. At six, he reaches for me with his arm but I think it is reflex. I ease back out, walk in the kitchen and click the coffee ON. I put four slices of bacon in the skillet. I'm as quiet as a church mouse. I take my coffee to the porch and sit in my chair. My wedding day is here. I am overjoyed that in a few hours I will be Mrs. Boyd Price. Bo appears in a pair of boxers. "Come back to bed Mrs. Price."

"Feeling better? I released the nurse at midnight last night."

"Thank you for taking care of me last night. I am much better now."

"Need coffee and breakfast?"

"I need other things, but my bed partner departed."

"You can unseal the vault tonight when I have your full attention. How 'bout some coffee or orange juice?"

"Both."

"Scrambled or over easy?"

"Scrambled."

We are eating breakfast and he said he's going to his mothers to shower and shave and pack after we finish.

"I really feel better," and he takes my hand and kisses my fingers. "I love you. Have I told you enough lately?"

"Well, you didn't mention it last night but I forgive you. You can make it up to me tonight."

"And I will. It's a promise."

We clear the table and he helps me put the dishes in the sink. He is standing behind me and kisses my neck. "I'm leaving, unless you want me to stay."

"Well, put some clothes on before you get to your mothers, okay?"

He rubs his beard on my face. "Sure you want me to shave?"

"Pretty sure."

He kisses my nose. "I can't find my phone or keys."

"Last night, I brought them in for you, you don't remember?"

"No."

"I guess you don't remember making love like a mountain lion either."

"Funny, I would have remembered that. See you later Mrs. Price. He kisses me deeply and says bye, D."

Its My Party And I'll Cry If I Want To

*I*t's time for my shower, I am going to take my time and afterward I am going to moisturize like crazy. Of course, one saturation of lotion does not make up for years I should have been doing that. I'm blowing out my hair and I am going to roll it in some jumbo rollers to add fullness. I finish packing my hair dryer, and my case of makeup, and put on a pair of capris and a cool blouse. I lock the house. The next time I enter this door, I will be Mrs. Boyd Price. My bag, my phone and all my nerves leave at once. I turn into the fernery. It looks like a wedding is taking place. Julie and Stephanie are working. I am moved beyond words as I drive up.

They greet me at the car and I get out singing "Here comes the bride."

"This is a beautiful garden."

Julie takes my hand and leads me to the deck. The arch at the embankment looks like a movie set. Lush, cascading greenery everywhere. Staggered thick fern pots in specimen condition dot the path. The water in the glass vases hanging on the shepherd hooks sparkle when the morning sun rays hit the glass. The wide coffee colored and white ribbons puddle on the ground.

"Julie, Stephanie, you have made my wedding day so special and I love you guys." We do the group hug and everyone is filled with big emotion.

"Ya'll go now, and get back here on time," I command them.

All the linens are on the tables, along with silver chafing dishes. There are white glazed ceramic signs in calligraphy labeling the brunch items one can choose; very classy. The centerpieces are so beautiful on the Battenberg. I am thrilled. The cake table is decorated and ready to receive the cake. Flowers that go on the cake are sitting there in a filled tray of ice to keep them cool. The cake is a surprise as Rene has told me on several occasions and to my surprise I am still clueless.

Love And Forgiveness

I go inside the house about ten thirty and a feeling of butterflies is within me. My clothes are already in the room where I am dressing. I ask Rita if she would tell Denise that I would like to see her in my room as soon as she arrives. Denise knocks on the door and comes in all dressed in white and khaki.

"Oh, you have arrived early and I imagine you are surprised. We are taking that family picture but we have a new family member in about one hour."

"To say the least."

"I wanted it to be this way and it seemed a perfect time to tie the knot at a Sunday Dinner when all the family would be here."

"Denise, I am the happiest I have ever dreamed possible."

"I can see that, I'm happy for you."

> "That's what I want; your best wishes because my heart is full and I want to start my marriage with hope and love for my family. Bo has erased my scarred heart by loving me, and showing me that love and forgiveness trumps wrong and injustice. My ardent request is that we begin anew as sisters again because having family united is the

biggest part of the journey of life. I blame no one anymore for my past sorrow. It is a new day, a fresh beginning. Now wish me the best life ever and I want you to see
my ring." I hold up my hand to show her but instead she
grabs me and hugs me and tells me she loves me.

"I'm borrowing Mom's room to get dressed so I better get started." It's
a beautiful day. I take a deep breath. It wasn't as hard as I thought. It
was my voice but God was directing my words. I feel his presence and
look up and say, "Thank You Lord for your guidance and providing me
courage."

Rita enters and brings me my bouquet and the gardenia for my hair.
Julie has designed my bouquet with Italian ruscus and crème peonies
and gardenia blossoms with subtle spikes of lily grass and ruscus. It is
heaven. Rita tells me she saw Denise very teary eyed. "Did ya'll argue?"

"Not at all. All is well. She wished me the best and said she loved me."

"Do you need help getting your dress on?"

"I need to pin up my hair, but I want it kind of loose, and
then add the gardenia, could you help me please?" Rita
sees my dress on the bed and tells me it is beautiful and
it is so me.

"That's what Julie said too, I feel Mom's presence in
here. Do you?"

"Don't get me all weepy. Is this what you wanted for your hair? Let me
add a little hair spray for you."

"Perfect. I need to finish my makeup. How does everything look out
on the patio?"

"The man of the hour arrived a couple of minutes ago with his family. He gave this gift for me to give to you. He looks quite dapper. His
mother is quite elegant and is wearing a hat. I've not been introduced to
Bo's sister."

I begin opening the box and peek inside. Wow, diamond drop earrings that barely drop from my ears. Dazzling is an understatement. *I hope my Pizza Hut manager isn't embezzling.* There is a sweet note handwritten in the box, "For My Everything." Tears fill my eyes.

Rita gives me a hug. "You are being so spoiled. Dolly, you are going to be impressed with the food. We all know how persnickety you are."

"I knew the brunch food would be. Mother is a class act Rita."

"Do you have your vows ready?"

"Yes. Are you going to walk out there to music?"

"I told Justin to use his judgement. On second thought, I might want to rethink that now." I laugh to myself.

"Do you need anything before I leave? Something old...something new?"

"Thank you, no, *been there, done* that. I already have the something blue and I look at my ring. She leaves, and I look at my vows once again and say them over to myself one more time. I walk out the door and look back and tell Mom bye.

Everyone is down at the lake waiting on me except Justin. I smile, and he winks at me and I begin making my way down the path to the lake. I breathe in my bridal bouquet that is so fragrant with the gardenias Bo has ordered for me. I look for Bo and he breaks from the group and comes up the path to walk me. We pause for a few seconds and look in each other's eyes. He whispers to me, "Ask me."

I look puzzled and then it hits me. "Still captivated Detective?"

"More than ever D. He kisses the side of my hair. "You are the most beautiful woman." We walk together and I look at everyone dressed in white and khaki and it is a beautiful group. Amanda has scattered petals everywhere and I think Julie has scattered some also. I take a deep breath, and look at the man of my dreams. He has khaki suspenders on and his mini gardenia bud is attached to his suspender. He is wearing a fun tie, khaki with white polka dots. I smile real big. He hasn't taken his eyes off me nor I off him. We reach the deck and embankment and he hasn't let go of my hand yet.

Reverend Young begins. "We are in the presence of God and the spirit and love of the Diamond Family to unite in marriage Amelia Dollene Diamond and Boyd Franklin Price.

Bo, you may begin."

"I have found my magnolia, open and full of beauty and pure in heart. I offer you a lifetime of respect, and love and faith and shelter. You are my everything my beautiful D and I look forward to growing old with you. I love you."

Reverend Young gives me a nod and I feel myself getting emotional.

"You reached the core of my soul to love me Bo and understand me. You repaired shattered dreams and trust and I do trust you unconditionally. My heart is overflowing with love for you because you are kind and calm and grounded, everything I need to be invested forever. I love you more."

The rings please. Bo hands me a gold band for me to give him. I slide it on his finger and whisper, "You think of everything."

"Bo, you may present your ring to Dolly."

"You sparkle like the diamond you are, pure and rare. I give you this ring as a symbol of our love that encircles our life." He takes my hand and slides off my engagement ring and places it on top of my engagement ring and slides both at the same time back on my left finger. It is another circle of diamonds around my engagement ring and I cannot believe it is possible for it to become even more beautiful. I cannot stop the tears. Bo produces a handkerchief for me and pulls me to him, and holds me. He looks over to the minister. Reverend Young is rushed..."by the power vested in me, go ahead and take care of your bride Bo."

My arms go around him and he kisses me passionately. "Mrs. Price, I love you."

"Ditto Detective, I cannot speak."

Reverend Young announces, "It is my pleasure to present Mr. and Mrs. Boyd Price."

Bo has his arm around me and we and we commence to greet and hug everyone. I walk over to Juan and Maria. I am grinning ear to ear. His suit jacket is red and silver, with large red roses embroidered all over and silver threads. He looks like he rented it from Porter Wagner. His pants have black satin stripes down the sides and he is holding a black and silver sombrero in his hands. I am honored he is wearing his best to my wedding. Maria is dressed in red and black and silver also. Her hair is pinned up with a large silk rose. Her shoes have silver tips at the toes. They are in full Spanish regalia and I hug them both. Juan kisses both cheeks and I am elated.

Mother and Rachel and Everett all hug me and say they are happy for me and Bo. Bo kisses the side of my head again, "I am the happiest I have ever been."

We hear the music get louder and Reverend Young encourages the guests to go on up to the tented area for the reception. "The Diamond family is taking a family picture and they will be up presently."

Roan is shaking Bo's hand Tom and Denise join us to offer best wishes. Bo shakes Tom's hand and leans in to hug Denise, "it's nice to see you again."

Bingham and Carly are making their way to us, "Aunt Dolly, you pulled the ultimate surprise on all us. You look like a queen, wow, I hope that ring is insured."

"I hope so too."

Bo hears us and tells me only a thousand more payments to go.

The photographer lines up the family in front of the arch. Everyone decked out in khaki and white is so impressive. He takes several pictures and then he tells us we are good to go. I see Detective Mullins with his wife and kids. The police chief is here and I must thank him for calling me that night. I've seen him around town and always think he has a certain rusticity to him; his dialogue short, a bit gruff all around.

Mr. Fox waves to me and smiles.

The music is playing romantic tunes and I grab Bo's hand and take him down the dock to the end. I take a deep breath.

"D. What is it?"

"I'm overwhelmed, getting a second wind. I wanted to tell you how handsome you look; how beautiful my ring is. I wasn't expecting anything else. My diamond earrings are beautiful and allow me to feel like a queen. *You* make me feel like a queen. Thank you for everything." He puts his arms around me and holds me tight. "You are my queen, this is just a start. Let's go and eat and say hello to everyone. You ready Mrs. Price?"

"I am."

Bo and I are walking up the path to the brunch area. Janet and Rachel are standing together. Bo kisses them both on the cheek. He has his hand in mine the entire time. I hug them and Rachel says she loves my dress. Janet echoes her sentiments. "It was a beautiful ceremony, Dolly, we love you and Bo together. Welcome to our family." Everett is holding Amanda and he puts her down and she runs over to Detective Mullin's kids. Everett says it's his turn to kiss the bride. I turn my cheek to him and give him a hug. "Congratulations, Bo and Dolly."

"Thank you all."

My family is already eating and seated at a table. *Big surprise.* Bo leads me to the buffet line. I notice a spiral cut ham with pineapple and cloves studded in heart designs all over the outside of the ham. A gentleman is preparing Eggs Benedict on demand. There is a potato and sausage frittata, along with a spinach and Swiss cheese quiche. I help myself to a couple of the colorful fruit skewers. In martini glasses, Greek yogurt parfaits are topped with that awesome granola Janet makes. Under glass cloches, there is a large pedestal cake stand of chocolate iced donuts with sprinkles on them. A heart shaped sign is below it, labeled Bo and Dolly, first date. I am touched with sentimental thoughts. Bo sees me and squeezes my hand. "I asked mother to have some here."

"We must eat one then or we can share." I kiss him and he grins. A tray of decorated pastries and apricot and walnut scones are on a silver tray next to the donuts. On the other table is a large crystal bowl holding shaved ice. Another crystal bowl filled with caviar rests upon the ice. All of the caviar accompaniments are here; minced onion, capers, and chopped boiled egg. A tray of toast points and water crackers lineup in rows beneath the bowls. It is a beautiful presentation.

I look over at the silver service coffee station which includes a pedestal bowl of turbinado sugar. "Your idea also?"

"I might have mentioned it." Another server is making bloody Mary's and pouring mimosas. The fountain is filled with pink champagne, and glass champagne flutes flank the fountain. I eye the wedding cake: three small tiers on an elegant silver cake stand. A silver and crystal monogram "P" on the top with the fresh gardenias that Julie has added. A silver place card holder holds a white card written in silver, Graham Cracker Cake. Glass candle wick dessert plates are stacked all around. We are sitting at the table with Bo's family.

"Janet and Rachel, I am in awe of your thoughtful and attention to detail, and every effort you have made. Every dish is sublime. I am so blessed." Bo and I begin eating. We start by both taking a bite out of the donut. We give each other a kiss with it still in our mouths and laugh. If guests are watching us, we don't care. It is silly sentimental goofiness. I point to Bo's face like he has something on his chin. He shakes his head no likes he's not falling for it. I point again, I'm serious, and he wipes it instantly.

Roan stands up and taps his glass with his utensil. "Our first introduction was a fishing trip where the girls out fished us and Bo and I caught sunburn. I knew he was going to fit in, we welcome him into our family and encourage him to try, just try and get a rein on Dolly. Unbridled, she is hard to handle. A toast everyone to Bo and Dolly." Bo gives him a thumb up sign.

Janet stands up to follow Roan's toast. "We love your spirit and southern spunk Dolly. It is refreshing and we welcome you my dear Dollene to our family. We'll try to keep up. Cheers, and raises her glass, Congratulations."

"Thank you."

The photographer asks if we can cut the cake. "Of course, Bo pulls my seat out for me and we cut a piece and we give each other a bite.

"What kind of cake? Darn, that is good. This might beat my favorite of Hummingbird cake."

"It's Grandma Gert's recipe. Graham Cracker."

The photographer mentions a toast. The server hands us a glass of champagne. Bo taps on his glass and everyone stills. "Thank you, friends, for celebrating the best day of my life. All of you are special to both of us. Our family is important and that's why we chose Sunday Dinner day. We hope to have more of these at our house with all of our families together. Now I'd like to dance with my bride, our song. He leads me to the dance floor and Justin is right on cue. *When a man loves a woman, can't keep his mind on nothing else.*

Mr. Fox asks Janet to dance, and Carly and Bingham, and Rhett and Scarlett join in. The dance area is full like my heart. Bo is nibbling on my neck.

"I think you need something more to eat." Bo is still in my ear, *when a man loves a woman, spend his very last dime...*

"Have you spent your very last dime?"

"No, not yet D. We need to catch a plane by six, maybe leave at five?"

"Plane? Where are we going?"

"Georgia, Savannah. He kisses my nose. That dress is a bit revealing Mrs. Price and you look beautiful in it."

"I'll take all compliments Detective."

"Tonight, I am going to tell you my first impression meeting you, remember in my office?"

"Yes, I want to hear it."

The song is ending and he pulls me so close and kisses my ear. He takes my hand and leads me to the table. Janet returns to the table and invites Mr. Fox to sit at our table.

Mr. Fox smiles at us, "Congratulations you lovebirds." I introduce Bo, and he stands and reaches to shake his hand, "Thank you, sir."

"Mr. Price, you have found a diamond, a real gem I think."

I smile, "What a nice thing for you to say, Mr. Fox."

"I look forward to getting to know you and your family," and he glances at Janet.

We snack some more and Bo says he's going to get cake for us.

"No need to get up son, the server will bring it to you." Janet motions and the server brings over cake for everyone at our table. Janet asks if the server can take cake all around to the other guests.

Rene is walking towards us, "Love the cake Rene, you did surprise."

"Aunt Dolly, you look gorgeous, I love your earrings."

"A wedding gift from Bo, I told you he has impeccable taste."

She picks up my hand to look at my band. "I am so stinking jealous."

"No, you're not, you're happy for me," and I smile because I am the happiest.

Rene addresses Mrs. Price, "Our family is so impressed with the brunch today. Thank you."

"You are most welcome."

All our guests seem to be having a grand time. The music is fantastic and the folks keep nibbling on the food. It is a little past four. I hope our photographer has captured our families enjoying life and our special day.

Julie approaches me and says she will stay a while and help Rita and anyone else that is helping break down the tables, take my car to the store, and come back on Monday to finish up.

"I could not have done anything without you and Stephanie. From the bottom of my heart, thank you my dear friends."

"Dolly, have a wonderful honeymoon. I'll see you in a few days."

Bo reaches in his pocket and he has an envelope for Julie and Stephanie. "Thank you, ladies, I'll bring her back safe and sound." He makes me so proud.

"Are you ready to go D?"

"I'll meet you in the house to get your bag. Okay?"

"Alright."

He is there in a couple of minutes, and gets my suitcase. "Have everything in here?"

"Yes."

He smiles and leads me outside to his vehicle and we are gone. I thought the goodbye would be more tearful. I hope everyone is still having a good time and haven't noticed we have departed.

"We'll stop by home and you can change. If I see you undress, we may be delayed and miss our flight. How does that sound?"

"The missing the flight or changing my clothes? It sounds like it's one in the same my dear."

We are here, and I take my case to get my purse out, and I'm changing quickly to a pair of jeans and a denim jacket. Bo is on the phone all the while removing his suspenders and tie. He looks around and I am ready.

"Thanks Steve, and he hangs up. Have everything D?"

"Yes, I grab a couple of bottles of water and lock the front door. Bo is holding my door open for me. "In you go, Mrs. Price." I am seated and Bo tells me to buckle up. He leans his head in and places a soft kiss on my lips.

Honeymoon Heaven

*I*t's almost an hour drive to Sanford airport. Allegiance Airlines has a direct flight to Savannah and it is a small airport and we don't have a problem. Bo hands the tickets to the agent behind the counter.

"Mr. and Mrs. Price, we will be boarding first class in a few minutes."

I look at Bo, "did she say first class?"

"Yes, I thought it would give us more privacy, and he winks at me."

"You do think of everything. I'm starting to feel inadequate."

The agent motions for us to board, followed by a general intercom announcement that all first-class passengers can begin boarding. Our seats are on the first row. Immediately a stewardess brings us two glasses of champagne, "Congratulations Mr. and Mrs. Price."

Simultaneously, we say "thank you."

I reach down in my purse and retrieve my little present for Bo. I set it on the tray. He looks surprised. "I have a wedding present for you as well. Bo unwraps it and opens it shyly. "It won't bite," I tease him.

He picks up the money clip and reads the inscription, "Invested Forever, D." Leaning in to me, he kisses my neck, then my lips, "You put some thought into this, I will cherish this always. I love you. Did everything go today like you wanted?"

"I didn't have many responsibilities except for getting there on time. When my sister Denise got there, I asked to see her and I had a talk with her."

"You did?"

"I followed your advice," he takes my hand and squeezes it, "I told her I wanted to start fresh and I blamed no one for the past anymore. She told me she loved me. I didn't want to to-open any old wounds."

"You feel good about it?"

"Yes, you were right."

"There is so much I want to talk to you about tonight D."

"You want to talk?"

"Well, in between your nursing duties. I'm still under the care of a doctor you know. Lots of bed rest, I think was the doctor's orders."

"While you are sleeping then, I will be shopping."

"I'm not letting you out of my sight. I will take you shopping."

"You might want to check your credit card bills first."

"We're good."

"We are? I admit I have been a little concerned. You have spoiled me the last few weeks."

We did not notice our flight was ending and we are landing. In a few minutes, we are at baggage claim and outside taking a taxi.

"Azalea Bed and Breakfast, downtown, please."

The driver acknowledges and says "Welcome to Savannah. I hope you have an enjoyable stay."

"Thank you."

"Bed and breakfast?" And I am looking at my new husband.

"Yes, ma'am. Does that suit you Mrs. Price?"

"I'm sure, although I don't recall any other options being offered. You did get two beds, didn't you? I know you still need rehabilitation, undisturbed sleep and all that."

"It's the all that I need the most, and he is looking into my very soul. We have a late start in life and I want to make up for lost time."

The driver pulls up, and unloads our bags and takes them in for us. I look around and this place is beautiful and cozy, so romantic.

Bo gives the guy a tip, and the guy thanks him profusely.

A very pleasant lady talks to Bo as I wander around. They have a library, a beautiful dining room, a big enclosed porch overlooking a pool, lush with privacy plants and gardens surrounding it.

"We have a few minutes before we go out. "Let's freshen up in our room first."

"We're going out again?"

Yes, you'll like what I have planned. He puts his arm around me and we head up the stairs. The honeymoon suite is lovely. It's dark woods and crisp white décor. I smell gardenia and look over at a pillow and there are blooms resting on the top. I pick them up, "for me?"

"Everything is for you." He takes my hands and put them both around him towards his back. "You are a dream I hope I never wake up from D." His lips are on mine and there is no separating us for several minutes. I am not ready to end this passion but he swats me on the backside. "Let's go."

"Go?" I look at the bed, and look at him. "You want to leave?"

He grins, "We have the whole night when we get back. C'mon."

We go downstairs and walk out hand in hand. There is a horse drawn carriage coming along the street.

"I'd like to do that one night while we're here."

"How about now?" And the carriage stops. "For us," Bo says.

"Really?" I am smiling from ear to ear.

Bo helps me up and puts his arm around me and tells the driver we're ready. It's a beautiful way to view the historic Savannah. The driver makes a few comments along the way. We're taking in all the sights and people walking. The horse stops at a coffee shop, and Bo exits to go get us a couple of lattes. There is cool in the air now that dusk is here. I outstretch the blanket that is on the seat. Bo hands me a coffee and the driver continues. We are out a couple of hours, and have made it back to the Azalea Inn. Bo helps me down and gives the driver a hundred-dollar bill.

"This is for you."

"Thank you, sir."

He turns to me, "are you hungry? I think we have missed our supper here. But I think we can have a snack brought up to your room. I'll check at the desk. You can go on up. I'll be right up.

Our bags have been unpacked, and our clothes are neatly arranged in the dresser drawer. There is a giant bath tub that beckons me. White robes and slippers are on an antique table and one gardenia is laying on the stack.

I'm in, completely immersed when Bo walks in. "I see you have found your comfort zone."

"While you are there, I'm taking a quick shower. Enjoy," and he leans over and kisses my neck.

"Thank you for the gardenias."

"You are welcome D."

I am still there when he steps out of the shower and puts on a robe. He smiles and shakes his head like he does not understand this whole bath obsession. There is a knock on the door and someone brings a tray in. I hear him say thank you.

Bo comes back in and says it's time for me to get out.

"Already? You're not going to join me?"

"No, he reaches in and pulls me up, and out. I am reaching for a robe and he pulls me in his arms, lifts me up and takes me to the bed.

"Hey, I'm wet, all over."

"I know and I don't care. He lays beside me, you smell heavenly, and I cannot wait any longer. He is kissing me and kissing me. There is no telling Bo anything except I love him and hearing it back.

"I get up about three, and go to the bathroom. I feel ravaged and I love it. I remember the negligee, Julie's gift. I'll put that on and in the morning, I can surprise him. I am awakened a couple of hours later to Bo whistling between his teeth. "Geez, where did that come from?"

"I am sleep deprived, are you intending on raping me again?"

"Yes, and you will like it. That nightie or lack of it has given me energy. He is taking charge and I don't like it, I love it. About nine o'clock in the am, I lean over to him, and say, " I think we have missed breakfast."

He kisses me and says "No, I had mine. But I am ready for a mid-morning snack." He lifts me up in his arms and starts again. "Mrs. Price, you satisfy all my hunger."

It's almost noon, and this little rag doll needs a shower and a toothbrush. I am barely in the shower, when Bo joins me. "Your alone time is over." He takes the shampoo and puts some on my head and starts to wash my hair. He lathers me up all over and then shampoos his own hair.

I put some conditioner in my hair and finally rinse. He is holding me now and ask me if I have finished.

"I'm being rushed," I think.

"No, not at all, and he holds me tight and kisses me oh so slowly, and slower and deeply.

"Are we going to be here all day in the bed?"

"No, we're leaving, get dressed before I change my mind."

I'm almost dressed when my cell goes off, crap, I need to charge it. I answer it but tell Rita I need to plug in to the charge.

"How are the newlyweds?"

"Great."

"What city are you in?"

"Savannah, we're staying at the Azalea Inn and Breakfast. Very nice. Did ya'll get everything picked up from the wedding?"

"Yes, everyone pitched in and helped."

"Denise is on the warpath again. I thought on the day of the wedding, she might have had a change of heart but her mellowness was short lived. She is calling for a special meeting when you get back to divide the personal belongings of the house. She has already taken some items from the house and claimed them for her new office."

"You're kidding."

Bo turns around and looks at me. *He mouths, Is everything okay? I shrug my shoulders.*

"When is the meeting?"

"She is planning on this for Sunday. When are you newlyweds going to be home?"

"On Thursday."

"We can talk then."

"Okay, bye."

"What's going on?" Bo can see I am thinking about Rita's call.

"It's Denise playing superintendent again, I don't think she can help herself. My parents never intended for their affairs to be so complicated. I believe they simply wanted their family to stay together as a close family, but we're all being pulled in different directions. Denise wants to make major changes in the operation and there is really no need. The company is making money for all of us, and we don't need the homestead but it will run down without someone living there."

"Do the Sunday Dinners have to be held there, is that part of the inheritance agreement?"

"No, just that we have a Sunday dinner."

"Why not let Juan and Maria move in the house to make it their home. They need a bigger home since their family is growing, and Juan told me he would like to live closer to his work."

"That is a good idea Bo. I'm going to run that by Rita and Denise. I smile at Bo. "I might keep you around for a while."

"I hope so, I'm not worn out yet. Are you ready?"

We walk out of the Inn and onto the street. "Are you ready for some lunch?

"Yes, I am," and we find a cute lunch place and order soup and sandwich.

"Dolly, when we get home, you need to decide if you want to build a new house or buy another. What do you think about an 'our house' for our new life together? If I didn't like law enforcement so much, I could work as an investment manager. I have done really well with my own stocks. I have been investing since my very first job as a teen. My dad let me buy stocks when I was young. I saved, did extra jobs all my life, had stocks that paid off, like Microsoft, and I reinvested.

"Oh, I've been worried you were embezzling from Pizza Hut."

"I also have my inheritance from my grandparents that I have never touched. I made money off the sale of my house with Dina. She left without anything from our marriage. For a short time, I kept that separate, in case she filed something against me, but eventually just put that money in the pot. I can build or buy from the interest I have collected without touching the core of my savings. Plus, I have my salary, and extra money I make from the sheriff's department. I know you are independent, but you can slow down or quit working if you want. I have already added you to my life insurance policy and health insurance which is one of the best offered around. You can save that money that you are spending on that. I know I am throwing a lot at you, I don't want you to worry about money or finances."

"Call me crazy, I'm seeing a Jaguar in my future, I'm kidding of course. I'm not quite ready to give up poking posies. I really thought you could become one of my delivery people on the holidays."

"If it keeps me sleeping with the boss, sign me up."

"If you will feel better in an "our house," then we can do either. You're serious about needing closet space?"

"Yes, I need a closet. I think we have tied up this table long enough."

We leave the restaurant and window shop along the way.

"I've got tickets for the Savannah Theatre tonight, "The Beat Goes On." We can go to the Olde Pink House for dinner early before the show."

"That sounds nice."

There is a jewelry shop that captures my interest and we stroll in.

"I'm thinking of a bracelet with a monogram charm on it for Julie and Stephanie as a thank you for helping us with the wedding. A saleslady hears me and brings a tray with gold and silver bangles that a charm can be attached to. I select a style and ask if she has the appropriate letters for the girls. "It's exactly what I would like to get. Please wrap them up for me" Bo is at another counter looking at tennis bracelets. "Do you like any of these D?"

I pull him from the counter, and look into his eyes. "Yes, I like all of them. But I don't want you to buy me anymore jewelry just yet. You just gave me these diamond earrings, which I love. Please, another day, another occasion. I insist. I just want you, not a ton of gifts. Okay?"

He hugs me and sighs and kisses my ear. "I love you."

We go to pay for my gifts and Bo produces his American Express.

"Bo, I can pay for this."

Bo takes my hand, "will you let your husband take care of you?" I realize he has his pride and this is not a time I need to demonstrate my independence.

"Thanks, baby. I know they will like them."

"I think it's time we get back to the Inn to get ready. He takes my hand, and we walk back taking in the beauty of Savannah and it's warm and friendly residents.

The woman at the Inn greets us and reminds us there is a complimentary happy hour at four-thirty. She asks Bo if we have everything we need in our room.

"Everything, thank you."

In the room Bo holds me, "it's hard for me to keep my hands off you."

I hope and pray we will always be this in love. Want to get a quick shower?"

"Yes."

We're dressed and going downstairs and Bo calls for a taxi.

"Would you like a glass of wine before we go"

"Thanks, no. I'm happy to wait outside taking in the sights. It's a short ride to the Olde Pink House and there are a number of people waiting. Bo has made a reservation through the Inn and we are seated.

"Would you like for me to order? I have been told they have an excellent halibut dish."

"Sounds great."

The waiter asked if we would like a cocktail.

Bo answers white wine for both of us please. We're going to have the halibut please with mashed rosemary potatoes and asparagus. Salad for both of us with raspberry vinaigrette. Thank you very much."

"Is that okay D?"

"You do like to take charge of me, don't you?"

"Too much?"

"No, I'm just realizing we've learned a lot about each other in a short time." and I smile.

Dinner is exceptional, and we talk more about our house and what we want. We have been engrossed in dining and our own conversation, we did not notice the abundance of people inside and outside waiting to dine.

We decide to walk the two blocks to the theatre. An usher takes us to the second-row seating.

"I hope you are properly impressed, Mrs. Price."

"Detective, I don't know when you had the time to plan all this for me."

He takes my hand in his, I've got my whole life planned around you," and brings my hand to his lips and kisses my hand sweetly. *Believe me, I know I have won the state lottery.*

The show is entertaining and filled with music of our era. Super talents give their performances their all, engaging the audience to sing along with them. Bo and I are enjoying ourselves, and the show last almost two hours. We walk outside after the show and Bo motions for a taxi to take us back to the Inn.

"That was great Bo. Doesn't it make you wander what the kids of today are going to be listening it in twenty years."

He smiles that awesome grin, and says "he has no idea."

When we arrive at the Inn, Bo leads me up to the room, "I think my bride is tired tonight."

"A bit," I take a nightie that Rene had given me at our little lunch into the bathroom. I come out shortly and Bo is already in the bed. "Wow, more sexy nightwear." He holds my head up to his, and kisses me till I can't breathe. "Goodnight, D."

He lays back and he turns over with his back to me. *What? What just happened?* With hands closed, I knock on his back like it is a door "excuse me, you kiss me like that and turn away? And you were saying that I am tired?" *Oh, no, I will not be ignored.* I get out of the bed circle around to his side and he is laying there, eyes wide open, amused as hell that I am the one wanting him to love me. He grabs my arms and pulls me back over him into the bed, laughing,

"So, you need more attention, do you?"

"Well, I didn't put this nightie on to be ignored. My ego is pretty much deflated now."

"I shouldn't have teased you, I didn't know what you'd do. I don't want you to think I expect it. I want you to want me too."

"There may be punishment for this little prank. Right now, you are wasting time," and I laugh too, because I love his playfulness.

In the morning, Bo is playing with the ribbon on my nightie, and he begins talking. "You know that first time I saw you in my office, I was enthralled with you. Your confidence in yourself was so sexy to me. I stayed on task but I made a note to myself, that you were a complex creature that I needed to know. Your sisters were equally complex. I mentioned you and your family to my mother and she filled me in some."

Oh, I am a sleepy head, and I ask him if his mother had mentioned, "in the mornings I need coffee before conversation."

"You just won't do Dolly, I'm trying to give you a compliment, and all you think of is coffee. He smacks me on the lips, "coffee it is."

He picks up the phone and orders breakfast for us both for the room, says thank you and hangs up. He rubs my lips with his thumb. "You haven't asked me in a couple of days Dolly, I don't mind telling you without being asked, I'm completely captivated and love you so much." He replaces his thumb with his lips.

There's a knock on the door, "Your coffee fix has arrived. If only I could be your fix in the morning, "

"Awe, poor guy, your time was last night."

Yes, it was my love," and he gets up to get the tray at the door.

I get up and go to our little table. Bo sets the tray down and pours me coffee, adds sugar and cream. He puts a napkin in my lap. "Enjoy." He is eating breakfast and I'm on my second cup of coffee.

"Today is our last day, what would you like to do?"

"I don't have an opinion. Has my concierge no plan?"

"Let's go down to River street where they have a cobblestone river walk with shops and restaurants and we can just hang out."

We get our showers and leave within an hour. Another taxi takes us where throngs of people are all about jogging, shopping and enjoying music on most every corner. We eat lunch on a rooftop lounge and watch the boat traffic in the waterway. Mid- afternoon, we go back to the Inn and decide to cool off in the pool. The cabana boy delivers wine spritzers several times, and we are back in the room by five.

"You got sun today D."

"Yes, I can feel it on my shoulders.

"Tired? Want to take a nap?"

"I think I will take a power nap."

"While you are napping, I'm going downstairs and call the station and Mother to see if all is well."

When I wake, Bo is reading a paper and has the television on but no volume.

"What time is it?"

"Almost eight o clock."

"Lordy, I cannot believe it."

"Feel rested?"

"You should have wakened me. Everything okay at home?"

"Yes, are you hungry?"

"Not that much."

"How about a hamburger?"

"Okay, you sure you don't mind, not going out?" He picks up the phone and orders it.

"How's your mother? Recuperated yet?"

"She said all of your family was very complimentary, and to thank you for the big bowl of potted white orchids. She told me the card said from both of us. He smiles and tells me, "Thank You. Apparently, Mr. Fox said he would be here in town Sunday and invited her to the Sunday dinner."

"Oh my, I imagine there will be some claws out, especially with the splitting of furniture, etc. Your mother may get a real sense of our family's dysfunction."

"Seriously?"

"Didn't you say this morning that we Diamond girls were all complex?"

"I did. What do you want from your parent's estate?"

"There isn't any furniture I wanted until you told me that we're building a new home. Now I can probably use some of it. I'd like to have my mother's cookbook, maybe a roll top desk that they have had for years. She has some beautiful China sets, including a glass candle wick setting with all the accessories. I like old dishes. In some ways, I believe I am old fashioned. Does that surprise you?"

"Not at all. Do you think you and your sisters want the same things?"

"It's possible. Until recently, and I'll be honest, without your gentle prodding, I was saturated in bitterness about Denise and out of spite, I would deny her anything."

"Prodding?"

"I said gentle. On our wedding day, I never uttered the words cheated, or anything near it. I said I was moving on with a full heart, something like that."

"Did Denise apologize?"

"No, it is not her makeup to admit wrong doing, I suppose that is true for any one of us girls."

There is a knock, and Bo opens the door. "Supper is here."

The Inn is delivering on all its promises to provide relaxation, comfort, and quality amenities. The hamburgers are hot, and the Inn has seen to every detail. Bo and I prepare our own bun tops with mustard and mayo, pickle, tomato and purple onion. I cut my burger in half, and offer to do the same with Bo's. I take a few of the vegetable chips. It is all very tasty.

"What time do we need to leave tomorrow?"

"Our flight is at nine. We need to be at the airport at seven forty-five a.m."

"Did the police chief say there are any problems.?"

"One or two. I can't really talk about them."

"Oh, okay."

"I might have to be out of town next week a couple of days."

"You serious?"

"Yes." I know he can see I am concerned.

"I know what you are thinking." I look down, and Bo tells me to look at him. "Dolly, what happened last time was an isolated incident. There has never been a problem in my long career. I follow every safety procedure. I am not a rookie or a risk taker. I want you to believe me when I say these things to you." I look down again.

He slides his chair over to mine and cups his hands around my face. "I don't want you to worry about my me or my job. Promise you won't worry."

I look straight into his eyes and soul, "I cannot promise you that."

He brings my mouth to his and sighs, "I don't know how to convince you D," and he kisses me. I want more of his kiss and put my arms around him. He releases his lips on mine, "I'll be safe and return to you. I promise you," and he gives me small kisses all along my cheek. "Want to get a bath while I get a shower?"

"Yes, that will feel good."

I am thinking about what he has said, I am aware I am losing some of my independence and that aspect scares me too. Bo kisses the back of my neck right before he steps in the shower. I lather up and rinse down and lay back at the back of the tub reflecting on the last few days, my honeymoon, and wondering what daily married life will be. God has blessed me with this incredible man that treats me with respect and kindness and so much love and passion. I am a lucky woman. Bo steps out with towel on and leans down to smooch. Are you ready to vacate?"

"You don't want to join me?"

"I want you to join me, here's a towel for you. Or do you want me to take you wet all over again?"

"Well, that was exciting, but not again. I step out and dry off with him watching me.

"Are you losing weight?"

"A gentleman never discusses a lady's weight."

"I wasn't going to discuss it, I just noticed you are losing weight. I don't care about what size you are. Whatever you are happy with, I am happy with."

"I'll remember that. I always tell my friends the man that brings me chocolates will win my heart. I'll know then he doesn't care how big I get."

"If I weren't busy now," and he takes me in his arms, "I'd go out and get you some right now, but like I said, I am busy for the next few hours."

"Hours, you say?"

"Don't bruise my ego, or it might be just a few minutes," and he laughs.

He lays me on the bed and takes each of my hands and puts them both over my head and holds them there and nibbles my ear, and kisses my cheek and finds my lips. I am his without further discussion. I just enjoy.

Bo is always on time and he wakes me gently. "Time to get up, sleepy girl. Your coffee will be here shortly." He has showered and in his boxers. I hustle to the shower and get in and out.

He is dressed, and has my coffee fixed. I sip some of my coffee and start dressing, then apply my makeup and put my hair up in a barrette. I put my last clothes and personal items in my suitcase. I pour another cup of coffee. Bo gives me a kiss, "I'm going to the lobby, check out, call a cab. Can you be ready when I return?"

"I can, captain my captain."

He winks and leaves. I check around the bathroom, the shower and all around for any last-minute items, and visit the sandbox. I have finished the pot of coffee, and grab my toothbrush out and brush my teeth again.

Bo knocks and enters. "Ready, Mrs. Price?"

"Yes sir."

He glances at me again. "Did you say sir?"

"Bless your heart, you can't help yourself, you're always going to be on time, on schedule, on task. Love you."

"That's all it takes. Love you too."

It's a short ride to the airport, and we are in the boarding area quickly. Bo checks in, and then turns me and asks if I want more coffee. We wait about thirty minutes and then the agent calls for first class.

"Good morning," I say to the stewardess. She points to our seats. "I'll bring coffee. Orange juice?"

Bo answers "yes, please, for both of us."

The stewardess brings a morning paper, coffee and offers us cream and sugar. "Would you like some bottled water?"

"Thanks, please," and I smile.

Bo takes my hand, kisses it and puts it back down. He starts reading the paper, all the way through to the stock page. I never get the paper at my house. "Do you read the paper every day?"

"Yes," he smiles. "At the department. Why?"

"Just curious. Would you stay longer in the morning if I started receiving the paper?"

He kisses my nose. "Probably no. If I stayed later, I probably wouldn't be reading. You know, making up for lost time."

"I see. I thought I was captivating, not trying to set a record."

"You do both and picks up my hand again."

The flight seems quick and the captain announces it is cloudy in Sanford and we will be landing in less than fifteen minutes. I finish my water and the stewardess collects the empty bottle and everything else.

I ask Bo if he is going to the department when we get home. "Yes, aren't you going to the store?"

"Yes, and if I I wanted to stay and read the paper with you?"

"I could make headlines with you, but not read." He grins. We unbuckle and deplane.

In baggage claim, Bo takes charge and grabs our bags and we make our way to the Tahoe. Bo opens the door, and tells me to buckle up.

"Geez."

Bo starts the Tahoe and turns on the air conditioning. He takes out his phone and makes a call while we are sitting in the parking lot.

"I'll be there in about an hour and a half, thanks, Steve, yes, we had a great time. This marriage thing suits me, and he looks over to me. I think I'll keep her."

He pulls out in the traffic and we are on our way. I pull my phone out, turn it on, and I call Julie.

"Hey, hey, this is your great white leader, returning home broke. Have you made any money while I was gone? What? The electricity has been turned off? I look at Bo, can I borrow some money?"

Bo pulls out his wallet and credit card and hands me his American Express and hands it to me. "Yeah, I think I'll keep him. See you in an hour."

Our eyes meet and we both snicker. "Are you cooking for me tonight?"

"Of course, what would you like? Beef wellington? Coquile St. Jac? How 'bout some round steak and rice and gravy?"

"I will eat something light for lunch. Are you okay for lunch?"

"Yep, I'm used to eating at work, by myself, all alone, no companionship, makes me wonder why I got married."

"Well, certainly not for lunch, I know this for a fact."

He drives to the back of my store, opens the door, and sets me down. I'm in the open door and leaning against the seat. He leans in and kisses me, a nice wet kiss, "I'm going to miss you this afternoon."

Bo says hi to Julie. "Here she is, safe and sound." He gives me a short kiss on my forehead. "Call me if you need me."

"Well?" Julie is searching my face for answers. "How was the honeymoon? Spill your guts!"

"It was awful, worse than anything, he is so cheap. He didn't want to spend any money on ...Julie interrupts, "you are so lying."

"Yes, I am, he is incredible Julie. I am so blessed and I am going to make him happy every day or I hope to."

"I am so happy for you Dolly, and.... the honeymoon part?"

"Julie, this is not like you, wanting to know intimate details. Better than the best, I hope I make him happy."

"Everything is okay here, however Rita has called three times, and said for you to call her as soon as you get here. Denise has called once."

I ring Rita and she answers the phone immediately. "Are you sitting on the phone?"

"Almost. You're not going to believe this. Denise calls me and wants to know if Bo signed a pre-nuptial. She says she's going to take him one to sign, thinks you are stupid for not consulting her about the jeopardy you placed your sisters in with the farm trust."

"Are you kidding me? Is she even here?"

"Yeah, she got here this morning. She is questioning whether you had the money to put on that wedding, suggesting you have had Mom's necklace and maybe sold it, to pay for the wedding. She told Rhett 'something wasn't right' about the whole thing, the wedding out of the blue, pardon the pun Sis. Rhett thinks that Denise believes Bo is a gold digger."

My blood pressure is rising. "Okay, I have heard enough. What do you think I should do?"

"Dolly, do you have a pre-nuptial?"

"No, it never occurred to me, never, but I will tell you. I am not concerned in the least."

"Well, if you're not concerned, neither am I. I support you."

"Let me rephrase that last statement. I'm not concerned about Bo's finances only that he will be attacked by her. I know how Denise can ferret for information until she finds what she can use against you. She can be irrational, even dogmatic. I don't want him to feel he needs to explain or justify. I don't know what she is basing her accusations on."

"She says detectives don't make inordinate amounts of money."

"I told her he has already retired from FDLE. It didn't seem to faze her. She called Mr. Fox, and is calling all the area pawn shops, even did a google search for the necklace at pawn shops."

"I'm telling you she is off the chain."

"Do you think I should call Bo? I think he is busy this afternoon. I don't want him to be caught off guard, and yet I don't want him to think our family is so crazy."

"Too late, and speaking of crazy, Denise thinks we should expand the fernery on the land Daddy has reserved for conservation around the lake."

"Expand? Why? We can't handle the operation now. Juan cannot handle any more. By the way, Bo has a great idea for Juan. When I told him we were going to empty out the house, he suggested we give or loan the residence to Juan for his family and start having the family dinners at our own houses. Does that sound like anyone that wants to grab the family business?'

"You have to admit you guys got married pretty fast Dolly."

"Yes, we did, but sometimes you just know when a person is genuine and kind and you just respond to it, it's like God is steering us all the way. If you knew how he responds to my volatility about Denise, how he handled my relationship with the captain, then you'd be convinced and understand what I know to be true. Trust is the hardest for me, and time after time, he has proven himself worthy."

"Don't be surprised if she waltzes in there and demands you go get a pre-nuptial."

"I'm not going to bother Bo this afternoon. I'll talk to him about it tonight at dinner."

"On another subject, I froze some of your wedding cake and took it out of the freezer for you today and I have some pictures Rhett took from the wedding in an envelope. Look at them. You guys are all starry eyed."

"That's us, starry eyed. We had a great honeymoon, just easy and spontaneous. I am so happy. I have found my true love Rita."

"I know it. I see it every time I am around you two."

"Okay, well this is some kind of news flash. I'll keep you posted. Is the Sunday dinner this weekend?"

"Oh, Bo talked to his mother and she said Mr. Fox has invited her, so I guess he is planning on coming. I told Bo it might be an eye opener into our family dysfunction. I'll stop by your work and pick up the photos and cake. Will that be okay?"

"Yeah, yeah."

I have missed lunch and I am hungry. Julie offers me a slim fast bar.

"I need to go to the grocery store and get groceries for the house and fix my husband supper tonight."

Julie tells me she isn't expecting any help from me today anyway."

"Oh, I almost forgot." I reach in my purse and pull out the presents for her and Stephanie. "Something from Savannah for all you did for me."

Julie opens it and is thrilled. She loves it. "It is too much with the money Bo gave me."

"I saw him give you an envelope, but he hasn't told me what he gave you."

"Five hundred dollars each. I was shocked. Frankly, I'd rather work for him."

"Very funny."

"Okay, I'm off to the store and to Rita's. Did you hear the drama?"

"Parts of it."

"To be continued…. and I roll my eyebrows."

The store isn't crowded and I zip around. At the checkout, an old friend sees me and offers congratulations. "This is the biggest news around town. Nobody knew it happened until it was all over. There are a lot of ladies out there who thought he had an out of town girlfriend."

"Oh, I didn't know."

"Wow, that ring is something special. Best wishes Dolly, you deserve happiness."

"Thank you."

The cashier butts in and said she just noticed my ring too. "That is beautiful, I bet your husband didn't buy that around here."

I smile, write a check and hurry to my car and drive to Rita's workplace. I park in front of Rita's office and go in. Rita's secretary greets me and says "Congratulations,"

"Thank you, we are very, very, happy."

Rita waves me in and hands me the envelope, and then the picture. It is a wonderful photo under the tree of Bo giving me my ring. He looks so handsome. I think my eyes are flooded with emotion. "There is significant detail of my dress, don't you think?"

"I think it is great of you two. Here's the cake."

"I just left the store, and I am cooking round steak tonight, I'll call you tomorrow."

I am home and start dinner. I put on a pot of rice, clean the yellow squash, chop some onion for the squash, make a salad, tea and prepare my round steak. I set the table and chill a bottle of wine. It's about six o'clock. My phone rings. It's Bo.

"I'm going to be home around six thirty. Is that okay?"

"Of course."

I decide to make a hoe cake on the stove top. It's basically a big biscuit cooked in a skillet. This way I don't have to turn on my oven. I begin frying the steak, so when Bo gets home, I will already have the kitchen sort of cleaned up. I flip the hoe cake and it is perfectly golden. I put some honey on the table for the hoe cake. I'll save the graham cracker slice for a late snack so I can light a candle on it. I am determined to keep the romance going.

I hear Bo unlocking the door. He is singing, 'honey I'm home, and I've had a hard day.. give me a cold one and ....

"Are those the correct words?"

"I don't know," and he gives me a big kiss. "Hello."

"Hello back. Supper is ready. Want to wait a few and have a beer? Or I have wine for supper."

"Yes, wine will be good. We can eat if you're ready. Let me go wash my hands." He puts down a file folder on the table.

I put supper on the table and he comes to the kitchen and helps. "This looks amazing, and I'm starved. I had a visitor today that was a surprise."

"Someone wishing you congratulations like I've had all day? Of course, everyone is looking at my ring, not my happy face."

He smiles. Chief Thunder happy too, glad to be in wigwam with my yellow hair. He kisses my forehead, and opens the wine and pours us a glass. "To us."

"Who was your visitor? I hope it wasn't the safety instructor."

"Not exactly, it was your sister Denise."

I gulp loud.

"Easy there."

"Yes, she called and asked if I was available and she came into my office. She appeared before I had an opportunity to call you to see what was up."

"Yeah, Rita exploded the bomb shell to me on the phone." I fix Bo's plate and we begin eating. I will use restraint and let him tell me in his own time. Denise will not ruin my first dinner home.

"What is this?" and points to the hoe cake.

"It's called hoe cake. You can eat it with butter or honey."

He smiles when he sees the honey, because we purchased the honey from the Savannah Bee Company on our honeymoon.

"I have never had it, or squash with onion for that matter. It's full of flavor. Round steak is one of my favorites," and he sips some wine.

I am eating salad and meat and I am anxious. Bo seems to be of hearty appetite and enjoying everything. "Did you speak to your mother?"

"Just a few minutes. I was fielding calls and then Denise came in. She is not very diplomatic, is she?"

"Really? Could have fooled me."

"Yeah, she came in with a folder."

"Is that it?" I am reaching for it.

"Um, no. That's mine."

I put it back in its spot.

She starts out by saying that "she is in charge of the family trust. And I quote, "This is a family trust, fairly simple but iron clad."

"Iron clad? I didn't quite understand where she was going with her statement. She went on about how her sister, meaning you, don't realize the ramifications of your own actions."

"What?"

"I believe she thinks you married into a wrong class Dolly."

"I am so sorry, I did try to warn you about our family dynamics."

"Oh, she is bold, brought a pre-nuptial back dated before the wedding date."

I gasp.

"She said she was politely asking me to sign it, for your well- being, that is if I cared about you. I answered the polite way would have been for her to give it to you to give it to me and ask me to sign it."

"What did she say then?" I'm pouring myself some more wine, and Bo some too.

"She dismissed it."

"I asked her if she minded if I read it first."

"She fully expected me to."

"I read it, scratch out the date and put in the correct date, initial it and sign my name. I reach in my drawer, and pull out my financial portfolio, copy it, and tell her I don't need any of your money. She looked completely dumbfounded. I get up and show her the door, and tell her it was nice seeing her again."

"You're not kidding me."

"No. It's all right D. I am glad to do it."

"What did the document say?"

"It's standard, basically absolves me of any financial interest. What we have Dolly goes beyond an amount of dollars."

"You did not have to do this."

"It's done. We can move on. I guess I won't be able to borrow any money from you."

"I am not amused."

"D. I have prepared a pre-nuptial for you to sign for me as well."

I swallow hard. I didn't see this coming. He reaches for the file folder. "It's got a lot of legal eagle garb in it. It's pretty clear though, even a simpleton can understand."

"A simpleton?" The hair on my back is raising.

I open the folder. This agreement between the party of the first part. Boyd Franklin Price, and the second party, Amelia Dollene Diamond Price, and I continue scanning the paper.

Amelia Price promises to be indebted to Boyd Franklin Price forever, to love him, and give him her whole heart, trust and believe he will support her, help spend his money to make him happy and provide him with humor, and zeal for life and a lifetime companionship. I gasp again, and look at him. "You are crazy beyond belief."

"I wasn't crazy until I married you. Will you sign please?"

There is a pen in the folder, and I sign my name. Amelia Dollene Diamond.

"There is a name you forgot to add. Price. P-R- I- C- E."

It will be the first time I have signed it and I smile. He passes me over another piece of paper. "It's our checking account signature card for the bank. Please close your personal account. There is no your money, or my money, only our money. Are you good with that?"

"The store?"

"That's yours of course Dolly, build your bank account up and if you want me to invest some of your money for you, then I will."

"I don't know what I did to deserve you."

"Dolly, don't be discouraged with Denise, or anybody. Don't give her any power to control your feelings. Let's keep our goals on what we want out of life, our aspirations, where our love takes us."

I am shaking my head yes. "You are right, I know. Except for that simpleton comment."

Bo starts laughing and cannot contain himself. "I worked on that word to goad you and it worked."

"You think you are clever trying to push my buttons, seriously? You need to remember how creative I am, and that paybacks are just that. Paybacks Detective."

"You only call me Detective when you are trying to make a point."

"Do I? and have I made my point?"

"It's crystal clear. On another point, I'd like to compliment you on dinner tonight. I experienced something new. I really enjoyed it."

"Compliments get you gold stars, and stars can be redeemed for rewards."

"Is there a chart somewhere I can see my progress?"

"Perhaps." I get up to clear the dishes. I load the dishwasher and put away the leftovers. "Do you want me to make you a lunch for tomorrow?"

He has a deer caught in the headlight look. "I will not be here tomorrow. I will be back around nine in the evening."

I look away and continue to put away dishes and food. Bo brings some dishes to the sink, and comes up behind me and holds me and kisses my neck. "I'm sorry, don't be upset. I don't like upsetting you." He kisses the back of my head. I turn around and I am emotional.

"I'll be fine," and I am whimpering.

"You don't seem fine."

"I am fine."

"Show me you are alright."

I look up at him, and kiss him lightly.

"Is that the best you can do?"

"You are really pushing the envelope tonight."

"Just so you know, I am never going to let you be mad at me." He picks up my face and kisses me so passionately, I must respond.

"I love you Dolly so much."

"I love you too."

"I'm going to get my shower, want to join me?"

"Let me finish up here."

He turns to go into the bedroom and bath. Soon, I hear the shower running. I pour the rest of the wine bottle into my glass and stand over the sink and just stare. I wipe the counters, and re wipe them. All the food is in the refrigerator except the cake. I start cleaning the sink with Barkeepers cleanser. I am thinking and wiping and full of angst. I drink the rest of my wine and put the glass under the water, add detergent and start washing it. Hell, I can do this. I'm a strong woman. It just makes me sad and I know I will worry. For the first time in a long while, I wish I had the captain with me. I know I have a new captain. I'll get through this. I can and I will.

I head for the bathroom. A bath will relax me. Bo is finishing and shuts off the shower. I turn the bath water on and add some bubbly.

"I was hoping you'd come shower with me," and he sounds disappointed. Bo puts a towel around his waist.

I can't speak. I don't want him to know how twisted I am inside. He senses something, he always does. He turns off my water. I already have my robe on.

"Okay, we need to get this out, let's talk." He picks me up and takes me to the bed, and sits with me. He puts his hand around my neck and pulls my face to his chest. He sighs that heavy sigh. "Dolly, I missed you all afternoon. I couldn't wait to get back to you tonight. And tomorrow, it will be the same. I'll be home before nine. You look frightened and you are withdrawing. I will be in the next county and I will be home before nine, I promise."

"You smell good."

"Well, that's a start, I'll take it." He takes my lip and bites it gently. You are my everything D. You have been through so much more in life than worrying about me getting hurt. It comes with my job; the possibility is always there. We can deal with this just like I will deal with all those holiday hours you work. Yes, I have seen you guys working late at your store. I know it will come again, and then it will be me worried about you, but I'll cope. You can cope too." He opens my robe up and puts his arms around me. "Are we good?"

"Yes, good." He pulls on my lips and kisses, and kisses and kisses me hard. *Yes, I'm good.*

I go back in the kitchen, get his cake, a fork, light a tiny candle and grab a glass of water. I take it into the room and he is sitting up fiddling with the television. He smiles.

"Graham cracker." And I hand it to him. "I'm going to get a bath."

"Wait," and he feeds me a fork full.

"Yum," and I head for the bath. I put the hot water back on, and lather up. I feel better and put a cold face cloth on my face and breathe in. I don't know what is wrong with me. I have moved from strong to weak. Perhaps another visit to Dr. Mallory should be scheduled soon."

I hear the TV get louder. I get out, dry off, and put my robe on. "Ready for lights out?

"Yes, come get in on my side D."

I am on his side, and he reaches into my robe and lifts me on the bed to him. He tastes sweet. "Thank you for the cake, and for supper, for caring about me, for loving me, and for trying to understand. I'm not going to let anything happen to us. Turn over, and let me massage your neck and back. You are so tense."

It is just what I need to settle down and relax our first night home.

It's six o'clock and I hear the shower running. Without fail, Bo is always an early riser. I start the coffee, and some bacon and put a bowl of grits in the microwave to cook. I am finishing my first cup and the bacon is crisp and ready to drain. I pour Bo a glass of orange juice, and set it on the table with his silverware. I turn the fry pan on low and wait to find out how he wants his eggs cooked this Friday morning.

I am pouring my second cup when I smell Bo's cologne. He whispers in my ear, "Good Morning Yellow Hair." He nuzzles my neck. I turn around, "Good Morning Chief. One egg or two? Scrambled or over easy? I have grits too."

"One, sunny side up and grits." He grabs a cup of coffee too. He is clean shaven and dressed in a Sherriff's department polo.

"Different job today?"

"Yes," and the answers stop there.

"Do you want toast with jelly?"

"Okay, but I can get it."

I take his plate to the table with another cup of coffee for me and sit down with him.

Bo asks me what I have planned for today.

"Catching up on work. I going to call Carly today and discuss her wedding."

"Carly is the one marrying Denise's son?"

"Yes, his name is Bingham. And we have the high school prom tomorrow night so I will be making corsages all day and most of tomorrow."

"You have to work on Saturday?"

"Yes, and remember we have the Sunday dinner this weekend."

"Is this guava jelly?"

"Yes, my mom made it. It was her last batch she made a couple of months ago."

"Why aren't you eating breakfast with me?"

"I wasn't hungry right now, just wanted coffee."

"Did you sleep well last night?"

"It was one of the best nights. The massage was a special treat for me."

"Me too," and he snickers.

"I'm thinking two gold stars were earned last night."

"I want to see the rewards chart soon, so I can set myself a goal."

Bo finishes his coffee. I am going now, and I will take a cup to go. "Thank you for breakfast this morning. Tomorrow I will fix breakfast for you."

He takes his plate to the sink.

"Are you going to eat here tonight, or will you eat before you come home?"

"If you want to eat late, we can go out for pizza, or I can eat beforehand and kidnap you for dessert. Door one or door two?"

"I'll have pizza here for us and dessert."

"Okay, give your husband of exactly of six days a proper send off to work." I put my arms around him and we kiss each other for a longer than usual time. "I'll miss you D."

He is gone, and I busy myself cleaning up the kitchen, and get a glass of water and go back to the shower and get ready for work. It will be a busy day working on one corsage after another. I have had a nice four-day getaway and so it is time to plant myself at the store and produce some work.

"Good Morning Julie." I enter with a happy heart.

"Want some coffee?"

"Yes, thanks." I grab some corsage orders and begin working. Currently we have 31 orders for prom. To be sure, more late orders will follow. All through the day, Julie and I take turns answering the phone. I make the wristlets and every once in a while, she joins me and packages and boxes what I have made, checking my work to be sure the colors are correct. The oldies are playing on Pandora and we talk about some of the expensive dresses the parents are buying their kids for the big dance. We eat lunch while we work, a slim fast bar and a diet soda is my choice of lunch today. Julie tells me how beautiful my wedding was, and that folks in town are surprised the two of us got married without anyone knowing we were dating.

"All I know is I am the luckiest woman alive. Today, I need to call Carly before she goes to work."

"You better stop and do it now, because it already half past two."

I step to my desk and try to reach her. Carly answers. "Aunt Dolly are you back from your honeymoon?"

"I am, had a wonderful time. We went to Savannah. How is the bride holding up?"

"I just want to tell you your wedding was phenomenal, and beautiful and so classy. Everyone of course was surprised but you guys looked like a wedding poster, so much in love."

"We are. Is Denise being cooperative?"

"It's better, like I mentioned last time we talked."

"Well, listen, I have an idea about the centerpieces. We could use a low glass terrarium bowl with five calla lilies deep inside the bowl encircling the bottom, sort of like chasing callas around the bottom. It's contemporary and uses the same flowers as the picture, unique and relatively inexpensive. I can make one, take a picture on my phone and shoot it to you. For the bridesmaids, we can use three callas and green hanging amaranthus. All that will be a different look and compliment the vintage theme you've got going. Oh, I just remembered you're probably coming Sunday, so I can make a sample for you to take home to show your mom and grandma. That will include them on the wedding plans."

"Aunt Dolly, you are the greatest."

"Tell it to my husband," and I am laughing.

"I bet he already knows."

"Anyway, we can put that centerpiece on the crocheted table toppers."

"Can't wait to see you. Do you have any pictures yet from the wedding?"

"Some candid shots and a few good black and white photos which showcases the beautiful ferns."

"Great, I'm on my way to work, feeling excited now. Thanks, and see you Sunday."

It reminds me I have that photo in my car, and I forgot to show Bo. I go to my car and grab it. I show Julie.

"Wow, this is a beautiful photo of you two."

"I love it, I wonder if I have a frame out there in the store, I'm going to put the picture on my nightstand and see if Bo notices it tonight."

"Good idea."

Julie goes out front. 'Fed Ex is here."

"O really?"

For you, probably a wedding present.

I open it and it is a three-pound box of See's assorted chocolates. Attached is a small card. "The more you eat, the more I have to love."

Julie shakes her head in disbelief. "Hasn't he noticed you've lost weight?"

"Yes, it's his way of teasing me. Julie, my husband remembers everything I say. Want a chocolate? Aren't you thankful we had a slim fast for lunch?"

I return to the bench making corsages for a couple of hours more. I tell Julie I will never understand why these kids wait till the last minutes to order their corsages."

"Because they are kids, and they live in an instant world."

"You are so right. I am finished for the day." Julie comes over and boxes the last one and sets it in the cooler.

My cell rings and I am thinking it is Bo. I pull it from my jeans pocket. No, it is Rita.

"What up girl?"

"Is that any way to answer the phone?"

"I knew it was you, good grief."

"Have you heard from Denise?"

"No, but she went to see Bo, and asked him to sign a pre -nuptial back dated before the wedding."

"She didn't."

"I'm afraid she did."

"I think at this point you call that a nuptial, not a pre-nuptial."

"Is Bo angry?"

"Not at all, I think he said he found her undiplomatic and impolite, something like that. He signed, gave her his own financial overview, sent her on her way, after he corrected the date. Bo won't sign anything questionable with an incorrect date. As Bo says, it's done, let's move on. He is focused on us, not our family drama."

"Speaking of drama, what are we having for dinner Sunday? I counted fifteen people or so. Since we are dividing up things, why don't we have something like lasagna and a big salad, and garlic bread, so we can carry on our business, and then not have to slave over a stove for an hour and a half."

"I guess I can make the lasagna Saturday night and put it in the refrigerator. Rita, can you make a gigantic salad? and I'll do the bread Sunday in the am. You call Denise. I just can't deal with her right now. I'm sure she will show up with plenty of attitude, ready to parcel out objects, items she discerns who will get what. Bo told me Mr. Fox invited his mother to come to dinner. Janet is rather refined, and it might be an eye popper for her to witness us girls feuding over relish trays and furniture. I want you to bring up the idea of Juan taking over the house idea. I don't want Denise knowing that was Bo's idea given the latest development."

"For sure. What are ya'll doing tonight? Want to go out to dinner with Roan and me?"

"Thanks, no. Bo is out of town till nine. We're having pizza at home when he arrives."

"Oh. Okay, we'll see you on Sunday. Bye."

Julie has shut down the store and is waiting on me to lock up.

"I'll see you tomorrow Julie, I'm headed to the grocery store."

"I put your chocolates in your car."

"Oh good, I've got an idea to play a joke on Bo tonight."

She shakes her head again, "you guys are having too much fun."

At the grocery store, I get all the ingredients for lasagna, and Cuban bread, and some staples, and arrive home in an hour. With groceries in my hand, I pull open the door and smell cleaner. Rounding the hallway, everything is spotless. Merry Maids card on the kitchen counter again. Yes, it was last Friday when they were here last. Is this going to be a weekly surprise? He won't get an argument out of me. Right now, I hate messing up my kitchen. I turn on my oven to cook crème brulee. It has four ingredients and it's quick. The ramekins are in my pan and I add a water bathe and set the timer. There are three choices tonight for dessert; Chocolates, Crème Brûlée or me."

I go ahead and start my tomato and meat sauce for lasagna in a big pot. It can simmer for a couple of hours. I have a glass of white wine and think back to my days of the captain when he kept me company on the weekends. My life has changed so much.

I place the wedding picture on the night stand on his side of the bed. Now for my joke. I take all the pieces of chocolate and put them in a zip lock bag. I stage a trail of brown crinkle paper ramekins all over the floor and put the box lid and rest of the papers on the bed. It looks like I have been eating chocolate for hours. I'll show him 'more of me to love.' My cell in my pocket startles me. It's Bo.

"Hey, just calling to let you know I'll be there in twenty minutes. Want me to pick up the pizza?"

"No, they are delivering. Everything go alright today?"

"Yes." *And that is my answer, short and to the point.*

"See you in a few." I look around and it is comical, all the wrappers scattered about with the bulk of them laying across the bed. I take a picture with my phone to show Julie tomorrow.

I'm taking out the crème brulee out of the oven and out of the water bath and hear Bo driving up. I rush to the bathroom and shut the bathroom door.

Bo comes in "Hey, something smells good." And then I hear him giggling. He is in the bedroom." Oh, my lord, what have I done. He calls for me, Dolly?"

"I'm in here," I moan a little, "feeling sickish,"

I hear him say, "I guess so." He goes somewhere, and I come out. Where is he? He appears with the trash can and starts picking up the papers. He looks at me and I am laughing my head off. He starts laughing and says, "you're not sick." He gathers me up and kisses me. "Hello. This is very funny stuff. I assume you still have the chocolates."

"Assume nothing with me. More of me to love? You should be ashamed."

"I'm shamelessly in love." He pulls me to him. I think a nice thank you is in order." I energetically kiss him, "thank you baby, ready for a cold beer?" The doorbell rings. "Whoops, the pizza is here." I open the door and give the guy a tip. "Dinner will be served."

We're eating pizza on the porch by candlelight, talking about *my* events of the day *not his*. "Are you tired?"

"A little, mostly from driving, and being outside in the sun."

I know this is the end of the conversation about his work out of town.

"Tomorrow I'm going to finish your greenhouse, and mow Mother's yard. You still working tomorrow?"

"Yes, at least till three."

"What's cooking?"

"Meat sauce for lasagna on Sunday. Are most of the guys in the department married?"

"Even split, I'd say."

"Do all of you guys work out together?"

"Do I look like I work out?"

"I think you probably do, you have a nice physique, but I don't know when you do."

"At different times. Sometimes at lunch, and some in the late afternoon after my shift. I had to meet a lot of physical requirements for FDLE, so I guess I've always been in shape."

"Is our married life like you thought it would be?"

"All I know is I can't wait to get home to you in the evenings, that it is hard for me to leave you in the mornings. I am having the most fun, the best sexual relationship ever, and I look forward to every new day because you make every day memorable." And you do it so effortlessly. I am a kid in a candy store, trying new flavors., and I love it. I Love You."

"That was quite a testimony, Detective. The bar has been set high for me to maintain, but I will try and be up for the challenge. Let's start with fun and sexual, and memorable."

I stand up, and take Bo's hand, and lead him to the boudoir. "Shower first and then we can start making memories."

"See, this is what I am talking about, you are too good to me."

We are in the shower and things are steaming up, this man of mine is so special. It is a win, win situation.

The Ultimate Surprise

Neither one of us stir until six o'clock. I am still on my side and he is behind me with his arm over me. I wish I could sleep in today, I think I'm just tired all the time. I'm not used to cooking for two and spending all my time with a husband. I didn't realize how happy I could be.

Bo is awaking and kisses my back. I turn around and face him. With eyes still closed, I point with my finger and pat to my neck. That's where I like him to kiss me. I bury my head in his chest and kiss him. I mumble, "can't we sleep in today?"

"Of course, you can go back to sleep."

I am still wrapped in his arms and so satisfied. I am sleeping away and do not realize he has left the bed, showered and is preparing breakfast. I smell coffee, and that is an instant alarm for me. At the dinette, Bo is checking stocks on his phone. An empty crème brûlée cup is on the counter beside him.

"Breakfast is ready, Cheese Grits and bacon and eggs."

I make my way to the coffee pot, and he stops me and holds me, and kisses my forehead, "Hey, you were tired. Am I wearing you out? I don't think you are eating enough. Have a seat. I'll get your coffee."

"Looks good Chef Price. Tastes good too, you have got my coffee down pat, one star for coffee, two stars last night. Bonus, one star for letting me sleep."

"I see you checking your stock. Are you making any money to offset what you spent on our wedding?

"Don't worry, we're good."

"Oh, the architect has our plan ready for the house. He said he would drop it by your store. I told him I would be in the yard most of the day. If you don't mind, and since I know you're busy, I will eat lunch with mother since I'll be mowing."

"Okay, who is the architect again, his name?"

"The Kimball Group, Miles Kimball."

"Oh, okay, did you remember the porch?"

"Of course."

"And my kitchen?"

"Yes ma'am."

"You're a good boy."

"If you want more coffee, you better start eating some of your breakfast," and he is giving me the do it or else look.

"Minus one star chef, coffee service can be improved."

Bo is snickering. "Alright then, I'm getting it, you start eating." He gets up and fixes me another cup.

"Thank you, I have eaten my egg, and part of my bacon. How was the crème brûlée?"

"Excellent, I couldn't resist."

"What time are you going to be home? Maybe three or four."

"Would you like to go out for dinner tonight, maybe ask Rita and Roan?"

"I'll call, that will be nice, since I have to cook for the dinner tomorrow. That is so thoughtful."

"Go ahead and get your shower, I'll clean up."

I'm in the shower, and out and dressed in record time. Bo is on the back porch.

"Bye baby," and I walk toward him and put my arms around him.

"You smell fetching," he says.

"Hold that thought," and I lean up and his lips are already there waiting, "have a good day D."

"You too."

"When I arrive at the store, I call Rita and see if they are available."

I am at the store and immediately I phone. "Hey there. Bo told me to invite ya'll to dinner, are you available?"

I don't know if Roan can take anymore of ya'll gushing at one another."

I'll call you back before noon."

"Bye."

I head for the bathroom, "something I ate doesn't agree with me."

When I come out, Julie looks at me and says, "Do you have the flu?"

"I don't think so."

"It's going around."

"I'm fatigued for some reason and I guess I've lost some weight."

Julie stands there and looks at me.

"Do I look that pale?"

"You look like you've seen a ghost. Dolly, are you nauseated?"

"Yes, how did you know?"

"Just a guess. Listen, I need to make this delivery quick before I get started. "I'll be right back. The orders are on your bench."

"Okay."

She takes the planter and loads up.

Right now, I have seven more to do. I have two finished ready for her to check. I hear Julie drive up; she walks in and hands me a sack.

"For me?"

"It certainly isn't for me."

"I like surprises." I reach in and pull out a box. It is an EPT test. I look at Julie.

She is shaking her head yes.

"But I haven't had a period in over four months. I am probably menopausal."

"This test is pretty accurate. I think I'm seeing a ghost now. It only takes a minute."

I walk in the bathroom absolutely shocked at the mere thought of being pregnant. In less than two minutes, I'm out with test in hand and set it on the table. A gentleman enters the store asking to see me.

I walk out front, "Hello, I'm Dolly, how can I help you?"

He extends his hand, Miles Kimball, the Kimball Group. And I hope I can help you, with building this dream house. He hands me rolled up papers. These are your house plans. Boyd asked me to drop them by. Very nice store you have. I'll tell my wife to come in here. She's always redecorating our home."

"Thank you, that's what we women do best. Well, thank you for the personal delivery. Boyd and I appreciate it".

With papers in hand, I rush back to the back to look at the test laying on the counter. It isn't there. Julie has it behind her back.

"Are you ready for the answer?"

"I don't know, I can't believe I even took a test. What does it say?"

Julie smiles, "Positive, your pregnant." She brings it from behind her back and it reveals 98% positive. I sit down in the chair.

"Are you happy?"

"I am numb. I just never thought. We have just been screwing like bunnies, with no care in the world, I don't think either one of us ever thought we could have a child. I'm old."

"Apparently your body doesn't think your too old," and she is all smiles and giggles.

"Put that test in the bag and throw it in another bag and then in the shop trash."

Julie giggles again. "I can throw it in five bags, and vacuum seal it. "It won't change the results."

"How did you know? What made you think about going and getting that, that test thingy?"

"It just hit me, you looked green, you've lost weight, you've had some high and low moods, I really don't know. Are you going tell him soon?"

"Julie, I have no idea."

"Are you happy or....?"

"Well, I am happy in love. I don't know how Bo will feel. I believe he'll be happy. We both feel a little robbed in life, that's why we got married so quick, and now this."

"Who was that guy?"

"Who?"

"That man just in, the papers?"

"Oh, the architect with house plans in hopes of building our house."

"Does the house have a nursery?"

"I believe it's three bedrooms."

"Well, that's good, you found out just in time."

"Julie, I don't feel so good."

"Honey, you probably have morning sickness. We have some saltines here."

She hands me over three and a glass of water. "Did you have anything greasy this morning?"

"Yes, bacon and cheesy grits."

"Let those saltines work their magic and drink that water. I'll get you three more."

I get up and go back to my corsages. "Heck, those kids will be coming in and I need to get them finished. Within an hour, I have them done and I haven't spoken a word in the last hour.

I look at Julie.

"Your color looks better now. Has the nausea passed?"

"Yes, but I guess the pregnancy is still here. What am I going to do?"

"Well, in nine months, you are going to deliver and then you are going to be a good mommy." Julie giggles again.

"How am I going to tell him?"

"Take those plans, open them up, and in one of those rooms, write in the box nursery, and when he is looking them over, it will be the biggest surprise ever."

"Yeah, it is that. Biggest surprise ever."

"Did you put that test in the garbage?"

She giggles again.

"Julie!"

"Yes, I did."

"No one can know until I tell Bo."

"Dolly, let's order some lunch and just relax. What sounds good?"

The door opens and in walks six kids, picking corsages up.

My cell phone rings. It's Rita.

"Hey there. Roan says yes. He really likes Bo, what time?"

"Dolly, are you there?"

"Oh, yeah. Okay let's plan on 'sixish, we'll pick you up."

The kids are gone.

"Dolly, How 'bout some soup and a sandwich. Are you feeling better?"

"Yes, a lot, how long do I have to go through this?"

"I'd say about three to six weeks. Everyone is different."

"It's only mornings, right?"

"Usually. You need to eat. Want some soup?"

"I'll go get us something. Can you wait on those kids?"

"Yes, I'm fine now."

"I'll be back soon."

Julie is back in 10 minutes. "Here, there are kids getting ready to come in, start eating this soup. and part of that sandwich. You'll feel a lot better."

"And I do. The soup is tasty." Chicken and rice. I bite into the chicken salad sandwich and it is also good. She got me some Jell-O, and yogurt. I eat all the Jell-O, and the yogurt and half of the sandwich.

Julie has finished waiting on the high school kids. Only two more pickups remain.

"Can I have a glass of wine?"

"Now?"

"No, I mean while I'm pregnant, expecting."

"I think so, every so often, I guess. Ask your doctor."

"What doctor?"

"You are pitiful."

Now I am laughing. "Well, it has been a shock to me, let's look at these plans."

I roll them out and put weights on the corners. The first picture is a drawing of the outside.

Julie is eating and looking at the same time. "Very pretty. Looks like it has a lot of southern charm with that wrap around porch."

The next drawing underneath shows the inside. "Here you go, mark this one room, closest to the master bedroom."

"Should I put it in big letters?"

"No, just small ones, how 'bout going around the inside room and writing nursery, nursery, nursery all around. Do you have a pink pen and a blue pen?"

"Yes, I do. What? alternate the colors?"

"Yes, that will be cool."

"What if Bo thinks I'm lying, I mean kidding him?"

"Want me to dig in the trash?"

"That won't be necessary."

"He'll take one look at you and he'll know. The doctor might give you some pills, if you can get in next week."

"Oh, I'm getting in next week, if I have to call all day long for an appointment. I'll call the Chief of Police to escort me down there, you can be sure," and now I am laughing.

"Okay, now this is the Dolly I know."

I start writing in the plans, hope Mr. Kimball doesn't mind my markings, and I roll them back up, with the drawing on top."

"It is two thirty p.m. Have all the corsages been picked up?"

"One more to go, go on home. I wish I was there tonight to be a fly on the wall."

"Maybe, not tonight, maybe this afternoon. We're taking Roan and Rita out tonight."

"Remember one glass of wine until you see the doctor. Julie walks over and hugs me. "It will be just fine. Do you have any saltines at home?"

"No, I'm going to the store and get some, something on each aisle. I'm just kidding!"

I'm in the store and Bo rings me on the cell.

"Hey baby."

If you only knew, "Hey there. I'm at the store, need anything?"

"Great, yes I need some razors, and deodorant."

"What kind?"

"Gillette for both."

"Do we need beer?"

"Checking... yes. Are we going to dinner with the in laws?"

"Yes, I told them sixish."

"Did Miles show up with the plans?"

"He sure did."

"Have you looked at them?"

"I was 'kinda busy."

"Will you be here in thirty?"

"Yes."

"'ll get my shower. Love you."

"Me too." *I mean ME TWO.*

I make my way around the store; razors, deodorant, beer, saltines, can't help myself looking at all the baby stuff. It is all too much to take in. I hurry along and pick up another Cuban bread, and a Kings Hawaiian bread, maybe I'll make French toast tomorrow morning.

I'm going to leave the paper in the car, and stall a bit. I take the groceries in. Bo takes them from me. He has just gotten out of the shower I can tell because he hasn't shaved yet. We set them down, and he puts his arms around me. "I thought about you all day."

"Did you? That makes two of us."

"You thought of me too?"

"Something like that."

He leans down and kisses me with so much passion.

"You are romantic this afternoon."

"Yes, I am. He rubs his stubbly beard against my neck. "Are you attracted to lumberjacks?"

He is tickling me with that stubble.

"Yes, fiercely, they are my favorite type."

"I knew it, I'll never shave again."

"Not so fast there, Z.Z."

"Who's that?"

"Z. Z. TOP, the singers."

"Oh, oh, only you could think of that."

There is another crème brûlée dish on the counter. "I think I have found my true loves' favorite dessert. It's good for you. I don't put that much sugar in my recipe. Just eggs, and milk.

How was lunch?"

"Great, she was glad to see me. She misses me too, but she is happy for me."

I put the groceries away and he gets a beer. He follows me in the bedroom.

"Oh, guess what I noticed this afternoon?"

"The closet space I made for you?"

"Yes, I noticed, and the picture. You wanted me to notice it without telling me."

I walk over to the picture and pick it up. Bo is standing behind me. "Rhett took this picture, I really love it."

"Me too." He puts his stubble beard against the back of my neck again, and it tickles. He grabs me up and falls on the bed with me in his arms.

"You have present for Chief Thunder? Tomorrow is one week anniversary. I take now."

He rubs his beard on me again.

"Yellow Hair have strong medicine, must give in small amounts."

"Chief Thunder need to be strong."

"Yellow Hair check arms for muscle. Very strong chief."

"Chief redeem stars now."

I kiss him because he is so darn cute and that's all it takes for us. He thinks I'm beautiful and I feel beautiful when he makes love to me.

"Yellow Hair thinks Chief take advantage, was supposed to be small amount."

"Chief strong now, take Yellow Hair for shower."

"Good idea."

We soap up each other and wash each other's back. "Yellow Hair has black eyes. Very strong medicine." He kisses me again.

"I tell him to get out of here and let me wash my makeup off."

I'm done, only to put makeup back on again for dinner. It was worth it and it was so much fun. I'm getting ready, and Bo is having another beer.

"Hey Dolly, want a glass of wine?"

"Thanks, no. I'll wait till dinner and have one with Rita."

"Can I wear shorts, or do I need to wear jeans?"

"I don't know, where are we going?"

"I thought we could go to that new steak house on the way to Deland. It's not that far."

"Better wear jeans. Roan will be mad if you wear shorts and he doesn't."

I put on fuchsia top and white capris. I am ready. It's about five thirty p.m.

Bo is ready too. "Hey, did you, bring the house plans?"

"Oh, I'll get them, they are in my car." *I feel butterflies.*

I go outside, and get them. I added a pink rubber band and a blue one on the rolls.

He places them on the table, "Did you like Miles?"

"Yes, very personable."

"Did he explain his vision?" *I'm sure he didn't envision my revisions.*

"Here it is. This is the outside drawing. There's a wraparound porch. Nice big wide entry. "Big steps for you to decorate all your seasonal stuff." *That's a big star.*

"Love the windows, don't you? and the side garage completely camouflaged, so you can't see into it."

"Garages, plural Bo, there's four."

"We need them, one for boat, one for each of us.

He flips to the second page. *Gosh darn, I am nervous.*

"Here's, the foyer, brick arches on the left, matches the brick in the kitchen and the outrageous stove unit you want."

"Outrageous? first you tell me I can have what I want, then you begrudge me something to cook on."

He grabs me up and kisses me. "I'm just teasing."

"Here's the sunken living room, brick fireplace, large French doors opening to the back patio. Two baths here. Master bed room. Do you think it's too big? I don't want to play hide and seek in there with you."

"I love the fireplace in there, needs a bear rug."

He looks up and laughs. "We don't need a bear rug, baby." *There's that word again.*

"French door here too, Miles marked this nursery. Strange."

"Uh, yeah."

"He put it in pink and blue ink. We didn't discuss this."

"You didn't?"

"Well, no, we don't need a nursery. I don't know how he got mixed up."

"Maybe he doesn't know what I know. Bo is still puzzled. He flips his head around, "what you know?" He looks back at the drawing. He looks back at me.

"I think it took a little longer for it to sink in with me."

"Are we going to have a baby?"

"Well, I am going to have one, and it is your baby." He takes me in his arms, and kisses me everywhere. Looks down at my belly, my face, my belly, my breasts.

"Oh god, Dolly, don't play about this, are you sure?"

"I took a test today, 98 % positive. It took me two hours to get over the shock."

He is squeezing me, he kisses me so softly, wets his tongue on my lips, he is so tender. D, you have put me in the clouds, I may never come down. I never dreamed we could."

"Me either. I was thinking I was menopausal. I was sick this morning, Julie said I looked like a ghost. I was nauseated, and she had a hunch.

She got a test at the drug store and brought it in to me. I was, am dumb-founded. He is kissing me everywhere. Bo, I thought you wanted to hear me."

"Oh, Dolly, I have heard every word you've said. Are you happy D about it?"

"This is so soon Bo. I need to go see a doctor, and sort this all out."

"It all makes sense now, I've lost weight and I'm tired and sleepy. My moods have been high and low."

"It makes perfect sense now. Have you told anybody?"

"No, not before you. After Miles dropped the plans by, Julie and I decided to decorate the room. Well, I need to back up, Julie knows. She figured it out. She fed me saltines this morning and tomorrow she said I'd probably have the sickness again."

"Oh D, I can't quit kissing you."

"I know, and if you don't shave, my facial skin is going to be rough."

"When do you think, you got pregnant?"

"It could have been any day or morning or night. We have been ac-tive bunnies before we got married, there was that three days we missed before the wedding."

"Can we start telling people?"

"I guess so, probably family."

"Yes, family, maybe we can take these plans with us and show Rita and Roan."

"Okay."

"Do you feel okay to go out?"

"Of course, I will let you know when I don't. Don't worry, we will know more next week."

He still has me in his grip. "D, I don't know what else to say, the hap-piest day of my life is when you married me, now this is my big bonus, a child with someone I adore. I love you baby and my baby." He is so tender and gives me soft kisses everywhere.

"Are you shaving before we leave?"

"I'm getting right on it."

We pick up Rita and Roan ten minutes after six. I sit in the back with Rita.

"How are the newlyweds?'

"We're good."

Bo blurts out, "We are great!"

Roan feels the need to comment, "Bro, that newness will wear off, just saying."

"That comment wasn't exactly an endorsement for your wife, Roan."

Bo looks over to Roan, "I've been meaning to ask you, where did that name 'Roan' come from?" Roan laughs, and says his granny named him after her favorite horse.

Bo laughs.

I notice Bo is just exuberant. He keeps looking at me in the rear-view mirror.

We arrive at the restaurant, and go in. Everyone orders drinks.

"Wine spritzer for me please." I am the first to order. The waitress takes our food order, and Bo brings out the plans.

Rita says she loves it, "looks very classy and she loves the entry. What is that pink and blue room?" She asks.

"Well, we don't know what color to paint it."

"Well, just paint it blue, Dolly likes blue, her whole house is blue." Roan quickly adds.

Rita looks over at me, I nod my head yes. She screams out.

"What's wrong?" Roan jumps up, "Is there a mouse?"

We are all laughing but Roan. Bo hands him the plan. "You might want to take a better look."

"Dam, this is a news flash. Congratulations Bro and Dolly. Wow."

"Wow is right." Rita says.

Bo puts his arm around me and looks at me. "Wow, is right."

I tell them I just took a test today. We'll know more next week." Our salads arrive and we talk about the wedding, Savannah, and future fishing trips.

The waitress brings our steaks. Bo suggest I check mine. It is fine. I love the attention he pours on me. I guess it is new love that makes us crazy for each other.

"Rita, what is on the agenda for Sunday Dinner besides eating? Is Denise bringing up the expansion proposal?"

Roan looks concerned. "For the life of me, I do not understand the need for the company to get bigger."

"I'm hoping Mr. Fox will be able to dissuade Denise about her plans for the company."

Rita inquires if I have made the lasagna yet.

"No, I started the meat sauce and I had a batch of crème brûlée made, but I have a rat in my kitchen who likes it. He says he needs to keep his strength up."

"I see. Do you think we need some green beans?"

"I'm afraid we do. Will you have time to make them?"

"After church."

Boyd looks at my plate, "you have not eaten much tonight. Please eat some more."

"I ate the outer edges, and it is a little too rare in the center for me to enjoy it. I guess I was premature in saying it was fine."

The waitress brings a tray of desserts to tempt us, but no one is interested. Promptly, she brings the tab and hands it to Bo. Roan immediately insists he get the bill, something about the last time. Bo tells him, "fry me some fish and we'll call it even." Roan asks him when he would like to go fishing. Bo said that it would be two weeks before he had another weekend free. Roan said it was a plan.

We leave and Bo opens my door, and he kisses my cheek.

Rita asks Bo when were we starting on the house.

"Soon, now I will be pushing them."

"That isn't necessary. I'd rather them do it right than hurry and make mistakes."

"Are you going to repeat the blue and yellow color scheme in your new house?"

We haven't discussed any of that.

Bo hears her, "I trust Dolly completely, whatever she wants. I don't want her wearing herself out though."

"Absolutely, you are right." Rita is in full agreement. "Dolly, you are older, and this may be a difficult pregnancy. You need to be concerned and reduce your work load."

"I know. I'll listen to my doctor. I am still in shock that we're having a baby."

We are dropping off Rita and Roan at their house, and I get out of the car and hug them and get back in the front. We will be home in ten minutes.

Morning After Meds

I need to get a few things done before I retire for the evening, but Bo will have none of it. Finally, I tell him he needs to go watch TV, because whatever I get done tonight, I won't have to do to-morrow. I drink a big glass of water while I am putzing in my kitchen.

I walk in the bedroom, and Bo opens his arms for me to come to him.

"My beautiful sweet D, I just want to hold you so close. I want to go to the doctor with you next week. Please don't shut me out because you think I'm too busy, or for any reason. We are going to be older parents, but we're up to the challenge, aren't we? We're both active, and I can help you in every way. I don't want you to be stressed. And you need to eat and feed this baby," and he grins. He brings my head to his chest and he kisses my head, I love you, I love you, I love you. He brings his lips to mine, he is so tender and soft, so gentle like I am fragile.

"Do you want a bath? Tell me, I will draw one for you."

"No, I am just going to wash my makeup off, and I'll be back, for a back and shoulder rub."

"You got it."

I feel a bit anxious, but I know it is temporary. I slip into bed beside him with one of my sexy nighties. I may be pregnant but I desire this man all the time, and want him to feel the same.

"When you wear something like that, I get excited, and I want you, every inch of you. I hope you will always want me too."

"I hope you will want me when I am nine months pregnant."

"Don't you ever doubt that, you are the woman for me always. Now let me give you a back rub and tell you what you mean to me."

It is six thirty and I am on the floor heaving in my toilet. Oh Lord, I feel bad.

Bo rushes in, "I hear you, and you need to drink some water, so it won't be dry heaving."

I tell him I need a few saltine crackers. He is back in a flash, pushes my hair back from my face, and gets me a cold, wet face cloth. "Hold that on your forehead. I am going to lift you up off the floor so you can sit here on the chair. Do you have those crackers down? Just sip that water, a little at the time. He sees a hair clip and pulls back my hair and clips it. Did you just feel sick and get up?"

I nod my head yes.

"Geez, you look pale. Just sip D. and let that cracker dissolve in your mouth. Are you cold? Do you want your robe?"

I have my eyes closed, with my head hanging down. Bo takes the face cloth and wets it again, folds it and pats my forehead and cheeks.

"C'mon I want you to lay down, maybe the worse is over."

I slip in the bed and lay still, he pats my forehead with the cloth, and it feels cool.

"I'm better, give me a couple of minutes.

Bo puts the covers on me, and kisses my shoulder. "Call out, if you need something." I nod my head.

I guess I am out an hour, and I get up, and put my robe on. Bo gets up from the table and walks toward me.

"I'm good, I feel okay, do you have coffee love?"

"Yes, please sit, how 'bout some oatmeal this morning?"

"Okay, that will be good for a change, and I will make you some French toast."

I busy myself making French toast because the sickness has passed. I tell him where the syrup is while the toast is grilling.

Bo sets the table and I pull out the meat sauce from the refrigerator. Bo is gazing at me and smiles. "You gave me a little scare. I was worried. Tomorrow I'll be more prepared. How 'bout some orange juice?"

"Thanks, no."

"I was thinking Dolly, maybe some smoothies would be good for you in the morning. They are packed with protein and fresh fruit, and then maybe you could drink a little less coffee? I must be grimacing. "Now, we don't need that extra head coming out now, it might scare the baby. "We both laugh. He leans over and kisses me, "Good morning."

"Thanks for being nurse Bo. You have a lot of hats you wear. Detective, Chief, Chef, Nurse, and soon Dad."

"I can't wait D."

"I know, I sense it."

I put the boiling water on for the lasagna noodles, add salt and a little olive oil. Time for breakfast. "Oatmeal huh?"

"I thought it might settle your stomach, but you need some protein, some yogurt?"

"I'll get it," I pass by the oven and turn it on, and head to the refrigerator and get some yogurt. My turbinado is already on the table.

I sit back down and mix all with my oatmeal. "How is your toast?"

"It is fantastic, trying to figure out the base bread."

"It's Kings Hawaiian bread."

He takes my hand and kisses all between my fingers. "There is nothing more important to me than you D. I will take care of you."

"I know, and I love you for it." I take the dishes to the sink. I'm cooking noodles and get all my ingredients out to layer the lasagna together. I take three sticks of butter out and put them in a bowl to soften and add lots of cloves of garlic for the garlic bread."

I finish two pans of lasagna and cover them with aluminum foil. The crème brûlée is ready to go in the oven and then I am off to the shower while they bake.

I am deep in thought and I know God has blessed me with a precious baby with the man I love so much.

I'm out and put a wrap on and go check my oven timer. I have time to blow dry my hair. Bo has cleaned up the kitchen, loaded the dishwasher, I see him outside on the phone.

I am dressing and putting on makeup when I hear the oven timer go off. They are done and overcooking them makes them watery. I have exactly fifteen servings including the ones I made the other night. I put all of them on a long platter and set them in the garage refrigerator. The bread is the last thing to do, and it won't take long.

Bo is back, "What time did you want to leave?"

"If we eat at one, I need an hour to cook the lasagna so I think we can leave at 11:30 and I'll be right on schedule."

"You have been busy this morning."

"So have you, thanks for helping in the kitchen."

"Are you feeling okay now?"

"Oh yeah, the sickness passed, once I had eaten crackers."

Big Dinner Big News

The irrigation pumps are running at the fernery and the outdoors smell earthy from the wet ground. I see Denise and Tom
are already here separating some of the furnishings into stacks.
I turn on the oven and set the lasagna pans in to cook. Bo greets Denise
and shakes Tom's hand. Tom is polite and ask where we spent our honeymoon. He and Bo are having conversation on the porch. This Sunday
Dinner should prove interesting with the division of personal effects
of Mom and Dad's lifetime together. I notice many dishes that register
special occasions and specific dishes Mom always served in them.

"Denise, is all your crew coming?"

"That was in the will, wasn't it?"

"A simple yes would be sufficient. Is something wrong today?"

"It's just a long drive over here and I didn't get much sleep last night."
*Well, I had morning sickness when I woke up, but I still managed to get you and your kids a
lunch prepared. GO figure.*

I put on the tea pot and when Rhett arrives, I'll ask…

"Oh, you have arrived. Rhett, could you take the Polaris and go down
to the fernery and fill up the cooler with ice. I have some beer in my car
and if you could ice that down, it will be appreciated."

Scarlett is setting the table without being asked and I suggest she add some salad bowls, some people might not like salad in their plate with lasagna.

Rene and Robert arrive as well, and Rene says she has brought a big fruit salad. I give her a big hug and whisper to her that her mama has taught her well.

The phone rings and I look at Denise. "I thought we had these phones cut off."

"Not yet, I've been a little busy. Other things are taking priority Dolly." *like expansion that we don't need.*

Scarlett answered the phone and said it was Bingham, Tom Jr. and Carly, going to be fifteen minutes late.

"Who's going to be late?" Rita is asking as she enters with her salad and dressing. Roan is carrying a big pot of green beans and turn on the stove for the beans to keep them hot.

Roan wants to know if the canteen is open yet. "It's one o'clock somewhere. I'll go ask my brother n laws if they would like a cold beer."

That has a nice ring to it, his brother n laws. Mom and Dad are smiling looking down at the family gathering up on a Sunday for family fun times. *Let's hope it will be fun.* The brawling had subsided but there remains accusations and animosity between the sisters. *Mom, I am trying to extend the olive branch, but Denise is like a snapping fire, get too close and I will get burned.*

Rita asks Denise about the three piles lined up down the hallway.

"Just trying to group duplicate items in separate piles for each of us, to keep or distribute to our children. *Children, I did not discuss with Bo if we were announcing today, gosh, he needs to speak to his mother first.*

I find him on the porch and he puts his arm around me. "Need help?"

"Not really, just wanted a second of your time, I lead him out the door.

"Are you planning on telling anyone about our addition? Your mother is coming with Mr. Fox, and maybe while the sisters are in the study or sometime, you could slip down to the dock and tell her privately.

Watch her to be sure she doesn't fall off though, in case she is shocked, dazed and stumbles." Bo looks concerned I may be right.

"I'll tell her she needs to update her will for another grandchild, and let it sink in. You sure you don't want to tell her together?"

"This is your time with your Mother, make it special."

"You are always so selfless D."

"No, I'm not, you bring out the beast, I mean best in me."

Rhett is back and Bo meets him on the sidewalk and helps him bring in the cooler.

I see Mr. Fox and Mother in the driveway and keep wondering if this is a blossoming romance or two older people enjoying companionship. Mother is carrying a white rectangular platter.

I hug her, "Welcome to Sunday Dinner Mother."

"I brought some marinated asparagus with peppers."

"This is beautiful Janet, I know everyone will enjoy this. The family is still raving about the wedding food."

"I haven't had a moment to check on you dear, since you returned. All is well?"

"I'm, I mean, we're very happy. In fact, the happiest. I am a lucky woman. I thank God every day for putting us in each other's path. Mr. Fox, glad you are here." He smiles and opens the door for me and Janet. "You can place that plate on the table Janet."

I look at the clock and put the bread in.

Bingham and Carly are here along with Tom Jr. Carly brings in a shopping bag. *I just remembered I was going to make a sample of the centerpiece and I have completely forgotten, heck, where's my head? Maybe we can go the store and I'll show her.*

Carly gives me a big hug, and Bing too. Tom Jr. taps me on the shoulder as he passes by to the porch. "Aunt Dolly, married life agrees with you. You are positively glowing. *You should have seen me this morning, that is if green is a glow color.* Carly brings out a Tupperware container. "I need a plate for these; they are goat cheese and honey, balls rolled in chopped walnuts. I made them. I'm learning how to cook."

"Thank you, Carly, and I see her studying my face and she is curiously smiling.

"Is everyone here?" I look around and don't see Bo, or Janet.

"Well, we can all go to the dining room. Girls, if you'll help me get all the food on the table everyone is in the dining room and I am pulling out the bread. Bo and Janet are coming indoors, and she looks like she has swallowed a canary. She hugs me and tells me she loves me and that she'll talk to me later.

Bo is beside me, "want me to get that baby?" And Bo takes the bread from my hands and gives me two thumbs up. *Maybe it is him who has swallowed the bird.*

It's just me alone in the kitchen. I look up and say, "Mom, here's to another Sunday Dinner." and I take my place next to Bo where everyone is standing to say grace.

Surprisingly, Tom asks to say the blessing.

"Lord, I am so thankful today. I have two sons that have graduated college now, and a new thoughtful daughter n law on the way. Everyone snickers a little. I have a wife who has reconnected to me, and will try to do the same with this family and remember what Blu and Ellie taught these girls about family and loving hearts and respect. We thank you lord for these sisters, all different branches but connected to a big sturdy trunk and roots that are deep in this beautiful land God gives us to enjoy. We are thankful for all of the helping hands that bring us this Sunday dinner that we may enjoy and embrace the diversity of our family and love one another. Amen."

Mr. Fox joins in louder, "Amen." His comment is appreciated by all.

"Roan, can you cut the lasagna into squares and everyone start passing your plates that way because that roaster is plenty hot. Perhaps, we can pass the other side dishes the other way. "Everyone, Janet brought the asparagus, Rene brought us this gorgeous fruit salad, and our newest food network star, Carly, brought the goat cheese balls. Rhett, brought... well, he brought Scarlett who was here early helping me get everything organized. Thank you one and all. Enjoy."

The food is all delicious and there is conversation all about; our honeymoon in Savannah, Carly's wedding, Tom Jr's new job at an engineering firm. Robert is going to be the new athletic director at the high school and Rita and Roan are planning a trip to Africa. Denise is sewing again and making the tablecloths for Bing and Carly's wedding. *Imagine that.*

I announce, we have crème brûlée for dessert, and I'll go get it." I bring out the platter from the refrigerator and sprinkle a tablespoon of half brown and half white sugar on some of the ramekins. I torch those with sugar to make that crunchy top on top of the cold crèmes.

I place it in the middle of the table. Everyone is helping themselves. Robert stands up and taps the side of his iced tea glass and says he has an announcement. *Oh.*

"After paying off our student loans, and both of having good jobs, and after three years of blissful marriage, my first wife Rene, and we all chuckle, is pregnant. Everyone is surprised and offering congratulations. Robert adds it's due in eight months. I look at Janet and she is all smiles.

Bo whispers in my ear, "should I go next?" I nod my head yes. *Sing canary, sing.* Bo stands up and taps on his glass. I have an announcement as well. After paying for our honeymoon, and keeping Dolly working to support me, and marrying the best thing that has ever happened to me. As miraculous as it is, and we are so sure God has touched our lives, Dolly and I are having a baby too; about eight months from now also. You can hear a pin drop and almost instantaneously everyone is rip roaring, and excited and laughing. *This is a hellava Sunday Dinner, Mom and Dad.*

We all stay at the table, eating and talking. Denise stands up and taps on her glass.

"No, I'm not pregnant." We all hear Tom say, "Thank you Lord Jesus."

Denise continues, "Thanks to the grapevine, Bo has a suggestion for our family which has been on my mind. His idea is that we let Juan and his growing family move in here to Momma and Daddy's house to live where he is closer to work. Perhaps, we can travel for future dinners to the sisters' homes or whoever would like to host the Sunday dinner. It can be a picnic or a BBQ, whatever the host and hostess has in mind from this day forward. Mom has made her point about the necessity and the importance of family unity with her stipulation of required attendance." She looks up to the heavens. "We get it Mom." Everyone is amused. "On another subject, and as overseer, I wanted to expand along the land that we own, but in talking to Juan, whose heart is this company, who talks to these living plants like Daddy used to do, I realize it's always been about the land, never to be raped, but used as tool to provide income. When income becomes secondary, we must look to preserving that which is precious to us, the land. Juan explained to me Dad's mission, to use the land conservatively and save some for the future. That's why he never planted that east block around the lake. I believe that is why he donated thousands to the university each year to ensure that agricultural families like ours have the latest technology and information about fighting disease and understand the chemicals and the development of new fertilizers that are introduced for our specific crops. It is all about giving back, paying it forward and protecting the land. I would like to establish a scholarship this year for a student who expresses interest in farming or growing products here in Florida. We can set aside an escrow account that we enhance every year. With a generous stipend for the sisters each year, Blu Diamond Farms can generate enough income to do all that. What do ya'll think?" We all shake our heads yes. Finally, we can agree.

"A reminder, we have stuff to divide today, so let's get to work. If you want something, go put your name on it."

"Rita, Denise, I think we can leave all the kitchen stuff here, and just take special bowl or something that is meaningful to us. I don't think any of us need utility dishes. I would like to have Mom's cookbook. "Aunt Dolly, Carly is eager as ever, I would love to be able to cook like all of you Diamond women."

"Carly, you can read, can't you?"

"Yes, of course,"

"Then you can cook, be a sponge and absorb cookbooks, recipes, magazines. You'll learn how to cook. Wanting to know and learn is all you'll ever need."

I take some of the soiled dishes into the kitchen and start loading the dishwasher. I go to a drawer and get Mom's cookbook and take it to Carly. "Here, start being that sponge."

I take another load in and when I return, she announces different recipes and different family members comment that they remember when. Mom's cookbook is an old Better Homes and Gardens edition that has a big envelope after each section to keep index cards and newspaper clippings. Mom's cookbook is stuffed with recipes from days of old. There's a lot of history in that book.

Rene helps bring in dishes, and she asks, "Aunt Dolly, did you have any idea?"

I know what she is talking about. "No, Rene, I never thought it would be possible, just took the test yesterday, but this morning I was a sick puppy. I have been tired and its unlike me, and I have lost weight. Julie is the one that bought the test after she saw me pale yesterday. Bo is so happy," and Bo comes up behind me and puts his hands on my shoulders. "Yes I am."

He turns to Rene and hugs her. "Congratulations to you and Robert too. I didn't mean to steal your thunder but we knew and it would be silly to hold it inside."

"As if you can, hold it," and I put my arm around him.

Carly yells out, squealing in the dining room, and everyone rushes to see what the problem is. She has the cookbook open and pulling some recipe notes out of one of those envelopes and out comes Mom's missing necklace.

"What's this? Oh my goodness!"

We three sisters respond in unison, "Mom's Necklace." A small handwritten note is attached.

"If you are finding this, you are looking in the right place to keep your marriage together. Take care of your husband, and cook and eat as a family. Hoping my daughters will share and wear this as a symbol of sixty-five years of respect, love and joy in a beautiful family."

"We will Momma, we will."

Sunday Dinner Recipes

Yellow Squash Casserole

8-10 yellow summer squash

I packet (sleeve) of Ritz Crackers, broken up

3-4 Tablespoons butter

3 Tablespoons chopped white sweet onion

I Egg

3 cups shredded cheese

Salt and Pepper to taste. Cook squash in small amount of water and drain. Do not overcook. Pour into mixing bowl.

Sauté onions in butter, and add to squash mixture.

Add crackers crumbs, egg, onions and drop by big spoonfuls in greased casserole dish.

Top with cheese, Bake At 350, thirty to forty minutes.

Grandma Gert's Graham Cracker Cake

2 sticks Butter

2 cups sugar

6 eggs, separated

4 cups Graham Cracker Crumbs (one box)

4 Tablespoon plain flour plus one tablespoon

4 teaspoons baking powder

½ teaspoon salt

2 cups whole milk

I teaspoon vanilla

2 cups chopped pecan pieces

Beat egg whites until stiff, set aside.

Cream shortening and sugar, add egg yolks to shortening mixture.

Mix one tablespoon flour with nut pieces as this keeps nuts from sinking in batter.

Mix dry ingredients together. (cracker crumbs, baking powder, salt, and flour) and then add to creamed mixture, alternating milk with dry ingredients. Always start with flour and end with flour.

Add good vanilla.

Fold in egg whites and nuts (don't over mix)

Pour into greased and floured 9" layer pans. Bake 25 minutes. Cool. Use cream cheese icing between layers. Top entire cake with whipped cream if desired. Use chopped nuts on top. (optional)

Hummingbird Cake

3 cups all-purpose flour

2 cups granulated sugar

1 teaspoon baking soda

1 teaspoon ground cinnamon

1 teaspoon salt

3 eggs, beaten

1 and ½ cups vegetable oil

2 teaspoons good Vanilla

1 8 oz can crushed pineapple, undrained

2 cups mashed bananas (4-5)

2 cups chopped pecans

Combine dry ingredients in a large bowl, add eggs and salad oil stirring until dry ingredients are moistened. Do not beat. Stir in vanilla, pineapple, 1 cup chopped nuts and bananas. Spoon batter into three well-greased and floured 9" pans. Bake 20-30 minutes or until Cake tests done. Remove from pans and cool completely. Spread frosting between layers, on tops and sides. Sprinkle remaining cup of nuts on top

Frosting

16 oz. cream cheese (2 packages) at room temperature

1 cup unsalted butter, room temperature

7 cups 10x confectioners' sugar

2 teaspoons good vanilla

Strawberry Cake
1 pkg. white Duncan Hines cake mix
1 small box strawberry Jell-O, (3 oz.)
¾ cup corn oil
¾ cup water
4 eggs
½ cup fresh or frozen strawberries, mashed

Mix together and bake in layers 25-30 minutes in well-greased and floured pans
or sheet cake at 325.

Icing
½ stick butter
1 8 oz. package cream cheese
1 box confectioners' sugar
½ cup fresh or frozen strawberries

Poppy Seed Muffins. Makes 12
2 cups all-purpose flour
¼ cup poppy seeds
½ teaspoon salt
¼ teaspoon baking soda
½ cup butter (1 stick)
¾ cup sugar
2 eggs
¾ cup sour cream
1 ½ teaspoon good vanilla

Preheat oven to 375, grease one 12 cup muffin tin.
Combine flour, poppy seeds, salt, and baking soda in small bowl. Using mixer, cream butter and sugar until thick and light. Beat in eggs one at a time, blend in sour cream and vanilla. Gradually beat in dry

ingredients. Spoon batter into prepared tin. Bake about 20 minutes, cool 5 minutes in tin on rack, remove and cool completely.

Sautéed Green Beans

Snap ends of beans and remove any strings, wash thoroughly.

Put on a big pot of boiling water.

Add beans to boiling water and cook 6-10 minutes.

Immediately drain and place in pan of ice water to stop the cooking process. This retains the bright green color. Drain thoroughly and pat dry with paper towel or air dry.

In large Dutch oven or wok, drizzle olive oil and sauté fresh garlic slices together. Add green beans and stir constantly until desired tenderness is achieved. Salt and pepper to taste.

Coconut Cream Pies (2)

Dock or fork-pierce large unbaked pastry shells like Marie Calendar's, and bake accordingly. These are deep (big) filling pies, so plan your crust accordingly. Southerners do not cut or serve tiny pie portions. Cool shells completely.

1 ½ cups granulated sugar

12 tablespoons cornstarch

½ teas salt

3 cups half and half

3 cups whole milk

1 cup evaporated milk

1 cup water

7 tablespoons butter

8 eggs separated

2 teas good vanilla

1 ½ cups coconut plus coconut for top of meringue to brown (use can, or bagged coconut)

Separate eggs and set whites aside for meringue.

In saucepan, place sugar, cornstarch and salt, slowly add all the liquids, stirring all the while on medium heat. As mixture starts to thicken, be sure you are stirring to keep from sticking. A big slotted spoon works best, but remember liquid is hot. Once the filling thickens and is bubbling, mix some of your hot milk mixture into your bowl of yolks and temper, once tempered, slowly add yolk mixture to thickened milk mixture and cook another five minutes. Mixture should be thick.

Place entire saucepan in a shallow sink of cool water to cool down. Keep stirring to cool down all the mixture, not just the outside) Once some of the heat has reduced, add butter and vanilla and stir in. Cool down more, and then add 1 ½ cups coconut. Stir in, and be sure custard filling is cooled before adding to pie shells. (adding coconut before saucepan and filling has really cooled down results in thinner filling, because the sugar content in sweetened coconut will add liquid when hot) Prepare meringue by whipping egg whites in mix master. When stiff peaks appear, add 4 tablespoons granulated sugar, pinch of salt, and 1 ½ teaspoon good vanilla.

Spoon by big spoonfuls on top of both pies covering edges, top with coconut, place back in oven to brown, about 15 – 20 minutes to set meringue, and be golden on top, about 375degrees.

Southern Hot Water Cornbread
Boiling water,
1 cup white Cream meal
½ teas salt
2-3 tablespoons of can milk (aids in browning)

Add boiling water **slowly** to form stiff dough, use the back of a big spoon, or wooden spoon to make dough, this will make a stiff dough. Make logs of dough and flatten out right before you lay them in hot oil. Fry till a golden brown. Dipping your fingertips in a cold bowl of ice water will keep dough from sticking to your hands as you form into flat logs or patties.

Crème Brûlée
1 cup sugar
6 eggs
4 cups half and half
1 teas good vanilla
Pinch salt

Blend all with mixer, pour in ceramic ramekins, and bake in water bathe about 35-45 minutes depending on depth of your ramekins.

Check for slight jiggle when you remove them from oven, over baking makes custards watery.

Southern Flour Hoecake with honey or marmalade
2 cups self-rising flour
¼ cup Crisco
¾ - 1 cup buttermilk
Pinch of baking soda (anytime you use a sour milk, add a pinch of soda)

In bowl, place flour and Crisco, and soda. With clean hand, mix buttermilk slowly into bowl, cutting in shortening, work fast with hand, until a shaggy dough appears, over mixing biscuit dough will make hoecake tough.

Heat cast iron skillet with small tablespoon of Crisco or bacon fat. When skillet is ready, spoon batter into 8-9" skillet, flip with wide spatula, regrease before turning over, or spray with Pam, place a few tablespoons of butter on top while the other side is cooking. Turn out on plate, place a silver knife underneath to keep hoecake from sweating on plate, tear or cut into desired portions.

Accompany with your choice or honey, jelly or syrup.

Snow Pea Salad
1 package baby frozen English peas
1 package green fresh snow peas, ends trimmed and cut into pieces
Small purple onion diced or one half of a large purple onion

1 small can water chestnuts, chopped and drained
4-5 slices crispy bacon cooked and crumbled

Combine all in bowl, mix together ½ cup mayonnaise and ½ cup sour cream, and teaspoon sugar,
Sprinkle some Italian seasoning into dressing if desired. Sprinkle salt and pepper over snow pea mix, combine dressing into snow pea mix and refrigerate, serve cold.

Uncle Lex's Flank Steak Marinade (or London Broil)
2 Tablespoon sesame oil
1 Tablespoon brown sugar
1 Tablespoon balsamic vinegar
2 Tablespoons Kikkoman soy sauce
1 teaspoon crushed garlic
1-2 teaspoon meat tenderizer

Mix all together and marinate flank steak 2-3 hours in plastic bag or Tupperware with lid. Turn often.

Goat Cheese Log or Balls
1 package goat cheese
1 package cream cheese
3 tablespoons honey (tupelo is best)
Add chopped cranberries, if desired.

Mix all together and shape into a log or individual balls and roll in finely chopped walnuts.

French Onion Soup
In Large saucepan, place 2 Tablespoons of olive oil and 2 Tablespoons of butter, and 2 tablespoons of plain flour. (for some thickening) Heat until blended. Add about 4-5 whole sliced sweet onions to oil and begin to sauté. Add 2 Tablespoons of turbinado sugar to the onions and

caramelize a few minutes, slowly on a low to medium heat, so you don't burn the onions. Add salt and pepper to taste, a bay leaf,
1-2 cups of red wine (or a small one individual serving bottle)
1 box liquid beef stock

Simmer 2-3 hours so the flavors will be robust and stock can be reduced
When you are ready to serve, place a toasted baguette slice in bowl, add soup, and top with
Gruyere cheese. Bake in oven till cheese is melted. Be generous with your cheese.

Crab Cakes with Dill sauce
1 pound plus (does not have to exact) lump meat crab (if it is big lumps, chop some for even cooking and it will help the cakes hold together)
2 eggs
2 Hellman's mayonnaise
1 teaspoon Dijon mustard
1 teaspoon Worchester sauce
Several drops of tobasco sauce
1 teas old bay seasoning
¼ teaspoon salt and pepper
¼ cup finely chopped celery
2 tablespoons chopped green pepper
½ cup panko crumbs
2 tablespoon minced purple onion

Heat skillet till hot, add a couple tablespoons of olive oil and 2 table-spoons of butter, reduce heat so you won't burn them, mix all ingredients together, let rest in refrigerate, melding flavors for an hour, shape into patties, and cook 2=3minutes per side till golden, serve with dill sauce on the side
Dill sauce: In a small bowl, mix equal amounts of quality mayonnaise and sour cream or yogurt (if you're cutting calories) add 2 sliced scallions, chopped tomatoes for color, and 1 tablespoon chopped fresh

dill, 1 teaspoon lemon juice and a couple drops of tobasco sauce. To make thinner, add a tablespoon of milk, can be made ahead and refrigerated.

Guava Marbled Cheesecake makes 10" cake

Place a guava paste brick in microwave to soften it. Cut up chunks of paste are easier to melt and puree. Drain one can of grocery store guava shells, reserving liquid in another saucepan.

In food processor, add drained shells, and paste, add 2 tablespoons lemon juice and puree to a thick pourable or be able to spoon it comfortably.

Make a graham cracker crust and pat in a large well buttered cheesecake pan.

In mixer, mix 5 packages of softened cream cheese, 2 cups sugar and 5 large eggs one at the time

Add 2 tablespoons good vanilla.

Spoon some of the cream cheese mixture over the crust, then spoon some of the paste mixture, alternating all the time. You can swirl some of the big spoonfuls with a knife to distribute the paste. Don't be afraid to put a lot of guava, keep adding cream cheese spoonfuls around and adding paste till you run out. This is a big cheesecake. Bake an hour to hour and half till set. Bake at 375 for 20 minutes, and reduce oven to 350 for the rest of the time. Every oven is different.

Use the juice, and taste if it sweet enough, thicken a bit with cornstarch and juice combined till thickened. Add to applicator bottle when cooled and criss cross ribbons on top of cake.